Shoemaker, Willie. 7/94

[MYST.] Stalking horse.

$21.95

DATE			
FEB.23.2001			
JUL 2 6 2008			
APR 1 8 2011			

Stalking
Horse

Stalking Horse

Bill Shoemaker

Fawcett Columbine
New York

A Fawcett Columbine Book
Published by Ballantine Books

LIBRARY OF CONGRESS CATALOGING-IN-PUBLICATION DATA
Shoemaker, Willie.
Stalking horse / Bill Shoemaker.
p. cm.
ISBN 0-449-90595-0
1. Horse racing—Fiction. I. Title.
PS3569.H5716S7 1994
813'.54—dc20 93-22125 CIP

MANUFACTURED IN THE UNITED STATES OF AMERICA

First Edition: April 1994

10 9 8 7 6 5 4 3 2 1

To all my racing fans,
with special thanks to Dick Lochte
for his help in putting it together

CONTENTS

Prologue

I WAS ON a smart, powerful Thoroughbred named Cajun Desire and the track was crowded and I had a sense that the grandstand was jammed with screaming fans. I was in complete control, sitting chilly. Biding my time. Saving wear and tear on the animal.

Passing the ¼ pole, we were third in line, one away from the rail. Time to move.

We edged closer to the number-two horse. I could hear the jock chirping in its ear, making that little whistle sound that passes for conversation between rider and animal. Whatever he was saying wouldn't do him any good that day.

It began to rain. A minute ago the sky had been clear. Now it was as gray as wash. And as wet.

It didn't matter. I liked the rain. Cajun Desire liked the rain. I laughed as we closed the gap. Cajun Desire's muzzle was inches away from the number-two horse's girth.

The rain was coming down in buckets now. But we weren't getting wet. There was mud flying everywhere, but it wasn't touching us. We were winners.

Cajun Desire took us neck and neck with the number-two horse. And then we eased past, not even winded. The lead horse was two lengths away. He was a big animal who moved like a merciless machine. I didn't recognize him or his jockey, which seemed strange.

We thundered past the ⅝ pole. "Now, old boy," I crooned to Cajun Desire. "Now you do it for me. Now you show 'em what you've got."

And Cajun Desire replied, "You're calling it, Coley."

"You betcha," I told him, not in the least surprised to find myself chatting with my mount. There was definitely something wrong with this picture. But I was too happy to try to figure it out.

We caught the big horse just as we were turning for home. He'd moved away from the inside rail and I ordered Cajun Desire, "Just ease on in there, boy, and we've got this sewed up."

The horse did as he'd been told and we squeezed between the big Thoroughbred and the rail and pushed onward. In another minute we'd be the front-runner. But the rain was pouring and there was a wall of water forming across the track. I pulled in my head and hugged the horse and we burst through the water wall. I said, "Take us home."

And Cajun Desire replied, "Sorry, Coley, no can do. There's something in the way."

It was an accident, a car wrapped around an oak tree. And there was someone in the car. Someone I cared for. Lit from beneath by flames coming up through the floorboards. The car's passenger looked at me and waved just before a tremendously hot white light enveloped the car. And Cajun Desire. And me.

"Sorry, boss, we lost," the horse said. And I closed my eyes.

★★★

When I opened them again, I was in l'Hôpital Evangeline, sharing the room with a member of the Thibodaux, Louisiana, constabulary. He was young and eager and asked me a few questions that I understood fully but was incapable of answering through the painkillers. What I replied sounded vaguely like "Umrah awawa balawaba."

Not having an ear for the language of chemical change, he departed, to return a while later with a beautiful blonde who seemed interested in my case and two other men. One, whom I vaguely recognized through the haze, studied me with a look of utter disgust on his big, square mug. The other, who was garbed in white, held up fingers, shone a light in my eyes until they watered, and tapped my knees with a rubber hammer. Finally, he turned to the blonde and the squarehead and said something about my being moved to All Saints Hospital in New Orleans, where they were better equipped to handle burns and concussions. The blonde looked concerned. The squarehead looked annoyed. The young cop looked relieved.

I slept during the apparently uneventful trip to All Saints, woke up as I was being wheeled into a private room where a pair of detectives from the New Orleans Police Department awaited with *their* questions. The blonde, who had accompanied me, somehow talked them into leaving.

They were back the next day when I was alone and defenseless. "Yoah name Colman Killebrew?" the older one asked.

"Ahyer," I replied.

"You a resident of the state of California, city of Los Angeles?"

"Ahyer," I repeated.

"Can you tell us what you been up to since you arrived heah in Louisiana?"

Actually, I couldn't. At least not at that precise moment. They must have realized that by my slack jaw and dazed expression. They nodded to one another and left me to the medical profession.

They did not return. Not even when my brain started to work again.

In their stead came two men so average in height, looks, and dress that they might have been brothers. Phil and Bill Bland. Not their real names. If they ever gave me their real names, it must have been during one of my less lucid periods. They were members of the Federal Bureau of Investigation and they brought their own stenographer to capture any pearls of wisdom I might be inclined to drop.

They had no personality to speak of, the brothers Bland, but they knew their business. They were not interested in my name, which they already had, or my state of residence, ditto. They weren't interested in the years I'd spent as a somewhat successful jockey, or why I no longer rode. They weren't interested in me at all, just in what I could tell them about a few murders that had taken place during the past couple of weeks and two million dollars or so that had gone with the wind.

Their questions were clear, pertinent, and endless. They went at it for precisely two hours each morning, after which they would depart. The blonde would then enter, sit on the bed beside me, and soothe my fevered brow with her cool, healing hands.

Her name was Lea.

She stood five feet eleven inches in her stockings, when she wore stockings, which was rare. She was intelligent, intuitive, compassionate, and karate-tuned. I shall never cease to be in awe of her.

Six days into my hospital stay, when the bandages had been removed from my head, and the tape keeping my arm strapped to my side had been exchanged for a sling, and the painkillers and tranquilizers had been replaced by Tylenol, the feds decided to leave me in peace.

They didn't say why.

Lea told me it was because they had all the information they needed to close out their case.

"I wasn't very candid with them," I informed her.

She nodded. "I'm sure they know that by now."

"I was very clever about my omissions," I said. "When the Feebs feel you've been uncooperative, they sometimes put in a call to the IRS, just to get the last laugh."

"Better notify your tax man," she replied. "They know you've been pulling their chain."

"How?"

"Daddy told them everything."

That figured. Daddy, a genuine reprobate named Raymond Edgar Starbuck, had apparently dedicated his life to making mine as miserable as possible. One of the reasons I'd played so coy with the Bland brothers was that I didn't think Starbuck wanted them to know too much about his dumb scheme. So naturally he'd confessed all, probably putting a spin on the events to shove me deeper into the soup.

"When I was under the spell of chemistry, I imagined I saw him standing at the foot of my bed," I said.

"You didn't imagine it."

"Is he still here?"

"No. He flew out as soon as he could."

"Good," I said. "What was he doing in Louisiana in the first place?"

"He came . . . I'm not sure why he came. He said something about trying to minimize the mess we made. But I think he was worried about us."

"There must be some other reason. Maybe it was so that he could call me a liar to the FBI."

She tsk-tsked and shook her head. "Actually, he didn't call you a liar until he'd flown back home. He gave his deposition to two gentlemen from the Los Angeles Bureau."

"Anything in it I should know?"

"Quite a lot," she replied. "Oh, Coley, I hope you realize that I've always wanted to be more open with you about . . . this whole business."

"It might have saved me a few bandages."

"Daddy didn't trust you," she said flatly. "But then, you didn't trust him either."

"With damn good reason."

She shrugged.

That day she was wearing a short, bright red dress with white polka dots. She was as fresh as morning coffee and as healthy as a frisky filly. She'd probably spent an hour in her hotel's gym and another jogging a few miles around the city. "You look exhausted," I told her, petting the bed beside me. "You ought to stretch out and rest your weary—"

"You're hopeless," she said. "Do you want to see the transcription of Daddy's interrogation?"

"I'd rather have you cradle me in your arms. Like you did when we were waiting for the ambulance."

"I thought you were dying."

"I was. You cradled me back to life. The Indians say—"

"You're not only hopeless but pathetic," she cut me off, picking up her big white purse from a chair. From it she removed a stack of pages nearly an inch thick.

I frowned at the pages. "I never knew your daddy to be such a blabbermouth."

"When he wants to be," she said, placing the stack on a table next to the bed. "Of course, he kept *some* secrets."

"Oh?"

"The transcript should be enough to occupy you for a few hours," she said. "I'll be back at six to fill in the blanks."

She started for the door.

"Lea?"

She turned.

"When you come back . . ." I gave her my wounded-waif look.

"Yes?"

"Could you bring me an oyster po'boy or some gumbo? This must be the only place in New Orleans where they don't season the food. I might as well be in Anaheim."

That evening we dined on seafood gumbo and crawfish pie accompanied by a dry white wine that Lea barely touched and I swilled. Starbuck's deposition had been as infuriating as it was illuminating, filled with crucial data that he'd hidden from me. But I was determined not to let anger interfere with our intimate little dinner. At least not until I had extracted as much additional information as she was willing to impart.

We talked until ten-thirty, when a large orderly arrived with my sleeping pill.

He frowned at the dirty dishes and went ballistic when he saw the nearly empty bottle of wine. He scooped it up and ordered Lea out. Harrumphing with indignation, he went out himself and took his sleeping pill with him.

I could have used it. Or another bottle of wine.

I turned out the light and rested my head back on the pillow. But sleep didn't give me a tumble.

I've never counted sheep. When I was young and naive and still had a career in racing, I would count Thoroughbreds crossing the finish line. With me in the saddle, of course. That night, I decided to do something a bit more constructive with my insomnia. I sifted through the various events that had resulted in my stint in the hospital—the things I was witness to, the things Starbuck described in his deposition, the final pieces of the jigsaw that Lea provided over dinner.

By the time the morning nurse arrived with my cold and lumpy breakfast oatmeal, I had the whole thing pretty well sorted out.

PART ONE

How I Got into This Mess

1

THAT FATEFUL MONDAY night had started innocently enough, without even a hint of Starbuck or his dumb, dangerous scheme. A simple repast at my restaurant, the Horse's Neck, followed by five minutes of chitchat about the next day's card with the horse players and track owls who keep the cocktail lounge noisy and smoky and alive. Then I was off across town on an errand of mercy.

No street gang followed with harmful intent. Nobody shot at me on the freeway. The earth did not shake or bounce under the Cherokee. The worst the newscast on the car radio could come up with was an oddball item about an unidentified adult male being kicked to death by a horse at Santa Rosita racetrack. It held no meaning for me. It had been seven years since I'd set foot on racetrack soil.

I figured it for one of those rare, lucky L.A. nights. Which was fine, because I would be spending most of it at a poker table. Not that luck has much to do with poker the way I play it.

The game was being held in an office on the nineteenth floor of one of those Century City glass-and-concrete slabs resting on land that was once a part of the backlot of 20th Century Fox studios. The floor-to-ceiling windows provided a nice view of an 1898 New York City street that had been constructed seventy years after the fact, at no little cost, for the movie *Hello, Dolly!*

The view was enhanced by the fact that there were no blinds on the windows. Not much furniture in the place either, except for a portable bar, a card table with a display of cold cuts, an official Diamond Jim poker table, and enough chairs for seven players plus the bartender and our host, Joey Kingman.

Joey was a pale, bald-headed man in his mid-fifties. He made his living finding appropriate locations, such as a vacant office space, for high rollers to indulge their illegal gaming lusts.

That night the invited included a real-estate guy from the Valley named Bob something, a movie producer I'd never heard of named Winston Mezzero, two brothers, Phil and Will Wheeler, who sold tires, Jay Grady, an actor who'd more or less retired after making a few million in a TV sitcom a decade ago, Maurice Adams, a television evangelist, and me, Colman Kille-brew, a former jockey turned restaurateur and general good sport.

Ours was not a friendly game of poker. We were not friends. At least they weren't my friends. They were part of Joey's regular group and had been meeting at various locations on the first Monday of the month for about a year. I was sitting in for a regular who'd complained to Joey after the last session that he thought Jay Grady, the big winner for two games in a row, had been enhancing his luck. He, the missing regular, would return only if and when Joey could assure him that the game was straight. So there I was, doing Joey a favor when I would have dearly preferred being in the comfortable little apartment over my restaurant, studying the sports section of tomorrow morning's *L.A. Times*.

During the first hour, the chips seemed to be hopping across the table to Grady's pile. He was an annoying, baby-faced man with a nervous laugh and a generally abrasive personality. That can be a definite plus in poker, provoking players into taking the game personally, wanting so hard to grind Grady's face into the green felt that they ignore the odds.

That might have been why Grady was such a big winner. But it wasn't.

He was seated to my right. Continuing around the table, counterclockwise, were real-estate Bob, Mezzero the movie maven, the Reverend Adams, who blessed the deck instead of cutting it, and the Wheeler boys, Phil and Will. We'd each started out with five thousand dollars in chips. Mine, which had been donated by Joey, had been reduced by a quarter. There were no really heavy losers just yet, but we were all down except for Grady, who smoked a cigar roughly the size of his ego and blew its acrid fumes into my face whenever he got the chance.

"This looks like my night," he said wetly, indicating his trip fours and reaching across the table with both hands to rake in the chips.

Will Wheeler, who'd held the losing pair of kings, sighed and asked the bartender for something called a Woolly Navel. The bartender, a dour soul named Ruben, replied, "No got. And I ain't got no goddamn piña colada, neither. How's 'bout a gin and tonic?"

"With a slice of lime?" Will asked.

Ruben just glared at him.

"Why don't we all take five?" Joey suggested. "Get a little food, a little drink, take a little whiz."

They agreed. While some went off in search of the bathroom and others hit the food table or began crowding Ruben, Joey motioned me to a far corner next to a floor-to-ceiling window that looked out over the city. Somewhere out there was my apartment, empty and beckoning.

"What do you think, Coley?" Joey whispered.

"You first," I whispered back.

"Well, the obvious thing is that the guy wins every damn time he deals."

"Yes," I said. "That is the obvious thing. What about the pickup cull?" I was referring to a method of cheating in which a player grabs the discards and uses them to set up a stacked deck for the next deal. In a heavy pro game, they'd cut off a guy's fingers for picking up the discards too early. But this was supposedly recreational poker.

"Jeez, is that how he's doing it?" Joey moaned.

"That and an overhand shuffle," I told him.

"The son of a bitch," Joey hissed. "I got a good mind to shove that goddamn cigar down his throat."

"That would be a bit premature," I said. "Let me take care of it."

"Hey," Jay Grady shouted from his chair at the table. "We didn't come here to eat and drink. We came here to play. I'm on a streak and time wasted is dinero lost."

Joey gave me a you-sure-you-know-what-you're-doing? look. Some guys live to worry. I responded with a supremely confident smile.

For the next forty-five minutes nothing extraordinary happened. Grady won a little more, always on his deal. Joey's nervousness increased and his eyes caught mine imploringly from time to time. I was fed up with him. But I was determined to do the job.

At just past ten, the price of poker really went up. The game was five-card stud, with Grady dealing. Phil Wheeler, who was as conservative as his brother was a plunger, dropped after looking at his hole card. Real-estate Bob and I said adios after two cards were exposed. The others seemed to be glued to the pot.

By the next-to-last round of betting, Will Wheeler was showing an ace of clubs, a queen of hearts and garbage. Grady displayed a king of diamonds and a pair of nines, and judging by the way he was throwing hundred-dollar chips onto the pile, he had another K-boy in the hole. Adams the evangelist showed all spades, but even with the Lord's help, he would probably not fill his flush. And the producer, Winston Mezzero, was pinning his hopes on a pair of sixes and an ace of hearts.

His jaw clamped firmly on a new unlit cigar, Grady spun out the final cards. Will picked up a queen of spades, the evangelist a lowly but welcome deuce of spades, Mezzero paired his ace, and Grady drew a club king. By the time the round ended, another several thousand dollars in chips had been added to the pot.

It was a very interesting table. Five-card stud does not usually produce so many bettable hands. But this was not a usual situation. Mezzero's two pairs—aces and nines—allowed him to open the bet. His clear blue eyes studied the cards on the table. He was in his thirties, a lean pretty boy with curly black hair, garbed in the film-industry-uniform dark Armani suit, white dress shirt open at the neck, a Cabo suntan, and enough gold jewelry to fully leverage the shadiest of savings and loans. His long, tapered fingers gracefully plucked two one-hundred-dollar chips from his pile and the race was on.

Grady, without hesitation, raised that by a thousand dollars.

Will Wheeler's hand went to his chips, but his brother grabbed it. Phil Wheeler shook his head and, surprisingly, Will shrugged and folded his cards.

The evangelist studied the board briefly and made his contribution, calling the bet. Mezzero saw Grady's thousand and raised it another two thousand.

Grady frowned and looked at Winston Mezzero's cards. "Wheeler showed the ace of clubs," he mused. "No way you could have pulled the case ace of spades." With a confident wink, he tossed in a three-thousand-dollar raise.

The evangelist shook his head. It was hell to hold a flush in a five-card game and discover it probably was not the winning hand. With the merest smile, he turned over his cards.

Mezzero, now going head-to-head with Grady, asked pleasantly, "How deep are you, Jay?"

Grady looked down at his chips, which he'd kept neatly

stacked. "Nine grand in front of me and another thirty in my pocket, *Winston*."

"Then that's my bet," Mezzero purred. "Thirty-nine thou."

Grady blinked and stared at the smiling movie producer. "You're bluffing, you bastard," he snapped. "You couldn't have that case ace. I got you beat."

"Right," Mezzero said sarcastically. "Like you're gonna make a comeback." He removed a packet of thousand-dollar bills from his coat pocket, counted out the proper number of bills. Joey was right at his side to exchange the cash for chips.

White-faced in fury, Grady pushed his chips to the center of the table. Then he got a thick pad of folded thousand-dollar bills from the pocket of his shirt and threw them onto the pile. Joey started to reach out to remove the cash from the game, but Grady snarled, "Leave it there, Shylock. I'm taking it right back."

He stared across at Mezzero. "Well?" he demanded.

Mezzero's long fingers turned over his hole card. It was the ace of spades.

"Dammit!" Jay Grady shouted, and leapt to his feet, nearly overturning the table. "Dammit!" he repeated.

"Want me to light that cigar for you, Jay?" Mezzero asked as he pulled in the pot.

Grady turned to Joey. "I'm out of here. And I'm not sure if I'll be back next month."

"I'll call you."

"Yeah," Grady said, glaring at Mezzero. "Call me."

As the door slammed behind Grady, Will Wheeler shrugged. "Most of that was our loot, anyway. He's been hitting us hard the past couple of games."

"But this does make the cigar-chewing bastard an overall loser," his brother added. "Good on you, Mezzero."

Mezzero smiled heroically. Joey gave me a confused look and I shrugged. He was definitely in the wrong business.

Another half hour passed uneventfully. I seemed to have inherited Grady's earlier penchant for winning on the deal. I was up nearly seven thousand dollars as I cut the cards for Will Wheeler. But I was tired of all of the games being played at that table.

When it came time for Phil Wheeler to deal, I shuffled the cards for him. He announced that he was going to play draw poker. I gave the deck one more flutter and passed it to Will, who cut for his brother.

The cards with their tiny octagon-patterned backs sailed out across the felt table. I picked up my five, but I didn't really have to look at them. Instead, I watched Winston Mezzero as he discovered what he thought the fates had sent him.

He was very professional. His blue eyes only widened for a fraction of a second. It's not every night a guy gets dealt a straight flush, even a small straight flush. He slumped in his chair, with a blank expression on his handsome face. But I spotted the pulse in his neck pounding away. If you see that pulse when a player looks at his cards, it's a pretty good sign that he's holding something extraordinary. If the pulse doesn't start throbbing until he bets, chances are he's bluffing.

Mezzero opened for a hundred. I saw him and bumped him a few hundred, friendlylike. The others all folded, even Will. While stacking the deck, I'd picked out a hand for him that was so terrible not even St. Francis of Assisi would have had any faith in it. I wanted to make sure that it would be just Mezzero and myself, bumping heads.

We kept raising one another coyly but continuously until there was about five grand in the pot. When it came time to draw, Mezzero glanced at his cards and said, unemotionally, "I'll play these."

The other players were impressed. Phil Wheeler asked, "What can I do for you, Coley?"

"I think I'll keep these, too."

This amused the others greatly, except for Joey, who looked at me with an expression sadder than a Saint Bernard's. Oh, ye of little faith.

Mezzero started off the new betting round with a thousand-dollar chip, and we went at it for a while. My stack of chips dwindled. Eventually, Mezzero said, "You got about seven thou left in front of you, Killebrew. That's my bet."

I added my chips to the overflowing pot and asked, "How deep are *you*, Winston?"

He cocked his head and smiled. "A little deeper than you, pal. Say thirty-five grand and some change."

"Before we sat down," I said, "I gave Joey thirty-six thou to hold for me, didn't I, Joey?"

Joey stared at me, ashen-faced. He had no idea what I was up to, but he was stuck with me. He gave a very forlorn nod.

"I'll raise you thirty-five grand and some change," I told the movie producer.

Joey shuffled over to his cash box and withdrew thirty-six thousand.

Mezzero looked from Joey to me. Then he flashed his bleached teeth in a shark's grin. He pushed all of his chips into the pot, along with a stack of G-notes that managed to cover the bet. I showed him the bad news, a straight flush in hearts to the ten.

He did not expose his cards, but I knew what they were: a straight flush in spades to the nine. The odds of being dealt a straight flush in a game of draw poker are somewhere around 15,942 to 1. The odds of being dealt a straight flush and being beaten by a *higher* straight flush are definitely off the charts.

I wanted Mezzero to know he'd been nailed. I wanted him to know I'd caught him fingering the discards and shuffling them for Jay Grady, stacking the deck so that Grady would win on his deals.

What I hadn't been sure of was whether Grady was in on the scam, since he'd walked away from the table twice before as the big winner. Mezzero answered that question when he cleaned Grady's plate. Letting Grady win was like putting money in a bank for the past two months. When the right time came, Mezzero withdrew all the funds and maybe a few thousand more of Grady's private reserve. And I had done the same thing to Mezzero.

He rose, glaring at me. He said, in a voice barely above a whisper but loud enough to be heard by us all, "You cheating little runt."

Phil Wheeler frowned and said, "I dealt that hand. Nobody cheated."

Mezzero ignored him. He turned on his heel and left the room.

The sound of the slamming door prompted the TV evangelist to say, "Well, I think it's time I returned to my flock. I'll just cash in these paltry little blue boys." He pushed three royal-blue one-hundred-dollar chips across the felt.

"It's time we all headed out," Will Wheeler said, and the others agreed, though the night was still relatively young.

Joey seemed to be in a daze. He turned to me for help. He'd had to dip into the bank for the thirty-six grand I'd used to nail Mezzero. He was short about five thousand dollars. I slipped him the cash to cover the chips.

Fifteen minutes later we watched the bartender, Ruben, departing with the leftover food and booze. Joey was folding the table. "You sure Grady wasn't in on the deal?" he asked me.

"I don't think so, but why not play safe? Don't let either of 'em in your games anymore."

"It used to be gamblers were more honorable," he said.

I wondered what world he was talking about.

"I'm sorry about Mezzero calling you a cheat."

"Coming from him, it was a compliment," I said.

"Well, you did me a good turn. Tell Johnny I appreciate it." It had been Johnny Rousseau, my not-so-silent partner in the Horse's Neck, who'd asked me to do Joey the favor.

"I'll tell him," I said, heading for the door.

"Don't forget your winnings," Joey said. "You sure as hell earned 'em."

"Spread it out to the guys who were taken by Mezzero," I told him, and realized at once that there was no way he could.

"I can't let 'em know I allowed either a cheat or a ringer in the game, Coley. Go on, keep it. It's more'n forty large."

"I never took a dime I didn't earn on the up-and-up," I said. "Donate it to the homeless."

"It's your moolah," Joey replied, giving me a you've-gotta-be-nuts look. But I knew that he'd honor my request.

Feeling even holier than the evangelist would, come Sunday morning, I rode the elevator down to the basement where I'd parked my Jeep Cherokee.

I was heading toward the shiny maroon wagon, thinking about the comforts of home, when Mezzero stepped from the shadows. His nice long fingers were wrapped around a pistol that was pointed at my chest.

"You've got one minute to give me my money, little man," he said. I'd played cards with the guy. I knew he wasn't bluffing.

2

THERE ARE TIMES to screw around and times to cut to the heart of the matter. "I don't have it," I told him.

A growl came from deep down in Winston Mezzero's throat and his finger tightened on the trigger. "But I know where it is," I added hastily.

He hesitated, then relaxed his finger. "Show me you don't have it," he ordered, moving closer.

The situation was not promising. As soon as he was convinced that I wasn't holding his money, he'd probably shoot me and then go after Joey. I reached for my right pants pocket. "Easy," Mezzero warned.

I edged my hand in slowly, then, just as carefully, withdrew it. Using considerably more speed, I threw an assortment of loose change into his face and dropped to the left.

There are those instances when size works to your advantage, even away from the track. Like when you make a small, fast-moving target. In the low-ceilinged garage area the shot sounded as loud as a mini-bomb. But the bullet missed me by a furlong.

Unfortunately, I couldn't get past Mezzero to freedom. And even if I was able to keep dodging until he ran out of bullets, he'd still be able to club me to death with the gun.

"Little man, you're dead," he hissed.

Suddenly, we were illuminated by a pair of bright, blessed halogen headlights. And a female voice was shouting, "What's going on there?"

Mezzero kept his eyes on me, but he began moving slowly until he could at least get a peripheral view of the newcomer. I was afraid to look away from him.

"I asked what's going on," the woman's voice continued.

"None of your goddamn business," Mezzero snarled, letting the headlights reflect off of his gun. "Just get your ass out of here."

I heard a car door open, and I had to see what kind of a woman would ignore the order of a guy with a gun. Blinking in the light, I observed a deeply tanned blonde who might have been seven feet tall get out of the car and start toward us. She was wearing white shorts and a dark blue halter. Her hair was gathered in a ponytail by a matching blue scarf. She was a California girl and a half.

Mezzero circled until he could keep his eyes on both of us. The giantess didn't pause for a second. She kept walking toward him. He looked mightily confused. A gun was supposed to make people, especially bystanders, listen up.

The blonde was only a few feet from him, totally ignoring the weapon. By the time he made up his mind to point it at her rather than at me, she'd pivoted on her left heel and kicked back her long, lovely right leg, driving *its* heel into Mezzero's privates.

With a shriek, he folded over. She did a little hop in the air, spun around again, and clipped the side of his head with her right foot, spiraling him into a cinderblock wall. His gun skittered along the cement floor a second before his body hit the deck and stayed there, motionless.

The blonde took a few steps, bent down, and picked up

Mezzero's gun. She turned to me and asked, "Is that you, Mr. Killebrew?"

I had never seen her before. I would have remembered. I said, "I think so."

"Would you mind getting into my car?"

"You don't suppose he's dead, do you?" I wondered, not caring much either way.

She crossed to Mezzero and used her foot to turn him onto his back. We could both hear his ragged breathing. "Broken nose," she said, disinterested. "Maybe a concussion. Broken hand."

"Blue balls," I added.

"Yes," she said with a smile, "that, too. Shall we?"

I shrugged and followed her to the car, a cherry-red Saab convertible with the top down. She tossed the gun casually onto the backseat.

"Well?" she asked as I stood there beside the car. "Aren't you getting in?"

"I was waiting for you to open the door for me."

With an elaborate gesture she threw open the door and bowed. She looked very good bowing. I got into the Saab and she slammed the door after me.

As we shot through the garage exit onto Century Park West at about sixty mph, I pointed to her cellular phone and asked, "May I make a call?"

"As long as it's under a minute."

I reached Joey Kingman as he was packing up. I told him that Mezzero had turned homicidal and suggested that he find his car quickly and be off. Then I replaced the phone and turned to the blonde. "Am I allowed to know where we're going?"

"To the Marina," she replied. Marina del Rey is a peninsula next to Venice that boasts a number of million-dollar beachfront shacks, a nice harbor, and one or two good restaurants, but it's best known for its mating bars.

"Great," I told her. "We can sip a couple of Harvey Wallbangers and see if we have compatible birth signs."

She gave me a fleeting smile. "Guess again."

"Why don't you just tell me what you've got in mind?"

"Don't you like surprises?"

"No. And I don't know anyone who does, except the fat guy on 'The Today Show.' "

"I love them," she said. "Especially when they're on somebody else."

3

IT TOOK THE blonde about fifteen minutes to make the half-hour drive to our destination on the Marina del Rey peninsula. The house had been built on the sand, with the beach and the ocean for its front yard. It was a solid-looking, two story-structure made of rough-hewn, weather-bleached wood and smoked glass.

An elderly Asian in white flannels and a midnight-blue blazer opened the door for us. The blonde called him Choo-Choo. He called her Miss Lea, which I supposed, made him some sort of butler. She handed him Mezzero's gun and told him to take care of it. He nodded and took it away, holding it daintily with thumb and forefinger and wrinkling his nose.

"Follow me," Lea said. As if there were any other option I'd choose.

We moved swiftly down a hall decorated with antique portraits of jockeys, through a large, masculine living room with a huge picture window facing the beach and ocean. It was furnished with white canvas stuffed chairs and a matching sofa and the hardwood floor was almost covered by a nice, quiet Oriental rug of deep purple. A captain's table in one corner was piled with magazines and racing forms.

A series of paintings of championship Thoroughbreds decorated the bleached-wood walls. Back in the good days, I'd ridden a few of the depicted horses into the winner's circle, including the great Spectacular Bid.

I got barely a glance at an unlighted dining room before being ushered into a wood-paneled den that was crowded with files, piles of papers and folders, riding boots, tack, a poster from the Bloomfield Open Hunt Horse Show, a blue-and-yellow scatter rug, several soft leather chairs, covered with books and papers, facing French doors that, if their blinds were open, would have provided a nice view of the Pacific.

There was an ancient table, possibly antique, that was housing a computer, a fax machine, three phones, a copier, and two or three other serious-looking gadgets that I couldn't immediately identify. Against the wall opposite the French doors there was an extra-long brown leather couch that had a caved-in middle.

All that took up about half the room. The other half was occupied by a massive black oak desk with gold corners and the man seated behind it. His name was Raymond Edgar Starbuck. The last time I'd seen him had been seven years before, sitting at another desk, telling me that it was the decision of the California Racing Commission that I no longer be allowed to earn a living as a professional jockey in the United States.

He seemed pretty much the same. He certainly hadn't grown smaller. He made the huge desk look like a Parsons table. He'd been hunched over it, frowning at a bronze statue of a bearded cowpoke riding a bucking bronco. One huge manicured hand was holding the statue upside down while he examined the belly of the horse through Benjamin Franklin glasses that were too small for his large, square face.

His pale blue eyes shifted from the bronze to me. With apparent regret, he righted the statue and placed it on his desk. "I hope Lea didn't interfere with your game," he said. "I asked her to wait until you were finished, but she's an impatient gal."

The blonde stared at him languidly, refusing to take the bait.

"Her timing was just fine," I told him. "She even helped me with a little problem I was having."

The pale blue eyes turned on Lea. "I'm sure she'll tell me all about it later," Starbuck said, making it sound like a reproach. "Right now there are more important matters. I've got a job for you, Coley."

"I have a job."

He glared at me and his high forehead wrinkled. "That's what you call it? Playing front man for a Vegas wiseguy?"

Seven years ago I would have jumped the desk and gone for him, right then, regardless of the fact that he had maybe a hundred and twenty-five pounds on me, not a lot of it fat. But I'd mellowed some during my stint as a restaurateur. So I used words instead of action. "I don't front for anybody," I informed him. "I paid for my share of the Horse's Neck. And Johnny Rousseau doesn't belong to any organization that I know of, except maybe the Vegas Better Business Bureau."

The big man shrugged. "I've heard different."

"Well," I told him, "you've heard wrong before."

"For nearly twenty years, when I was chief steward with the Jockey Club, part of my job was to check out every race, jockey, horse, or owner that seemed just a little bit, uh, questionable; and there were a lot of those. The last five years, in business for myself, I've been going one-on-one with some of the slimiest thieves who ever set foot on racetrack turf. I sorta know when the information is on and when it's sour."

"Even Einstein slipped up on his addition every now and then," I said.

He settled back and laced his fingers on his stomach. "Einstein had a lot on his mind. I keep a clear head."

"Clear meaning empty?"

He ignored the insult. "How'd you get hooked up with Rousseau, anyway?" he asked.

It was none of his business, but I couldn't think of a reason not to tell him. "No big story. When you're a top jock, there are hundreds of guys coming around to slap your back and buy you beer. But when you take a fall, nobody calls. Except Johnny. He asked me what I wanted to do with my life and I told him I thought a little restaurant in Hollywood might be nice."

"And is it?" Starbuck asked.

"Not as nice as the feeling you get when a thousand-pound Thoroughbred carries you past the finish line, but nice enough these days. Is it okay if I sit down?"

"Yeah, sure," he said. "Lea, throw the junk off one of the chairs for Coley."

The blonde walked gracefully to one of the leather chairs, tilted it, and dumped its contents onto the floor. Then she scooted the chair across the hardwood until it rested behind me. I slipped onto it. "Is there anything you don't do well?" I asked her.

"She makes lousy breakfast," Starbuck said.

"Ah," I said, leaning back in the chair.

"What's that supposed to mean?" he asked with sudden anger.

"It means 'ah.' "

Lea smiled at me. "I'm his daughter," she said. "You don't think I'd take up with anyone that pigheaded if I had a choice?"

"I was wondering," I told her. "Daughter, huh? That's amazing."

"I didn't bring you here to discuss my family, Killebrew," the big man snapped. "I want you to join me in this project."

"I liked it better when you called it a job," I said. "And I didn't like it much then."

"It'll be fast and easy and it'll be well worth your while."

"What do you want me to do?"

"Your specialty," he said. "I want you to fix a race."

4

I WISH I could tell you that without another word, I stood and walked from the room calmly and with dignity. But the fact is that, my image of myself as a mellow restaurateur notwithstanding, I leapt from the chair and grabbed the bronze statue with the intention of bouncing it off Starbuck's square head. Before I could put that plan into action, I felt a big blond body pressed against my back without any friendliness. Then a sharp jab in the side of my neck made me lose all strength in my right arm.

The bronco statue dropped to the desk with a clunk, bucked, and rolled over onto its side. I fell onto my chair, equally numbed.

Starbuck had barely moved. He shook his head disgustedly. "Get a rein on your emotions, man. You're behaving like a barroom bruiser."

Through clenched teeth, I said, "I've never fixed a race in my life and I've never knowingly been involved in a fix. And I think you are goddamn well aware of it."

"All I'm *aware* of is what the facts tell me, Killebrew," he said, leaning back in his chair, insufferably smug.

Rubbing my neck where the Amazon had poked it, I rose. "You can put your *facts* where the sun don't shine," I grumbled. Then I turned, waited for Lea to take a back step out of the way, and headed for the door.

I nearly made it before Starbuck crooned, "I know where you can find Francie Dorn."

Not much else could have stopped me. Francie Dorn. Green eyes laughing. Bright red curls crowning a lovely oval face. Milk-white skin, powdered with freckles. Black heart.

We'd lived together for nearly five months. The last time I saw her was that morning seven years ago when I left our apartment for the track to ride a horse named Wilder Walk. She never watched me race. Said it made her too nervous.

After my "accident," I expected her to be there at the hospital. I was surprised that she didn't show up during the two days I was there under observation. I was not surprised to find she'd moved out of the apartment.

She left no note.

Starbuck was grinning at me when I turned to face him.

"You know how the world works, Coley," he said. "You do something for me, and I do something for you, like putting you in touch with the woman who ended your racing career."

"I thought *you* ended it," I said.

"That's always been your problem. Betting the wrong horse."

"These days I only bet on sure things."

"Then you're not interested in Francie Dorn anymore?"

Lea wrinkled her nose in mild disgust as she glanced at her father.

"I'm interested," I said.

"Enough to play my game with my rules?" he asked.

Lea's aristocratic face was expressionless now. Her intelligent brown eyes were studying me.

"Why don't you tell me exactly what you want done," I said to her father.

5

IF STARBUCK HAD smirked or smiled or done anything to indicate that he was feeling good about yanking my chain, I might have taken a walk, Francie or no Francie. But he skipped the gloating and got down to business. Leaning back in his chair, he asked, "Ever been to Bucktown?"

I'd been to a couple of Bucktowns, but I assumed the one he meant was the suburb of New Orleans where a couple of ex-Confederate officers beat the post–Civil War blues by building what was to become one of the most famous racetracks in the country. There was a cemetery where the old track used to be, but historic Magnolia Park had been reborn several decades ago a few miles away, centered on a mile-wide peninsula surrounded on three sides by a generally unpolluted Lake Pontchartrain. "I know the place," I told Starbuck. "Spent a season there. Rode a few winners. Fancy Feet, Cayenne, Dream o' Me."

"I didn't ask for your autobiography. But I'm happy you're familiar with the track." He bounced the chair forward and began to sift through papers on his desk.

"It's been about nine years," I said, "but Magnolia Park shouldn't have changed much. A fast track. Good crowds. The gent who runs the operation, Cal Bouraine, is a charming old rascal who's convinced he makes the world's greatest mint julep."

Starbuck continued shuffling through the goat's nest on his desk. "They've got this annual feature race."

"The Dixie Derby."

He nodded, then relaxed as he got his mitts on the paper he'd been searching for. He paused to contemplate it, then slipped it into one of his desk drawers. "The derby carries a heavy purse for a medium-size track," he said. "One hundred thousand dollars. The favorite is an animal called Cajun Desire, sired by Cajun Caesar. I want you to try to arrange it so Cajun Desire loses."

"Seven years ago I told you I always played straight. Nothing's happened to change my mind on that."

"You fell in with a bad woman, Coley," he said, as if he were bored with the explanation. "She cashed a lot of tickets on that race. She wouldn't have if you'd won on Wilder Walk."

"Some evidence to snuff out a career," I snorted.

"You made your bed," he said, waving a dismissive hand. "Look, you don't have to actually fix Cajun Desire. All you have to do is go through the motions."

"Why?"

"Because the animal is owned by Remy Courville."

I looked properly blank. "Who's he?"

"A guy who likes to think of himself as a Louisiana business-man and horseman," Starbuck replied. "But he may be some-thing else entirely. His family carries a lot of clout in the state. His late father served a term as lieutenant governor. His sister, Roberta, owns a plantation that supplies nearly a fifth of this country's sugar. Remy has his own plantation that he's turned into a breed farm.

"On the surface, the Courvilles seem to be merely your aver-age white, elitist, alligator-tough Southern family. But an article last year in a New Orleans paper linked Remy to a nasty little scheme involving land fraud in Florida. It also mentioned that he's got a hair-trigger temper. I want to shake him up."

"Why?"

"Because that's what Mrs. McGuinn is paying me to do," Starbuck snapped.

"Clara McGuinn?" I asked, surprised. She was a solid–as–a–rock woman of middle years who'd been calling the shots at Santa Rosita raceway since her husband's death in the early seventies. I'd been a guest in her home many times, not only when I was riding high, but after I'd acquired my pariah status. "What's Mrs. Mac got to do with this?"

Starbuck's chair squeaked as he leaned back. He scratched his graying head and said, "Santa Rosita's had a couple bad seasons and Mrs. McGuinn is in the middle of a proxy fight she probably won't win unless we can reverse the odds a bit."

"This Courville is trying the takeover?" I asked.

"It's not that simple," Starbuck answered. "A company known as Southern Boy Supplies and Services is attempting to gain control of Santa Rosita Track Operating Company. Southern Boy is a Cayman Island corporation that took over Magnolia Park in Bucktown, Louisiana, a couple seasons back."

I frowned. "What happened to old man Bouraine?"

"Stroked out about three years ago. Without him, Magnolia Park started to slide. But since Southern Boy stepped in, it's become a cash cow. It was in trouble and now it's prospering. That sort of credential looks impressive to Mrs. Mac's shareholders, who are pretty disgusted with Santa Rosita's present bottom line. But she's not too anxious to step aside."

"I wouldn't think so," I said. "It's not easy to give up your life's work."

Starbuck pretended to ignore my comment. "There's something off about Southern Boy. It's been impossible to discover the names of the principals. There's no way in the world you can get any information out of the Caymans, especially when bankable funds are concerned. So I figured that the other end was the place to poke around. With Mrs. McGuinn's approval, I sent a local private investigator, Irwin Matthes, to Louisiana on a snooping expedition. He worked his way into the operation at the track and sniffed out a rumor that Remy Courville sits near the head of the boardroom table at Southern Boy."

"How good is Matthes?" I asked.

"The best," Starbuck said. "But he must've overplayed his hand, because he called me this morning to say he was heading home immediately. I need a replacement."

"What happened?"

Starbuck stuck a finger behind his glasses and rubbed his right eye. "I wasn't here when he called. Choo-Choo took the message. I'm meeting with Matthes tomorrow morning for a little debriefing. All I know now is that he's out of the game and I'm sending you in."

"Let me get this straight," I said. "You want me to try and fix a race because you think Remy Courville's company is pushing to take over Santa Rosita? I don't see what good a fixed race is going to do."

"It's simple," Starbuck said. "You start trying to put in the fix. Then Courville finds out about it and we see what he's made of."

"Suppose he doesn't find out?"

"We'll make sure he does," Starbuck said. "And the person who enlightens him will earn Courville's undying gratitude. And maybe his confidence."

"In other words, you want me to be your goat," I said.

"I'd call you more of a stalking horse."

"Meaning what?"

"When a political party wants to change the odds in favor of their man, they throw in a new candidate, a stalking horse that kicks up a lot of dust, gets everybody all perplexed. Then, when he's done the damage, the horse gallops away and their man is a shoo-in."

"So who's your man?" I asked.

Starbuck looked over at his daughter, who was leaning against the wall with her arms crossed. "Lea's my man," he answered with a wide paternal grin.

"So," I said, after an appropriate pause, "Lea drops the dime on me and gets very close to Courville. Then what?"

"I go through his garbage cans," Lea said, "and see what I can find that'll get him out of Mrs. McGuinn's hair."

"You're assuming that Southern Boy has some ulterior motive for wanting to take over these tracks," I said to Starbuck. "Suppose there's nothing? Suppose Remy Courville is just a good ole boy with a lot of loot who likes to own racetracks and knows how to run them profitably?"

"If that's the case," Lea said, "maybe I'll marry him."

"He's already married," Starbuck snapped at her. "But even

if—" The ringing telephone spared Lea the end of that sentence. Starbuck identified himself, then tucked in his chin and listened for a while. Every now and then he'd ask "When?" or "Why?" and once he went all out with "What are the details?"

To beat the boredom I winked at Lea and she gave me the sort of smile you bestow on a mental case.

Finally, with absolutely no change in his expression, Starbuck replaced the phone and asked, "Are you with us, Coley?"

"You don't know how this Courville will react," I told him. "He may have me arrested. He may have me worked over. Or worse."

"Lea will keep you informed of Courville's reaction," he said. "If it gets too rough, you can catch a plane out."

"Like Matthes."

Starbuck stared at me.

"What's *really* going on here?" I asked him. "What makes this Courville guy so important you'd put your own daughter at risk?"

He looked at the tall blonde with what seemed like genuine admiration. "Lea is the most self-sufficient human I know. Don't worry about Lea. As for my motive, it's simply to do a job I was hired to perform. Now if that's all . . ." He picked up a notepad and turned the top page back.

"There's still the awkward discussion of how much I'll be paid," I said.

"For maybe two weeks' work? Five grand plus expenses," Starbuck replied without looking up as he scribbled something on the notepad.

"Ten's my price," I told him.

He grunted and nodded agreement so quickly I realized I should have asked for more. I said, "Suppose it takes a third week?"

"It shouldn't."

"But if it does," I insisted, "I want another five grand."

He nodded again.

"And the whereabouts of Francie Dorn," I added.

"Of course," Starbuck said, looking up at me over his Ben

Franklins. "If you asked her real pretty, I imagine she might even help you spend the ten thousand."

I didn't bother to reply. I faced Lea. "Will you drop me off at my car, or shall I call a cab?"

6

AFTER FIVE MINUTES of using her Saab to send dozens of fear-frozen Marina del Rey yuppies back into their mixer bars, Lea Starbuck asked me, "Well, did you do it?"

"It?"

"What my father accused you of."

I cocked my head in contemplation. "Not exactly," I said. "Were you trying to hit that guy on the cycle?"

Lea stared at the leathered longhair whose polished chrome machine had barely escaped the Saab's bumper as she barreled into the right lane. He swerved and gestured menacingly with a clenched fist. She blew him a kiss and said, "Missed with at least a foot to spare. Anyway, we're talking about you and Dad."

"Your father and I probably won't be doing one of those telephone commercials," I said. "The one where old friends keep in touch."

"What makes him think you threw a race?"

"It wasn't just any race," I told her. "It was a Breeder's Cup at Santa Anita."

"And you say you didn't throw it, exactly."

"Do you do much riding?" I asked.

"Very little. It's my father's game, not mine. Why?"

"I was trying to think of the best way to explain what happened."

"We both speak the same language," she said. "Keep it under four syllables and I bet I can get the drift of it." The Saab buzzed onto the Santa Monica Freeway, followed by angry horn blasts of which Lea seemed blissfully unaware.

I said, "It was a hard-luck race. I had trouble getting away from the gate and found myself trapped behind a pack of horses. Then a hole opened. You don't get much time to decide if the hole's wide enough. Maybe three seconds. I went for it and that was a mistake."

"What happened?" She was not vitally interested, merely curious.

I decided to tell her anyway. "A pretty nasty crash. A jockey named Dewey Lane broke his leg and two horses hit the turf. Mine, a powerful three-year-old named Wilder Walk, had to be put down."

"Were you hurt?"

"My pride mainly. A dislocated shoulder and a minor concussion. But they let me live, if you call it living."

"And Dad thinks you did it on purpose?"

I nodded. "He was chief steward at the time and called for an investigation. Wilder Walk was the favorite."

"That was the only reason he had—your horse was the favorite?"

I chuckled. "There was one other thing," I said. "The woman I was living with—"

"Francie Dorn?" Lea interrupted.

"Yeah, Francie Dorn. Evidently she had bet quite a lot on the horse who'd been favored to show, Mighty Rose. Only she bet him to win, which he did."

"Ah!"

"Ah, indeed." I could see Century City's high-rise buildings in the near distance. I wondered what the odds were that we'd make it in one piece.

"How much did she win?"

"The figure eighty thousand sticks in my mind. But that was

just the total of the bets your father knew about."

"And Dad assumes you got a share?"

"No," I said. "He knows I didn't. A team of accountants convinced him. So he came up with another theory. I was in on the deal, but Francie ran off with all the money."

"Did she?"

"Run off? Absolutely. By the time I woke up in the hospital after the fall, she was long gone."

"So without any real evidence, and without any witnesses, Dad put you out of racing."

"You got it." We were zooming along Little Santa Monica Boulevard now, seeing how close the Saab could get to the parked cars.

"But you must have fought it. Your lawyer should have been able to do something."

"That's where it gets a little complicated," I told her.

Her fine, high forehead wrinkled. "In what way?" she asked.

"I was not completely blameless."

"Ah," she said, as if her world suddenly made sense again. "Well, then . . ." she added, hoping that that would prompt some sort of defensive reply.

When it didn't, neither of us said another word until we descended into the underground parking lot where my maroon Cherokee was waiting, apparently unmolested.

"I don't see your homicidal friend," Lea announced, her eyes probing every square inch of the well-lighted area. "Suppose he's gone home?"

"When you get kicked that hard in the balls," I said, "home is where you usually want to go. Or a hospital. In any case, thanks for a swell evening."

She waited until I'd started to open my door to ask, "What do you mean you're not completely blameless?"

"We could go somewhere and talk about it over a drink," I suggested.

"Somewhere like your apartment?" she asked cynically.

"I was thinking of my restaurant," I said.

She defrosted a bit. "Oh. That's a possibility, I suppose."

"It has a back stairwell that leads to my apartment," I told her with a smile as I stepped from the Saab. "Follow me."

"I know the address."

"Follow me, anyway," I said. Then I remembered her driving, and added, "But not too closely."

7

IT WAS JUST past the witching hour when Lea and I parked our cars in the nearly empty lot next door to my restaurant, the Horse's Neck. I decided on the rear entrance to avoid the handicappers in the cocktail lounge, who, at that time of night, would certainly be in the bag and either overly friendly or belligerent.

As we strolled through the kitchen, which was in its clean-up-and-good-night phase, Antony, the head chef, glared at Lea as if he expected her to steal one of his fry pans. He was going through a difficult divorce and his opinion of women, even long-legged blondes who were with the boss, was unshakably negative.

Jack Hayward, whom you may remember as John Fitzhugh Hayward, a jowly British character actor who'd appeared in a million movies over the past five decades and starred briefly as a confidence man in a 1950s TV series, spied us as soon as we entered the empty dining room. He serves as the restaurant's maître d' when he's between pictures, which has become nearly his permanent situation.

"Ah, I see you found the blackguard," he said to Lea as he bounded toward us, his rosy face beaming.

"He was right where you said he'd be," she told him.

"Bravo," he said, as naturally as I've ever heard the word. "Well, may I fetch the handsome couple potables from yon bar?"

When Jack had wandered off with our order—a cognac for Lea, a framboise for me—I asked, "What story did you feed him to find out where I was?"

"A variation on the one about me being a friend from out of town who simply had to see you before I flew back," she said. "Don't be cross with him. He held out until I told him how much I enjoyed his performance in *Eve Ate the Apple*."

Jack played a butler in the movie, which was one of his favorites. "Your dad was right. You can take care of yourself just fine."

When the noted thespian returned with our drinks, he didn't say a word, merely made a little gesture with his hands that was similar to the one the pope uses to bestow his blessings on the crowd.

Lea blew him a kiss and the old fraud blushed. Then she turned her eyes on me and raised her glass. "To the future," she suggested.

I clinked to that.

She took a sip of cognac and said, "So finish telling me about the race."

Her persistence was praiseworthy, but I could have done without it. What to say? "I was off that morning," I explained. "As soon as I put on my shoes, I knew it. It had been a very wet night. Lots of booze. I still felt woozy and I knew damn well that my reflexes were off. And if they hadn't been, I would not have tried to push my mount through an opening that narrow. So I can't say truthfully that I was without blame for what happened."

She frowned. "Would you feel guilty if you'd had a head cold, or an ear infection that threw off your equilibrium? It sounds to me like you did what anyone would do who was trying to win a race. You saw an opening and you went for it."

I sipped my framboise and wished that she were right.

She asked, "Did you ever consider that you wanted to share the guilt with Francie Dorn because that made you feel like you were still together?"

So much for her being right. I was experiencing the stirrings of lust in my heart and I thought she could give me information about her father that might prove useful and I was actually beginning to like her. So I didn't call her theory dumb schoolgirl psychobabble. Instead, I said, "We've been talking about me all night. Now let's hear the Lea Starbuck story."

"It's nothing nearly so . . . eventful. I was born in Great Neck, Long Island. When I was a tot, Dad, Mother, and I spent summers and falls there while he was a steward at Aqueduct and Belmont Park. 'The Big A and the Medium-sized B,' was what he called them. Winters, we'd move to Saratoga or out here for the Santa Anita season."

"Must've been tough to make friends with all that moving around," I said.

"As soon as I started school, Mother and I stayed put and Daddy did all the traveling by himself."

She told me a little about her schooling, her life with Mother, and a few amusing vignettes about Starbuck that I think were attempts to make me dislike him less. They failed.

"What made your dad go into business for himself?" I asked.

"Mother died. A heart attack took her very quickly and she was gone before he was able to fly back to Great Neck.

"Her death hit him very hard. He sold the Great Neck house, ended his stewardship, and did nothing for nearly a year. Then Worldwide Insurance, which has a special department that provides coverage for members of the racing profession, hired him to recover a Thoroughbred that had been stolen from a farm in Lexington—Robber Baron."

"I'd heard that Worldwide got the animal back from some pistoleros down in Mexico. I didn't know it was Starbuck who found the horse."

She nodded proudly. "After that success, he became too busy to mope around anymore. And when I finished college the following year, I went to work for him."

"Why is he so anxious to get the goods on this Courville guy?"

"Part of it is the money," she replied matter-of-factly. "Mrs. McGuinn is an old friend. But she's also paying him a lot, and

Dad has never been vague where money is concerned."

"What's the other part?" I asked.

She frowned and shook her head. "I don't really know. I wonder if your old girlfriend has something to do with it. Dad spent an enormous amount of time tracking her down."

"Why?"

She shrugged. "Unfinished business, maybe. What about you? Haven't you ever tried to find her?"

"I don't suppose I've spent more than four or five years at it."

Her eyes were suddenly very bright. "To kill her or to kiss her?" she asked.

That *was* a question. I hadn't been very wise in the ways of the world when I met Francie, but my wins had given me enough of a taste of celebrity to spot manhunters from a furlong away. And she'd gotten past my defenses.

Sure, she'd been vague about her past. And there was an impulsive quality about her and a fearlessness that at times seemed a little odd. But that only added to the excitement. Once, when we were at a party at the home of a top breeder, she dragged me into our host's bedroom, insisting we make love immediately. That accomplished, she proceeded to poke around the room, opening drawers, dancing, and mugging with articles of our host's and hostess's clothing.

She discovered a little gun in the drawer of a bedside table. She removed it, grinned, pointed it at me, and pulled the trigger.

The weapon made a click—the loudest click I'd ever heard.

"What the hell are you doing?" I managed to croak.

"I knew it wasn't loaded," she told me. "I could tell by the heft. I grew up with guns. My father sold them."

She replaced the pistol in the drawer and slid back into bed with a cat's smile. "How do you feel?" she asked. "Happy to be alive?"

"That. And angry. And anxious to be out of here."

"Relief and anger and anxiety," she said, pressing her body against mine. "Tell me they don't turn you on."

Considering the position we were in, it would have been foolish to lie.

Our time together had been like that. Unpredictable. Wild. Dangerous. I don't know if I loved her, but I'd definitely been infatuated with her. Was I still?

That was more or less the same question that Lea had asked. "I won't know until I see her," I replied. "And maybe not then."

Lea nodded and shifted her stare to the dregs of cognac in her snifter. "Would you like another?" I asked. "Upstairs?"

She hesitated. "No," she said finally. "I'd better go."

I stood as she pushed her chair away from the table. "I booked you on a Delta flight tomorrow night at nine," she said. "The ticket will be waiting for you at LAX."

As we walked away from the table I was following her a bit too closely. She turned suddenly and I almost bumped into her. She had a crooked smile on her face. She moved closer and stooped a little so that I didn't have to stand on my toes to kiss her.

It was a pretty good embrace, all things considered. When it ended, she took a deep breath and said, "We don't have to be work slaves when we get together in New Orleans, do we?"

"I bet we could take a night off," I suggested.

"At least that."

I followed her through the kitchen. It was empty now, except for Antony, who had removed his apron and chef's hat and was slipping into his sport coat. He glared at Lea.

At the back door we kissed again, and I said, "See you in Dixie."

I watched her as she moved gracefully across the parking lot to her convertible. When I turned, Antony was staring out of a window at the departing Saab.

"That woman, Coley," he said, and then he began to sputter as if his words were too inadequate to express his emotions. "That woman," he tried again, "she got the most beautiful legs I ever see."

"Yes. They're something, all right."

But he would not be denied. "It's like they carved out of some kinda perfect wood. And polished by hand."

"You should relax a little, Antony," I told him. "Pour yourself a drink. Take a nice, cold shower."

He didn't hear a word I said. "Oh, *madre*, if she was my wife, even for just a few weeks, she wouldn't need to hire no goddamn lawyer. I *give* her the goddamn house just for the pleasure of those fine legs."

"That reminds me," I said, and headed for the large refrigerator, where I found an herb-baked chicken drumstick I'd been saving since lunch.

I took it and a glass of milk up to my apartment. They say if you eat just before going to bed, you're liable to have a nightmare.

That night I dreamed about Francie Dorn.

PART TWO

Starbuck's Story

8

I EMPLOYED KILLEBREW *because I was up against the wall. It didn't matter that the guy had a reputation worse than Shoeless Joe Jackson's. In fact, that was just the kind of reputation I needed and I didn't know how to list that in a Help Wanted ad.*

That's how Starbuck described our genial, one might say familylike, business relationship to the FBI after everything got messy. But according to the verbatim transcript of his interviews with Agents Joe Mossbach and Wheeler Deemes, which Lea passed along to me in the hospital in New Orleans, he wasn't quite as forthcoming on the subject of my predecessor.

MOSSBACH: *"The man you hired before Killebrew, what's his name?"*
STARBUCK: *"I'm sorry. What?"*

MOSSBACH: *"Name. This investigator you hired. What's his name?"*

STARBUCK *(hesitating):* *"Matthes. Irwin Matthes. Anyway he went down there to New Orleans. . . ."*

MOSSBACH: *"We're gonna have to pay him a visit."*

STARBUCK: *"You won't want to do that."*

MOSSBACH: *"Oh, no? Why?"*

STARBUCK: *"Fact is, the poor sod's dead."*

MOSSBACH: *"Dead? Dead how?"*

STARBUCK: *"Accident."*

DEEMES: *"What kind of accident?"*

STARBUCK *(mumbling):* *"Kicked in the head by a horse."*

DEEMES: *"Did you say 'by a horse'?"*

   Silence.

DEEMES: *"You have to answer in words, Mr. Starbuck. The tape doesn't pick up nods."*

STARBUCK: *"Yes. He was kicked by a horse."*

MOSSBACH: *"This wouldn't be the guy that got his brains scrambled at Santa Rosita? About three weeks ago?"*

STARBUCK: *"The same."*

DEEMES: *"And you and he were working for Santa Rosita?"*

STARBUCK: *"In a manner of speaking."*

MOSSBACH: *"And you think it was an accident?"*

STARBUCK: *"That's what the Torrance Police Department decided after their investigation."*

DEEMES: *"Did they talk to you before arriving at that conclusion?"*

STARBUCK: *"No."*

DEEMES: *"And did you offer them the information that the late Irwin Matthes had been investigating this Southern Boy Supplies, thereby making his death seem somewhat more than accidental?"*

STARBUCK: *"No."*

DEEMES: *"Why the heck not?"*

STARBUCK: *"It was my job to assist the management of Santa Rosita. An accidental death was bad enough for business. A possible murder would have turned the place into an empty cavern."*

MOSSBACH: *"You never know. People like that kind of morbid stuff. A murder might have been good for business."*

STARBUCK: *"I didn't care to make that decision, and since I had no hard evidence that it wasn't an accident . . ."*

This was a blatant lie. By then, Starbuck knew damn well that Matthes had been murdered.

MOSSBACH: *"When did you find out about Matthes's death?"*
STARBUCK: *"A few hours after his body was discovered. A friend called me while I was in consultation with Mr. Killebrew."*
DEEMES: *"What friend?"*
STARBUCK: *"I . . . it's odd, but I don't seem to recall."*

As much fun as it was reading about how the Feebs pushed Starbuck to the wall, it was not very enjoyable to discover how badly I'd been misled by the son of a bitch. He'd received the news of Matthes's death—Matthes's unquestionable murder—while I was sitting there in the room with him. But instead of warning me about the kind of people we were dealing with, he didn't let out a peep.

Instead, we cut our deal and he sent me off with his daughter like a lamb to the lions.

Then, as Lea was later to reconstruct the scene, as soon as we were out of his house and out of his hair, he dug through a desk drawer for his Colt Police Special and black leather holster. At least *he* would have a fighting chance if things got rough.

He attached the holstered handgun to his belt, grabbed a rumpled sport coat from a hook, and left the room. As he barreled through his spotless kitchen the houseman, Choo-Choo, looked up from his late dinner to see him snatch a handful of bagels on the run.

I'd assumed that Starbuck was a Seville or Lincoln Town Car sort of guy, but I'd underestimated him. Comfortably ensconced behind the wheel of a Bentley ragtop, he glided from his garage with one hand on the wheel and the other on his car phone.

Before he hit his first red light, the aristocratic voice of Mrs. Clara McGuinn had answered his call. Their conversation went something like this:

"I'm free to talk now," he said. "Lay whatever more bad news you've got on me."

"Nothing beyond what I already told you," she answered, rather testily. "Your man, Mr. Matthes, was found dead in a barn at my track. And the police are convinced that one of Jay Fairsea's animals is responsible. It's been all I can do to keep them from putting the poor beast to sleep on the spot."

"Have they identified Matthes?" he asked, making a clean turn onto the Santa Monica Freeway.

"His wallet was missing, and I have matched the police in playing dumb, as per your suggestion."

"Let's keep them stupid for a few more hours."

"That shouldn't be hard," she replied scornfully. "They're considering hoofprinting the horse."

"I'm gonna snoop around Matthes's apartment before they get their mitts all over everything," Starbuck said, moving impatiently past a small import.

"Let me know what you find."

"I'll try to make it to your place before midnight. Will you be able to shake the lawmen by then?"

"I'm leaving now," she replied. "I've had my fill of observing law enforcement at its most obtuse."

"What makes you so sure Fairsea's horse didn't do the job on Matthes?" he asked.

"A horse may have inflicted the damage on the poor man's skull," she answered, "but the heels of your Mr. Matthes's shoes clearly indicate that he was dragged through the mud into the barn. And I doubt that even the smartest Thoroughbred who ever lived would have been able to attack him and then hide his body in another location."

"You *do* use your eyes, don't you, Clara?" Starbuck told her. "You should have been a sleuth."

"That may be my midlife career change, if I lose my racetrack."

"That's not gonna happen."

"I suppose that's why neither of us is worried," she replied dryly, breaking the connection.

9

THE WILLOUGHBY APARTMENTS where Matthes lived was a three-story stucco building in Hollywood on Kings Road. With no legal parking place in sight, Starbuck wedged the Bentley into a space next to a hydrant and got out without bothering to lock the car. As he approached the Willoughby's glass-front doors, a deliveryman was exiting carrying a bright red warming box labeled DELVECCHIO'S BOSTON PIZZA.

The man was thin and sallow and looked as if he hadn't eaten a pizza in his life. Starbuck stopped him with, "Did you just drop one off at my place? Mott in 3-C?"

The skinny man shook his head. "Naw. It went to Grace in 4-B. Somebody'll be along with yours soon. I'll check when I get back to make sure."

"Thanks," Starbuck said.

He watched the man stroll to his truck, get behind the wheel, and start the engine. Then he pressed the button for 4-B.

There was a short wait, followed by a click and a woman's voice saying, "Yeah?"

"Grace, this is Delvecchio's again," Starbuck replied, vaguely imitating the delivery boy's laconic speech. "I shortchanged you on your order. I owe you another two bucks."

The buzzer sounded and he entered the building.

He didn't have to consult the directory, which was in a brass frame on the left. He moved swiftly through the empty pale-green-and-white lobby and, ignoring the elevator, took the carpeted stairs to the second floor.

The door to apartment 2-D was slightly ajar. Starbuck put his credit card back into his wallet. He used the tip of one brown suede shoe to push the door open.

The apartment was in darkness.

Starbuck drew his Colt from its holster and stepped warily but swiftly past the bright doorway into the darkness.

He reached beside the door for a light switch, but his hand touched only smooth wall.

A door slammed at the rear of the apartment.

Starbuck rushed forward, banging his knee on a wooden chair. Cursing, he arrived at the rear of the apartment flying blind. He followed the hum of a refrigerator and opened its door. The interior light led him to the apartment's back exit.

He went through it in time to hear footsteps slapping down the cement stairwell.

Adrenaline testing his arterial walls, he bounded down the stairs in pursuit. He stepped out into a narrow walkway and paused to gawk at the sight of a tall redheaded woman in a jogging suit as she struggled with a rear gate.

He shouted, "Hey, stop right there."

The woman did not stop. She rattled the gate frantically and finally got it open.

Grunting, Starbuck ran to the gate just as it swung back and closed with a snap. The woman was halfway down the alley slipping into a fairly new little toy car. Starbuck thought it was some sort of Japanese product; he couldn't tell them apart. This one's engine turned over right away and the redhead was roaring off with a screech of rubber.

Breathing heavily now, Starbuck made a mental note of the car's plate, a California vanity job consisting of the word KNEADY.

He put the Colt back into its holster and retraced his steps to Apartment 2-D. There, he used the glow from the fridge to find a light switch.

In sudden brightness, the rooms looked as if they'd been hit by a tornado.

In the den, which had been used as an office, the cushions of a beige sofa had been ripped, the sofa itself gutted. Drawers had been pulled from a desk and from a bright green filing cabinet.

A Stone Age computer monitor lay on its side. Starbuck straightened it and turned on the machine. A message appeared on the monitor: INSERT START-UP DISK. He looked at the desk. There didn't seem to be a start-up disk. In fact, there were no disks at all. Not even scattered on the floor with all the file folders and papers, some of them bearing the name of the occupant of the apartment, Irwin Matthes.

In the equally devastated bedroom he noted lipstick on a pillowcase. New or old? Also among the debris were cigarettes with lipstick on the filters. The cigarettes were recent. There was still smoke in the air. Probably the jogger. But did joggers smoke?

He didn't know very much about Matthes's private life. Had he a girlfriend? Somebody he trusted?

There was a small study that Matthes had been using as a TV room. The set had been dragged to the center of the floor. Its back had been removed.

Books had been pulled from half the shelves. Starbuck didn't like the fact that whoever had done the search had not pulled all the books from the shelves. It made him think that whatever the searcher had been looking for had been found.

He bent down and began poking through the books. Then he studied the titles still on the shelf. He was trying to figure out which book had been the last that the searcher had grabbed when the phone rang. Matthes's recorded voice announced that he was not at home and requested that the caller please leave a name and number. The caller did not respond to that request. Starbuck heard him say, just before hanging up, "Nobody there, Sarge."

The police had finally ID'ed Matthes's body.

Starbuck used a handkerchief to press the answering machine's playback button. He waited for the clicks and whirls. There were no incoming messages. Either that or the machine had been cleared.

He pushed the redial key.

There was a series of clicks, then a pause, then a ring. A voice with a built-in sneer answered, "Hotel Brentwood."

It was the new camping grounds for incoming celebrities: two pale blue towers overlooking a prime section of westside residential property with upward of two hundred rooms. Since the phone couldn't tell him which of the two hundred Matthes had called, Starbuck hung it up.

He wondered if it were possible to pry a guest roster out of the hotel. Maybe a name would ring a bell. He'd put Lea on it in the morning.

He took one final look around. Time was running out. He left the apartment, careful to wipe the knob with his handkerchief.

The first police car arrived on the scene just as the Bentley pulled away from the curb.

10

LESS THAN HALF an hour later the Bentley was parked along a quiet, tree-lined street in Beverly Hills. Starbuck was slouched behind the wheel, idly nibbling a bagel and watching the gate to a walled mini-mansion directly across the way. A machine embedded in the burled wood of his dash played a cassette tape of Johnny Mercer singing his own compositions.

"Accentuate the Positive," "Glow Worm," "Blues in the Night," Starbuck knew the words to all of them. According to Lea, her father had known them for years, had sung them often to his wife, Lily, who'd always been amused at how such a gravelly voice could carry a tune so charmingly. He stopped singing after Lily's death. But only a few weeks before, he'd seen the Mercer tape advertised in a magazine and he'd sent for it on a whim. Lea thought it was because it reminded him of her mother.

The gate to the mini-mansion swung inward and two figures passed through it. One was tall and feminine, the other short and canine.

Clutching a leather leash attached to the collar of a frisky medium-sized dog, Clara McGuinn looked up and down the street. Starbuck got out of the Bentley and joined her.

He regarded the dog, an English harrier named Skitter, with some wariness. At their last meeting the dog had urinated on his two-tones, doing such a thorough job of it that he'd had to throw the shoes away. He leaned forward, ready to knee the mutt, if necessary.

Clara, a frown of apprehension hovering over her soft, purple eyes, glanced back at the gate and said, "We'll have to be quick. Barry knows I never take longer than fifteen minutes to walk Skitter, especially this late."

"Why didn't you just level with him and tell him we had business to discuss?"

She was distressed. "We have our ways of coping with situations," she said in a tone that closed out that subject.

Barry Gallen was her junior by at least a decade. They'd met about three years before when Gallen, an executive at a cable network, had set up a deal to televise the races at Santa Rosita. I didn't know him, but I'd seen him around. He was a handsome, self-assured guy who talked a little too loud. But the story was that he seemed as genuinely smitten with her as she was with him.

Just a few months after they started seeing one another, he moved into the home she'd shared with John McGuinn for nearly thirty years.

From the time of John's passing until her romance with Gallen, Mrs. Mac had kept her life away from the track rather private. Gallen made it considerably less so, establishing an overbearing presence in the clubhouse and at dinner parties that her friends and associates somehow managed to tolerate out of affection for her.

Gallen, however, had demonstrated very little tolerance for most of Clara's cronies, particularly those he felt socially beneath him. I'd heard he played it especially high hat with Starbuck, if not for that reason, then because he suspected, with some justification, that Starbuck's fondness for Clara ventured beyond the platonic.

As she and Starbuck strolled that night past multimillion-dollar homes belonging to film stars and sports figures and dope dealers, the burly man found some small solace in the fact that she hadn't actually married Gallen. "Have the police come up with anything more?" he asked her.

She shook her head. "It was perfectly dreadful, and you didn't make it any easier, Ray, telling me to stay mum about Mr. Matthes."

"They've identified him," he informed her. "I barely beat the squad car to his apartment."

"It's so dreadful. What in the world was your Mr. Matthes doing at the track at that hour, anyway?"

Starbuck had been wondering that himself. "I don't know," he said simply. "I assumed he'd call me when he got in town, but he didn't. Instead, he phoned somebody at the Brentwood Hotel and then went to the track. I wonder why?"

"Maybe he didn't go there voluntarily. Maybe his killer deposited him there to lay even more bad publicity on my doorstep."

"More likely he was lured there. By what? The promise of information?" Starbuck scowled. "How'd he and the killer get in, anyway? Don't you have watchmen over there?"

"Of course we do," she said. "They just don't seem to have been terribly efficient. The police think Mr. Matthes entered from a hole in the back fence. No telling how many people have used it to wander around the grounds. There is even evidence that trespassers have been using the track at night for jogging, for God's sake."

Starbuck's thoughts went immediately to the woman in the

jogging suit who'd been in Matthes's apartment. Then they bounced back to the track. "Do you know the watchmen personally?" he asked.

"One of them, Larry Mullen, has been with us for aeons. He's the son of one of my husband's track cronies."

Starbuck knew the crony, Pat "Irish" Mullen, an old jockey agent who'd passed away at least a decade ago. His son would have to be in his fifties. "What about the other fella?"

"Louis Naylor. A six-year employee. Formerly with the San Diego Police Department."

"What were they doing while all hell was breaking loose?"

"They say they fell asleep."

"Both of them?" Starbuck asked incredulously. "Well, Clara, I sure hope you don't mind me doing a quick background on 'em."

"Do what you feel is needed," she said. Then she added, "Are we in agreement that Mr. Matthes's death was not an accident?"

He watched the harrier gleefully bestowing its corrosive urine on a healthy shrub. "No question about it," he said.

"Am I in danger, Ray?"

"You're at least two steps away from it, the way I figure. Matthes was murdered because he discovered something. The killer probably thinks he died before he could pass on his discovery. But if not, the trick will be for Mr. Death to find out who Matthes was working for. You don't have to worry unless somebody bumps me off, Clara. Then you can start wondering if they know who *I'm* working for."

She gave him a very worried look. He tried a reassuring grin until it began to hurt his face. "I wasn't trying to scare you, lady. Just the opposite. Nobody's gonna try to do me any harm." But he *was* armed. "Anyway," he went on, "our association, if that's what it is, has been kept pretty much under wraps."

She nodded. The dog tugged at the leash. "We'd better head back to the house," she said.

"I can find you a good bodyguard," he offered.

"I'd rather have a gun," she replied.

"Have you ever used one?"

She smiled frostily. "You don't know much about my girl-hood, do you, Ray?"

"Not much." It surprised him that he didn't. They'd spent quite a bit of time together over the years and talked about nearly everything. He knew she drank vodka and tonic without lime. He knew she liked the symphony, the Lakers, Pink's hot dogs, automobiles with plenty of legroom, the Democratic party, Sunday hats, and people who talked about things other than real estate or the movie industry. He did not know why she thought she was in love with Barry Gallen.

"Let it suffice to say I can shoot a gun," she said, bringing him back to the moment.

"I'll have one sent around in the morning."

"No," she told him. "You'd select one of those little lady pistols. I'll find my own weapon, thank you."

At the gate to her home he said, "I had a brief meeting with George this afternoon." Her nephew, George McGuinn, was the head accountant of her company.

She nodded. "Did he use that favorite phrase of his, 'a very downside picture'?"

"Not more than twice. Must be part of the working vocabulary they teach 'em at Yale."

"George went to Harvard," Clara said.

"Even worse," Starbuck said. He'd met with the tall, gangly, ultraserious young man in the study of George's three-room bachelor apartment in Santa Monica. While others his age were out enjoying the sunshine and beaches, George was entombed in a room with blinds drawn to keep the outside world at bay, surrounded by ledgers, spreadsheets, computers, stacks of software, half-consumed cans of diet cola, and Snickers candy-bar wrappers rolled into tight little balls.

George's eyes, behind thick glasses, looked weary, his clothes rumpled. Starbuck noted that he wore both belt and suspenders, an ultraconservative touch that he found depressing in one so young.

"He's quite clever, really," Mrs. Mac said. "Top of his class. Brilliant with computers."

"He looks like he's been spending too much time at the keyboard," Starbuck said.

"The boy is so darned serious. But at least he's found time to get himself a girlfriend, not that he'd ever mention it to me."

"Then what makes you think he's got one?"

"Women know these things, Ray. Besides, a friend saw them together. The lady was described as 'Madonna on the hoof.' "

Starbuck was vaguely impressed. "That may be the reason he looks like he's been livin' on No Doz."

"I'm sure she has contributed to his lack of sleep. But the main reason for his run-down condition is that he's been burning the midnight oil putting together a financial report for a stockholders' meeting in thirteen days."

"He mentioned the report," Starbuck said. "The question he couldn't answer was why Santa Rosita continued to lose money last season even though attendance was holding."

"It's the recession. People don't have as much betting money as they used to and the darned Lotto gets a hunk of that. And operating costs have soared to the moon," she said. She bit her lip as she stared at him. "Time seems to be moving so quickly these days, Ray. Is there any chance you'll have something that might help me at the meeting?"

"I'm sending a new man to New Orleans tomorrow to do the job Matthes didn't quite get done."

"Do I know him?"

He hesitated, then told her about me.

"I've always been so fond of Coley," she said. Or I hope she did. "I hate to see you put him in so perilous a situation. Isn't there anyone else?"

"I need somebody with a lousy reputation."

"That he has, thanks to you. I'm surprised he agreed to do it."

"Well," the bastard replied, and I bet he gloated, "I made him an offer he couldn't refuse."

"I won't ask its nature. I prefer not to become too disenchanted with your methods of operation." She shook her head again. "Poor Coley. He's had so much bad luck. I hate saddling him with more."

"Coley knows how to land on his feet."

"Except one time," she said.

"That was his fault, not mine," he replied defensively.

"I suppose it was." She put a hand on Starbuck's arm and gave him a smile he would later describe as wan.

"Never in this world would I have sent you a lady gun," he told her.

Her smile grew warmer.

Then she bid him good night and went through the gate and into the house where Barry Gallen awaited her.

On the drive back to the Marina, Starbuck turned up the volume on the Johnny Mercer tape, but he didn't sing along. He wasn't in much of a singing mood.

PART THREE

I Head South

11

I SPENT THE next morning preparing for my trip of unde-
termined duration, paying bills and canceling appointments.
Jack Hayward agreed to keep the restaurant functioning and my
head bartender, Lew Roselli, said he'd be glad to oversee his end
of the operation, including the hiring of a new waitress, something he'd been pressuring me to do for about two months.

At noon, a messenger dropped off an envelope from Starbuck
that was filled with photocopies of press clippings and other
material pertaining to the Courville family of Louisiana. I de-
voured the information with a light seafood-salad lunch. By far
the most interesting article was a splendid piece of yellow journal-
ism from a weekly newspaper called *Grits*, penned by someone
with the improbable name of Ambrose Bierce Jones.

It began with old news. In the early eighties, the then-governor of Florida had announced that in an effort to improve state finances, a small section of the Everglades would be drained and offered for sale. Representatives of a company called Florida Futures, which numbered on its impressive board the two state senators in charge of the 'Glades project, approached several wealthy developers with the suggestion that, for a sum, they would be given special consideration in the bidding process for the land.

There is no way of knowing how many of the developers paid Florida Futures for services that failed to materialize, only that when the land was finally auctioned, several disgruntled suckers stepped forward to complain bitterly to the senators that they'd been fleeced.

According to the article, the senators knew nothing about any under-the-table negotiations by Florida Futures. Yes, they were on the board of that organization, but its purpose, they'd been informed, was to act as a nonprofit company dedicated to care for the homeless of the state. Florida Futures had nothing to do with real estate.

FF's executives and representatives were no longer to be found at the expensive office suites in Miami. The only ones left to answer charges were the senators, several members of the entertainment world, sports figures, and captains of industry who not only believed they'd been helping the homeless but had contributed heavily to that needy cause. None of them were brought to trial, but the notoriety was punishment enough for their gullibility.

So much for past history. Journalist Jones's update on the decade-old crime was prompted by his brand-new "astounding discovery that local sportsman and entrepreneur Remy Courville, then barely out of the Harvard Business School, had been one of the masterminds behind Gladegate."

This remarkable conclusion was based solely on the word of an "elderly but extremely lucid man, let's call him Lucien," who contacted the reporter and met with him at a New Orleans bar. Lucien claimed to be a confidence operative from Chicago who'd been brought to Florida by Courville to be part of a scam that had been designed to net millions. The figure, reporter Jones noted, was in excess of twelve million dollars. Lucien's payoff was thirty thousand, the same as most of his associates. Courville and his cronies at the top, none of whom Lucien knew, walked away with at least nine million.

The police of Florida were no longer interested in Lucien's statement, since the statute of limitations on the crime had expired. But "in the interest of justice," Ambrose Bierce Jones approached Courville with the confidence man's accusation, only to be "bodily thrown" out of the horseman's French Quarter restaurant.

The article ended with Jones's claim that it was being published "despite threats against myself and my loved ones."

What a fun trip this was going to be!

I was booked on the last flight to New Orleans that night. On my way to the airport, I made one stop at the Beverly Wilshire Hotel, where a tanned, handsome guy in a tuxedo was pacing in the lobby waiting for me. My partner in the restaurant, Johnny Rousseau, was in town from Las Vegas for the evening to attend a charity dinner honoring Dodgers manager Tommy Lasorda.

"You didn't buy that tux in Vegas," I told him.

He grinned, displaying teeth so even and white they would have been the envy of any film star. "No. It comes from this little shop on Curzon Street. The tailor used to outfit Cary Grant." In spite of his polished exterior there were still the rough edges of South Philly in his voice.

"Okay, partner, I'm paying two-and-a-half a plate tonight. What's so important I had to miss the appetizer?"

I explained that I would be out of town for at least a week, maybe longer. Then I outlined the way the restaurant would be run in my absence.

"I've got a new playmate," he said. "So I'll be hanging around L.A. awhile. I'll drop by the Neck ever' now and then to keep 'em on their toes. Where you off to?"

"Down south to New Orleans," I said. "I want to check out the operation of Magnolia Park racetrack. You familiar with it?"

"Familiar? I never been there, but I've heard of it."

"Ever hear of a guy named Remy Courville?"

"What team does he pitch for?"

"I understand he might be one of the owners of Magnolia Park."

"I don't keep tabs on that part of the South," Johnny said. "But I've got this cousin on my mother's side who should know Courville if he's worth knowin'. Name's Jackie Parnell. He's some sort of politician down there. A real nut case, Jackie."

"Nut case?"

"When we was kids, we lived down the street from this rinky-dink store where the old guy sold cheap magic junk. Jackie had this thing about it. Every nickel he got, he'd take it down to the store. He had the bottom drawer of his dresser filled with magic tricks. You know, the rings that break apart and the shell-game stuff. He could make cards and birds disappear. Hell, he even made this kid's cat disappear.

"The family went down south when my uncle Jack got sent to New Orleans, for work. Uncle Jack made people disappear. But he never got caught at it, and now he's gone himself and Jackie's in politics."

He moved me to the front desk, where he borrowed a pen and a sheet of hotel stationery. He scribbled a phone number on the paper, folded it, and handed it to me. "I'll tell Jackie you're gonna call. Anything else?"

"One little thing." I gave him a quick rundown of my run-in with Winston Mezzero.

"What a schmuck," was his apt response.

"I'm concerned he might make trouble for your friend Joey Kingman," I said.

Johnny nodded and told me not to worry. He'd take the wind out of Mezzero's sails. "Now, if that's it," he said, "I'd like to get back to the dinner before Lasorda makes his speech."

"Take lots of notes," I told him. "I want to know every word he says."

12

KNOWING STARBUCK, I was not surprised to find I'd been booked in the tourist section of a red-eye that had a forty-minute stopover in Dallas. I considered paying for an upgrade, but the flight was far from full, which meant I could probably stretch out for a snooze. And I wasn't in the mood for unlimited drinks and overly solicitous flight attendants.

On the way to Dallas I watched maybe ten minutes of a Stallone movie about gangsters that was supposed to be funny, then found three consecutive empty seats, pushed up the armrests, and made a berth on which I slept fitfully until we touched down.

With that stop, the flight lasted more than five hours. Losing another two hours because of the time change, I arrived in New Orleans at a little after five A.M. There didn't seem to be any porters awake, so I dragged my luggage out into a very early New Orleans morning that was as hot and muggy as a sauna.

The only cabdriver waiting at the stand looked like he was half in the bag. He needed a shave and his eyes were bloody and he was sipping from a go-cup that read HUGO'S BAR. His fiery eyes took me in and he stopped drinking long enough to say, "Uh-oh, I guess this is gonna be a *short* trip."

I didn't bother to reply, merely turned on my heels and reentered the terminal to rent a car.

The yawning clerk, a guy with unnatural platinum hair and an attitude, handed me a city map with the keys to a T-Bird. "You have chosen well, suh," he said in a rich Southern drawl. "The Thundahs have the best air conditioner on the lot."

By the time I got to use it, I'd sweated away three or four pounds. But the clerk was right—the air pouring from above and beneath the dash was icy.

I studied the city map for a few minutes. New Orleans didn't seem to offer that difficult a terrain. I took the Airline Highway, with its billboards and fast-food shacks and dubious motels, as far as it went, then continued along a more industrialized Tulane Avenue until it hit South Rampart. That street, famed in song and story, led me to Canal, once *the* downtown business center, but now, by the looks of it, just another inner-city collection of uncared-for old buildings.

Conditions improved the closer I came to the river, until, right at the foot of Canal, an assortment of recently erected architecture seemed to drag the city, kicking and screaming, into the 1990s. Part of this was no doubt the result of the state's recent legalization of gambling. A little thing like that can turn around depressed property values almost overnight. Of course, it can also lower the quality of life in an area. But it certainly does brighten a hotel lobby.

Mine, La Belle Epoque, was in the middle of a cold but clean concrete cityscape, a purposely antiqued high rise facing the muddy Mississippi, where gaming ships were scheduled to dock nightly. I'd rarely seen a friendlier bunch of desk clerks, each wearing a lapel button reading GUESTS ARE ALL WINNERS AT LA BELLE.

I was surprised to discover how big a winner this guest was. Starbuck had put me into a well-appointed suite with a good view of the river and, as the bellhop was quick to point out, a small kitchenette, in case I should want a break from the high-cholesterol delights of the city.

It was still too early to make any calls, so I removed my pants and shirt and tested the bed. It was a little softer than the one I'd been used to, but it served its purpose well.

I was awakened at ten, New Orleans time, by the door buzzer. My young bellhop, a red-headed fellow named Harold, wheeled in a tray filled with croissants, oatmeal, eggs, sausage, orange juice, and coffee that smelled better than any perfume I could remember. "Compliments of a lady," Harold told me, his simian features twisted into a genuine monkey grin.

His gloved forefinger pointed out an envelope on the tray. It read, *Hope the suite is to your liking. Dad thinks you're in a broom closet. See you soon, Lea.*

I tried to keep the smirk off my face as I asked Harold for a newspaper.

"Yessuh. You prefer *USA Today* or the *Picayune?*"

"I'd prefer the *L.A. Times*," I told him. "But I'll settle for the *Picayune.*"

He reached down to the tray under my breakfast and brought forth the *Picayune.* "Compliments of the hotel, Mistah Killebrew. But I can head ovah to Gilbert's Newsstand to see if they got the L.A. papers."

If I'd accepted Harold's gracious offer, I could have discovered that the body found in the barn at Santa Rosita racetrack had been identified as Irwin Matthes. That just might have moved me to step gingerly out of Starbuck's scenario by catching the next flight home. What I did instead was to say to Harold, "I think I can live for a few days without the news of earthquakes and gang shootings."

He spotted my luggage on the floor, right where he'd deposited it earlier that morning. "You want me to lay out yoah clothes and stuff for you?"

Again, I declined his assistance. I found my wallet in my pants pocket, fished out a fiver, and passed it to him. "Thanks for everything, Harold. I'll keep in touch."

He flashed one final monkey grin and disappeared, leaving me to eat my breakfast and read my newspaper all by myself.

I turned to the sports section and glanced at the names of the reporters and columnists. None was familiar, an indication of how long it had been since my last trip to the Crescent City.

There was a short piece about a trainer named Levy who had seven horses running at Magnolia Park that afternoon and boasted that at least five of them would wind up in the winner's circle.

There were the results of yesterday's races at Magnolia and the lineup for today's nine events. Somebody named Mike Mixon made his Leaky Pirogue Picks, which included a filly named Francie Fair in the sixth.

In a column titled *From the Pelican's Beak*, which combined track information with general racing gossip, a name popped out at me as if it had been printed in neon. *Local sportsman and financier Remy Courville, son of the late James G. Courville, former lieutenant governor of this state, and his wife, the former Joan Bienville, last night hosted the annual And They're Off charity dinner-dance at the Fairmont Hotel. The $200-a-plate affair was to benefit the Tanmark Clinic's efforts to perfect a vaccine to combat endotoxemia, the number-one killer of horses.*

The mention of Courville prompted me, once I'd gobbled up my breakfast, shaved, and showered, to drive to the nearest public library, a very ugly modern brick building on St. Charles Avenue. There I sifted through an assortment of Courville-related articles in the *Picayune* and various other Louisiana publications. There wasn't much more to be gleaned than in the material Starbuck had provided, except for the sort of public-relations notices that had appeared in that morning's paper. Social notes. Notable public works.

I did discover, however, that the restaurant Courville owned in the Vieux Carré was called Le Cavalier. The Horseman. If nothing else, the guy was definitely consistent in his fondness for horseflesh.

My plan was to drive out to Bucktown to take a tour of Magnolia Park. But first I found a pay phone. I had two calls I wanted to make before the day got away from me completely.

The first was to Ambrose Bierce Jones at the offices of *Grits*. His voice sounded more wary and less Southern than any I'd heard since I hit town. When I told him I wanted to speak with him about Remy Courville, he was positively guarded.

"About what?" he asked.

"About whatever you can tell me," I said. "I'm starting out fairly fresh, except for your fascinating account of the scam down in Florida."

"What's your interest?"

"I'm from Los Angeles," I said. "I'm scouting subjects for the series 'Face Up.' " The show was devoted to real-life crime and criminals. Although it was high in the ratings, I'd never actually seen it, but I was confident I knew enough about it to seem convincing to Ambrose Bierce Jones.

He agreed to meet me at Magnolia Park at one-thirty. "I'm six-three and black," he said. "How'll I know you?"

"I'm just the opposite," I told him.

"Hell, I'm an investigative reporter," he said. "I'll find you."

I depressed the switch hook, wondering if being seen with Jones was such a good idea. I decided it was. I was there to shake Courville's cage, and being spotted with his least favorite journalist would be a fast way to get that done.

I fed the pay phone another coin and dialed the number of Johnny Rousseau's cousin, Jackie Parnell.

A woman's voice answered. I asked for Jackie. "Minute," she said. I heard her shout, "Honeeey, it's for yew."

Jackie moaned and griped all the way to the phone. When he spoke into the receiver, he sounded like a mixture of Deep South and South Philly. "Yeah, who am I talking to?"

I identified myself. Jackie's voice grew instantly friendlier. "Johnny says you and him are partners, kinda."

"We own a restaurant together."

"You not involved in the casino?"

"No. I haven't been to Vegas since Elvis died."

He chuckled. "Man, I haven't been there since Louie Prima died. What kin I do you for? Something about Remy Courville, Johnny says."

"I want to find out how he operates," I told him. "I may try to work out a business deal with him."

"Oh, son, you sign a contract with Remy, you lucky to get away with your fountain pen."

"You know him then?"

"I know of him," Jackie replied. "When I was a state senator, I met him a couple times, I guess."

"You're not a senator now?"

"Ex-senator. Got my butt whipped by a black guy. And he got beat by a Ku Kluxer. That'll tell you something about the state of politics hereabouts. But I can still wheel and deal when I want. I suppose we should get together."

I suggested dinner that night and invited him to bring his wife.

"Wife?" he replied indignantly. "Hell, son, I lost my wife when I lost the election. That was my secretary answered the phone, and I got to put up with her all day, I sure as hell don't want supper with her. Where you plannin' on eatin'?"

"How's about Le Cavalier?"

"Remy's place? Good choice, if you don't mind wearin' a coat and tie," Parnell said. "I know how casual it is on the coast, but here in New Or-leans, they try to keep the ole values alive."

"I'm wearing a coat now," I informed him. "And I've got a tie at the hotel."

"I'm proud of you, podnah. Now, if we was to arrive at Le Cavalier aroun' eight-thirty, you might even get a chance to catch the man hisself, Remy the Great, in action."

"Eight-thirty it is," I said.

"We can meet in the bar," he suggested.

"How will I recognize you?"

"Cousin Johnny says you used to be a jockey. It might be easier if I find you, assumin' you're still jockey size."

"More or less," I said. In fact, I was maybe twenty pounds heavier than I was in my racing prime.

"Then I'll see ya when I see ya, podnah," Parnell said, clicking off.

13

ACCORDING TO A book I read one stormy spell during my last stint in New Orleans, the Creoles have always been heavily into racing. As early as 1804, it was established as an organized sport locally, and even before the Confederates fired on Fort Sumter, the Crescent City boasted a quintet of the finest tracks in the United States.

Shortly after Lee took the place position in the war, one more track was added to the list. Major William "Buster" Broussard and his comrade in arms, Major Greydon "Teets" McQueen, both of the late Confederacy, feeling especially fortunate to have escaped the conflict with their skins intact—their commanding officer, General Stonewall Jackson, was mistakenly shot by his own forces only yards from where Buster and Teets were biding their time—decided to push their luck by constructing a new racetrack to be called Magnolia Park.

Regrettably, Buster's heart gave out on him before Magnolia made a name for itself. But Teets lived to see some of the greatest jockeys in the land battle it out on his turf. And his son and grandson carried on the tradition until the Great Depression, when Magnolia Park went into bankruptcy and the turf was tilled and consecrated and retitled Magnolia Cemetery.

It was just after World War II when realtor Calman Gregory Bouraine, Sr., having amassed a rather awesome amount of loot from house-hungry returning GIs, agreed to provide his ne'erdo-well son, Cal Jr., with the cash to re-create Magnolia Park at its present location.

It was the smartest thing the old man ever did. His son may have been totally worthless at just about every other job he undertook, but he knew how to run a track. According to Starbuck, he kept it a one-man operation, which is why his death took such a toll on the establishment.

Judging from the crowds rushing toward the turnstiles to give their money away, it had weathered the bad times and was meeting the competition of the lottery and gaming clubs. I paused at the entrance to scowl at a bronze statue of a jockey riding a rearing alligator. I didn't remember it from before, and it was the sort of thing a jockey would remember. The hordes of eager bettors barely gave it a second's glance. Maybe they were used to jocks on 'gators. I found it pretty degrading for both participants.

Other than the statue, the place didn't seem to have changed very much. The layout was as before. From the top tier of the glass-enclosed grandstand, those few not in the grip of racing fever could look past the track where magnolias blossomed in its neatly landscaped center, past the vast array of parked cars, past a collection of seafood restaurants sitting on stilts, all the way to the gray-blue, sailboat-dotted waters of Lake Pontchartrain. Racing and sailing, just two of the events that the self-proclaimed "Sportsman's Paradise" had to offer.

The grounds had been designed in standard style, with the grandstand providing a clear view of homestretch and finish line, and with the clubhouse offering the best view of all. Except, of course, for the view from the back of a galloping, bighearted Thoroughbred.

I hadn't been to a track since my riding days ended. What would have been the use? I'd never been much of a bettor, and frankly, I'd never felt very comfortable on the spectator side of the rail. That day was no exception.

I took my racing form and my beer cup and moved to a position where I could eyeball the crowd without bothering anybody and wait for Ambrose Bierce Jones.

He wasn't hard to spot—a long and lanky black man garbed in white, button-down oxford shirt and black chino pants. He had a tape recorder hanging from one shoulder and looked vaguely lopsided because of a folded notebook half-stuck into his right pants pocket. His nose and mouth were sharp and small and seemed to belong on another face, not necessarily a black one. His hair was fairly conventional by the day's standards, no geometric shapes, no zigzag patterns. His concession to hirsute creativity was a small goatee that made the area above his mouth seem oddly naked.

He greeted me with caution, but he accepted the offer of a beer. When I returned with the cup, he drained off half of it in one gulp and belched almost politely. "Well," he said, "what exactly's on your mind?"

I noticed a strip of black adhesive over the top of his tape machine. Before answering his question, I reached over and switched off the machine's record button. The adhesive had been to hide the red power-on light. He gave me a don't-blame-a-guy-for-trying gesture.

If he was carrying a spare recorder, I hated to think of where he might be hiding it. I didn't really plan on saying anything that would have been particularly self-incriminating, but with him being a journalist of dubious ethics, I didn't really want our conversation in his collection.

"Now that we're just two guys talking," I told him, "I'd like to know what you know about Remy Courville."

"For 'Face Up.' "

I nodded.

"Will I get on camera?" he asked.

"Is that part of your deal?"

He nodded enthusiastically.

"I'll make a note of it," I lied blandly. "So tell me about Courville."

He pointed out a vacant box a hundred or so feet from the rail. "That's where he usually hangs out during the season," he said. "Must be busy somewhere else, probably scamming some poor son of a bitch. Too bad. I'd like to have said hello."

"Did he really toss you out of his restaurant?"

He nodded. "He would have tossed me even if I hadn't written the piece. It's just about the only place left in the Quarter where you have to be free, *white*, and twenty-one to get served."

"That's against the law," I said.

"No shit, Perry Mason," Jones said bitterly. "But there's law and there's Louisiana law. Very different and not just because of the Napoleonic Code."

"Is that why you were baiting him? Because he's a racist?"

"I wasn't baiting him."

I grinned at him. "Of course you weren't. Some guy whose real name you won't use came out of hiding for the first time in ten years and decided that of all the hotshot reporters in the country, you were the one to talk to about Remy Courville's involvement in a well-known Florida scam."

"What're you saying?" Mr. Ambrose Bierce Jones was pulling back from me now. I didn't want to lose him.

"I'm saying that your article about Gladegate smells a bit off."

"Then what the hell are you wasting my time for?" he snapped.

"I'm not wasting your time, Ambrose," I said. "My boss at 'Face Up' doesn't care if your story is true, half-true, or coke dream. It was printed, and that gives it all the validity we need. But I have to know what we're dealing with to figure out if it's enough to get Courville on the griddle, where we want him."

He waited for the track announcer to tell us a little bit about the next race. Then he said, "A guy bragged on this girl I know that he and Courville put together the Everglades scam."

"This braggart have a name?"

Ambrose shook his head. "Woman wouldn't tell me. She's afraid she'll come into it."

"I assume that since you went to the trouble of keeping her out of your story, she means something special to you."

"Assume what you want. She's not part of the story."

I nodded, liking him a little better now. But not well enough to level with him. "Anything else about the braggart?"

He frowned and said, "He told her he'd schooled with Courville."

I got us two more beers. "We're going to need something more on Remy," I said. "Something current."

"He's a player. Screws anything that breathes. But that's not exactly a crime yet. Otherwise, as far as I can tell, the man is staying frosty. Managing his breed farm. Running his horses. Doing his bit for charities. Financing racist politicians. That sort of stuff."

"Is that true about the politicians?"

He shrugged. "Hell, the only politicians we got who don't hate the black man are black themselves. And the deals some of them make, you begin to wonder if *they* don't have white sheets hanging in the closet."

"So your statement that Courville backs racists is basically bogus."

He grinned. "Basically," he agreed.

"What about his involvement in a company called Southern Boy Supplies?"

Ambrose shrugged and gave me a blank look.

"Southern Boy owns a large piece of this place," I added, hoping to pique his interest.

He remained blasé. "So? As far as I know, Magnolia's clean."

"It was when Cal Bouraine ran it."

"Yeah. Must have been, because crooks usually don't have the money problems Bouraine had," Ambrose said. "This place was goin' down fast."

"Magnolia Park was losing money *before* he died?"

Ambrose knew he'd supplied me with some new information and it pumped him up. "So my uncle said. He worked the clubhouse during those days, waiting tables. I remember him telling us that even the busboys were worried that the track was going to go bust. Uncle thought that old man Bouraine was under so much pressure that's probably why his head exploded."

Nice sensitive turn of phrase. I said, "Business looks great now."

"Uncle said the concessions didn't fall off that much, even in the crunch. Offtrack betting and TV cut attendance, but there was still a lot of activity in the clubhouse."

"Maybe somebody was emptying the till before it got to the accountants."

"More likely folks didn't have the kind of loot to throw away that they used to. Whatever, things changed immediately when the daughter, Delia Bouraine, took over. She turned things around almost at once."

"How, I wonder?"

"Hell if I know. Magic?"

"You don't recall your uncle mentioning Southern Boy Supplies?" Ambrose shook his head. "Could I talk with him? Is he working today?"

"He's working. But not here. Uncle Martin's got a pretty good job with a restaurant chain in Atlanta. He was let go here at the track when they pink-slipped everybody last year."

"There was a mass firing?"

"The clubhouse staff, the concession people, some office workers. Maybe you're right about folks stealing from the track. That'd explain why Delia Bouraine decided to bring in a whole new team." He looked at his watch. It was a Swiss Army timepiece, the kind everybody seemed to be wearing that year. "I gotta get out to Lake Vista, get a statement from a guy about some rats somebody found in a bakery he runs down on Rampart, in *de ghetto*."

"Big story?" I asked.

"Everything's relative. You want to pursue the Courville piece?"

"I'll let you know," I told him.

"Right," he said cynically. "I got a nose that's very sensitive to bullshit. And it's twitching something fierce."

"Sorry you feel that way about it," I said. "All I can tell you is what I said at the jump. If we pursue the segment, I'll make sure you get on camera."

He shrugged. "Well, at least I got two beers out of it."

He took one last look at Courville's empty box and wandered

off. I stayed until the sixth race to put fifty bucks on Francie Fair's nose. The filly, a three-to-one shot, won in a walk. With a name like that, the others didn't stand a chance.

14

AT THE DINNER hour, the French Quarter seemed to be just waking up. The streets, which had been swept clean of the lunchtime tourist trash, awaited the nightly deposits of go-cups and paper napkins. The barkers were dusting off their spiels. The strippers, glimpsed through partially opened doors, looked relatively awake and energetic. A young jazz trumpeter in a candy-striped blazer stood in the doorway to a club eagerly fingering his horn. The tourists were still in curiosity mode. Hungry rather than thirsty. Once they'd fed, they'd face the decision to go back to their hotels or go crazy in some club. An amazing number usually opted for the latter.

Bourbon Street had a little more neon and a little less style than I remembered from eight years ago, but so did most of the world. It was also hotter and more humid.

If I'd had my choice, I'd have headed toward Galitoire's, a bright, mirrored restaurant with, in my opinion, the best food in town. Or maybe even Antoine's, where they served an appetizer called oysters Bienville that was so rich I had to choose between it or a main course. The irony was that in the old days I was forced to be very careful about my diet, because even an extra pound could make the difference in a close race. That night I was free from dietary restrictions and could swill oysters Bienville until I passed out, but once again work was making that impossible. My destination was Remy Courville's restaurant, Le Cavalier, known, according to the guidebook, not so much for its fare as for its "clubby, sporty ambience."

That same guidebook had noted that there was a city council that had to approve of any exterior changes made to buildings in the French Quarter. Courville must have kept them as happy as clams. The facade of his establishment was nothing if not historic looking. The three-story structure on Iberville Street near Royal was as crusty looking and ancient as the hand of man could make it. Bricks of a faded red peeked through cracks in the gray stucco. A sort of green mildew seemed to be crawling up from the sidewalk.

The front of the place was a doorless wall, the lower part of which was interrupted by only two unshuttered, mullioned windows with dirty yellow, opaque panes. The upper floors were treated to more conventional, if not more modern, portals.

A tasteful wooden sign swung from a metal bar poking from the corner of the building. On it, a blond guy wearing a silk shirt, jodhpurs, and a wide smile waved from the back of a leaping stallion in a Zorro-like pose. LE CAVALIER, the sign read, EST. 1988.

I passed beneath it, along a brick walkway to a heavy wooden door at the side of the building that swung open with amazing ease. Tendrils of icy air mixed with the humidity, and I almost expected the condensation process to take place right there in the doorway.

Le Cavalier's main dining room resembled a softly lit country inn. It was packed with a very urban crowd. The conversation clatter was amplified and spread around by a low ceiling. One long wall was covered by a trompe l'oeil painting of the stands at Churchill Downs, with a crowd of life-size fans observing a race in progress in the distance.

I was not surprised to find that the bar area was decorated in the style of a tack room at a stable—rough wood, leather saddles, and reins hanging from hooks on the wall along with etchings and photos of Thoroughbreds and jockeys.

One of the men at the bar raised a hand and waved me over. Jackie Parnell looked less like a politician than anyone I could have imagined. What he looked like was Howdy Doody. A brush of bright red hair, a moon face covered with freckles, a pale blue suit with white piping on the lapels, a white cowboy shirt, and a string tie. The toes of blue-dyed lizard boots poked from beneath his narrow cuffs.

He'd been entertaining the two women sitting next to him with close magic. As I approached he removed a ring from the brunette's finger without her or her dirty-blond friend noticing it.

He shoved away from the bar, extended a hand—the one without the ring—and shook mine vigorously. He did not seem to know the names of the women, but he introduced us anyway. Then he explained to them that as much as he regretted it, we'd have to leave them to pursue "a very impo'tant business matter."

He took a few steps away, then turned, reached behind the brunette's ear, and "found" her ring. While she replaced it on her finger, giggling, he reached behind the dirty-blonde's ear and discovered a small white card. "My phone number, darlin'," he said.

As he sauntered to our table, me following in his wake, he said, "A fact of life I learned in politics, Coley—it never hurts to advertise."

We'd worked our way through a couple of gin and tonics, two bowls of good, thick seafood gumbo, about a loaf of French bread, a couple of medium-broiled steaks, and much of Jackie's political history when he suddenly stopped talking. I looked up from my coffee to see if it was food or drink or perhaps cholesterol overload that had stemmed his monologue and found him staring at an arriving party of seven that was being seated at a large table across the room.

I did not have to be told that the man at the head of the table was Remy Courville. His tall, athletic frame, his handsome, unlined, tanned face and longish blond hair were the same as those of the horseman on the wooden sign outside. He bristled with all the ego and confidence that money and power can buy.

"The pale brunette with the cheekbones is his wife, Joan," Jackie whispered. A model's cheeks she had all right, and large, luminous brown eyes and a generous mouth.

"Recognize anybody else?" I asked.

"Me? Hell, I recognize nearly everybody. I'm in the people business. The older broad with the scowl is Remy's big sister, Roberta." She was a small, compact woman with a vaguely marsupial face, wearing a shiny green dress designed to accentuate her full breasts. With her was a too-pretty young man with a cultivated permanently bored expression. Jackie identified him as "Norell Travers, Junior. Picture's always in the papers with some debutante or other. He's a banker, used to be the youngest VP at Olympia National, till he got older. Of course his daddy, Norell Senior, is president of the establishment."

Jackie didn't have to give me the name of the ancient in the dark blue suit who was running a big-knuckled hand through dank gray hair. I'd have known that weather-whipped wrinkled mug anywhere. Granville "Granny" Hayes, one of the best horse trainers in the business. I'd worked with him a time or two in the past.

Jackie's overvalued memory drew a blank on the other couple, a show-business-sleek pair, both of them tall, expensively dressed, physically immaculate, white teeth glistening as they smiled and chattered.

I asked Jackie if he'd mind switching seats so I could observe Courville's table without giving myself a stiff neck or Remy something to wonder about. That accomplished, I focused in on young Courville, who appeared to be charming, fastidious, and the perfect host. Up to a point.

One of three attractive young women at a table near Remy's began staring at him, then lowering her eyes and flirting. He began to flirt back, winking, making funny moues with his mouth. It was a fascinating exhibition, made even more spell-binding when Joan Courville became aware of it.

She turned to see the recipient of her spouse's facial contortions and spied the girl. She glanced away quickly and attempted to rejoin the conversation at her table.

Apparently dissatisfied with just the harmless winks and blinks, Remy gestured with his thumb, indicating the front door. The young girl was no novice at that sort of thing. She immediately stood up, murmured something to her friends, and made her exit. Remy gave her a couple of minutes, then excused himself from his table and followed her out. Joan Courville did not watch him go.

"That's some marriage Remy's got," I said to Jackie.

My freckle-faced tablemate had been occupying his time by playing with a piece of string, knotting and unknotting it singlehandedly. He said, "Her friends call her Saint Joan for puttin' up with the putz. I understand he's even been known to slap her around a little."

"Why doesn't she do an El Paso?" I asked.

Jackie shrugged. "Maybe it's the money. Maybe it's the religion. Maybe, and I don't wanna go too radical here, but maybe she loves the guy."

"Yeah, maybe," I agreed with a sigh. "What's her background?"

He cocked an orange eyebrow. "I'm not sure. She's not from heah. Georgia gal. Socialite, I expect, though I don't really know. Looks like she comes from money. Lots of class."

I thought so, too. Though I imagined that being married to Remy might wear some of that away eventually. "Well," I said, "I've had a better meal than I expected and got a good long glimpse of Remy. Not bad for just one night in New Orleans."

Jackie said, "If those gals are still in the bar, I think we could turn this into an even more memorable evenin'."

I shook my head. "I've had as much fun as I can take tonight, what with jet lag and all," I told him. "But don't let me stop you."

"Oh, I won't do that, podnah," he said, and snapped his fingers for the waiter. I paid for the meal and we started out.

At the door I heard someone calling my name. Granny Hayes was rising from the Courville table, a white napkin tucked into his shirtfront, a big smile on his face.

He kept repeating my name as he walked across the restaurant to shake my hand. "What in the world you doing in this humid, crime-ridden, roach-infested city, Coley?" he asked.

"I wanted to see what kind of races you guys run down south, Granny."

The door opened behind me and Remy Courville reentered the restaurant, looking a bit rumpled and self-satisfied. Granny stopped him. "Mr. C, I want you to meet an old friend o' mine."

Courville's pale blue eyes moved from my shoes to my hairline. Then some slot fell into place and he smiled. "I remember you," he said. "Killebrew. Colman Killebrew."

I gave him my most polite smile.

"You made some money for me once, when I was still at Harvard."

"I hope it was a bundle," I lied.

He put his hand on my shoulder, not a gesture that I liked particularly. "C'mon over to the table, have a drink and meet my guests," he said.

I looked at Jackie and started to say something. But he winked and gave me a good-bye salute, sauntering back to the bar to look for his two lady fans.

At the table Remy introduced me to the pretty couple, whose names were Mark Vetter and Joleen St. James. It was impossible not to look down the bodice of Joleen's dress, so I did, wondering if she and Mark were married. Remy provided the answer. "Mark's visiting from the West Coast; Joleen's a local gal." He then went on to introduce me to his sister and the continually bored Norell Travers, Jr., and finally, to "my eternally suffering wife, Joan."

He added, "This guy, Coley Killebrew, rode one of the finest races I've ever seen. The Vosburg Handicap at Belmont. The horse was named Evensong. Must have been twelve years ago. A helluva race. I cleaned up."

"It wasn't a bad ride, if I say so myself," I replied. Evensong had been a difficult animal, slow out of the gate. I'd chirped, cooed, done everything I could to get him to cooperate. And cooperate he did. Once he got going, it was only a matter of bumping a few other lesser animals out of his way. A fine victory and one of my fonder memories.

I drew up a chair between Granny and Joan Courville. Norell Travers, Jr., leaned forward and said, "I follow racing very avidly, Mr. Killebrew. I remember reading about some problem you had at Santa Anita."

"Some problem, yes," I agreed.

An eyebrow went up on Travers's mildly decadent face. He smirked. "I wouldn't want you to break Remy's heart, but, strictly *entre nous*, did you fix the Belmont race, too?"

His "*entre nous*" also included the table, of course. And maybe even that whole section of the restaurant. Granny Hayes made a little grunt of displeasure. Remy Courville scowled at Travers, but remained silent. The others seemed to ignore Travers's rudeness, probably because they'd come to expect that sort of nonsense from him.

I shrugged good-naturedly and asked, "How well do you know horses, Mr. Travers?"

"Well enough," he said. "I've been riding since I was six."

"Do you know where the horse's frog is?"

He sneered. "It's part of the beast's foot, on the bottom near the heel."

I looked properly impressed. "What about the poll?"

"I just love games," he said archly. "The poll is located on the horse's forehead, just below the ears. But don't think these dumb questions are going to change the subject."

"I wasn't changing the subject," I said. "I just wanted to test your knowledge of horses."

"Why?"

"Because I wanted to make sure you knew what everybody at this table probably knows."

"What's that?"

"The part of the horse you resemble."

I stood up, bid the members of the party good-bye, and left the restaurant without a backward glance. But just before the thick oak door slammed shut, I heard Remy Courville give out a loud whoop of laughter. I was smiling myself.

PART FOUR

Starbuck Carries On

15

"I was hired to look into the business affairs of Southern Boy Supplies, not poke my nose into what seemed to be an accidental death at a racetrack. I don't go looking for trouble, gentlemen."

—RAYMOND EDGAR STARBUCK,
in reply to questions from Federal Bureau of Investigation agents
Joseph Mossbach and Wheeler Deemes

STARBUCK MAY NOT have gone looking for trouble, but what he neglected to mention to the FBI stalwarts was that he'd phoned a pal named Janis Doyle at the Department of Motor Vehicles requesting the name and address of the owner of the

California vanity license plate KNEADY that he'd observed in the alley behind the late Irwin Matthes's apartment.

At ten that morning Janis called back with the information. " 'Ninety-one Toyota, registered to Mildred Drucker. Jeez, Ray, the lady's a redhead, green eyes, five-nine, a hunnert and forty pounds of fun. Thirty-nine years old, though. Getting up there.''

"Just give me the lady's address, Janis," Starbuck snapped. "I promise I won't ask her to the prom."

His next call was to Lea. When he'd finished passing along the information Doyle had provided, he added, "She's probably at her job, whatever that is."

" 'Kneady'? She either works in a bakery or she's a masseuse,'' Lea replied. "I'll find her."

"The other thing I'd like you to do today is drop by the Hotel Brentwood and get me a list of the guests for the past couple nights."

"No problem," she replied, filling him with fatherly pride, admiration, and just a touch of curiosity.

It took Lea nineteen minutes and a folded hundred-dollar bill to secure a computer printout from the hotel's billing file. She left it on her father's desk together with a Post-it reminder that she'd taken the money from petty cash.

Two hours later she was seated in the Saab, parked on a sunbaked street in Torrance, California, observing a voluptuous redhead marching in the direction of a Toyota Corolla that bore the plate KNEADY.

The woman had just exited the Landry-Morganthau Chiropractic Clinic. Her tanned bare midriff separated a very full electric-blue halter from slacks that fit more snugly than Batman's tights.

Lea turned off the Saab's engine, quieting both radio and air conditioner, and stepped into the sizzling glare of the noon sun. She took her time strolling toward the redhead, who stood at the door of her car digging into a leather thong purse for her keys.

"Mildred Drucker?" Lea asked.

The redhead spun around. She seemed startled. Then annoyed. "That's right," she replied roughly.

"My name is Lea Starbuck, Miss Drucker. I'd like to talk to you."

"Talk about what?" Apprehensive now.

"About what you were doing at the apartment of the recently deceased Irwin Matthes."

Mildred Drucker unlocked the Toyota's door, slipped behind the wheel, and jerked the door shut. She speared the ignition slot with her key. She twisted the key. There was the whine of a starter giving its best. But the engine wouldn't turn over.

Lea stood directly in front of the car. She was waving something. A distributor cap.

Mildred Drucker took a minute to consider her situation. Then she pushed the car door open and stepped out, snarling, "What the hell do you think you're doing?"

The problem, as Lea later explained it to me, was that she wasn't certain if she was confronting Irwin Matthes's murderer or a girlfriend or a combination of both.

She stood her ground and said, "Just trying to get your attention, Mildred."

"Okay, you got it. Now what?"

"Now I'd like you to drive with me to meet my father."

"Oh, sure," Mildred said sarcastically. She extended her hand. "Gimme the distributor cap, Blondie, before I get really mad."

"You're involved in a murder, Mildred. And my father and I are the only ones standing between you and the police."

Mildred Drucker dropped her hand. "Police? Murder? That guy wasn't . . . It was the goddamn horse . . . it almost took me off, too."

"You were there?" Lea asked. "At Santa Rosita that night?"

"So what if I was?"

"Irwin Matthes wasn't killed by a horse," Lea said flatly.

"The papers say the police are calling it an accident." Mildred seemed to want that to be the truth.

"The police and the papers are wrong. The body was dragged into the stall after Matthes was dead."

Mildred brought her hand to her head and leaned back against the car. "Oh, Christ . . . I knew it."

"Knew Matthes was murdered?"

"Huh? Oh, no. I knew there was something screwy. And now she's gone and it's my fault?"

"Who's gone?"

"I . . . who the hell are you, anyway?"

"I gave you my name. My father and I are investigating Mr. Matthes's death, and we think you may be able to help our investigation. If you don't cooperate with us, we can always get the police to do the job."

It was a bluff. Starbuck would not go to the police.

The redhead remained motionless, something on her mind.

"You didn't kill him, did you, Mildred?"

"Me? Why the hell would I kill a guy I didn't know? This is bullshit," Mildred snapped. "Gimme back my distributor cap. I gotta go see about something."

Lea moved past Mildred, reached into the Corolla, and popped the hood. She began to deftly replace the distributor cap.

Mildred watched her in confusion. "How'd you find me?"

"You're not that hard to locate. We did it. Matthes's murderer can, too."

Mildred licked her lips.

Lea closed the hood with a snap and rubbed her hands together to dry-wash a few oil smudges. "Well, Mildred, how about it?"

"I can't go with you now. I've got to check up on something. Then I've got patients all afternoon. Maybe after work, this evening."

"What time?"

"I guess I'm through at five," Mildred said. "Where is it I'm supposed to meet you?"

"Right here. At five," Lea told her.

Mildred Drucker reluctantly agreed. She got into her Toyota and drove away.

Her destination was a new pink-and-white stucco apartment building a couple of miles south of the clinic. Lea watched from her car as Mildred walked to the iron gate, picked up the intercom phone, and dialed five numbers. She gripped the phone impatiently for nearly a minute, then slammed it back on its hook and turned to her car.

She saw Lea's Saab across the street and her face reddened. Without word or gesture, she got into the Toyota and drove back to the clinic.

She called it quits at four, exiting with a stuffed duffel bag. Lea was parked directly behind her car.

"Good," Lea said. "You got away early. I was getting a little bored out here."

"I have to go see about a friend," Mildred said.

"You can do that later."

"But she's . . ."

"She's what?"

Mildred slumped, defeated. "Nothing. You and your old man want to talk, let's talk."

16

STARBUCK SPENT THE afternoon searching copies of itemized bills of the guests of the Brentwood Hotel. Immediately, he ruled out single male guests, reducing the two hundred and twelve bills to a mere one hundred and thirty-six. Next went the "Mr. & Mrs." listings. Forty-two remained. Of them twenty were doubles occupied by couples of similar gender. Of the remaining twenty-two single women, seven were well-known celebrities. That left him with fifteen likely candidates.

He shuffled through them, noting that three had settled their bills with cash. One of them had paid for a phone call to Irwin Matthes's apartment. Her name, according to the printout, was Fiona Dawson. Her home town was Coral Gables, Florida.

Starbuck dialed the phone number she'd given the hotel. It belonged to a fish market in Boca Raton.

With a sigh, he put all the bills into a folder and moved on to other tasks, important and trivial. He was on the plank deck just outside of his office pouring seed into a bird feeder when Lea led Mildred Drucker around the corner of the two-story bleached-wood house. The big redhead took a look at his Day-Glo aqua T-shirt, baggy shorts, and flip-flops and she relaxed a notch. Lea surmised it was the flip-flops that got through to her.

Starbuck put down the bag of seed, wiped his fingers on his shorts, took Mildred's hand, and gave it a hearty shake of welcome. "Can I get you something, Mildred? A cigarette?"

"When you spend your days beating people into shape, you don't mess up your own body with tobacco," she replied. That meant the stubs in Matthes's apartment hadn't been hers. She added, "I haven't had a coffin nail since high school."

"That wasn't so long ago, I bet," he said with a wink. "And do you feel the same way about alcohol that you do about tobacco?"

The side of her lip curled up. "I'm a masseuse, not a nun," she said.

Starbuck looked relieved. He yelled for Choo-Choo, who exited from the house as if he'd been waiting anxiously for the call. The Asian took an order for "a batch of gin martinis for Mildred and me," then disappeared back inside the bleached-wood building.

Starbuck led the redhead to a chair that faced the sunset.

Lea found her own chair and observed the dynamics carefully. She was always amazed by her father's many moods, real or improvised.

"That sky at sundown's really something, isn't it?" he asked Mildred.

She had to agree that it was.

Choo-Choo returned with a tray containing three martini

glasses, several olives speared by toothpicks, and a pitcher of clear but potent liquid.

Starbuck handed a full glass to Mildred. "You look like a two-olive lady," he said. As he plopped the olives into the gin he asked, "What can you tell me about Irwin Matthes that I don't already know?"

"God's truth, I never set eyes on the man while he was still breathing," she replied, accepting the drink.

"Then . . . ?" He clinked his glass against hers.

Lea, who was left to pour her own martini, watched them both with amusement.

Mildred took a healthy gulp of her drink and croaked, "Oh, damn, but your guy does good work with gin," indicating the direction of Choo-Choo's departure.

Starbuck's eyes flicked to Lea. She could tell how impatient he was, but he was hiding it very well from his guest.

Finally, with the help of the martini, they got the full story. Mildred and her dearest girlfriend, one Lannie Luchek, well fueled with jug wine at a lounge near Santa Rosita called the Paddock, had decided to take a moonlit jog around the racetrack.

"And you jogged past Irwin Matthes?"

"There was this goddamned crazy horse," she said. "It came out of nowhere. Biggest damn horse I ever saw. It attacked us and I ran away from it and found the poor son of a . . . the poor guy back in the stables."

"Was he dead?"

"I hope to tell you."

"That must have been a shocker," he said, trying to keep it friendly, conversational. No sense of inquisition. "What happened next?"

"I got the hell out of there."

Mildred was almost finished with her martini. Starbuck casually brought the pitcher to her glass and filled it.

"How'd you know where he lived?" he asked.

She blinked and stared at him. "That was *you*, wasn't it? In the alley behind the building. You got my license-plate number, and that's how you found me."

"How'd you discover Mr. Matthes's address, Mildred? Did you know him?"

"Never laid eyes on him before that night, like I said."

"So?"

Mildred took another bite of martini. "I found this envelope folded up inside his shoe. I mean, his shoe had fallen off near his body and I saw this white paper sticking out of it. An envelope. With some strange stuff scribbled on it."

Lea realized her father was leaning forward in his chair, trying not to look too eager. "I don't suppose you still have the envelope?"

Mildred hesitated a second, then reached into the leather thong purse beside her chair. She removed a plaid cloth billfold and from it extracted a section of an envelope. She handed it to Starbuck.

He studied it for a few seconds, turning it over, frowning. Then he handed it to Lea.

It was an envelope from a company called the Buttersoft Leather Factory. The label with Matthes's name and address looked computer-originated. A bulk-mail postal indicia.

She turned the piece of envelope over. On the nonprinted side was scrawled in blue ink, $x =$ *gross win pool minus take or net pool* . . . $y =$ *favorite bet . . . breaks to a + dime.* . . .

Mildred's eyes went from Lea to her father. She downed the last of her martini and said, "I couldn't make heads or tails of it, can you?"

"I'm not sure," Starbuck said. "Lea?"

"A betting system?" She shrugged, handing the envelope back to her father.

"You don't mind if we hang on to this, do you, Mildred?" Starbuck asked, slipping it into the back pocket of his shorts.

"Be my guest," the big redhead replied, slurring slightly now.

Starbuck filled Mildred's glass again and went back at it. "You still haven't told us why you went to Matthes's apartment."

"I was trying to find out what I'd got myself into," she replied. "I was worried."

Starbuck was losing patience with her. "You must have been

very worried. Matthes's apartment looked like a garbage dump."

"Hey, it was like that when I got there," she shot back defensively. "Everything all thrown around. I didn't find anything. I didn't even know what I was looking for. I should have been out trying to find Lannie."

"Who?"

"My girlfriend, Lannie. Like I said, she was with me at the track."

Starbuck had forgotten about the friend because she hadn't seemed important. But he was interested in her now. "What made you think your friend needed finding?"

"When the horse came at us, she ran into the stands. But when I went looking for her, she was gone. Then I heard the police siren and I had to get out of there. Back at the Paddock, her car was gone.

"I called her when I got home, but all I got was her dumb answering machine with Barry Manilow singing 'I Go to Rio.' "

"Maybe she was sleeping," Starbuck said.

"If she's home, she answers. She'd rather talk on the phone than sleep."

Another swallow of martini.

"And . . . ?" Starbuck asked.

"And I got worried and I figured maybe something was weirder out there at the track than just a horse going nuts. That's why I went to the guy's apartment."

"You still haven't heard from Lannie?"

"She hasn't been in to her job. I drove over to her place during my lunch break. Your daughter knows. She wasn't there. I been phoning every hour. That goddamn song."

"Is there someplace she might be? Her parents? A boyfriend?"

"What parents? And she wasn't seeing anybody special. Anyway, if she'd gone off, she'd have called. I'm her closest friend." Mildred looked like she might cry.

"Why don't you describe her for us? And then Lea can make a few phone calls to see what we can find out."

Mildred sniffed, rubbed at her eyes, and began to provide them with a physical description of her friend Lannie Luchek. While

Mildred rattled off such attributes as hair color, age, size, etc., Lea did not bother to take notes. Like everything else, her memory is well trained.

"Any birthmarks or scars?" she prompted.

"She has this red spot on her right shoulder. It's like the Russian guy's forehead, that kind of birthmark."

Lea nodded and went inside the house. By the time she returned, the martini pitcher was nearly empty and Mildred and Starbuck were discussing the sudden drop in temperature once the sun disappeared.

Lea locked eyes with her father, then turned to Mildred. "I'm sorry, but your friend's dead."

"Huh? What'd you say?"

"They're holding Lannie Luchek's body at the morgue in San Pedro," Lea said calmly. "She was discovered in the harbor this morning. They think she fell in by accident. Her car was parked by the docks. She'd been drinking."

Mildred looked stricken. She stood up too suddenly and would have fallen had not Starbuck steadied her. "Got to go to her," she said, trying to twist out of his grip.

"Hold on, Mildred," he said. "Use your head."

"They've already identified the body," Lea said. "There's nothing more you can do except to let the wrong people know that you were the other woman at Santa Rosita with Lannie."

Mildred stared at them, terrified. "What the hell is going on?" she wailed.

Starbuck relaxed his grip and guided her back onto her chair. "I don't know," he told her. "Until I do, maybe you should take a trip somewhere."

"I've got a cousin in Riverside."

"Riverside's not far enough." Starbuck turned to Lea. "Call our pal Paco down in Cabo," he said. "Tell him I'm sending him a new masseuse for his hotel."

"Poor Lannie," Mildred said, eyes flooded with tears as she rose from her seat. "She didn't even want to go to the goddamned track. It was my idea."

Starbuck put his arm around her and eased her down onto a

chair. His brow was furrowed. Lea thought he looked genuinely moved by the woman's tears. My guess is that if he was moved by anything, it was the realization that he was going to have to hide not just one but *two* murders from the police.

PART FIVE

I Get the Job

17

I DON'T KNOW if it was the unfamiliar bed, or the air conditioner, or that weasel Travers's insult, but I tossed and turned most of the night and eventually gave up the idea of sleep altogether.

At about four, two on the West Coast, I dialed a 310 prefix and a phone number.

"Starbuck residence," Choo-Choo answered, sounding as fresh as a daisy.

I gave him my name and told him I wanted to speak with the master of the house.

"Mr. Starbuck sleep."

"You and I are awake," I said. "Why shouldn't he be?"

Choo-Choo, a born diplomat evidently, chose to remain

silent, so I added, "This is important. You'll have to wake him."

"Not a good idea."

"Maybe not, but it's got to be done."

A few minutes later Starbuck's phlegm-thickened voice was growling, "What the hell is it, Killebrew, that couldn't wait till morning?"

"It *is* morning here," I said. "You sound a bit hung over."

"Hung over? It's so early I'm still drunk, dammit. What are you doing up at this hour, anyway?"

"Trying to figure things out."

"What's to figure?" Starbuck wanted to know. "In all my years at the track I've only heard of two ways to put in a fix. You corrupt jockeys or you doctor horses."

"Maybe, but the problem is, Starbuck—I'm not going to fix any race, or even pretend to."

He cursed for about a minute before shouting, "Then what the hell *are* you gonna do?"

"I met Remy Courville last night at dinner."

Silence from Starbuck's end. Either he was too furious to speak, or he was mulling over the implications. Finally, he asked, "So what?"

"So, I'm going to work for him."

"You son of a bitch. This is my own fault, thinking I could trust you, even for a second."

"Lighten up, Starbuck," I suggested. "I'm still wearing your colors. It's just that I'm running this race my way, not yours. Yours would have left us at the post. By working for Courville, I can see how things are going at Magnolia Park and I can check out the Southern Boy Supplies connection, firsthand."

More silence. Then he allowed, "There are advantages to your plan, I suppose. When do you start?"

"I don't know. He hasn't hired me yet."

"What makes you think he will?"

"*You* hired me. And look at the way *you* feel about me. Courville acts like we're old pals. Anyway, with me on the inside, there's no need for you to involve Lea in this."

"What I involve Lea in is none of your goddamn business,

Killebrew," Starbuck said heavily. "She'll be in New Orleans by the end of the week."

"I don't need her here," I objected.

"You're in no position to make that kind of decision."

"What the hell does that mean?" I grouched back. "Is there something crucial you're keeping from me?"

"You know all you need to," he said before breaking the connection.

I stared at the humming phone for a few seconds, then replaced it and got out of bed. I could have pouted awhile, but I had things to do before daybreak.

18

AT FIVE A.M. a ragtag bunch was huddled along the outside rail of the track at Magnolia Park, watching the horses being put through their morning workouts. The sky was an unpromising charcoal gray. The air was humid and the warm wind off of Lake Pontchartrain carried even more dampness. It looked like we might be in for rain.

I wandered back toward the stables. A guy wielding a pitchfork told me that Courville's horses were being kept in Barn Nine. There, an apple-cheeked young jock paused in his conversation with a cement-faced lady groom to inform me that Granny Hayes was having his breakfast at the Feed Bag.

They'd repainted the little coffee shop since I'd eaten my last stale doughnut there, but they hadn't changed the furnishings. The chrome edge surrounding the long tan Formica counter was even more pitted with rust. The matching tables had about twice as many initials and other information cut into their tops. The plastic cushions on the chairs had tape patches on top of tape patches. The light tan linoleum showed sections of floorboard through worn spots near the door and the counter.

Three ceiling fans spun so slowly they barely bothered the flies, stirring air that was filled with a rich aroma of coffee mixed with frying foods—eggs, bacon, sausage, potatoes. This was prime time for the Feed Bag and the place was crowded with trainers and handlers and hotwalkers and other denizens who work the back side of the track.

Granny was alone at a small table near a window, scowling through pince-nez at the sports page of the *Picayune*.

His face lit up when he saw me.

"Sit down, young man, and have some mush," he said, grinning.

"Maybe a cup of coffee," I said, parking on the chair across from him.

There was no way I could stop Granny from ordering me a couple of eggs and Cajun hot links to keep my coffee company. When they arrived, he asked me what I was really doing in New Orleans.

"Looking for work," I answered. "Know of anything?"

"You're kinda overqualified for most jobs that're available," he said.

"Have *you* got anything?" I asked, before downing a bite of egg.

He sipped black coffee and shrugged. "Hell, I can always use a hand. Out at the plantation, I'm overseeing the stable manager and everybody else, it seems. Top o' that, I've got my hands full just training Remy's horses. And I'm slowing down. It'd sure ease up on me to have you around. But Remy's the man who does the hiring."

"Is that a problem?" I asked. "I got the impression that I was on his good side."

"He seems to like you well enough, but it wasn't too politic to piss off that Travers punk. He's in tight with Remy, and he spent most of last night grinding his teeth on your name."

"What's his tie-in with Courville?" I asked.

"I'm not sure, except that they were in college together. And there's a lot of business chitchat goes on between 'em."

"Travers is probably Courville's banker. I imagine the plantation must be pretty well mortgaged."

"Travers could be holding the papers, I suppose. But Remy's got more loot than he knows how to spend."

"Where's it all come from?" I asked.

Granny's face stiffened. "Family money," he said, lowering his voice.

"That's fine with me, as long as he throws some my way," I said cheerily. Then I changed the subject to a wonderful old guy named Josh Railsburg whom we both knew. It'd been Josh who'd shown me how to cross reins and sit on a horse, back when my colors were so new they rustled.

I waited for Granny to tell me about the time he and Josh had worked a winter on a ranch in La Puente, California. Then I asked, "Who's this Mark Vetter guy? I get the feeling I've seen him before."

Granny shrugged. "He's from your part of the country. Got a place on the beach out there. A pal of Remy's. Maybe from Harvard like Travers. Not a bad sort. Seems to know something about horseflesh. I think they're partnered in a few things. He and his fiancée been staying for the better part of a month out at Dogwood. That's the name of Remy's plantation. Over in Thibodaux, due west of here."

"Vetter's fiancée looks like she might be hard to rein in," I said.

"You mean the gal last night? Hell, she's not his fiancée. That gal's just some two-bit Beulah Remy fixed him up with for the evening. Remy's got a thing for hookers, and so do his 'friends' evidently. Vetter's gal's out of town on business. She's a real sweetheart, Felicia. Everybody likes her."

"Even Remy?" I wondered.

Granny's smile went away and his face closed down. "I suppose so," he said. "Like I just tole you, everybody likes her."

I got us off of that track and back onto one that was more comfortable for Granny—bygone days. While I cleaned my plate of breakfast eggs we reminded one another of some nights we'd spent on the town, the weirdness of owners and jocks we'd known, the sort of stories that were more fun in the recalling than in the experiencing.

"I better be getting back to the barn," Granny announced suddenly, looking at his watch. "Remy's coming out this morning to put the clock on Cajun Desire."

"Good animal?"

"Best I've seen in a while. Got him entered in the Dixie Derby and he's the hands-down favorite."

Over my protests he paid for my breakfast. "I'll sound Remy out about putting you on," he said as we walked out into the damp, overcast morning.

"I know you'd give me a good sell," I told him, "but I'd feel better doing my own pitch." I didn't want Granny to get any more involved in my business than he already had.

"Okay," he said. "Let's head to the barn, and when Remy gets here, take your best shot."

As we approached, a grizzled veterinarian with more hair sticking out of his ears than was on his head was using an ophthalmological gizmo to peer into the eyes of a magnificent chestnut colt. The young jockey who'd given me Granny's location was standing by, watching both man and animal with a fair amount of apprehension.

"Well, how's he look, Doc?" Granny asked.

"Purty fine," the vet replied, sticking his gizmo into a bag. He bent down and played with the animal's left leg, pulling it back, fondling the knee joint. "Purty fine," he repeated.

"This is the beauty that's gonna win the Dixie," Granny told me. "Cajun Desire."

"Nine hundred and ninety pounds of thunder," the young jock said, continuing to observe the vet. "I wish I was gonna be riding him."

"Mike," Granny said to the jock, "meet my old pal Coley Killebrew."

The boy nodded to me politely, and extended a well-callused hand. "Mike LeBlanc," he said.

"And that's Doc Robideaux." The vet petted the horse's leg, stood, and gave me one of those vaguely hostile glances I'd almost learned to live with over the past few years. He did not offer to shake my hand.

"There's a new binding you oughta be using, Granville," he said. "These are fine, and do the job. But there's better on the market." With that, he went into the small room Granny used for an office, found his leather satchel, and left.

"Pretty charming guy," I said.

"Oh, Doc's all right, in his way," Granny said.

"Are you a jockey, Mr. Killebrew?" Mike LeBlanc asked.

"Was," I said.

"One of the best," Granny added. "Averaged three hundred eight wins a year for a bunch of years."

The boy stared at me now. "Why'd you stop? You look like you still have a lotta good years in front of you."

"I ran into bad luck," I told him.

The kid was curious. He opened his mouth to ask more, but Granny cut him off. "Mike's just turned seventeen, Coley. But he's been riding real well and he's gonna be losing his bug this season." A novice rider carries a "bug," a weight advantage, until he has proven himself.

"Who's your agent?" I asked the boy. It's the agents who put jocks onto good horses.

He looked at Granny, who answered, "Bob Loubat was thinking about it, but Remy's taken a personal interest in Mike." Granny made an unconscious grimace, the significance of which was lost on me.

"How much weight are you carrying?" I asked Mike.

"Two," he replied, subtracting a hundred the way some jocks do. "But I'm working hard to get even lower." He was eager, anxious, and bright. I hoped Courville didn't screw up his career.

"We better get back to work," Mike said. "Nice meeting you."

Granny and I watched boy and horse head for the track. The old man said, "The kid really has it, Coley. You'll see. He reminds me of Johnny Longden."

As long as I'd known Granny, I'd never heard him express that much enthusiasm about a jock. It made me even more curious to see the kid do his stuff.

19

COURVILLE DIDN'T MAKE it to the track that morning. At six A.M., when he phoned to say he'd be arriving at noon, Granny and I were in his office, enjoying the air-conditioning and chicory coffee powerful enough to jump-start a dead battery.

" 'Sidetracked,' he calls it," the old man said with distaste after replacing the receiver. "I never can figure the fella out. I know how much the horse means to him, not to mention Mike. But he'll push all that aside just for a little poon."

"Some guys are horsemen," I said. "Some are ladies' men."

"I suppose."

"What's the situation with him and Mike?" I asked.

"He saw the kid ride at Saratoga, found out he was a Louisiana boy, and took a personal interest," Granny replied. "Mike's from Alex . . . uh, Alexandria," he explained, realizing that I was not terribly familiar with the territory. "Mom and Dad and little sister all burned up in a fire back about three years when the boy was off working at Breton Stables outside Lexington.

"Anyway, Remy and his wife, Joan, got to jawing with the boy and decided to sorta take him under their wing. They been going back and forth about adopting him. They don't have none of their own."

"I'm not surprised," I said.

There was a knock at the door.

Granny swung his feet off the desk and said, "C'mon in," loud enough to be heard over the air conditioner.

The woman who entered was a small brunette with a heart-shaped face and a Coke-bottle-shaped figure. She was wearing black linen slacks and a silky blouse that would have clung to her body even if it hadn't been a hot, humid day. She was smiling, but as she looked from Granny to me and explored the other vacant areas of the tiny office, the smile went away.

"Where's Remy?" she asked.

"He got hung up, Miss Bouraine," Granny said. "Should be here by the first race, however."

"Oh." She was more than mildly disappointed. Then she put on a smile. "I'm Delia Bouraine," she said, taking a step toward me and extending her hand. I stood and accepted it.

"Coley Killebrew. I knew your father, Miss Bouraine. He was a good man."

She nodded and turned to Granny. "Please tell Remy I stopped by."

"Sure will, ma'am. Anything I can help you with?"

"No. It looks like my new office manager has flown the coop and Remy said he might be able to find me another. I don't suppose you're an expert on keeping an office running smoothly, are you, Mr. Killebrew?"

"You never know until you try," I said.

"Possibly not. But I am hoping for someone who's been trying for a while. Nice meeting you."

I repaid that compliment with one that sounded similar. I counted to fifteen when the door closed behind her and asked Granny if she was another of Remy's ladies.

He got that uncomfortable look again. "I don't know, Coley. And truth is, I shy away from the part of Remy's life that don't concern the work I do for him."

"You don't think his playing hide the salami with the owner of the track might impact on your work?"

Granny gave me a sour look instead of a verbal reply.

"Well," I said. "Since Courville won't be here until post time, I think I'll head out and let you get your business done."

He didn't seem sorry to see me go.

I caught up with Delia Bouraine just as she was climbing the clubhouse steps. She turned and looked at me with a mixture of cynicism and curiosity. "Yes, Mr. Killebrew?"

"I was wondering if we might have lunch together."

"It's barely seven A.M.," she said.

"I wouldn't want to wait until the last minute to ask you," I said. "You might think you weren't my first choice."

That earned me a smile. "I have lunch brought to my office at eleven forty-five," she said. "It's a humble repast, but you're welcome to share it."

"That's very kind of you."

She cocked her head. "You know, I think that's the first time anybody's called me 'kind.' I'm not sure I'm flattered." She gave me a very brief smile and went on her way.

When she'd ascended the stairs and entered the clubhouse, I turned to look out over the track. The morning sun was peeking through the clouds and it seemed as if it wouldn't be a day for mudders after all. New Orleans weather. Unpredictable.

Just like Delia Bouraine.

I yawned and decided to return to my hotel to catch a few hours' sleep. I had the feeling I'd better be wide-awake for my luncheon date.

20

THE SCAMP IS a tasty fish that's caught along the Gulf Coast. It's best prepared broiled, which is how it was served up on a conference table at the far end of Delia Bouraine's office, bathed in lemon butter and toasted almonds. By then, we'd agreed to call each other by our first names and we'd sampled an excellent chilled Chablis and a half-dozen oysters Rockefeller, nice plump oysters covered with a dark green sauce that tasted of spinach and watercress and onions and something a bit like anise.

I mentioned the sauce and she laughed. "Most of the guys around the track wouldn't know anise from alfalfa," she said.

"Just because you spend time with horses doesn't mean you have to share their tastes when you put on the feed bag," I told her, wondering how my restaurant was getting along without me.

"Well, it's not anise or licorice. It's good old rot-your-brain absinthe. I keep a couple of bottles in the kitchen for my own use. They say that Pernod tastes the same, but I can tell the difference."

"Has this country lifted the ban on absinthe?" I asked, as if I didn't know.

She gave me a Cheshire-cat smile. "If you have the right friend, bans don't matter much."

"That friend being Remy Courville?" I inquired.

She reduced her smile and said, "Perhaps I've been indiscreet in mentioning it. For all I know, you're working for the government."

"Hardly. Though I understand that the late J. Edgar Hoover liked his agents to be as short as him. No, I'm just a traveling man with a little understanding of horses."

"And people," she said.

"People fool me all the time. Horses, I usually know right where I stand."

She nibbled at her scamp and stared at me for a few seconds. She asked, "Are you involved with Remy?"

"I was about to ask you the same question."

She colored briefly. Instead of replying, she said, "I mean, are you working for him?"

"I'm thinking about it. Put in a good word for me."

She smiled. "You might not want that. Remy and I were . . . *are* friendly enemies. It's only this place"—she indicated the office and by extension the whole track—"that keeps us civil."

"I didn't know he was a part of the operation of Magnolia Park."

She took a sip of wine, swallowed, and said, "Not actually a part. But he's a very influential fellow in this state, and he has been helpful on occasion. Are we going to continue to discuss Remy, or shall we get a little more personal?"

"It's your office," I said.

"Tell me about yourself."

"What you see is what you get. My hair and teeth are my own. Various parts of my body have been broken or sprained over the years, but everything's working pretty well at present. I've been told I snore, but I don't believe it."

She laughed. "Why would anyone lie about it?"

"Like I told you—I don't have any idea why people do the things they do." I paused to watch her take a sip of wine. "You, for example. Why are you spending your days running this place when you could be out there somewhere having fun?"

She leaned back in her chair. "When I was growing up, I never was very interested in the track," she said. "Nor did Daddy, in his wildest nightmares, consider the possibility that I might take over for him. But he passed away suddenly. And Mother certainly wasn't the person for the job. It's all she can do to get dressed and out to the country club by afternoon. So, it was either take control or kiss Magnolia Park good-bye."

She stared at me and asked, "Has the business end of the track ever appealed to you, Coley? I could use some help right now. My office manager ran out on me without an hour's notice."

"As you mentioned this morning, it's probably not a good idea to hire a novice."

"You look like you could catch on pretty quickly."

"I'm not crazy about offices, Delia," I said truthfully. "I'm much happier out in the elements, in the company of animals."

"Offices are where the money is, if you know your stuff."

"Not necessarily. As much as your father knew about running this place, I understand it wasn't doing so well during his last years."

"That's absurd," she said, scowling. "It's always been a very successful operation. Recently, because of a few changes I've made, it's become even more successful. But it's never suffered."

"And what about your social life? Has that suffered from all the work and no play?"

"There's been . . . play," she said coyly. "I enjoy play. Otherwise I'd be eating alone."

"You should let your partners take over. Then you could really cut loose," I told her.

"My partners? What partners?"

I was about to slip in a question or two about Southern Boy Supplies, but I didn't get the chance. The door to the office opened and Remy Courville came in. He looked from Delia to me, studied the table, the wineglasses, and said, "My, my, Coley, I am impressed. The most I've ever rated has been a muffuletta and a bottle of Dixie."

"Come join us, Remy," Delia said. "We were just talking about you."

"Oh?" He pulled up a chair and sat facing us. He wasn't smiling now.

"I just offered Coley a job, but he said he'd rather work for you. Something about the company of horses."

"Granny mentioned he could use a little help back at the plantation," I told him.

He stared at me, his handsome face without expression. "What's in it for you?"

"A few bucks. More important, the chance to work with one of the best trainers around."

"A paid education, then?"

"Something like that," I told him.

"When could you start?"

I looked at my watch. "Is five o'clock this evening too soon?"

He laughed. "You and Granny can work out the finances. He'll also set you up at Dogwood. Maybe we can even get you on a horse one of these days."

"My time in the saddle is over," I told him.

"We'll see," he said. "Anyway, now that that's settled, you think you could leave Delia and me alone for a minute? We've got something important to discuss."

I looked at Delia. She seemed vaguely upset. She said, "If you wouldn't mind, Coley."

"Not at all," I said, pushing back my chair and standing up. "Thanks for lunch."

She gave me a distracted smile and I made my exit.

As I went through the door I heard her say, "Irwin Matthes has left town. Do you have any idea where he's gone?"

"Never mind him." Courville's voice was playful. "What's with you and the jock . . ."

That's all I could hear before the door swung shut behind me.

21

"MR. STARBUCK NOT here," Choo-Choo's voice informed me via long distance. I was standing at a pay phone not far from a grandstand beer stall.

"Where can I reach him?" I asked.

"Not know, Mr. Killebrew."

There was some muffled discussion on Choo-Choo's end and, suddenly, Lea was on the phone saying, "Hi. How's N.O.?"

"Slow track, fast people. I've got a question for your father."

"Try me."

"I fully intend to," I said.

There was a second's silence, then she said, "I mean, maybe I can answer your question."

"It's about my predecessor, the often-discussed Irwin Matthes. I just discovered he'd been working at Magnolia Park and I sort of wondered what he told your father about the operation."

She hesitated and replied, "He didn't say anything."

"Starbuck said he was going to meet with Matthes for a debriefing. He must've found out something."

"The meeting didn't happen," she said. "Coley . . . ?"

"Yes."

"Nothing."

"Thanks to many years spent in the Orient studying men's minds, I can sense you're trying to tell me something."

"Irwin Matthes is dead," she said.

"Plane crash? Heart attack? Hemophilia?"

"Murder." Her voice was appropriately lifeless.

"That was going to be my next guess. Any details you'd care to share?"

She told me about the body being found at Santa Rosita. "The police think he was kicked by a horse, but Daddy is certain it was no accident. I'm sure he meant to tell you."

"Maybe in a year or two, when he felt I was old enough to hear such things."

"He probably thought you'd use it as an excuse to quit."

"Bingo," I said. "You can take this as my official notification."

"Please stay," she said. "At least until I can get there."

"Get here? Are you crazy?" I calmed down enough to observe the area around me. A few handicappers going after brews. I lowered my voice. "Your father said Matthes was a top professional. And *he's* dead. It's time for us amateurs to dismount and leave the track."

"I'm not an amateur," she replied defiantly. "I can take care of myself. You've seen proof of that."

I had to admit that was true.

"And I don't quit what I've started. I'm disappointed to find out that you do." There was what sounded like sincere regret in her voice.

"My religion demands that I shy away from the near occasion of death."

"What you're saying is that you're afraid."

"I suppose so," I told her.

"And your fear is stronger than your desire to locate your old flame, Francie Dorn?"

She was definitely her father's daughter. The image of Francie fluttered through my head. My throat felt dry.

"Not to mention the fact that I probably saved your life the other night," she continued. "You owe me for that."

"Thanks for not mentioning it."

Granny appeared at the far entrance to the stands, scanning the gathering crowd. When he saw me, his face broke into a wide smile and he galloped my way.

"Don't leave until I get there," Lea's voice pleaded in my ear.

I did owe her something. And I wanted Francie's whereabouts. "I'll stay," I told her. "But you don't come here. That's out. It'll be difficult enough just worrying about my own hide."

She was silent for a few beats. Then: "I'll have to discuss this with Daddy. If you don't want me there—"

"I want you anywhere but here. I want me anywhere but here. Hopefully, when this is over, we can both be anywhere but here together."

Granny was only a few feet away when I replaced the receiver. "Hot damn, son, but it looks like we're gonna be workin' together," he said, putting his arm around my shoulder.

I found a spare grin from somewhere in the recent past and pasted it on my face as I let him lead me to the counter to seal the deal in beer.

22

IT WAS SHORTLY after eight that night when Granny and I arrived at Dogwood Plantation. The drive had taken a couple of hours, carrying us along a highway past a little town called Raceland, then west on state highway 1, plunging deep into the heart of Cajun country.

There were vast swampy landscapes where the water almost lapped at the edges of the asphalt and expanses of floating greenery dotted with sturdy, moss-strung oaks that looked as solid as sidewalk.

The sun slipped behind the Texas border just as Granny steered our formidable black Range Rover through the metropolis of

Thibodaux (population 15,810) with what seemed to me a fierce determination to beat nightfall. Regardless, my first view of Dogwood, the Courville compound, relied heavily on available moonlight.

A wire fence that went on for miles marked the outer limits of the property. The wire gave way to a high stucco wall that spanned the front of the plantation. Granny turned off the road to poke the Rover's nose at a thick plank door that had been built into the wall. He tooted the horn and a small panel about six feet off the ground slid open.

Eyes peered out through the opening. Then the panel slid back into place and the door swung inward. A big bruiser in white shirt, tight Levi's, boots, and a Stetson stepped around it. He had a large, round, baby face that he tried to square up with dirty yellow sideburns down to his jawline. He wore an elaborately stitched holster and his right hand rested casually on the butt of the pistol it housed. His other hand held a cellular phone.

He stepped out of the glare of the Rover's headlights and squinted at us. Granny mumbled, "Evening, Floyd."

Floyd paused—for dramatic effect, I assumed—and then nodded his head and hat at Granny. Granny eased the Rover past the big man and into the compound.

In front of us was another wall, this one Mother Nature's, made up of tall, thick trees and shadowy foliage. A winding shell drive led us around it and through a series of twists and turns until the main house appeared, a half mile or so from the gate.

It seemed to glow bone white in the moonlight, a two-story affair with no less than eight white columns supporting the roof. Mirror-image winding stairwells swirled up to the first floor, which I later learned was the house proper. The ground level had been used to stable horses when the place was built back in the late 1700s. Some Johnny-come-lately in the 1800s bricked in the lower part and turned it into another floor of living space, a sort of aboveground basement.

"Built for a Spanish queen," Granny told me. "Or so Remy says. Place is big enough for a hotel."

"I don't suppose that's where I bunk," I said.

He chuckled. "Hardly. I have me a little cottage back near the stable that's got an extra bedroom."

"I don't want to crowd you, Granny," I said.

"Hell, boy. With you taking some of my manager chores, I don't plan to be spending a whole lot of time here. There's more than enough racing going on in this part of the country to keep me busy."

I told him that besides the Fair Grounds and Magnolia Park in New Orleans, I knew about Evangeline Downs in Lafayette. And Louisiana Downs.

"You never raced at Delta Downs?" he asked. And when I shook my head, he added, "Maybe a hundred and fifty miles to the west, in a town called Vinton. Right next to the Texas border. They keep the track going year round. That's how Mike plans to rack up a lot of winners next year."

"Before they started Sunday racing in Southern California, the jocks would head down to Agua Caliente to grab a few wins," I told him. "It was rough down in Mexico back then, I gather. A lot of whip and slash."

"It can get a little rough around here, too," he said ominously.

We drove past a swimming pool glowing an eerie green from its underwater lights. Next to that was a pair of tennis courts. "Too many 'skeeters for much night swimmin' or tennis," Granny said. "You remember the 'skeeters?"

I nodded that I did. "And the damned Louisiana cockroaches," I said. "Real man-eaters."

"Yep, we got them in pro-fusion out here. Even bigger than in the city. Remy says he hopes they grow big enough he can throw a saddle on 'em."

"He do much riding himself?"

Granny shook his head. "Not so's you'd notice. But he does love the animals. It ain't just show with him, the way it is with some."

"You like the guy?" I asked.

"Hell, I've worked for worse," Granny said.

The horses were kept deep into the property, in a stable area surrounded by trees. They must've had to cut down quite a few willows and oaks and cypress to make way for the large barn, the pen, the long bunkhouse, several bungalows and a short circular track. But judging from the solidity of Granny's little house, the wood had been put to good use.

"I'll take you around after you stow your gear," the old man told me, leading me past a screened porch and into a comfortable living space that smelled of pine needles and cleaning wax.

The dark hardwood floors glistened with polish. Pale yellow walls were decorated with color photographs of horses, some carrying jocks, some standing free and tall. There was a fairly new TV set, a VCR, and a radio. A comfortable-looking easy chair faced the television. A couch of dark wood, topped by dark green cushions, sat before a long wooden table filled with magazines like *Horse Illustrated* and *Horseplay* and a couple of ancient copies of *Time* and *People*.

A small kitchen was to the left. My room was down a hall that ran next to the kitchen. It was no smaller than the hotel bedroom I'd been using and it looked much more homey. The single bed of dark wood had a horse's profile carved in the headboard. I poked the center of the mattress and it seemed solid. I dropped my bags at the foot of the bed and went back into the living room, where Granny was clicking on a window air conditioner.

"If you leave your door open, Coley, you'll get enough of this to stay comfortable. Otherwise it tends to heat up a little."

"I could just open my window," I said.

He grinned. "I thought you said you remembered the 'skeeters. They laugh at screens. The buggers come right on in, attack, and take no prisoners." He picked up a small spray can from a table and tossed it to me. "Better put a little of that junk on the exposed areas of your body if you wanna head out to look the place over."

The mosquitoes were, on that night at least, overrated. Or maybe the citrus-smelling ointment kept them at bay while Granny showed me the barn and introduced me to the animals and the humans who lived and worked there.

The bunkhouse consisted of two sexually separate but equal sleeping quarters for the men and women who were salaried members of the staff. "The majority of the workers," Granny said, "got their own places in town and get paid by the hour. But we got five or six folks who hang out here all the time. They don't have much of a life away from the barn, but they seem to like it that way."

"Don't you?" I asked him.

He chuckled and took me into the men's quarters, where a noisy bourrée game was in progress. I declined an invitation to sit in, but observed for a few hands as the vicious combination of poker and bridge devastated its losers and rewarded its winners. Out of habit, I watched to see if anybody was dealing from the bottom or crimping edges. Not that it mattered particularly, but the game seemed straight.

Granny headed back to his house and I wandered out into the night. I wouldn't have called it cool, but it was less humid than the city. The sky looked clear. Nothing between me and the moon and stars.

I wandered away from the barn area, kicking pine cones. I was feeling generally at peace with the world until a light flashed in my face, and an authoritative voice demanded, "What's yoah name, buddy?"

I gave my name and heard it repeated by the authoritative voice. Then the light was turned off and the voice said, "Sorry, buddy, but yoah face's a new one to me. Ah'll remember it next time."

My eyes were getting used to the darkness. He was a tall man dressed in the same outfit as the guy at the gate. Stetson, white shirt, Levi's, holster and gun, and cellular phone, which he'd apparently used to check my name.

He had a full black beard and black eyebrows that met over the bridge of his nose. Considering the part of the world we were in, I wondered if he was ever mistaken for a loup-garou. "You know my name," I said. "What's yours?"

"Jus' call me Johnson," he said. "It's what the boss calls me and ever'body else does, too."

"You been working here long, Johnson?"

"Little over a year. You just startin', huh?"

I nodded. "Pretty good place to work?"

"Not half-bad," Johnson said.

"A lot of ground to patrol."

"Yeah, but we got four of us on duty at all times."

"Why so much security?"

It was one question too much for Johnson. He gave me a tight smile and said, "If you take walks at night, Killebrew, you oughta stick around the barn area. Some of us get spooked easier'n others."

He gave me a polite nod that was evidently my cue to head back where I belonged.

Once again under Granny's roof, I asked the old man about the cowboy patrol.

"They're okay," he said. "But like all guys you give a gun to, they think they gotta behave like Humphrey Bogart with a hangover."

"Why's Remy need an armed security force?"

"These are rough times," Granny said. "Hell, just because a guy's paranoid, don't mean folks aren't out to get him."

"Who's out to get Remy?"

"You'd have to ask him that, Coley. He don't confide in yours truly."

"If he's so worried about people doing him harm," I said, "why does he wander around the French Quarter without his gun-totin' posse?"

Granny cocked his head to one side. "Never occurred to me," he said. "It's *his* business, in any case. You know, Coley, back when we worked together last, I don't remember you being such a curious cuss."

"Back then I was too stupid to be curious."

"Well, at this time and at this place, it may be stupid to be too smart." He gave me a wink and went to bed.

I stayed up for a while.

PART SIX

Starbuck Finds a Body

23

TWO THOUSAND MILES to the west, Starbuck had begun his day by sending a very hung-over Mildred Drucker on her way to Cabo San Lucas and at least a temporary job at one of the resort area's larger hotels. He then got out the Bentley and let it carry him to Parker Center, where he visited an old friend in the Los Angeles Police Department, a wiry, hyperactive, rodentlike man named Eddie Rafferty, who was also a hopeless handicapper.

Starbuck wondered if Rafferty might prevail upon both the Torrance and the San Pedro Police Departments to cough up copies of their case files on Irwin Matthes and Liandra "Lannie" Luchek, respectively.

Raising and lowering his shoulders while pacing around his

desk, Rafferty allowed as how the request was within the realm of possibility. He mentioned something about needing a new pair of sunglasses, which in Southern California police circles meant that the job would cost fifty dollars. Relieved that Rafferty did not need a new surfboard, Starbuck exited Parker Center and headed for home.

There, he discovered that he had missed a visit from Lea, who had arrived just in time for my telephone call. He tried phoning her. No answer.

Annoyed, he took off for her apartment in Venice, a beachside community slightly up the coast from his place in the Marina.

Lea was not there. A young man whom Starbuck recognized as Lea's neighbor was sitting in front of her building applying hot pink polish to his Great Dane's claws. The color matched his own finger- and toe-nails. He informed Starbuck that Lea was in the ocean swimming her daily five miles.

Starbuck was sitting on the beach under a lonely palm tree with his shoes and socks in his lap when she finally emerged from the Pacific. As she strolled across the sand, squeezing salt water from her long hair, he thought that she'd been swimming in the nude, which was a little extreme even for Lea. But as she approached he realized she was wearing little tan patches held together by matching strands of material. He wondered what her mother would have said. . . . The same thing he was going to say, probably. Nothing.

"Hi, Dad," she greeted him. "Are we having brunch together?"

He felt his stomach lurch. Too many martinis the night before. "I could handle coffee, maybe," he said. "I want to talk to you about Killebrew."

"What about him?" she asked, waiting as he tiptoed across sand that the sun was frying.

"He woke me up last night to tell me he's made his own plans," Starbuck replied. He perched on a bright yellow fireplug and tried to brush the sand from his feet while he gave her his slant on our phone call. He ended with, ". . . so Choo-Choo tells me he called again this morning and you talked to him. What's he want now?"

She gave him a detailed account of our conversation.

Starbuck reddened past sunburn into apoplexy. "That son of a bitch is going to blow this whole deal."

"It's your fault for not providing him with more information."

"All he had to do was follow the game plan. Now he damn well *may* be getting in over his head."

Lea didn't give him an inch. "Maybe he trusts his instincts more than he trusts you."

"Dammit, I'm the boss of this operation, not him." He tied his shoestrings and stood up. He took a few steps and it felt like he was carrying half the beach in his shoes. He marveled at the way Lea could prance barefoot over rocks and pebbles and shards of glass.

"At the very least you should have told him about Matthes," she said.

"I didn't want to scare him off."

"Well, he knows and he's not scared off," she said.

He studied her for a few seconds. "Did you tell him about the Luchek bimbo?"

Lea frowned. "That's a lovely way to refer to a woman who was just murdered."

"You're right. I stand politically corrected. Did you mention her to Killebrew?"

"N–no." She shook her head.

He smiled triumphantly. "Then I assume you have your own doubts about Killebrew's courage."

"He asked me about Matthes," she shot back. "If he'd asked me about Lannie Luchek, I would have answered truthfully."

He scowled suddenly. "Look, little girl, you and the jockey—"

"The ex-jockey," she interrupted. "I'm surprised you of all people would make that mistake."

"You and the ex-jockey aren't . . . you know?"

"Aren't what?" she snapped angrily.

"Getting . . . uh . . . involved, or anything?"

"No. But it wouldn't be any of your business if we were."

Blood was starting to pound in his head. "You don't want to waste yourself on—"

"Don't say it," she ordered. "I've heard it before. They're never good enough for me."

"Well, honey, you *are* special."

"And you're selfish."

He looked hurt as he nodded his big head. "Yeah, I guess I am. But I'm right about Killebrew. You know as well as I do that the main reason he's taking his chances in New Orleans is because he wants to find his precious Francie Dorn."

She had to agree, but it didn't make her any happier with him. She was so annoyed she invited the neighbor and his Great Dane, whose name was Duchess, to have brunch with them.

Duchess rested her huge head on Starbuck's thigh the whole time it took him to drink a cup of mediocre coffee. When he stood to go, he realized that the dog had drooled all over his pants.

24

"WASN'T YOU WEARING tan slacks this morning?" the ratlike Detective Eddie Rafferty asked as he handed Starbuck a collection of faxed sheets containing official police reports of the deaths of Irwin Matthes and Liandra Luchek.

Starbuck didn't answer him. Instead, he scrutinized the drooping pages while Rafferty watched and twitched and mumbled something about missing the opening race.

What Starbuck discovered was that neither the Torrance nor the San Pedro Police Department had put itself out in gathering information about the two decedents.

Matthes's death, at first thought to be the result of an accident with a spooked horse, was now being attributed to a blow from a blunt instrument, possibly a lead pipe. The weapon had not been found.

Matthes's body had been dragged seventy-two feet across the soft earth before being deposited in the stable at Barn Number Five.

There was an abundance of footprints in the earth in the vicinity of the homicidal attack. Most were standard riding boots or tennis shoes. The only vaguely odd prints were those identified as a woman's high heels.

Starbuck finished the sheets on Matthes and handed them to Rafferty. "The Torrance guys do a swell job. It doesn't even say where the guy got popped."

Rafferty squinted at the sheets. "Seventy-two feet from Barn Five," he said.

"Which direction?"

"I see what you mean," Rafferty said. "They measure off the distance, but they forget to get specific on the direction. What can you do today, the kids they're putting on the job? You notice this stuff about the footprints?"

"High heels? Yeah. You don't see too many high heels in that area."

"The Torrance detective I talked to said there were also jogging treads leading from the track," Rafferty said. "Out on the goddamn track, too. Two sets there. Small enough to be broads' feet. He said he told his lieutenant about 'em."

"There wasn't any mention of the joggers in the file."

"No," Rafferty admitted, chuckling. "The lieutenant who's in charge asked the detective if he thought one of the joggers went back by the barn, took off her running shoes, and put on her high-heel pumps. Because for the lieutenant's money, the position and direction of the pump prints made it pretty clear the dame in the pumps dragged the guy. So the detective didn't put anything about the joggers in the report. He didn't want to piss off the lieutenant, who likes things as clear and simple as possible."

Starbuck thought the lieutenant's appraisal of the situation was correct. It had been a woman who'd banged Matthes's gong. A woman wearing high-heeled shoes. A woman who left lipstick-smeared cigarette butts in Matthes's apartment. A woman who was staying in the Brentwood Hotel under the name of Fiona Dawson.

The San Pedro Police Department had decided that Lannie Luchek's death may not have been an accident after all. The fatal blow to the head had occurred before the body entered the water. But there were no wood splinters in the wound, which indicated that she had not bounced her noggin on the dock on her way into the briny. The investigating officers had discovered no blood or particles of flesh on the side of the dock.

Finally, there had been no water in Lannie's lungs. Even if death had been instantaneous with the blow, there should have been an intake of breath. The bottom line was that she'd been dead when she hit the drink.

Starbuck handed Rafferty the price of a new pair of sunglasses, knowing the cash would be gone by the fifth race. The big man then started for the door, but the cop stopped him with, "Ray, you think the two stiffs might be related?"

Starbuck folded the fax papers carefully and put them into his coat pocket. He hoped that Rafferty wasn't bright enough to ask for a comparison of the shoes Lannie Luchek had been wearing with the jogging prints found on the track at Santa Rosita.

Looking at the cop's twitching, puzzled face, he was convinced that would never happen. "I asked you if you thought they was related?" Rafferty repeated.

"Old son," Starbuck said, slapping Rafferty on the back with a heartiness he did not feel, "that's such a long shot, I can't even see *you* betting on it."

25

AT SIX FIFTY-FIVE that evening, Starbuck was met at the entry to the Santa Rosita executive offices by the track's chief accountant, George McGuinn, Clara's nephew. "My aunt called to say she'd be a little late," he told the detective. "She said you could just go down to her office."

"Are the others here yet?"

"Others?" George jerked back from the word. Starbuck realized that the young man wasn't in very good shape. The bags under his eyes had deepened since their last meeting and his pallor accentuated their gray flannel color. He was obviously under pressure from either the preparation of the stockholders' report or from the intensity of his new romance. Maybe from both.

Starbuck told him that the evening's gathering would include the two security guards who'd been on duty the night of Irwin Matthes's death. "I'm sure Clara wouldn't mind if you sat in, too," the detective added.

"Me? Lord, no. I've got enough to do without getting involved in things that don't concern me." He flashed a nervous smile, then added, "Her office is just down—"

Starbuck told him he knew where Clara's office was and the young man breathed a sigh of relief before staggering back into his work space.

Starbuck was a little relieved himself. George McGuinn's stress was draining. He was happy with the solitude of Clara's outer office as he lowered his bulk onto a large red leather couch facing the door.

He was sitting there, thinking about dinner and murder, though not necessarily in that order, when he heard heavy footsteps approaching down the hall. He hoped they signaled the arrival of Larry Mullen or Louis Naylor, the two night security guards, rather than a repeat visit with George McGuinn.

It turned out to be someone he hadn't considered. Barry Gallen, Clara McGuinn's "insignificant other," as Starbuck once described him, entered the office, smelling of bay rum and bourbon. He wore a lightweight tan sport coat over a blue oxford shirt with bright yellow tie. His cocoa-brown slacks showed a day's worth of wrinkles, but his face was smooth as a baby's, except for a few booze blotches. When he saw Starbuck sitting on the red leather couch, he went rigid.

"Hi, Barry," Starbuck greeted him with a pleasantness he was certain Gallen didn't deserve.

"Starbuck," the other man mumbled, then put himself into motion again, walking swiftly past him into Clara McGuinn's private office.

Seconds later he exited. "She's not here," he said, obviously confused.

"So I noticed," Starbuck replied. "We're supposed to meet at seven."

Gallen's pink-rimmed eyes hardened. "You and Clara?" He made it sound like an accusation.

"And a couple of other guys," Starbuck said.

Barry Gallen consulted his Rolex. "They're late."

Starbuck sighed. "The story of my life. I get there early; everybody else gets there late."

More footsteps.

This time they belonged to a doughy, ashen-faced man in a khaki uniform with the name of the track stenciled in red on his right shirt pocket. He entered hesitantly, as if uncertain he was in the right place.

"Larry Mullen?" Starbuck asked.

"Louie Naylor."

"Well, take a seat, Louie," Starbuck told him. "The show's running a little behind schedule."

Gallen looked at his watch again as if he expected the action to goose things along.

"Anybody bring a deck of cards?" Starbuck asked.

Gallen glared at him. Naylor smiled nervously.

Five minutes more of that and Starbuck decided to start defrosting Naylor's story.

"Must be a pretty boring job, huh, Louie?" he asked. "Patrolling an off-season track."

"It's okay."

"What's the setup? You and Mullen alternate patrols?"

Naylor started to answer, but Gallen overrode him with, "Any idea where she is, Starbuck?"

"Nope. The nephew might know."

"That twit doesn't know anything that doesn't come out of a computer," Barry Gallen snapped as he moved toward the door. "Tell Clara to call me when she gets here. I'll either be in the Jaguar or at home."

Naylor waited for Gallen to go, then asked, "Was that Mrs. Mac's husband?"

"He wishes," Starbuck said. Then he began questioning the security guard in earnest.

Clara McGuinn arrived fifteen minutes late, apologizing profusely. She'd been practicing at the Beverly Hills Gun Club, she explained, opening her bulky black purse and showing them a little Llama Comanche III snuggled into a pale blue designer holster.

She looked around the outer office. "Where's Larry Mullen?"

"We've been wondering that ourselves," Starbuck said.

"He usually beats me to the job," Louie Naylor told them.

"You know his number?" Starbuck asked him, then pointed to a phone on the empty desk beside the private office door.

Clara walked into her office. Starbuck stayed in the doorway waiting to hear the result of Naylor's call.

The security guard held the phone to his ear for nearly a minute, listening to the rings. Then he replaced the receiver and followed Starbuck into Clara's office.

"He's probably on his way," she said, gesturing the two men toward a couch and chair of matching soft rose-colored leather, facing her polished antique desk.

The room was a slightly lighter rose, the rug a darker shade. Twin windows behind Clara's desk looked out over the darkened track. Starbuck went to the windows, peered out, then turned. "Why don't you tell Mrs. McGuinn what you told me, Louie? About the coffee."

"It's just that you asked me what was different about that night," Louie said, perching on the edge of the couch. "And the coffee was different. The coffee in the machine in our room is like weak mud, and usually Larry takes a walk over to the Greek's for a carton that lasts us until morning, when the pancake house opens up. Then I go over there for doughnuts and a half carton of Joe. Actually, the pancake house has better coffee than—"

"Get back to that night, Louie," Starbuck prompted him impatiently.

"Yeah. Well, Larry's got this smirk on his face he gets sometimes that I'd like to wipe it off, you know. And he says he met this babe. That's how he talks. 'Babe.' He met this 'babe' who's half his age, who's got this big job, travelin' around the country. She's all over him like a cheap cologne. Very possessive. And she says she don't want him drinking store-bought coffee when she makes the best coffee in the world.

"So I think the guy's maybe gone off his nut. I mean, Larry likes women sure enough, but I been working with him for six years, and in that time I never heard of a woman liking *him*. But, irregardless, the night bell rings and we both go down and there's this lady in a new Olds out in the parking lot, with the engine running."

"What was she like?" Clara asked.

"She's in a new car," Louie replied. "I didn't get much of a look at her. Larry tells me she's shy, so I stay by the door and he goes out to get the coffee from her."

"The point is," Starbuck said to Clara, "the woman got out of the car to ring the night bell. Then she got back in the car because she didn't want Louie to see what she looked like."

"I figure she's a scag—you'll excuse the expression, ma'am— and that's why she's hiding. But, what the hell, she makes us coffee, even if it's not the best I ever had."

"What was wrong with it?" Starbuck asked.

"It's a little bitter. But if you douse it with Sweet'n Low it's not bad."

"So, after you drank this bitter coffee, you and Larry snoozed off?"

Louie Naylor nodded. "That is, I went back to the office with the coffee and Larry stayed with his lady. I poured myself a cup and I was working on that when Larry came back. Then it's kinda fuzzy because I got real sleepy and asked him if he'd take the first patrol and he said yes. The next thing I know, the cops are banging on the door downstairs and Larry and me are sitting at the table, waking up like it was morning and it was time to go home."

"What did the police say when you told them your story?" Clara asked.

Louie looked uncomfortable. "They said we wasn't very good night watchmen, falling asleep on the job. But I swear, Mrs. Mac, that ain't never happened before. Not the both of us going out like that."

"Did they talk to Larry's girlfriend?" Starbuck inquired.

"Well, you see, we didn't exactly tell 'em about her. Larry didn't want to get her involved, and what the hell . . ."

Starbuck faced Clara. "I'd better try to find Larry Mullen. Do you have an address for him?"

She did.

He was moving from the room when he remembered Barry Gallen's message. He turned and she looked up expectantly. "Something else?" she asked.

"No," he said with a grin. "Nothing important."

26

L ARRY MULLEN LIVED in Studio City, in the San Fernando Valley. His apartment was one of six that formed a
shadowy *U* around a small, lighted pool. Television noise
screeched from several of the lighted apartments, but Starbuck
saw no sign of life behind their draped picture windows and
closed doors.

The complex was named for the leader of an all-girl band that
was popular on television in the early 1950s. The numbers on the
apartment doors were flanked by metal musical notations. Mullen's was G clef—4—G clef.

A venetian blind had been lowered to cover his picture window, but the bottom of it had caught on something in the room
and a triangle of light snuck out onto the cement walkway.
Starbuck pressed the metal button beside the door and a dull
electronic bong sounded inside the apartment.

No one responded to it.

Starbuck tried the door.

It opened.

He took a quick glance at the other apartments, unholstered his
gun, and went in.

Easing the door shut with his foot, he took in a small living
room, barely furnished with a couch, chairs, and coffee table, all
pull-apart Danish. The light was coming from a chrome floor
lamp beside the couch. More light came from a tiny TV set
perched on a counter separating that room from a minuscule

kitchen. On its picture tube was some choreographer's idea of a Jamaican festival. Black dancers gyrating frantically with bright colors exploding behind them. The sound was off.

Starbuck walked cautiously across the electric-blue shag rug, looked over the counter into the kitchen, which was spotless except for the wrapper of a Snickers bar that had been rolled into a tight ball. It rested beside the open, empty garbage pail. A basketball shot that hadn't made the hoop.

Starbuck walked through the curved portal leading to a closet-sized alcove and two closed doors. He used the display handkerchief in his top pocket to open the nearest door. It led to a very neat lighted bathroom that hadn't been updated since the building was constructed in the forties. Music notes appeared at regular intervals in the pale blue tiles outlining the shower.

The walls of the room were also pale blue, the ceiling an off-white. The fixtures—basin and toilet—were pale blue, too, though the shades did not quite match. The water in the toilet bowl was a dark blue.

On a glass shelf, a tin of shaving cream, a razor so clean it looked as if it had never been used, and a comb-and-brush set were lined up like little soldiers.

Mildly disgusted by Larry Mullen's compulsive neatness, Starbuck backtracked to the alcove and tried the other door, which opened into darkness. He used the handkerchief to flip on the overhead light. This was the bedroom, with pale yellow the dominant color. It was a particularly claustrophobic room, made even more so by windows that were up high near the ceiling along the far wall. Its furnishing included a double bed covered with a rumpled brown corduroy spread, a chair, and a dresser. That left barely enough room to walk in and turn around.

Starbuck did not like the way the room smelled. A stuffy odor that stung the nostrils. He turned his attention to a closet door next to the bed and opened it with the handkerchief. Inside were several pairs of khaki pants and shirts, hanging in orderly rows, and an assortment of old shoes, including sneakers, grouped in pairs, with their heels pressed against one wall. At the rear of the closet, Larry Mullen's collection of *Playboys* was stacked in chronological order, at least two decades' worth.

Stepping back out of the closet, Starbuck realized what the odor was. The acrid smell associated with gunfire. He remembered B-movie detectives identifying it as "cordite." He wondered if that was the proper name for it, or just something a Hollywood hack dreamed up. No matter, that's what he smelled in Larry Mullen's bedroom.

He looked back at the bed and noticed that the rumpled cover was being stretched away from him and toward the separation between the bed and the far wall.

He edged around the bed and found an overweight man wedged between the bed and the wall. He was resting on his left side, arms and head tangled in a blood-wet clay-colored sweatshirt that he apparently had been removing when someone stuck a revolver next to the base of his skull and pulled the trigger. The blood, bone, and brain had been contained by the sweatshirt, a point that the compulsively neat Larry Mullen might have appreciated under other circumstances.

Starbuck tucked his gun away and bent down to touch the man's wrist. He was definitely dead. And had been for a while. Starbuck was not of a mind to disturb the bloody sweatshirt. Instead, he carefully removed the wallet from the corpse's back pocket. Inside were two twenties, four ones, a condom, and a packet of credentials carrying the name Lawrence Patrick Mullen.

Starbuck replaced the wallet in the pocket and backed away from the corpse. Then he retraced his steps to the alcove, where, using the display handkerchief, he turned off the bedroom light and pulled the door shut.

He paused at the bathroom and looked in again, staring at the toilet. The lid was up, but the seat was down. If he had never married, never lived with a woman, he would probably have found no significance in that. Maybe there *was* no significance. Maybe Larry had relieved himself. No! The kind of guy who cleaned his razor that thoroughly and kept blue water in his bowl would have replaced the lid after using it.

As he crossed the living room Starbuck noticed that a grown

white man in short pants had replaced the black dancers on the television screen. The little figure was crying and a beautiful woman in a bikini walked behind him and patted him on the head. As intriguing as this sequence was, Starbuck pulled himself away from it. He held the kerchief against the lamp switch and extinguished the light. Then he lifted a blind to peer out at the complex.

The water rippled in the pool as two figures pressed together in the shallow end. Mumbling a curse under his breath, Starbuck propped his backside against the edge of the couch and waited for the lovers to go back to their apartment.

Their passion increased, as did their stroking and caressing. Starbuck assumed it would not be long now. But he was wrong. The male propped the woman onto the steps at the shallow end of the pool and began to remove her suit. Then they made love.

Starbuck wanted to kill them both.

Eventually, all desire spent, the lovers retreated, arms entwined, to an apartment on the opposite side of the pool.

Starbuck still did not leave, thinking that other neighbors could have been watching the public display and remained glued to their windows, waiting for more.

Finally, his impatience got the better of him. Turning up the collar of his coat, and using one of his hands to cover the lower half of his face, he left Larry Mullen's apartment, shut the door with his handkerchief, and moved quickly out to the street.

He did not think he was observed. He hoped not, because his very distinctive Bentley was waiting at the curb near the front of the complex. He drove it as far as the nearest 7-Eleven store, where he used the phone to notify the police of Larry Mullen's permanent condition.

PART SEVEN

My First Day
at Dogwood

27

IT WAS STILL dark outside when I awoke to my first morning at Dogwood Plantation. Granny Hayes was in the kitchen, rattling pans and slamming cabinet doors. The air was cool and remarkably fresh. I felt better rested than at any time in recent memory. And the pan rattling segued into the sound of something sizzling on the stove, music to soothe the savage hunger.

Granny and I gobbled fried-egg sandwiches doused with Tabasco and washed them down with chicory coffee as pungent as incense. He did most of the talking, outlining the day awaiting us, explaining exactly what chores he expected me to carry out. He ended by saying that he was driving to Magnolia Park later that morning to supervise the arrival of a new filly that Courville had purchased.

"There's something I'd appreciate, Coley," he added.

"Name it."

"If you could spend some time with young Mike. Pass along a little of that hard-earned experience. I got a feeling the kid's gonna need it."

"I didn't notice him in the bunkhouse last night," I said. "Does he live off the plantation?"

"He's got a room up the main house," Granny said. "Like I said, they're treating him like an adopted son. Even got a tutor to come in afternoons to get him through high school. But don't let that give you any wrong ideas. The kid pulls his own weight and expects to be run hard. Nobody gets a free ride at this barn."

"What about friends of Courville's, like Travers Junior," I said. "If he decides to take a horse out, do I run him hard, too?"

Granny shook his head balefully. "It ain't likely he'll be doing that. But if he does, then pro-ceed at your own risk, Captain, is all I can tell you."

I found Mike sitting on the floor of the tack room working a conditioner into the tack he'd use that day and listening to a Cajun stable hand named Andrew describe the previous night's activity at a bar known as Lulu's Landing.

". . . and my little ma-ma look at me, yeah, and she say, 'I got me better lungwarts than that *cochon* up on the bar in the wet T-shirt.' And I tell her, 'Well, Ma-ma, you an' me gonna—'"

The Cajun saw me in the doorway and clammed. "See you later, yeah, Mike," he said, and slipped past me to go do whatever he was supposed to be doing at seven in the morning.

"Didn't mean for him to cut his story short," I said.

Mike smiled, studying his tack. "He'll finish it for me," he said. "Andrew'd much rather talk than work."

"Wouldn't we all?"

He raised his head. "Not me," he said with the seriousness of the young. "I love this. From the time I'm able to remember things, I wanted to work with horses. I didn't know if I was gonna be a trainer or a stable hand. I just knew how good I felt when I was around animals."

"Granny says you've got what it takes to be a winning jock," I said. "He's a guy who knows."

"The last few years, that's all I wanted out of life."

"But now . . . ?"

He shrugged and worked more conditioner into a strap. "Joan . . . Mrs. Courville thinks I oughta go to college. She's probably right."

"No reason you can't do both," I told him. "Athletes go to school all the time. It's not easy riding all week and studying, too. But it can be done."

"Yeah, maybe."

He got to his feet and picked up the saddle and bridle. I walked with him into the stable, where he began to ready a big gray gelding named Sly Boots. I left him to his work and paid a courtesy call on the barn manager, a squat, dark man with a bald spot surrounded by wiry gray hair. His name was Howard Ragusa.

I introduced myself, asked to see his daily operating schedule, and then began to figure out ways of becoming part of the landscape at Dogwood Plantation.

After getting acclimated to the system, I found myself near the small oval work track, watching Mike put Sly Boots through his paces. The kid balanced himself just like I used to, leaning slightly forward, poised and alert. I knew the exact moment he'd get down into the irons—that is, settle into the stirrups. I could almost feel the horse under *me*.

I must have watched them for ten or fifteen minutes, my mind a mixture of admiration and jealousy. When I finally pulled myself away and turned to go, I noticed that Mike had another admirer. Joan Courville was standing near the rail, smiling at the boy's progress, looking for all the world like a proud mother.

28

THAT EVENING GRANNY returned at seven and How-
ard Ragusa took us both to dinner at his sister's restaurant in
Morgan City, a pleasant little town not far from the plantation.
We talked horses for most of the night and I realized I'd forgotten
how much I enjoyed the subject when it was the animals themselves under discussion and not the purses they brought in or lost.

On the ride home, full of boiled crab and crawfish étouffée and
bonhomie, we told jokes and lied a little. We rolled into Dogwood at a little after the respectable hour of ten. Howard, whose
sister called him How-air, went to the stables, and Granny and I
headed for the cottage.

He wanted to turn in early, explaining that he wouldn't be
getting much sleep the following night. Remy had scheduled a
shindig at the plantation to welcome the return of his pal Vetter's
fiancée. That meant the old trainer would barely get to bed
before rising at the crack of dawn to drive into Bucktown and the
track.

An early night was fine with me. It had been a while since I'd
put in a full day of work.

I slept like the dead. For about two hours.

Then I was awake, staring at the reflection of headlights across
the ceiling of the room. It was not the lights that had awakened

me but the sound of a heavy vehicle crawling down the dirt road that ran near the cottage.

I slipped from the bed and moved to the window in time to see the truck lumbering over a ridge heading for the far end of the property. I threw on the same clothes I'd removed just a few hours before. On my way out I grabbed a pair of binoculars that Granny had hanging from a hook near the front door.

The light from the moon made it easy to follow the dirt road. But after a mile or so I spotted, not more than thirty feet in front of me, a pair of security cowboys standing together having a conversation about the Saints football team. I left the road and worked my way through the trees.

The next half mile proved a bit more difficult as hard earth gave way to Louisiana swampland. Ahead of me I could hear the sounds of activity. Men talking. Clatter and clang. I advanced cautiously, trying to disturb neither snake nor 'gator nor even muskrat.

When I arrived at the end of the protection of a copse of pecan trees, I halted. In a clearing several hundred feet away, three burly men were unloading boxes from what appeared to be a delivery van. Its tall metal rig bore the name SOUTHERN BOY SUPPLIES. The uniform, unmarked cartons—the kind used by moving companies—were being toted to a large cement bunker that had been constructed behind and slightly below a huge weeping willow. The moss drooping from the tree's ancient branches almost obscured the bunker.

Granny's binoculars took me past the bunker's open door into what appeared to be an office. I could make out a desk, a chair, files, and the cartons piling up along one wall.

Johnson, the hirsute security cowboy I'd met the night before, led Remy and Mark Vetter to the spot where the unloading was taking place. Remy regarded the bunker and the piled cartons. Then he poked his nose inside the van. "Looks like it's all here," his voice carried through the still night.

A man wearing bib overalls, a white undershirt, and a khaki cap handed Remy a clipboard. The horseman studied the sheet caught by the clip, then put out his hand, waiting for the man in overalls to offer a pen. When that happened, Remy signed the receipt with a flourish.

Finished with the loading, the three burly workers hopped aboard the trailer through its rear sliding door. A minute later they were gone.

Remy entered the bunker and dragged one of the cartons to the door, where an overhead light shone down. He dismissed Johnson with a curt order for him to make sure the truck had left the grounds.

Once Johnson had departed, Remy ripped open a carton lid. I adjusted the binoculars and focused in on rows of neatly stacked currency. Remy picked up one packet of bills, used his thumb to flutter its edges. Smiling, he tossed the packet to Vetter. "That should make her happy, don't you think?" he asked.

"It was a triple," Vetter told him.

Remy grabbed another packet and handed it to Vetter. "If only all of life was this simple, huh?"

"Before we start patting ourselves on the back too hard," Vetter said, "maybe we should make sure that the Hat didn't fill one of the boxes with something less negotiable. Like cardboard."

Remy started to object, but Vetter had a penknife in his hand and was cutting the tape on another box.

They opened all ten cartons and satisfied themselves that each contained money. I tried to make a rough guess at the total. Definitely over a million dollars. Maybe even two million.

Remy pushed the last lid back down and shoved that final carton across the cement floor of the bunker, away from the door. Then he pulled down his tie, unbuttoned his shirt, and yanked a neck chain clear of his clothes. On the end of the chain was a key. He reached inside the bunker to turn off the light, then used the key to lock the bunker door.

Vetter slipped the twin packets of money into his jacket pockets and Remy inserted his index and little fingers between his lips and whistled. In less than a minute another security cowboy, one

I didn't know, returned with a flashlight to lead them back to the main house.

I gave them a good head start, then began wending my way over ground and swamp. Back at the cabin, I removed my shoes before entering. I took the shoes into my bathroom and spent the next few minutes with wet toilet paper getting rid of the mud and clay.

Then I returned to my bed and contemplated businessmen who keep their working capital in their backyard in cardboard cartons.

PART EIGHT

Starbuck Applies the Crop

29

POSSIBLY DUE TO the number of murders committed each day in the City of the Angels, the shooting of a middle-aged security guard was not trumpeted by the media. If a leading public-relations firm had not spent much of the day employing its special talents and clout to keep the name of the late Lawrence Mullen's employer from the press, it might have been a different matter. NEW KILLING LINKED TO SANTA ROSITA RACETRACK, a headline might have read. Starbuck's mention of it caused Clara McGuinn to wince and her nephew George's weary eyes to blink.

The three of them were sitting in a black leather booth at Angelica's, a restaurant not far from the track. Starbuck had selected it for their dinner meeting because of its proximity and because the chef's grilled chicken with Italian parsley was one of his favorite dishes.

He sat to Mrs. Mac's left, sinking back against the leather and looking entirely too relaxed for a man who'd skulked away from a murder scene not twenty-four hours before. He lifted a small cruet and refilled his martini glass to the rim. "That's what I love about this place," he said, gesturing with the cruet. "They go the extra mile. Sure you won't have something to kill the taste of that chemical soft drink, George?"

Clara's nephew George, looking as uptight as ever in his button-down shirt, subdued striped tie, and business suit of banker's gray, held up a thin, slightly shaky hand. "I don't drink," he said. "It . . . befuddles the brain."

"That's why most of us drink," Starbuck told him. "Especially after listening to a report like the one you just gave us."

George, in fits and starts, had just taken them through the annual financial report that would be going out to Santa Rosita stockholders within the week. It was particularly grim.

Starbuck polished off his martini and imagined he could feel the juniper berries massage his brain cells before shorting them out. "I still don't understand," he said, "how the track could have turned a profit two years ago, with less volume."

"Operating costs," George muttered, looking into his soft drink.

"Maybe our pari-mutuel system is on the fritz," Clara said dispiritedly, reaching for her white wine.

The waitress arrived and they ordered. George asked for his steak to be cooked well-done, causing Starbuck's opinion of him to drop another few notches, though he allowed, "It beats candy bars. Clara, did you know that your nephew lives on colas and candy bars?" The reference was to the cans and candy wrappers Starbuck had observed in George's den.

"Th-this report has kept me so busy I haven't had time to cook for myself," the young man answered defensively.

"What about that gal of yours?" Starbuck asked. "Doesn't she cook?"

George paled and stared at him, mouth agape. "Wha-what are you talking about?" he finally got out.

Clara gave Starbuck an admonishing frown and turned to her nephew. "I'm sorry, George. I'm afraid I've been indiscreet enough to mention your lady friend to Ray."

"What lady friend? I don't know w-what you people are talking about."

"My mistake," Clara said, surprised by the force of his denial. "Lucy Dural told me she saw you and some very pretty woman on Rodeo Drive last week and I assumed—"

"It wasn't me she saw!" George interrupted. "When would I have time?"

"When do any of us?" Starbuck said as the waitress returned with a full cruet of gin. "I'll do the honors myself," he told her, taking the bottle and pouring its contents into his empty glass. He took a sip, smiled and said, "Enough of this 'girl' talk. Let's get to the business at hand. Or rather the lack of business at Santa Rosita."

George McGuinn seemed to unwind a notch. Starbuck asked him, "Could the pari-mutuel machines affect the track's profits?"

George coughed nervously. "I'm not sure what you mean."

"Bear with me on this," he told them both. "The bettor buys a ticket at the window; the seller punches a button, and when the ticket pops out, the machine registers the bet with the totalizator. Then what happens?"

"The computer sorts and totals the bet," George replied, "and sends the information to the calculating room, where another set of machines figures the changing odds on each horse. Then the new odds are relayed to the tote board."

"How do the machines figure the odds, exactly?" Starbuck wondered.

"George?" Clara turned to her nephew.

"The calculators deduct the track percentage and the state taxes from the gross win pool," George informed them. "Then, when the race has been run, the money bet on the winner is subtracted from the net win pool and set aside to be returned to the winning bettors. The remainder gets divided up by those same winning bettors."

"It's as simple as that?"

George nodded.

"These calculators are all computerized?" Starbuck asked.

The young man nodded again.

"Computers get viruses. Suppose your computer has a cold that's affecting the track's financial health?"

"Any major mistake would have shown up. Isn't that right, George?" Clara asked.

George blinked. "Absolutely," he said.

"Suppose it's not major? Suppose the computer just neglects to list every third two-dollar ticket sold?" Starbuck continued.

George cleared his throat. "We'd find out about it, mucho pronto, when we redeemed more tickets than we sold."

"What if the problem is more subtle than that? Maybe it's every tenth ticket."

"The same answer. We'd get back more tickets than we sold."

Starbuck mulled that over. Time to be more specific. "George, does this mean anything to you—'breaks to a plus dime'?"

George stared at him blankly. Clara said, "Why George, he's talking about breakage."

"Oh, right." George nodded. "Breakage. When the calculators figure out the earnings on each dollar that is bet, sometimes you wind up with pennies. But the track doesn't want to pay off in odd cents, so, in our case, we break to a dime. That is, the calculators automatically make the last digit of the amount a zero. If a winning ticket averages out to ten dollars and thirteen cents, for example, we pay ten dollars and ten cents."

"And what happens to all the extra pennies?" Starbuck inquired.

"They go into the amount set aside for the state and the track."

"How much are we talking about?"

"It's minimal," the young man replied.

"That's not exactly true, George," Clara told him. "It ranges from about five to ten thousand dollars a race."

Starbuck was staring at them.

"But breakage is profit," George said. "We don't *lose* money on it."

The late Irwin Matthes's cryptic note flashed before Starbuck's eyes again; . . . x = *gross win pool minus take or net pool* . . . y = *favorite bet . . . breaks to a + dime.* . . . He said, "I think we should bring in an independent computer guy to check out your calculators and see what he comes up with."

"I don't see how that could be the problem," George said.

Starbuck studied him for a moment, then winked. "Humor me, George. What harm can it do?"

30

FROM THAT POINT on, the dinner moved slowly and silently. And awkwardly. George picked at his steak. Clara barely touched her veal. And though his chicken was every bit as savory as he'd hoped, Starbuck wolfed it down without his customary delight in its taste.

Two hours later the bird seemed to be dancing the funky chicken on his stomach. A headache had driven every bit of the martinis' relaxing influence from his skull. He was sitting, cramped, in the shadow of the information kiosk at Santa Rosita racetrack, watching the employee entrance. His Bentley was parked at the other side of the lot, hidden by a Dumpster.

He'd been there ever since bidding farewell to the McGuinns at the restaurant, long enough for his night vision to have kicked in. Still, he heard the car before he saw it—engine purring, tires bouncing on the ridges of the parking lot. The dark Mercedes sedan glided into view and, almost immediately, made an abrupt turn, heading straight for the employee entrance. There it stopped and its engine ceased to function. The car gave a little buck and was silent.

The door on the driver's side opened and George McGuinn got out, carrying a black leather briefcase. He searched the grounds furtively, then, apparently satisfied with the stillness around him, he unlocked the employee door and entered the building.

Approximately fifteen minutes later he departed nervously, his briefcase under his arm. He started to unlock the car, and when he failed to hear the reassuring click, he frowned and tried the door. It was open.

Mildly puzzled, he slipped in behind the steering wheel, placed the briefcase on the passenger seat, and expelled the breath he'd been holding.

From behind his ear, Starbuck's voice whispered, "George, you degenerate little pissant, I'll have that briefcase, if you please."

George McGuinn looked as if he might faint. But he didn't. Instead, he cried.

Starbuck reached over the seat and grabbed the briefcase. He opened it and dumped its contents on the backseat. "Let's see now. We've got two Snickers bars. Little instant meals, huh? A goddamn Filofax, you acquisitive son of a bitch! And what's this? A beeper. Of course. And, sure, an electronic appointment book. And"—he held up a small cream-colored square of plastic—"the pièce de résistance, but what is it?"

George McGuinn blinked at it through his tears. "It—it's a computer disk."

"Indeed it is, Georgie. And what might be on it?"

George McGuinn opened his mouth, but no sound came out. He waited, caught his breath, and stopped sniffling. "No-no-nothing but my accounting program."

"You'll excuse me if I don't take your word for that," Starbuck said, slipping the disk into his inside coat pocket.

"You can't just—"

"Please, George. Don't insult my intelligence with some feeble protestation. You're in a really serious jam here. If my suspicions are correct, you've been helping to sabotage your aunt's race-track. But that's not the big trouble."

George McGuinn licked his lips and remained silent except for a loud sniff.

"The big trouble," Starbuck continued, "is that you've been a party to at least one murder, maybe three."

"Me? No! I . . . I don't know anything about a—"

"Georgie, Georgie," Starbuck said patronizingly. "If you're gonna eat candy bars, you oughta watch what you do with the wrappers. They're scattered all over your digs. And you left one of them in the late Larry Mullen's apartment. I bet it's occupying a little plastic bag right now in some evidence locker."

Starbuck opened the back door and stepped out.

"What . . . what're you going to do?" George McGuinn asked fearfully.

"Drag your worthless butt inside," Starbuck growled, yanking George's door open and pulling him from the Mercedes.

"Wait a minute," the young man cried out as he was dragged across the asphalt. "I left my keys in the car."

"Including your key to the building?"

George nodded.

Starbuck dragged him back to the car, reached in, and pulled the ring of keys from the ignition lock. Then he shoved George toward the employee entrance. He kept pushing him until they were inside the building.

A nervous Louie Naylor appeared, gun held in shaky hand. Starbuck said calmly, "Just us boys, Louie. We're gonna be burning a little midnight oil."

The security guard let out a grateful sigh and put his gun back in its holster. It took both of his hands to do it. Then he wandered back to his coffee and radio.

Starbuck turned to George. "Now you're going to give me a demonstration of how the computers work and what little tricks you've been using to undermine the operation."

"Suppose I cooperate," George said, trying to catch his breath. "What do I get out of it?"

Starbuck backhanded the young man across the face, using such force that George slammed into a wall. "You've got no bargaining chips, George," he said. "None at all."

Actually, Starbuck was annoyed with himself for swinging on the kid, rodent though he might be. He blamed his anger on the frustration he was feeling. There was no way he could pass along any useful information to the police about the candy wrapper or George's financial manipulations. Once it became public record that Clara's nephew was involved in a murder or two or three and had engineered the financial collapse of Santa Rosita, there'd be very little hope of her continuing to helm the corporation. He was being paid to keep her control intact.

Of course, if something were to convince him that George had actually killed one or all of the victims, that would be another matter. At the moment, however, Starbuck didn't see button-down Harvard-boy George as a stone killer.

About George's girlfriend he was a little more sanguine. There were indications—the high-heel indentations near Irwin Mat-thes's body, the lipstick-marked cigarette stubs in his apartment, Muller's coffee-making girlfriend, and the lowered position of the toilet seat in the meticulously neat victim's bathroom—that a woman was at the heart of the murders.

"I'm bleeding," George McGuinn said, starting to cry again as a drop of red dripped from his nose onto his coat sleeve.

Starbuck handed him a handkerchief. "Tell me about the woman," he said.

George McGuinn dabbed at his nose and stared at Starbuck. "There's no—"

"Don't make me hit you again, son," Starbuck told him. "There's a woman. And a hell of a woman she must be, too. Unless I'm wrong, and I seldom am, there are two other guys she wooed who are now snoozing big time."

"She couldn't . . ." George said, then dropped into silence.

"What were you doing at Larry Mullen's apartment?" Starbuck asked.

"I . . . I went there yesterday to see Larry. He wasn't there, but his door was open. The TV was on. I thought he'd just stepped out for a minute. I went in, waited for a while, and when he didn't get back, I left. I guess he was . . . there all the time."

"According to the coroner, he'd been shot and killed around three or four in the morning," Starbuck said. "Your girlfriend's been really busy."

"I told you. I don't have a girlfriend."

Starbuck sighed. It was going to be a long night.

PART NINE

My Best-Laid Plan

31

I WAS AWAKENED that morning at four-thirty A.M. by Granny, who was clattering around the kitchen and talking to himself. While I pried my eyelids apart and jump-started my heart with a cup of black coffee, he kept me entertained with complaints about having to put up with "Remy's crowd" at the evening's dinner party. Then, as I was refilling my cup, he seemed to take offense at my casual disregard of his problem and headed for the door in a huff. Before making his exit, he turned and said, "You might think about getting that workout track properly smoothed and raked. It's got holes in the ground as big as your head."

I passed along the order, sans pique, to Howard Ragusa, who informed me that the work had already been done. Mike LeBlanc and one of the staff had performed the task.

Feeling not exactly vital to the smooth operation of the stable at Dogwood Plantation, I made a three-minute phone call to New Orleans. A while later, at shortly after nine, having supervised a few minor chores and having made sure the schedule for the day was set in stone, I borrowed a stable Jeep and steered it into La Ronde, a little town to the east so tiny it wasn't even on the map. There was a country store, an ice-cream parlor, two video shops, and Maybelle's, a diner that was a block and a half away from the main truck stop.

Jackie Parnell was sitting at the counter, flirting with a waitress who couldn't have been older than fifteen. "Hiya, possum," he called when he spotted me in the mirror running along the back wall.

I took a seat next to him. We were the only customers in the place. He said to the waitress, "Make it the same for my father, here."

She giggled and went off to fill the order. Jackie asked, "So what was it so important we couldn't talk about it on the phone?"

He yawned. His eyes were puffy. "Did my call wake you?" I wondered.

He made an exaggerated gesture of looking at his watch. "Oh, hell no, Coley. I friggin' thrive on four hours' sleep, followed up by an hour's drive."

"I met you halfway," I told him.

"Okay, podnah. Here we are, together again, halfway between hell and a hernia. Now what?"

I explained to him that I'd been impressed by the way he'd slipped the ring off of the woman's hand the other night at Le Cavalier.

"That's nothin'. Jus' a little close magic." He removed a half-dollar from his pocket and began making it walk across his knuckles.

The waitress returned carrying a bowl of cream with some little white-and-gray lumps in it and a plate loaded with slices of French bread. "Here y'are," she said.

"What is it?" I asked.

"Oyster stew," she replied. "It's the ex-senator's favorite."

I turned to Jackie. "For breakfast?"

"Son, you're thinkin' like a Yankee. Yankees are inta a time-an'-place mentality. But in this part of the country, you take your de-lights when and where they happen. Maybelle's is famous throughout the South for its oyster stew."

I tried the stew. It was very good. Hot. Peppery. But it wasn't my idea of breakfast. I buttered a slice of French bread, and when the waitress went back into the kitchen, I asked Jackie if he thought he could steal the chain off of a man's neck.

"Courville's?"

I nodded.

"Easiest way would be to get some broad to bed him and take it then."

I said, "I don't want to use a cast of thousands on this. Just me and you."

"Why do we need the chain?"

I told him about the key and the bunker at the plantation. I did not tell him about the cartons of cash, because he didn't strike me as the kind of guy one trusted with that sort of information. "There's a desk in the bunker," I explained. "And a metal cabinet. I need to see if there are any files in there I can use."

Jackie nodded. "You care if he knows he's been ripped off?" he asked.

"I'd rather he not."

"Well, podnah, I could probably razoo this man's chain and key. But to do it I'd have to get close to him and distract him, and then we'd have to make a wax impression pronto and put the key back on him before he got wise and it'd be a very complicated setup. Why don't I just pick the goddamn lock?"

I told him that would be fine.

32

W E DECIDED THAT there was no time like the present for the break-in. That night's dinner party in the big house would occupy Remy and the others, Granny included. Jackie and I could burgle the bunker and be free and clear before the dessert was served.

The plan called for Jackie to check into a motel in the near vicinity. Naturally, he had a favorite, one bearing the dubious name of the Alibi Motel. "You've heard of beds with magic fingers," he told me enthusiastically. "At the Alibi, they even got bathtubs with magic fingers. And there's this honey who works the bar—"

"I didn't know you were such a finger man," I interrupted. "But, in any case, I hope you'll keep your mind on our boring little break-in even while sampling the Alibi's facilities."

"You know it, podnah," he said with a grin. It was not what I'd call a grin of affirmation. Regardless, I bid him and Maybelle's oyster soup a fond adieu with the belief that everything was in order.

And then, in the early afternoon, Hey Dude, a warmblood (a combination of cold-blooded draft breed and hot-blooded Thoroughbred) was discovered to have an abscess on its flank.

The animal was a show horse and a favorite of Joan Courville's. She made it clear to Granny that she would be most grateful if he would care for the beast personally.

Hey Dude's condition worsened in late evening, and with the

vet unavailable, Granny decided to spend the night with the warmblood. He was eager to do it. "Who the hell wouldn't rather have dinner with a horse," he told me, "instead of with a bunch of horses' asses?"

That was fine. But how was I going to duck out of stable duty and away from Granny's watchful eye long enough to get my thievery done?

Then word came down from the big house that threw my plans for a complete loop. Since Granny's absence would make thirteen for dinner—not a particularly desired omen for a host who felt very strongly about the importance of luck—Remy had tapped me to take up the slack.

It was apparent that this was not a request but a demand, regretful apologies not accepted. I borrowed the Jeep again and drove to the Alibi Motel.

The rain that had been threatening ever since I arrived in Louisiana picked that time to put in an appearance. It was one of those heavy, pelting showers and it sounded as if a kangaroo in golf cleats was tap-dancing on the Jeep's roof.

I got wet running the ten feet to Jackie's cabin and soaked waiting for him to open the door. "C'mon in, podnah," he said, standing there with a towel wrapped around his waist and a highball in his hand. "You look like a drownded skunk."

There was a naked blonde in his bed. She was eating finger-lickin' Southern-fried chicken and watching MTV. I said to Jackie, "You have an interesting style."

"Ever seen a body like that, Coley? Stand up, honey, and show Coley that dimpled rear end of yours."

The girl told me hello, placed her nibbled drumstick on a paper plate, and hopped from the bed. She did a little twirl. "When you're right, you're right," I told Jackie. "But do you think we could have just a minute or so of bachelorhood?"

Jackie walked to the bed and said, "Honey, what's your name again?"

"Jeri," the girl said. She pointed at a waitress uniform that was lying on a chair. It had her name stitched above the pocket.

"Jeri," Jackie asked, "do you figger you could maybe go in the bathroom for a while? Run yourself a tub or something while Coley and I have a little powwow?"

"Got some quarters for the fingers?" she asked. Jackie gave her a handful.

We both watched her make her exit.

"I tell you, podnah, you stick with Jackie and I'm gonna show you the secrets of life, I swear."

I could not disagree with him. Instead, I explained to him the circumstances that had conspired to force us to postpone our plans.

"Why postpone 'em?" Jackie asked. "Hell, man, this is perfect. You got an alibi and I can go right in there and do the job myself."

I hadn't trusted him enough to tell him about the money. I certainly didn't want him finding all that loot by himself. "You don't know what you're looking for," I said.

"Well, tell me."

"I don't know myself," I said truthfully. "I won't until I see it."

"I could go in and just clean out all his files."

I shook my head. "I don't want Remy to find out too soon that his files have been compromised. Why don't you and Jeri just have a good time here tonight and maybe tomorrow night . . . ?"

"Aw, man," he said. "I don't like to shoot the whole day and not get the thing done."

I pointed to the bathroom. "You call that shooting the whole day?"

"You don't understand, Coley. *That* is the icing on the cake. The cake is the job. I'm not here for icing."

I told him I was sorry but that we'd have to settle for icing. He sighed, hitched his towel tighter around his waist, and walked me to the door. "Well, hell," he said philosophically, "I guess things could be worse, huh?"

"We'll get it done tomorrow."

He opened the door and a gust of wind blew rain into the

room. Jackie squinted his eyes and peered out at the weather. "Man, this is almost nasty."

"Good day to take it easy and stay in bed," I said.

He grinned, then scowled as he looked out again. "Them birds are acting like they was on happy dust."

A flock of little birds—starlings, maybe—swooped, scattered, and almost collided into one another in a frantic effort to get out of the rain. Then they managed to form a solid phalanx and zoomed away. "Weather does weird things," I said.

"Around here it does, podnah. That's for damn sure."

33

THE RAIN DIDN'T stop. That night, as I was putting the dimple in my tie, Granny tore into our digs, wild and wet. Without removing his dripping yellow slicker, he rushed into his room. I followed him in. He was rooting around for something in a gladstone on the floor. A deck of cards.

"Things kinda slow in the stables?" I asked.

"That damned Hey Dude's comin' along just fine," he said with a wide grin on his rain-soaked puss.

"Then maybe you should go to the party."

"The hell you say, brother. You're all saddled up." He stood, slapped his back-pocket area, frowned, and moved to his chest of drawers, where he discovered his wallet. "Besides," he added, slipping the worn leather past the slicker and into the rear pocket of his Levi's, "you got no idea what a loser Ragusa is when it comes to gin rummy."

"What's with the weather?"

"You got eyes. It's raining like hell. That's the way it is down here, in case you forgot. Could keep up like this for days."

I followed him back into the living room, where he found a pinkish bottle of Cabin Still on the sideboy. He slapped that into his slicker pocket.

"If it continues, what'll happen to the Dixie Derby?" I asked.

"It'll be run. It'd take a hurricane to get 'em to cancel. Might even be to our advantage. Cajun Desire loves the wet. He's not just a mudder, he's a swimmer." He snapped up his moist slicker and started out. Then he paused. "You take care tonight, huh?"

I gave him an innocent look.

"Give that Travers fella a wide berth, you hear? He's a mean-spirited bastard, and he's already got you on his s-list."

"I'll do my best to charm him," I said.

The house was no farther than a quarter of a mile from our little cottage, but if I had not been holding an umbrella over my head, and if I'd been walking with my mouth open, I would have drowned. As it was, my shoes were carrying enough water to provide life support for a school of goldfish.

When you live in a drought area like Southern California, you forget what real rain is like. But evidently this downpour was pretty unique even for Louisiana. It was the main topic of discussion as I entered the comfortable living room where the guests were assembled for cocktails.

An old bird with silver white hair and a voice deep enough to make the crystal hum was telling Mike LeBlanc and a pretty brown-haired teen queen about the time the weather was so bad he had to paddle a pirogue down St. Charles Avenue to court his wife. Mark Vetter complained about the dampness affecting his sinuses, and Roberta Courville, Remy's sister, replied that if it increased the yield of her sugarcane crop, the dampness was fine by her and Mark might consider using a nasal spray her doctor prescribed that not only cleared up the sinuses but left you with a nice buzz.

Remy and his banking weasel, Norell Travers, were standing beside a large fireplace, possibly discussing the rain, but from their furrowed brows, I suspected their conversation was a bit more practical. I was about to aim my squishy shoes in their direction when Joan Courville appeared out of nowhere to greet me as if I were an honored guest.

Lavishing me with effusive thanks for gracing her gathering, she led me to the bar off the main room, where she left me in the care of big, pink-faced Floyd, who, dressed in a rented tux, was pretending to be a mixologist.

Armed with a scotch sour that wasn't half-bad, considering it was prepared by a hired thug, I reentered the party. This time I was roped in by the old, silver-haired gent, who was, it turned out, a congressman named John George Gossom. He was making a quick visit to his home state between sessions and he damn well had to drive all the way from New Orleans in the pelting rain to say hello to Remy and his sister, Roberta. Hell, considering their father, the late lieutenant governor, was his closest and dearest friend, they were like members of his own family.

Mrs. Gossom was one of those aging Southern belles who say little, evidently saving the muscles of mouth and throat for the regular sipping of an old-fashioned, which she clutched as if she were afraid someone would sneak up and snatch it from her.

The teenage brunette was Mike LeBlanc's hometown sweetheart. Her name was Julie Fontenot and she spoke with a charming Cajun singsong that increased with her enthusiasm. She was wildly impressed by the house, by the people, and by the way Mike seemed to fit in. She was telling me how much she'd been missing Mike—she'd seen him only twice since he moved in with the Courvilles—when Delia Bouraine made her entrance.

Conversation didn't exactly stop, but it did slow down a little. Even Congressman Gossom seemed impressed by the way Delia had fit her small, yet in some details overabundant, body into a dress so tight quite a lot of her seemed to be spilling over the top. I gave her a friendly wave and she flashed me a bright smile.

"Well," she said as she approached, "you're looking very suave for a man who prefers the company of animals."

"When in Rome," I said, and introduced her to the congressman, whom she'd known since she was a child. She smiled while he went on and on about their lengthy friendship, his voice wavering from time to time as his eyes drifted to her minimal neckline. During a half-minute break, while the congressman engaged in a necessary inhale, she leaned toward me and whispered, "You'd think he'd never seen breasts before."

"Your eyes are nice, too," I told her.

She started to reply, but those nice eyes lifted and moved to the right. I turned to follow their glance. Remy and Travers Jr. were staring at us.

"Excuse me," Delia purred. "I'd better go say hello to my host."

"Now there is a real flower of the South," the congressman exclaimed, somewhat redundantly.

Julie returned our conversation to a topic of more universal appeal. "I hear they got squalls in the Gulf," she announced.

"Joan said it's so bad the LaBordes weren't able to make it from Slidell," Mike added, not noticing that his use of our hostess's first name had brought a frown to Julie's face. The object of her concern was just a few feet away, saying something to her sister-in-law about hurricane weather.

"It's just a heavy shower, honey," Roberta Courville replied. "Makes the grass grow tall."

Remy drifted into the conversation with the news that the whole thing was being caused by a hurricane off Havana.

"I've felt better about hurricanes," Delia Bouraine announced, sailing into the group with cannons armed and ready, "ever since they began giving them male names."

"Should have started out that way," Roberta chimed in. "Men are such blowhards, anyway."

One of those sixth-sense reactions caused me to turn to the left and stare directly into the eyes of Norell Travers. The weasel's glare was so intense it made the hair on the back of my neck rise. But I managed a wide grin and saluted him with my scotch sour.

Remy began needling Mark Vetter gently about the absence of his fiancée, Felicia Deauville. The occasion for the dinner was to celebrate her return from a successful business trip to the East Coast. Her flight had been delayed by the weather, but she'd arrived and was in her room, getting ready for dinner.

"What's keeping her, Mark?" Remy asked. "If she's worried about making an entrance, tell her to throw on a bikini and a boa and just come on down."

Mark Vetter wasn't terribly amused. "Felicia doesn't like to be rushed."

Remy slapped him on the back and said, "Then you're lucky you've got staying power."

"What sort of business does Felicia do?" I asked Vetter.

"She's in public relations," Remy answered before Vetter could. "But I think she'd be even more successful in private relations."

Remy was drunk, of course. But he didn't seem drunk enough to account for the antagonism he was building up in his business partner.

Lightning flashed outside the windows, followed almost immediately by a crack of thunder that gave us all a moment's pause. Remy turned to me and asked, "What's the worst weather you ever rode in?"

I described a race at Santa Anita back in 1982 when a storm blew in from Hawaii and somehow hailstones got mixed up in the wind and rain and it was like getting hit by golf balls and a horse got knocked out cold and two jocks had to be treated for concussion.

"And were you hurt?" Delia Bouraine asked.

"No. I was too busy winning the race."

"You won that one, huh?" Norell Travers, Jr., asked. "Then you must not have had any money on the number-two horse."

Delia looked at him questioningly and Travers replied, "Our dinner guest here is sort of the Shoeless Joe Jackson of racing."

"That's very cute," I told him.

Remy began, "Look, there's no need for . . ."

I held up a hand. "It's okay," I told him. "Every time I sat down on a horse, some half-smart jockey would call me a name that was a hundred times more insulting than that. You learn to ignore it, because if you let names get to you, you lose your concentration."

Delia looked from Travers Jr. to me and her eyes were shining. "What would it take to make you lose *your* concentration, Coley?"

What a dangerous lady, I thought. "A little more than some overeducated, underdeveloped, pudgy dilettante with a smart mouth," I said pleasantly.

Travers's face whitened in fury and he teetered on the edge of carrying the situation further. But regardless of our differences in size and weight, I was an athlete and he was an out-of-shape weasel. And he knew it. He backed off, but the atmosphere was more highly charged than it had been by the thunder and light-ning.

It was eased somewhat by the entrance of Mark Vetter's fian-cée.

I was still watching Travers making a slow exit to the bar when Remy said, "Coley, here's something to lift your spirits. I don't believe you've met Mark's lady, Felicia Deauville. Felicia, this is Coley Killebrew."

I turned and looked into the beautiful, smiling face of my old sweetheart, Francie Dorn.

34

FRANCIE TOOK MY hand in hers, which was dry and warm and seemed to tingle, although that was probably my imagination. There was not even the barest hint that she might have known me at another time and another place or that my last vision of her had been in my bed, rosy from lovemaking, sending me off to ride a race still a little drunk and needing sleep. "Are you a horseman, too, Mr. Killebrew?" she asked.

"On and off," I replied. "But call me Coley. Most people do."

Vetter joined us, slipping his arm around Francie/Felicia's shoulders possessively. And Joan Courville informed us all that dinner was ready.

In the large formal dining room, our hostess made a thing out of assigning our seats. I found myself between Congressman Gossom's nonspeaking wife and Francie. Her fiancé was across the table, ignoring Delia Bouraine and Julie Fontenot, on either side of him, to stare at us. Not far away, Travers was shooting me a venomous glance while Joan Courville was saying something that Mike LeBlanc found absolutely fascinating. Outside the storm continued.

Before long, a different storm began to build around the table. Remy found the salad dressing a bit too vinegary. Then the service was too slow. "Can't you handle the goddamned kitchen staff?" he snapped at his wife. "Do I have to do everything myself?"

Joan Courville withstood the tirade for a while without turning a hair. So Remy upped the ante. "You're just like a god-damned mistress," he spat out. "You expect me to do everything for you. Well, maybe I would treat you as well as I treat my mistresses if you could screw as well as they do."

That was it for his wife. She stood, ashen-faced, and made a remarkably dignified exit.

Remy suddenly relaxed, sipped his wine, and said, "Anybody notice how the room seems suddenly brighter?"

Roberta Courville said, "Really, Remy, if you feel that way about Joan, why don't you just get a goddamned divorce? This routine is getting old."

Mike LeBlanc stood awkwardly. "Maybe I'd better see if she's all right."

"She's all right, boy. It's just a little set piece we go through. Sort of a mating ritual. But go on, if you must."

The young jockey loped away from the table, Julie Fontenot's anxious eyes following him.

"Young Mike's devotion to Joan is quite inspiring, don't you think?" Remy asked the table.

No one bothered to answer. We all sat quietly. The congress-man's face was a disturbing shade of purple. I wondered what it was that kept him from telling Remy precisely what he thought of his behavior. I suppose we all had our reasons for staying silent, good or bad.

Suddenly, Delia Bouraine snapped, "You know, Remy, you really are a snot."

He laughed. "Why, Delia, and I was just going to tell you how much I enjoyed looking at those big knockers of yours." He added, "I'm sure you'll appreciate this, Congressman—they feel as good as they look. Just like they were the real thing."

Delia rose, her face crimson. "They feel even better when they're offered willingly," she said through her teeth, "but you'll never get the chance to find out." With that, she left the room, too.

The table was beginning to look like the set for *Ten Little Indians*. Our host addressed the rest of us. "Well, chillun, don't wait for me to say grace, you just dig right in."

There was a flutter of nervous laughter, followed by a few halfhearted attempts at conversation. I decided to hell with it and dug right in. I was starving. As I savored roast as soft as butter I was aware of Francie staring at me. I dabbed at my lips with a napkin and said, "I understand you've been traveling on business."

"I used to work for Carbelli and Dietrich. It's a public-relations firm in Manhattan. Then I met Mark and that was it for Carbelli and Dietrich. But every so often one of my former clients has a special problem, so I fly in and offer whatever help I can."

It had been seven years, so I suppose she could have gone to New York and conned the agency into hiring her. When you're a beautiful, intelligent, heartless, basically immoral liar and cheat, public relations might seem like the perfect career move. But the vaguely Southern accent was certainly not real. Nor was the air of casual elegance. So maybe the ad-agency yarn was bogus, too.

"How'd you and Mark meet?" I asked. I was conscious of him being a third party to our conversation. We both were.

"One of those wonderful coincidences. We both got into the same cab on Madison Avenue, and . . ." I was suddenly struck by the memory of the woman she used to be—New York abrasive, but funny and earthy and unpretentious. And sexy. I remembered the lushness and the surprising strength of her body against mine. My face felt flushed.

Francie was staring at me and her triumphant smile told me she knew what I'd been thinking and that I had not quite gotten her out of my system.

Delia Bouraine returned to the table and, without a word, took her seat next to Remy and began to nibble at her food.

A short while later Mike LeBlanc rejoined the party. Remy put down his fork and asked, "Well, how's Mama doing?"

"Sir?" the young jockey asked, embarrassed.

"What's Joan up to? Not playing with my razor blades again, is she? Or maybe counting her Seconals?"

"No. But it's kind of you to ask, darling," Joan Courville told him from the door. Calm, composed, she drifted gracefully to her chair.

Remy eyed her suspiciously. "Not even a tear shed?" he asked.

She rewarded him with a smile that could have chilled a penguin. "No more tears," she said. "No more anything. There's nothing you can do to affect me anymore, Remy. Nothing you can do to force me to leave you. Except kill me, of course. And I wonder if you're above that?"

That ended the party.

The Gossoms made a swift, mumbling departure. Roberta Courville informed the weasel Travers that he was driving her immediately to her plantation on the other side of New Orleans. I excused myself.

At the door I turned and saw Francie staring at me with that knowing smile. I was halfway to the cottage before I realized I'd forgotten to open my umbrella.

35

I T WAS NEARLY midnight when I was awakened by the sound of my bedroom door squeaking open. A figure in a raincoat entered. My first, sleep-fogged thought was that Granny had decided not to spend the night in the stable after all.

I heard the snaps on the raincoat pop open and the coat hit the floor. Lightning flashed and I realized my visitor wasn't anything like Granny. Francie Dorn stood before me, her voluptuous body naked as the proverbial jaybird.

"I wanted to make sure you knew it was me, Coley," she said. The Southern accent and the airs were gone now.

I croaked, "You're taking a hell of a chance. Where's the boyfriend?"

"He drove away with Remy about a half hour ago. Said something about going to New Orleans for a meeting."

"This late? What kind of meeting?"

"How should I know?" she replied. "My guess is that they're shacked up with whores. That's the good old Southern way, isn't it?"

"You're asking me? I'm about as Southern as a snowball."

She slipped into the bed. Lightning flashed again. I felt the familiar rush as her full breasts touched my arm. Then the rest of her firm body pressed me from waist to ankle. "You're nothing like a snowball," she said.

I had no control over my body. I'm not sure I wanted any. At the same time I didn't want her to think I was a pushover. "Been busy the past seven years?" I asked.

"Oh? Is conversation on your mind?" Her hand moved between my legs. "You don't feel like it."

"Not right now," I said, pulling her closer. I'd meant to add, "But eventually." I got as far as "But even—" and her mouth covered mine. It was as sweet and as hungry as I had remembered. Soft, but demanding. Comforting and frantic.

She shifted on the bed so that I could roll onto her. Her body moved under me. She ended the kiss, panting, and said, "You," as if it were an accusation. "You didn't . . . forget me."

As if.

"You won't ever . . . forget me." Wide green eyes. A moan coming from those full lips. Her fingers dug into my back. No fingernails. She used to bite them to the quick. Maybe she still did. I hadn't noticed.

She leaned forward and her tongue licked my left nipple. I went over the edge. She laughed triumphantly as I entered her, as if she were the one in control.

As if.

★★★

We did finally get around to that conversation. I was lying on my back staring at the odd shadows on the ceiling caused by light reflected off the rain puddles. Francie was huddled against me. Granny's air conditioner kept us cool. The rain did its dance on the roof.

"I left you because I was scared, Coley," she said.

I gave her a skeptical look. "Scared of what?"

"Everything that was coming down. You were in the hospital. There was this son of a bitch from the track, Starbuck, who was hounding me, making threatening noises to my friends. So I did a Pasadena."

"With your winnings," I added.

"What winnings?" she demanded. "That was part of the problem. I had no money at all. And no prospects. I didn't know how badly you were hurt and I was afraid to come near the hospital because of that Starbuck bastard who was accusing me of all sorts of things. I hitched to San Francisco, worked in a café there.

"Eventually, I went east, back to Manhattan, where I knew some people who would help me straighten out without my having to worry about them copping to Starbuck. I stayed away from the tracks as long as I could, but as you know, Coley, I have this thing for the races. At Belmont, I met this nice, unattached older man, and what with one thing and another, he took me home."

"Older man? What about Vetter?"

She hesitated.

I said, "That story about the cab, I think that was Doris Day meeting Rock Hudson in some fifties flick."

She smiled. "You do still feel something for me, don't you, Coley?"

"Couldn't you tell?"

"That was sex. Sex hides . . ." She hesitated, searching for the proper words.

". . . a multitude of sins," I finished for her.

"Yes. I was going to say it hides all sorts of resentments. But it hides sins, too. Do you still love me?"

"Did you ever love me?" I asked, lobbing the ball back in her court.

"With every part of my mind and body," she said solemnly.

"Except for that little section of gray matter that convinced your loyal body to duck out on me."

"I don't remember you being so cynical."

"It's been that kind of a life."

"I happen to think cynicism is a turn-on," she said, her hand trailing down past my stomach.

Before it found its target, I grabbed it. She pouted. "Now that you're satisfied, you don't want me anymore."

"I don't want you any less, either. It's just that now we talk. Besides, just a few minutes ago you were telling me how satisfied *you* felt."

"That was a few minutes ago," she said.

"Speaking of the time, just how much do we have left?"

"A while."

"Then let's get back to your story about the old duffer at the track."

She pulled away from me and any evidence of playfulness left her. "He's not an old duffer. Rom's not more than sixty."

"And Mark is what—twenty-nine? Thirty?"

"Mark is his son." She looked at her raincoat. "I forgot to bring my cigarettes."

"I don't use them," I told her. "So you took up with the old duffer's son."

"It's not like you think. Rom got . . . sick. I think he's probably happy for both of us."

"I'm happy for both of you," I said.

"Don't be mean. It's been a mistake. Mark's a very . . . demanding man. I'm in a difficult situation. He wants to marry me and I just want out."

I lifted the rumpled sheet. "Your legs look pretty good," I said. "Take a walk."

"I tried. I haven't been on any business trip. What business? I was running away from the bastard. But his people found me and forced me back."

"His people?"

"The goddamned Mafia," Francie hissed. "Mark's father is Romeo Vetticino."

I stared at her for a beat. The name was not unfamiliar. Until the black and Latino gangs began filling their coffers with drug money, every crooked dollar spent on the West Coast wound up on Romeo Vetticino's counting table. According to my restaurant partner, Johnny Rousseau, he was a cold, brutal man that you didn't want to cross without significant reason. I said, "That being the case, why don't you put your coat back on and go home and we'll forget this little incident ever happened?"

"I love you, Coley," she told me. "I always will."

She seemed so sincere, I began to wonder if she might be. But I didn't pass the thought along. I just stared at her.

Angrily, she leapt from the bed. "You've changed," she said. "But I should have figured that when I found you working for a pig like Remy Courville."

"At least I'm not going to marry him," I said.

I was familiar with her temper and was ready for the slap. Even with that, her nails were barely inches from my face when I caught her wrist. When I felt the tension leave her arm, I released my grip.

She took back her hand, rubbing her wrist. She stared at me and her eyebrows formed a confused frown. "Who is she?" Francie asked.

"Which 'she' are we talking about?"

"Lea."

I had no idea what my face was doing. I said, "Who's Lea?"

"Maybe it's not Lea. But it sounded like Lea. When we were making love, you said, 'Oh, Lea.' It tends to spoil the moment."

"I wasn't aware the moment had been spoiled," I said.

"That's because I convinced myself that I'd misunderstood, that you'd called me 'dear' or something equally appropriate. But now I see you don't give a damn about me. Somebody else is ringing little Coley's chimes."

When I didn't answer, she shrugged, grabbed her coat from the floor, wiggled into it, and slipped her feet into her soggy pumps.

She stared at me. I still had no idea what to say.

She opened her mouth, thought better of it, turned, and rushed from the room. I heard the front door slam and started breathing again.

Did Starbuck, that loathsome bastard, know that Francie was mixed up with Remy and his pals? Probably not. He wouldn't have risked my meeting up with her while on the job. He would have assumed I'd let her talk me into throwing this race, too.

What *was* Francie doing there, anyway? How did she fit into the picture and how would it affect my situation? Regardless of my actions, my feeling for her went a bit deeper than she thought. Too deep for me to let her waltz into a trap Starbuck had set for Remy and Vetter.

And what the devil was Lea doing, sneaking into my psyche at crucial moments? I sighed. I was poking my nose into matters involving murderous businessmen, the Mafia, and millions in cold cash, and instead of using caution, I was behaving like a character in a Teenage Lust comic book. It was all that bastard Starbuck's fault, I lied to myself.

PART TEN

Starbuck Makes a Date

36

EARLIER THAT DAY, Lea, the object of my apparently subconscious affection, had parked her yellow-and-black motorbike in her father's garage, filling a narrow space between the Bentley and a three-year-old tan Mazda sedan that he used when he needed to blend into the automotive scenery. She removed her bumblebee helmet with its cosmetic antenna, shook out her hair, unzipped her shiny yellow jacket, and unveiled a T-shirt that read, LAST CHANCE SALOON, ELKO, NEVADA, in lettering that had nearly faded away. She pulled a key chain from her shiny green shorts and let herself in through the door connecting the garage to the laundry room.

Choo-Choo looked up from the *Los Angeles Times* as she strolled through the kitchen. "Your father is in the office already," he said with a certain amount of awe. "I don't think he been to bed yet."

She rolled her eyes, paused at the fridge to pour a glass of freshly squeezed orange juice, took one sip, and continued on through the house to Starbuck's office.

The big man was at his desk, several half-eaten bagels on a plate at his elbow. He looked up at her, eyes red-rimmed, black-and-gray hair lying flat against his skull as if it had given up the will to live. "I won't need you for an hour," he said.

"My, but aren't you Mr. Sunshine this morning. I realize you didn't exactly summon me at this early hour of nine-thirty A.M. I just felt the urge to stop by to see how my daddykins is feeling."

"You ever use the word 'daddykins' again in my presence and I'll disown you."

"Does that mean you'll disinherit me?"

"That, too," he growled. "Gawd, but it's been a night."

"So tell all," she said, sitting on one of the leather chairs facing the desk.

"I had to stand by while a little puke of a human, who should by rights be out at Lompoc making license plates, or whatever the hell they do at Lompoc, was told he was getting an expense-free European vacation instead."

"Goody," she said, "an immorality tale. I'm all ears."

He sighed, took off his glasses, and rubbed one eye and then the other with a thick knuckle. And he began telling her about George McGuinn's fall from grace.

She listened attentively, no longer feeling very larky. At one point she asked, "How exactly did he destroy the track's profits?"

"He jiggered the software program that operates Santa Rosita's computerized accounting system. When winning prices are established, the odd number of pennies is supposed to be decreased to the nearest dime, with the extras split between the track and the state. Thanks to Georgie boy, the figures were *increased* to the nearest dime. Not only was the track losing money on every race, it was giving the state a percentage of loot that wasn't ever there to begin with."

"But isn't it just pennies?" she protested.

"That's what curious George said, but Clara contradicted him to the tune of as much as ten thousand dollars a race. Since George is supposed to be the expert, that little bit of obfuscation would have made me suspicious of him, even if I hadn't already been."

"Why'd he do it?"

"Three reasons," Starbuck told her, "money, sex, and fear. The money was a flat quarter of a million dollars, to be delivered on the day that the track changed ownership.

"The sex had been administered by, according to George, 'the most beautiful blonde I've ever seen.' They'd met one evening several months ago. He'd been carrying a carton of soft drinks to his apartment when she'd asked for his help with a flat tire. He'd allowed her to come up to his apartment to call a service station.

"For nearly three weeks she visited him often at his place, providing him with the kind of sexual experience he'd only dreamed of. In the course of those visits she told him that a very dangerous man was in love with her. She wished there were some way she could escape his influence. Specifically, she wished she and George could run away to some tropic paradise."

"Oh, please," Lea interrupted.

Starbuck sighed, shook his big head sadly at George's stupidity, and continued his tale. Though head over heels in love, George was still enough of an accountant to mention that they hadn't enough money to get as far as the beach at Santa Monica. That's when the blonde outlined her plan. George had told her of his connection to Santa Rosita racetrack. She knew of someone who would pay a quarter of a million dollars if George would help him gain controlling interest in the track.

"And George didn't question the coincidence of all this?" Lea asked.

"Get George away from his computer," Starbuck said, "and he's less than an idiot. He didn't question anything as long as the blonde kept occupying his kip."

"Am I to assume she stopped?" Lea asked.

"Oh, yeah," Starbuck replied. "That's where the fear came in."

The blonde provided George with the computer program that was guaranteed to turn Santa Rosita's bottom line red. And as soon as it had been incorporated into the system, she began seeing him less and less frequently. Finally, the night came when she told him that the romance was over.

George couldn't believe it. First he was heartbroken. Then he got angry. If she left him, he would go to his aunt and tell her how he'd sabotaged the track's computer. The blonde replied that if he did, he would be killed. If, on the other hand, he behaved like a good little boy, he would receive the money as promised.

"And that was that?" Lea asked.

"Not quite. Last week his girlfriend showed up at his place again. She wanted him to do 'one little thing more.' He was to make sure that the employee door to the track would be open at eight P.M. two nights away. He asked her why and she refused to answer.

"He explained that there were security guards who toured the track every half hour, checking things like the locks. He couldn't guarantee that the door would be open when she wanted it, or that one of the guards wouldn't be around to get in the way of whatever she was hoping to do.

"She asked if the same guards were on duty every night. He replied that they were, at least on weeknights. She kissed him on the cheek and told him not to worry about unlocking the door. She'd take care of it herself. Then she was gone. It was the last time he saw her. But he heard from her again, the day after Irwin Matthes's body was found at the track. Georgie boy was, as you may imagine, a bit upset at his probable implication in a murder. She calmed him down and told him she had to see him.

"The address she gave him was an apartment building in the Valley. She'd told him the apartment door would be open. He was to enter, sit down, and wait for her to join him.

"He grew restless. He turned on the TV. Something about the place seemed odd, even unsettling. He was about to go when the phone rang. It was the blonde. He wanted to know where she was. She told him she wasn't coming. She just wanted to make sure he would keep his mouth shut about their involvement.

"George said he wasn't inclined to do that and she suggested he go into the bedroom of the apartment. With some reluctance, he did. That's when he found, as I did sometime later, the dead security guard, Larry Mullen.

"George didn't bother to take a good look. Frantic, he rushed back to the phone. The blonde told him that this had been an object lesson. If he talked, he'd wind up like Mullen."

"I can't exactly blame George for keeping mum," Lea said.

"If the little bastard had come to us earlier, none of this would have happened. We'd have nailed the broad."

"Does she have a name?"

"Fiona Dawson," Starbuck said with a grimace. "The same Fiona Dawson who was staying at the Brentwood Hotel the night Irwin Matthes called there. Only there is no Fiona Dawson that I've been able to find. At least not in California, New York, or Chicago. Definitely not in Florida, where she told the hotel she lived."

"What about New Orleans?" Lea asked.

He shook his head.

"Did George provide any crucial physical description? Scars? A tattoo of a skull on her belly?"

"George isn't the world's most observant witness. The little skunk is absolutely worthless."

"It won't be a total loss for him. He's getting a trip to Europe out of it. Does he need a traveling companion?"

He scowled at her. "You'll be traveling, all right. But not to Europe. I want you to fly to New Orleans tonight and make sure Killebrew is on the right track. If he isn't, set him straight."

"Why wait till tonight?" she asked.

"Because I want you to take a little drive with me."

"When?"

"I was gonna call you later, but as long as you're here . . ." He stood up, scowled, and pressed his fist against his lower back. "Dammit, but it's hell to grow old," he grumbled, stretching and causing various pops and cracks along his skeletal structure.

Apparently satisfied that his body was in sufficient working order, he moved from the room. Lea followed silently. "Where are we going?"

"To Malibu."

"Specifically."

"To Romeo Vetticino's place."

"Because . . . ?"

Starbuck paused in the kitchen to sniff at a pot that Choo-Choo had on the stove. "Because the blonde let it slip to George one night that Romeo was the guy behind the racetrack buy."

37

THE MALIBU HOUSE had a short but colorful history. Located on a promontory looking down on the colony, it had been built for just under a million dollars in the early fifties by a Vegas lounge singer, a friend of Johnny Rousseau's named Lou "Natureboy" Tortelli, who was shot three times in the head for being in the wrong hotel suite at the wrong time with the wrong woman. In the sixties, a TV mogul picked it up for a mere $2.5 mil, glassed in the front, then built a wall that blocked the view. He committed suicide, but it probably wasn't the lack of vista that drove him to it; the TV jungle can be a cruel one.

A rock musician moved in for just $2.9 million in the seventies, tore down the wall, and tried to fly to the ocean one night when both he and the moon were high.

Then the place languished on the market for quite a while.

When there's been that much fatal karma in one location, word gets around.

The house's present owner, the one Starbuck and Lea had made the drive to see, ignored the stories about the haunted house of death. Romeo Vetticino was not afraid of ghost stories. He was his own walking ghost story.

His and Starbuck's paths had crossed several years before when he'd been in the market for a Derby winner named Magic Cal. The Thoroughbred's owner had been opposed to the sale, until his two-year-old son went missing.

The owner brought Starbuck in to find the son. That didn't happen. In desperation, the owner sold Magic Cal to Vetticino. The next day, an elderly couple from Wyoming, in Southern California for a gathering of Unification Church ministers, found the boy sitting in their rented automobile, with a cardboard delivery tag attached to his overalls.

The boy was happy, healthy, and apparently none the worse for his fourteen-day adventure. Starbuck began to pursue the matter, but the boy's father told him to let it go, that Vetticino had paid a fair price for the horse and there would be nothing gained in pressing the case further.

But Starbuck didn't want to give it up. Denied access to the boy, who, even with his limited vocabulary, may have provided a clue to his abduction, the detective turned his attention to Vetticino.

A month into his apparently fruitless investigation, he received a notice from the IRS that he was going to be the subject of a total audit. Then came, in succession, a letter from the state that his license had been lifted because of an impropriety in a case closed long ago, a telegram from his bank stating that because he had failed to submit mortgage payments for the past six months, his home was now in foreclosure, and a confirmation of his request for the cancellation of his life- and health-insurance policies.

It appeared that some elusive computer hacker had been at work. Starbuck had the canceled checks and records necessary to refute all charges, but it took him nearly three months to straighten out his affairs. He had just accomplished that when he received a bouquet of red roses and a note that read, *Life can be simple or difficult. Your choice. R.V.*

Starbuck has always had a hard head. Lea thinks he inherited it. His father, a bad-tempered prairie dog of a man, refused to go along with the government's plan in the sixties to pay him for not raising cattle on his thirty-acre Montana spread. Even when, in retaliation, the IRS and other agencies literally took the ranch away from him, he'd continued to believe that he'd been right.

Starbuck's mother, whom Lea loved, was not exactly a push-over herself. A powerful woman who did a ranch hand's work during the day and painted delicate watercolors in the evening to relax, she gave her husband a concussion with a tenderizing mallet to convince him that their son needed a college education. The offspring of these two strong-willed, somewhat stoic West-erners was not the sort of man you threaten, not even with roses.

He found his own hacker who eventually worked his way past the passwords guarding the Vetticino business files. Unfortu-nately, the files were limited to the crime family's legitimate enterprises. The best Starbuck could do was to repay Vetticino in kind by corrupting the files enough to throw the man's compa-nies into temporary chaos.

They had not really met. Starbuck had seen Romeo, of course. At the track a few times. At restaurants. Once at a solemn high mass for a slain police lieutenant whom, everyone agreed, the gangster had disgraced by attending.

The last time he'd caught sight of the crime lord had been six months ago. Starbuck and Lea had been in the Malibu Colony on business. They and their client, the head of an independent film-production company whose underage daughter had taken up with a jockey, were standing in front of the man's home when a Mercedes convertible drove by with Vetticino in the passenger seat. The driver was an attractive red-haired woman whose face was familiar. The car had passed before Starbuck realized who she was—Francie Dorn.

The combination of Francie and Romeo was too much for him. He left Lea to handle the producer and drove back to his office, where he started a series of phone calls. By nightfall, Starbuck was faced with the frustrating discovery that Vetticino had been maintaining so low a profile lately that even his most reliable informants had heard nothing about him for months.

From a delivery boy who brought groceries to the Vetticino compound, Starbuck learned that "the bodacious redhead," otherwise known as Francie, "was sort of like housekeeper for the place. Telling the cook what to do and like that."

The boy, who visited the compound at least once a week, had never seen "the dude who owns the place."

And so Starbuck had let it go, making note of Francie's location and saving that information for the day when it might become useful. *Like a lure to wave under my nose.*

Now he and Lea were parked a hundred yards away from the gate to Vetticino's Malibu mansion. And Starbuck said a silent prayer that this time he might do the man some serious damage. *Maybe he could pressure Francie Dorn to help him bring the guy down.*

He opened the door to the Bentley and stepped out gingerly into the heat and sunshine. "If I make it inside the grounds, give me at least fifteen minutes to get back. Then use the cellular phone to bring out the cops. Call—"

"Eddie Rafferty. I know," she said.

The guardian of the gate was wearing a white short-sleeved shirt with epaulets, dark blue walking shorts, high white socks, and canvas sneakers. Even in the sneakers he stood several inches taller than Starbuck's six-foot-two. His long blond hair had been gathered in back in a modified ponytail. He relayed Starbuck's name to the main house—an off-white, two-story affair that had the rounded, vague look of a nondenominational mausoleum.

In response, a young woman in a very brief tennis outfit left the house and bounced toward them. Her jet-black hair was cropped short and her dark eyes looked playful. She was not, as he had hoped, Francie Dorn. "Please open up for Mr. Starbuck, Lars," she said.

Once Starbuck was past the gates, she introduced herself as Donna, a niece of Romeo's. Starbuck paused to let the Vetticino family tree take root in his memory. Romeo had only one sibling, a sister. "Luisa's daughter?" he asked, trying to pin down whether the girl was real family or just an honorary "niece."

"You know my mother?" she asked.

"By sight," he said. He recalled a formidable, big-boned woman, with an oddly delicate face. Married to . . . what was the name? Meyhew. Frank Meyhew. A lawyer with one of the downtown firms. Supposedly clean. But his daughter hung around Romeo's compound.

"Mother thinks this place is tacky," the girl said, as if reading his thoughts. "And Dad has forbidden me to set foot inside the gate. So, naturally, I practically live here." She led him into the mausoleum, through a sterile, milk-bottle-white entry, across a hall, and out onto a terraced area with a clear view of the coastline all the way to Santa Barbara.

She sat down at a table and asked Starbuck to join her. He glanced at his watch. "If it's all the same, Miss Meyhew, I'd like to speak with your uncle and I haven't got a lot of time."

"So busy. So dynamic." She smiled up at him and, by damn, she ran her tongue over her lips. Starbuck wondered how old she was. Twenty. Twenty-one. And flirting with him. Probably she flirted with everybody from the pool man to the guy Romeo had handpicked to become her husband, but Starbuck felt flattered all the same.

She said, "My uncle has spoken of you. He says you are a most persistent man, who will not let him rest until he is in the grave."

"Or until he stops monkeying around with the racing game."

She looked puzzled. "You mean his horses?" she asked.

She was a lovely, full-bodied young thing, but she had not been the reason he'd driven to Malibu. "I'd like to see your uncle, Miss Meyhew," he repeated.

"That is not possible, *Mister* Starbuck," she said, mocking his formality. "My uncle is . . . away. And if he weren't, he wouldn't see you anyway, because he absolutely hates your guts. Do you play tennis?"

"Not in the sunshine," he said. "And rarely at night. So the idea is that you're *it* as far as a spokesperson for the family?"

"That kind of flattery will get you nowhere." But she didn't seem at all insulted.

Starbuck sighed. "Well, then, what can *you* tell me about one of your uncle's girlfriends?"

"Girlfriend? My uncle has no girlfriend."

"Blonde. Green eyes. Goes by the name of Fiona Dawson."

She laughed. "Sounds like a British call girl. Like I said, my uncle has had no girlfriend, blonde or otherwise, for a long, long time."

"That's not true," he said. "He had one here about six months ago. Redhead. Maybe a little hard. Name of Dorn."

"Francie? That was six months ago." She waved an airy hand. "Your information is really very moldy, Mr. Starbuck. But I bet I could bring you up to date in just one night. Over dinner, say."

"Could you?"

"Could and would." She rose from the chair gracefully, invading his space so that he had to take a backward step or feel her breasts against his chest. He took a half step.

"How old are you, Miss Meyhew?"

"That's a rather rude question, but I don't mind answering. I'm twenty-four."

He wondered at what age a young woman stopped lying about how old she was and started lying about how young she was. Maybe Lea would tell him, if he broached the subject carefully. "What's this all about, Miss Meyhew?" he asked.

"Maybe I like older men," she said.

"Oh, I'll bet there's another, more believable reason."

She shook her head. "Such low self-esteem. We'll have to do something about that. But I'm not sure this is the place. Do you know the restaurant Stromboli? In Beverly Hills?"

"I could probably get out my guidebook and find it."

"Tonight at eight, *Mister* Starbuck."

He looked back at the building. "Since we're getting along so well," he said, "couldn't I have just five minutes with Romeo?"

She shook her head. "He really isn't here. I haven't seen him in weeks."

"Where is he?"

"Ask me again, tonight."

She led him back into the building. "I'm going to take a nice hot sauna right now. I don't suppose you'd care to join me?"

"I work too hard filling my body with impurities," he told her. "I don't like to get rid of 'em too quickly."

She grinned at him again, pressed her lips against her palm, and blew him the kiss. "Until tonight, then," she said. "Be there or be square."

At the entrance to the compound, Lars had been replaced by a normal-sized thug in a gray suit who smirked at Starbuck and whistled a tune as he opened the gate for him to pass through. It wasn't until he'd arrived at the Bentley that he realized the melody was "Ain't She Sweet?"

Lea was standing beside the car, leaning on the front bumper. "You just made it," she said. "I was about to call out the National Guard." She opened her car door and took a seat.

As Starbuck circled the Bentley he discovered Lars the gate guard's uniformed body lying on the lawn beside the car. The big man was unconscious but seemed to be breathing. Starbuck stepped over him and got into the vehicle. He gave Lea a questioning look.

"The big galoot tried to get fresh."

"Oh?" Starbuck replied, turning the key in the ignition and smiling at the resulting grunt and purr from the engine.

"He sidled over and said, 'The old guy's probably getting his ashes hauled inside, so why don't we make hay while the sun shines.'"

"He didn't really say that—'make hay while the sun shines'?"

"No."

"Or about the old guy getting his ashes hauled?"

"Actually," she said, "his English is worse than Lassie's. But I could tell what was on his mind. Just like I can tell what's on yours right now."

"And what might that be?" he asked, aiming the Bentley south along the Pacific Coast Highway.

"You're wondering if that overripe little brunette bimbo who was batting her eyes at you at the gate is seriously interested in your ancient and creaky body or if she's setting you up for Romeo."

"What do you think?"

Lea replied, "You don't want to know."

38

THE TWO-HOUR TIME difference between Louisiana and California meant that while Francie and I were celebrating auld lang syne, or whatever the hell it was we were doing, Starbuck was sitting across a white tablecloth from Donna Meyhew at an overpriced Italian restaurant in Beverly Hills trying to bring their meeting into some sort of focus.

He knew why he was there—to pick her brain about her uncle's activities. What bothered him was that he didn't know why she was there. Or why she'd kicked off her shoe and was running her bare foot up his leg under his pants. He was glad she'd picked the left leg, because he was carrying a little La France Nova, the world's smallest and lightest locked breech 9mm pistol, in an ankle holster on his right, not knowing what to expect from Romeo Vetticino's niece.

Through an appetizer that was some sort of cheese-and-lamb pizza, through an osso buco that was magnificent in both taste and size, through three rounds of Bombay Sapphire martinis and a bottle of the smoothest Chianti he'd ever drunk, he had quizzed her on her uncle while she played with his hand, told him how handsome he looked, asked him how much time he spent at the gym each day, and in general tried to flatter, cajole, and seduce him.

What he had learned was that Romeo had been away from the compound for several months. She thought he was back east, in New Jersey to be specific, selling off property that the family had owned for aeons but no longer needed. She had no idea when he planned on returning.

Was Francie Dorn with him?

She repeated her statement about Francie being old news. Yes, her uncle had had some sort of involvement with her, but the Meyhews despised the woman and eventually Uncle Romeo had come to his senses and sent the slut packing.

Did she know where the slut had gone?

She did not know, and cared less.

Did she know if her uncle was involved with a company called Southern Boy Supplies? Had she heard her uncle mention a man named Remy Courville? Was her uncle trying to purchase Santa Rosita racecourse?

The answers were no, no, and she didn't know but thought it highly unlikely. "Uncle Romeo is into selling these days, not buying."

Finally, when the tart tartan arrived, she gave a little wiggle and said, "That's all I care to say about Uncle Romeo. Now let's talk about us."

"You first," Starbuck said.

"Okay. What turns you on?"

"This apple deal," he said, spooning a good-sized mouthful of tart tartan toward his face.

"Is it that you're not into sex, Raymond?"

"I'm into sex, all right. But I don't much care for 'Raymond.' 'Ray' is fine."

"Well, *Ray*?"

"Let's say, for the sake of argument, that I am into sex."

"Fine."

She signaled the waiter, who'd been hovering near their table with a dedication seldom seen by Starbuck. "We're finished here, Gino. Bring us a bottle of Dom to go."

Starbuck got out his wallet and she asked him to please put it away. "My uncle owns this place," she said.

Starbuck felt a little light-headed as he slid behind the wheel of his Bentley. Still, he was certain that he was in control of his senses. He pointed the car toward the ocean, but Donna had a better idea. "Let's go to the Excelsior." It was an elegant little hotel in Beverly Hills that catered to European visitors.

"Why?" Starbuck asked.

"Because sex in a hotel room is better than sex almost any-where else I can think of."

So they headed for the Excelsior.

Twenty minutes later, as they stood before the hotel's recep-tion desk, the night clerk informed Starbuck that his "secretary" had made all the arrangements earlier that day and that the man-agement sincerely hoped their stay would be a pleasant one.

A bellhop who did not seem surprised that they had no luggage accompanied them up seventeen floors to the Honeymoon Suite at the top of the hotel. Starbuck was staggering, not because he had to but because he thought it was expected of him.

Donna took his hand and led him into a bedroom that had been designed to look soft and creamy and inviting. The bed was round with a satin cover. "Come here often?" he asked her.

"Only on very special occasions," she said. She placed the Dom Perignon on a dresser. Then she helped him remove his jacket.

She sat on the side of the bed and drew him down beside her and she kissed him gently on the lips while she undid his tie.

"Let's lie down," she said. And the bed was soft and comfort-ing under him.

She pulled off his shoes and then snuggled beside him, giving him playful little kisses on his ear and chin while she unbuttoned his shirt. Then she began kissing his chest and neck.

Starbuck had to admit he was enjoying the whole thing, but he was a bit uneasy about the gun strapped to his ankle. Fortu-nately, he was able to keep his pants on, no thanks to Donna.

"Excuse me for a minute," she said, "while I powder my nose. I'll be right back." Giggling. "Don't run away."

As soon as the bathroom door closed behind her, that's exactly what he did. He was off of the bed, gathering his shoes and clothes. He moved very quickly into the outer room, slipping on his coat and jamming the tie into his pocket. He was heading for the front door, when he heard the key turning in the lock.

He ducked behind a plump couch and watched as the door opened and two figures entered the darkened suite. First in was Lars. The big fellow had a yellow-and-purple bruise on his jaw and a bandage on his neck, courtesy of Lea. He did not seem happy to be there. Behind him came a young man in his late teens, pale and studious, carrying a small hand-held video camera.

They both moved toward the bedroom door and paused there, waiting.

The boy clicked on his camera. Starbuck tied his shoelaces.

Donna appeared at the door. She'd ripped the front of her dress and her panties were torn and dangling from one ankle. "The son of a bitch isn't here," she said.

"Where is he?" the boy wanted to know. Metal braces glistened in his mouth.

"How the hell should I know? I got him drunk. Then I left him in the bed halfway undressed, like we planned. I went to the bathroom to rip my clothes. But when I got back he was gone."

The boy turned on the light in the bedroom. He said, "You forgot to get him to drink the champagne. The champagne would have done it."

Donna frowned. "He was staggering, Frankie. I didn't want him to crash. Anyway, if you'd got here earlier, you'd have caught him."

"Any earlier, Don-nah," Frankie said through his dental hardware, "and we'd have been here before you. You screwed up with the champagne."

The poor children of Southern California, Starbuck thought. They're so used to seeing adults fall apart on two glasses of chardonnay, they didn't know how much a hard-hitter could put away and still navigate. He doubted that the champagne would have done the trick.

The trio entered the front room and Starbuck slipped his pistol from his ankle holster. But they didn't see him. "It was a stupid idea anyway, Don-nah," the boy said chidingly. "You don't even know if Uncle Romeo would have wanted you to do this."

"He wants this Starbuck jerk off his back. He's said so a bunch of times. A seventeen-year-old cries 'rape' and has the video to prove it? Uncle Romeo would never hear from the asshole again."

"Great. Only it didn't work."

"I was hoping it would make Uncle Romeo feel better," she said, moving toward the door.

"Has Mom let you see him yet?" the boy asked.

Donna shook her head and replied with some petulance, "Every goddamned morning she goes to visit him, but does she ever let me come along?"

"Let's face it," Frankie said. "Our mom's the Wicked Witch of the West. And Dad's so far out of it, he doesn't know shit. Our parents are dickweeds. Uncle Romeo is the only cool adult in the family."

They left the suite. Lars closed the door behind them.

Starbuck slipped the gun back into its holster and pushed himself upright with a grunt. He yawned, looked at his watch, and groaned.

In the lobby, he told the clerk he was checking out. The bill had his correct name and address. Donna had been remarkably thorough for a seventeen-year-old. Then he spotted the total. "Five hundred and twelve dollars and twenty-four cents? For one goddamned night?" he sputtered indignantly.

The cashier, a sallow man who looked as if he cut his own hair, gave him a polite but firm nod, then regarded him impassively as he handed over his credit card. Starbuck picked up the key to the suite and said, "I forgot something in the room."

At that price, he damn well wasn't going to leave the champagne for the cleaning crew.

PART ELEVEN

I Witness Trouble at the Track and Starbuck Visits the Sick

39

THE NEXT DAY the Louisiana sky was a smudgy slate. The gusty air blew droplets from the trees, but the rain seemed to have stopped, at least temporarily. The threat of it did nothing to deter the crowd at Magnolia Park, which gathered early and eagerly.

Thanks to scrambled eggs, toast, and coffee in the Feed Bag I was feeling in top form. As I wandered from Barn Nine to the stands, my mind played back the events of the previous night, pleasant and otherwise, and tried to separate reality from wishful thinking.

That pastime ended when I spotted a nasty tableau taking place by the south gate. Two of the track security guards were escorting a man out of the gate, followed by Delia Bouraine in full fury.

One of the guards had the man's right arm twisted a few inches over his head, forcing him to walk on tiptoe. The other guard was working on the left arm. The man was Ambrose Bierce Jones, the mildly hostile tabloid journalist I'd contacted on my first day in New Orleans. I wondered if I was responsible for his current predicament by hinting to him that Remy Courville owned a piece of Magnolia Park.

Delia waved Ambrose's tape recorder in the air and snarled, "Just throw him out."

"But Miz Bouraine," one of the guards said, "if the guy's a goddamned thief, then shouldn't we turn him over—"

"I'm no thief, you jive mothah," Jones shouted in his diplomatic way. "She's the thief. She and her loverboy, Remy Courville."

Delia stepped forward and kicked him in the ankle. "Take him somewhere and make sure he knows better than to ever come back here again."

The talkative guard said, "Ma'am? How do we do that?"

"Oh, my God. Do I have to draw a map? Give him a few bruises."

"Now, Miss Bouraine. You know your daddy—"

"You're fired, you son of a bitch."

The guard, a thirtyish guy with a broken nose and crooked teeth, dropped Ambrose's arm and stepped back. "Fine with me," he said. "Strong-armin' guys just because they piss you off ain't my idea of man's work, anyway." He took off his hat and spun it onto the dirt. "I'll go clean out my gear and find me a real job."

He stormed past me. Delia shouted at him, "Not after I've spread the word about you."

He wheeled. "Yeah? Does that mean you want me to spread some words of my own, ma'am? Like about the last time you wanted me to hurt somebody?"

She stared at him and said nothing. Satisfied by her silence, he made his exit.

Ambrose took that opportunity to twist out of the other

guard's grasp and stagger backward. The guard looked confused. His hand went to his holster.

"I don't want you to shoot him," Delia snapped. Then she slumped. "Aw, the hell with it."

She threw the tape recorder at Ambrose. It missed him and landed on the cement with a crash. "You get out of here and don't let me ever see you again, or I will have you shot."

She turned and stormed toward me. As she passed I said, "Morning, Delia. Problem?"

"My life's nothing but problems," she hissed, continuing on her way.

I watched the guard lead a somewhat pliable Ambrose off the property.

I followed them to the gate, where the guard stopped and Ambrose continued on down the street. I left the grounds, keeping a few paces behind him. When we were out of sight of the guard, I said, "What was that all about, Ambrose?"

He nearly jumped out of his skin. I guess he thought I was a leg breaker Delia had sent after him. When he saw it was only me, he relaxed. "Aw, hell, did you see that? She broke my goddamn machine."

I nodded. "What put the bee in her bonnet?"

He grinned in spite of himself. "I get a call from my friend this morning. She tells me that she spent last night at the Hilton, having a party with Courville's college pal and Courville and some nonpro named Delia Bouraine.

"They all got pretty high, and my friend says she heard this Delia and Remy talking about Magnolia Park. She didn't hear what they were saying exactly. But I remembered what you told me, that maybe Remy was a silent partner at the track."

"And so you did what? Came out here expecting to walk right in and confront Delia Bouraine about Courville?" I asked.

"Hell, do I look that stupid? No, I was subtle. I told her I was a bellman at the Hilton and I found something she left in the hotel last night. That got me into her office. *Then* I asked her if Courville was one of the owners of the track. That's when she blew up on me. I was just trying to loosen her up about the Hilton, so's she would answer my questions. But she had those track police guys in there in a New York minute. Told 'em I was trying to rob the place. What bullshit."

"Did your friend tell you anything else about last night?"

"You mean the sex stuff?"

I shook my head. "I mean the business stuff."

"Nothing. The only business she knows is the sex stuff. Missy Delia is quite a lady. Surprised even Courville with some of her tricks. This was their first romp, evidently." He cocked an eyebrow. "I phoned your goddamned TV show and they never heard of you."

I shrugged.

"Who the hell are you, brother?"

"We're on the same team, sort of," I said. "We want to bring Remy Courville down and I have a better chance of doing it. I'd appreciate it if you didn't get in my way."

"But who are you?"

"Just a guy you never met," I told him.

"Hey," he shouted. I didn't look back. I wondered how good a reporter he really was. Maybe he hadn't ignored a promising lead. I know I hadn't.

The ex–security guard was sitting on a bench in the otherwise empty employee locker room, gloomily tying the laces on a pair of Reeboks.

He looked up at me and bristled with anger. "What's your problem?" he snapped.

I held up my hands. "Nothing. I just thought you did the right thing out there."

"Yeah, sure. I always do the right thing." He was a Southern boy, and the words came out "rahyt thang."

"You said something about telling tales," I said.

His hands clenched into fists. "She send you here to try and convince me not to?"

"Do I look like I'd be very convincing? You've got a foot and a half and maybe eighty pounds on me."

He relaxed slightly. "Miz Bouraine don't have to worry, anyhow. She leaves me alone, I'll leave her alone."

"I gather this wasn't the first time she asked you to toss some guy around," I said.

"What makes it your business?"

"I like this track," I told him. "I wouldn't want to see her do something stupid that would hurt it or the memory of old man Bouraine."

He frowned and ran his tongue over his crooked teeth. "You knew the old man?"

"I rode here a few years ago."

He stared at me and nodded. "When she first took over, Miz Bouraine was okay, but lately she's been a real she-wolf to work for. And when her boyfriend dumped her—"

"Boyfriend?"

"Guy named Matthes. Worked in the office."

"He dumped her?"

"So I hear. She caught him with some other dame. It was just a couple weeks ago. Then he came in to clean out his desk and she got me and Phil to toss him out, like the black guy just now. She's calling Matthes a crook and a son-bitch and a lot worse. And she wanted him busted up.

"We didn't bust him up, though. Phil slapped him a little. Phil don't care, one way or the other, long as he keeps his job. But I don't do that kind of thing. I was brought up by the Jesuits and I stay as clean as I can in this town. That's probably why I won't go making any trouble for her."

He stood and picked up a dusty gym bag from the floor. "Guess I better go hit the pavement." He paused at the door. "Maybe this is some kinda phase she's going through, Miz Bouraine. But I'm still glad I'm leaving. Six years is a long time to stay at one job."

I remained in the locker room for a few minutes, staring at the floor, wondering who the woman might have been who'd made

Irwin Matthes lose his inside track to the workings of Magnolia Park.

A few hours later I found Remy and Mark Vetter sitting in the Courville box. Remy was doing the talking, gesturing wildly with his hands. From the expectant smile on Vetter's face, I assumed the subject was not too serious. Evidently Delia had not told them about her morning visitor. As I approached, Remy was winding up a joke: "And the farmer said, 'A pig that great you don't eat all at once.' " Vetter laughed and Remy chuckled and I uttered a genteel cough.

Remy spun around. "Coley, how you doin' this morning? You know the joke about the pig with the wooden leg?"

"I think I just heard the punch line," I said.

"Yeah. Right," Remy said, losing some of his high spirits. "So tell me what you and Granny have been conjuring up for our amusement."

When I had finished outlining Granny's plans for the Courville horses on the day's card, he nodded and said, "Remind the old man that I want him to use Mike as often as possible."

I told him I would and started to go.

"Sit awhile, Coley," Remy said. "Share some of your expertise on the horses out there. We need a few picks. I'll even lay a couple bucks on 'em for you."

I took a seat and began to go through the form with them. I supposed they were better handicappers than I was, but I made a few suggestions about the first two races. Then Vetter got tired of that and changed the subject to the fun and games he and Remy had played the night before.

"It was very intense," Vetter said, grinning. He turned to Remy. "But I still think you should have picked up something at the Blue Lagoon instead of—"

"I can always go to the Blue Lagoon," Remy interrupted him.

"You'd get a kick out of the Lagoon, Coley. You wouldn't believe the women."

"Every color, race, or creed," Remy added. "Whatever's your

heart's desire, you'll find it at the Lagoon."

"And they're all clean," Vetter added.

"A doctor on the premises," Remy said. "Not only to check the gals, but to take care of any customer who blows his pacemaker."

"We should have stayed there," Vetter said. "But Remy had his own punch."

"You didn't stay at this great place?" I asked, as if I couldn't believe it.

"Just to pick up Mark's little friend," Remy replied. "And this guy"—pointing to Vetter—"with a hundred beauties to choose from, he picks this bimbo he thinks looks a little like his Felicia, talk about having your blinkers on. Hell, he might as well have stayed at Dogwood."

"Felicia was too jet-lagged to play," Vetter replied. He was obviously annoyed by the memory. Then he brightened and added, "She doesn't know what she missed."

I stood. "I'd love to stay here listening to you guys all day, but I'd better get back to work."

"Okay," Remy told me. "But you know what they say about all work. . . ."

"Maybe we should bring Coley with us the next time we go to the Lagoon," Mark Vetter said. "You remember Joleen, Coley? She told me she had the hots for you. I bet she'd do you for nothing."

My smile was beginning to make my face ache, so I gave them a knowing wink and walked quickly from the box.

But I didn't get far.

Lea Starbuck, garbed in a formfitting white dress, a bright blue ribbon collecting her long blond hair into a ponytail, was waiting for me on the steps leading down to the barns.

She raised one eyebrow and said, "Hobbing with the nobs?"

"I told your father you weren't needed."

"Daddy doesn't trust you."

"That's his problem."

"You moved out of the hotel." She made it sound like an accusation.

"To live at the Courville plantation. This is no place for us to talk," I told her. "I'll meet you later at——"

"Well, well, well. Holding out on us, Coley?" Remy was standing a few feet away, looking appraisingly at Lea.

"Who's this handsome man, honey?" she asked in a Southern accent thick enough to support a bale of cotton.

Before I could reply, Remy brushed past me and had her hand to his lips. He introduced himself with mock courtliness. And she responded with the lie that her name was Lee Ann Stanton.

"And you and Coley are boyfriend-girlfriend?"

"Well, Remy, I suppose we are . . . if that's what you call it when you meet a person in a bar one night and you enjoy each other's company till morning. And you don't heah from that *person* again."

Remy bestowed one of his wolfish smiles on me. I wasn't flattered. "Coley, why don't you invite your *girlfriend* out to Dogwood for dinner tonight. Hell, it's Friday. Invite her for the weekend."

"I'm sure she's got other plans," I said hopefully.

"Nothin' I can't cancel," she replied. "What's Dogwood? A little ole cabin or something?"

"Something," I told her between clenched teeth.

"Great, then. It's settled." Remy was pleased to have closed the deal so swiftly. "We've got a spare bedroom in the main house for you . . . both of you." He grinned at me. "No sense bothering old Granny with another guest in the cottage."

"No sense at all," I agreed.

He winked at Lea and trotted away.

"That was a very stupid play," I told her. "I had something planned for tonight, and it didn't include being trapped at another dinner from hell."

Lea put a gloved finger against my mouth, then moved closer. She bent slightly and kissed me. It did wonders for my disposition. She drew back, whispered, "He's watching us from the stands."

What the hell, I thought. I circled her in my arms and gave Remy a real show. For a moment we both seemed to forget where we were or what we were doing. Then I pulled away from her and blessed her with a smile. "I'll pick you up at six, Lee Ann. Don't forget to pack an extra set of crinolines."

"Suite 1227, daw-lin'. An' come early," she replied. "I think mah daddy wants to know your inten-shuns."

40

AT THE MOMENT her "daddy" had other redfish to blacken, to coin a Cajun phrase.

He was slumped in his inconspicuous tan Mazda, parked along Highland Avenue in Los Angeles's Rossmore neighborhood, once the location of the city's wealthiest burghers. Some of the old money was still there, but it was sharing wrought-iron fences with the likes of Franklin Meyhew, who, it was whispered, had connections to the Vetticino crime family.

Starbuck yawned, nibbled a bagel, and hoped that the most direct connection would lead him to Romeo's new resting place before he ran out of patience and carbohydrates. He was assuming that Donna Meyhew had been speaking literally when she said that her mother visited the old man every day.

The gates of the Meyhew estate opened at eight-thirty to allow a sedate cocoa-brown Mercedes sedan access to the cruel outside world. Its driver was a male, in his early fifties, wearing a cellular phone in his ear. Franklin Meyhew.

His wife's red 450SL convertible didn't put in an appearance for another hour.

Starbuck let it lead him by half a city block until they hit

Coldwater Canyon Drive and it appeared she was headed in the direction of the San Fernando Valley.

For all its overpriced real estate, Coldwater was a speedway, and the little red Mercedes seemed intent on taking the gold cup. It zipped in and out of traffic along the narrow road as if Luisa Meyhew were looking for death in all the right places.

By some stroke of luck or magic, she eventually arrived unscathed at the crest of the drive and began her descent into smog-shrouded Sherman Oaks. Starbuck kept pace with her and hoped she wasn't going shopping at the Galleria.

On Ventura, the red Mercedes turned left toward Encino. It continued in that direction past the Galleria. In the suburb of Tarzana, it led Starbuck south past an assortment of twisting streets to a nonresidential neighborhood and a square building of no architectural distinction. It bore the legend ST. CATHERINE OF SIENNA, PEACE FOR THE AFFLICTED.

Starbuck gave Luisa Meyhew five minutes, then strolled casually into the building. In the shiny marble lobby, tastefully spare except for a statue of the building's patron saint looking properly beatific, an equally unpainted young woman with a pleasant, scrubbed face greeted him from a window in the far wall. The woman was clothed in a somber skirt and sweater. There was a bronze plate under the window that read, INFORMATION.

Starbuck smiled at the young woman and confessed, "I'd like to talk to someone about St. Catherine's." He was playing it by ear, having just become aware of the place's existence seven minutes before.

The scrubbed woman asked, "Is the sufferer a family member?"

"Oh, yes. My uncle Hugo."

"Of course," she said, as if she'd known the imaginary Hugo most of her adult life. "Let me get Sister Jerome."

Alone in the lobby, Starbuck gravitated to a pair of windowed doors. Through the glass panels he saw a room containing several sofas and stuffed chairs. Men and women, most of them in late middle age, sat on the sofas. A few stood at windows looking out. They didn't seem to be talking or interacting in any way that

Starbuck could tell. But they looked in relatively robust health.

"Can I help you?"

The voice belonged to a cheery, short, square nun wearing a summer habit. Even without a wimple or peaked veil, she transported him back to the classrooms of his youth. Dunce circles and palms stinging from eagerly administered rulers. To chase the images from his mind, he decided to think of her as an oil drum with a happy face on top. "I'm inquiring about St. Catherine's," he told her.

"Well, you've come to the right place. I'm Sister Jerome."

She extended a strong, callused hand and Starbuck took it. "My name is Jay Stratton," he lied.

"Sister Margaret said it was about your uncle?"

"Uncle Hugo Stratton, yes."

"Fine. Follow me."

She led him past a set of swinging doors down a shiny tiled hall decorated with portraits of saints, many of them in the act of expiring. Sister Jerome's destination was a pleasant, sunny office fashioned with contemporary furniture. She indicated that Starbuck should take a chrome-and-yellow canvas chair facing her teak desk. She removed a leather folder from a desk drawer and opened it to a printed form. She uncapped a gold fountain pen.

In response to a series of questions, Starbuck painted a picture of his "uncle," a man in his sixties, very active, very definitely of the Catholic persuasion, who had retired several years before.

"How long ago did he first exhibit symptoms?"

Starbuck stared into Sister Jerome's chubby unreadable face and said, "Two years."

"How much has the illness progressed?"

"Oh, pretty far along."

Sister Jerome nodded. "You will have to tell me the extent of his needs, Mr. Stratton. And be very specific."

Starbuck looked uncomfortable. "Before we get into all that, Sister, would it be possible for me to take a little tour?"

She gave him a brief smile and screwed the top on her pen. "Of course. We've very proud of our facility. I don't think there's another quite like it in all of Southern California."

★★★

There was an Olympic-size pool on the roof, where several of the "guests" were doing laps while others sat enjoying the sun. There was a music room, and a gym and a small theater. A clinic occupied two floors. There were numerous private and semiprivate suites. And, as Starbuck discovered on their way back to Sister Jerome's office, there was a section of the second-floor wing that was closed to visitors. Luisa Meyhew was just leaving it when they passed by. She nodded to Sister Jerome and stared blankly at Starbuck.

He waited until the Meyhew woman had disappeared into an elevator to ask Sister Jerome about the private sector.

"It's occupied by one of the main benefactors of St. Catherine's," she said.

"What's his name?"

"I'm afraid I'm not at liberty to say. Secrecy was one of the conditions of the donation."

"Isn't that unusual?" Starbuck asked.

She shook her head. "I wish it were. But some people feel that there is a stigma attached to Alzheimer's disease. Just because a relative is stricken with it, they feel it somehow reflects badly on the family as a whole."

Starbuck nodded, thinking to himself that Alzheimer's might have a more negative effect on one particular family's reputation than on others.

Armed with the name of the disease that his uncle Hugo was supposed to be suffering from, he quickly answered the remainder of Sister Jerome's questions and provided her with an address and telephone number as fictitious as the rest of his story. He left her with the idea that he would be calling her soon to finalize the arrangements.

She insisted on walking him to the lobby. But Starbuck, whose favorite saint was Thomas, was not about to depart without making sure that Romeo Vetticino was not lazing smugly behind that locked door, reading the morning line and sending his min-

ions out for pastrami and beer in time for the closed-circuit feed
from the tracks.

He waited for the nun to depart, then he strolled to the front
door. There, he stopped and began searching his pockets. Scowling mightily, he returned to the swinging doors. The scrubbed-
faced young woman behind the window called out to him, "Sir,
can I help you?"

"No problem," Starbuck told her. "I left my pen. I remember
the way."

He thought she may have shouted something else, but by then
he was walking swiftly down the corridor past the saints, then up
the stairwell leading to the second floor. At the door to the
private section, he hesitated, then entered.

He found himself in an empty anteroom with more portraits
of saints, a wooden table on which rested a tray with the remains
of someone's breakfast, and a closed door.

He went through the door.

Inside was a large living room, richly furnished in leather sofas
and chairs trimmed in dark wood. One wall was covered by a
floor-to-ceiling entertainment center with a huge television set
that was tuned to a daytime cooking show. The other wall was
mainly glass, providing a view of lovely downtown Tarzana.
Romeo Vetticino sat on a chair looking at neither window nor
television. The ceiling seemed to be what interested him, particularly one section of its northwest corner.

He looked tan and amazingly fit. He was wearing a swimsuit,
leather sandals, and a maroon terrycloth robe with white stripes.
Starbuck said, "Hello, Romeo, what do you know?"

The man turned his head slowly and stared right at him. There
was no life in the eyes. The man said, "I'm ready for my laps."

"You sure look ready," Starbuck said.

"I swim twenty laps a day."

"Not bad for a man your age."

"I'm ready for my laps."

There was a noise from the rear of the suite. Then footsteps.
Starbuck retreated to the door. He was going through it when he

heard a male voice shout, "Hold up, you."

Starbuck glanced back, saw a muscle monster in a white T-shirt and white pants enter the room carrying a beach towel that matched Vetticino's robe.

"I'm ready for my laps," Vetticino told him.

The monster dropped the towel and started toward Starbuck, who rushed out onto the second floor and ran and slid his way to the stairwell. Luisa Meyhew was on her way up. She gave Starbuck a strange look as he raced past her. By then the muscle monster was at the top of the stairs. "He was with Mr. V," the big man shouted to Luisa.

Starbuck did not pause. He could feel Romeo's sister sending eyeball darts at his retreating back.

In the lobby, he heard the young woman behind the window inquire about his pen. He did not stop to reply. It was only when he had left the building and was behind the wheel of the Mazda that he realized that the orderly, or bodyguard or whatever, was not still after him. Luisa Meyhew had probably called him off.

It was on the San Diego Freeway, socked into the usual everyday all-day traffic jam, that relief turned to frustration. Yes, he had discovered that Romeo Vetticino had retired from the game. But with Romeo obviously not the one behind the takeover at Santa Rosita, he was back at square one.

41

MY DAY WAS considerably less frustrating, all in all. After the episodes involving Ambrose, the security guard, and

Lea, the rest of the afternoon at the track seemed generally uneventful. But it had its interesting moments. Mike LeBlanc was set to ride a horse named Chilly Jilly in the second race and I discovered that I actually enjoyed watching the kid prepare for it. He had an instinctive way of communicating with animals. You could spot it as soon as he began rubbing the filly, petting her. Once he whispered something in her ear and the horse actually seemed to smile.

They cut a deal, he and Chilly Jilly. She'd leave the brain work to him and he'd trust her with the power. Together they formed a single unity. His seat and balance were perfect. I had to grin at his confidence. Both he and the horse seemed to be strutting.

The track was muddy and Mike wore three sets of goggles. You learned that lesson fast in a rainy climate. In L.A., I'd been racing awhile before I encountered my first muddy track. I'd barely cleared the gate when so much slush flew through the air that my goggles were plastered with the stuff. What do you do? You can't clean them. You can't take them off. I was totally blind when I brought that animal in third and figured I was lucky to have brought him in at all.

Mike whipped off his top set of goggles before passing the first post. By the turn, he'd dumped a second pair. He was in the homestretch before his final pair were coated. We didn't have to wait for the track announcer to tell us who won the race. Mike brought Chilly Jilly in a full head in front of the place horse.

Granny gave me an elbow in the side and said cheerily, "See what I told you. The boy's got it. He sure as hell reminds me of Longden."

He didn't remind me of Johnny Longden or Arcaro or any of those guys. Mike LeBlanc reminded me of *me*.

I told Granny about Remy inviting my girlfriend to Dogwood for the weekend and he did not seem happy. "You're setting yourself up for difficulty," he said.

I replied that it sure as hell hadn't been my idea.

He shook his head. "I guess not. When Mr. C wants something, he can be damn persuasive. But still . . ."

"I'd like to duck out before the last race to rent a car and go pick up my girl."

He agreed to take care of things at the barn.

It took me forty minutes to get to the rental place and do the paperwork. By the time I arrived at La Belle Epoque, the rain had started again. The hotel's awning managed to keep most of it off of my muddy track clothes.

I was halfway across the lobby when Harold, the monkey-faced bellhop, greeted me with, "Hey, Mr. Killebrew, back with us?"

"Just visiting," I told him, and slipped into a waiting elevator.

Lea opened the door to Suite 1227 with the phone to her ear. Into it, she said, "Here he is now," and handed the instrument to me.

Starbuck cursed away at me for a few minutes on general principle, then, with little change in tone, asked what I'd found out, if anything.

"After you," I told him.

"Me? Who the hell is hiring whom?"

"You*m* is hiring me*um*. But there are strange things happening out here, and unless you impart whatever knowledge you have, I won't know how to evaluate the information I have."

"Don't worry about the evaluation," Starbuck said. "That's my job."

"Okay, then, I have nothing to report."

Lea shook her head, but she was smiling. Starbuck screamed something that I didn't hear, because I was holding the phone an arm's length from my ear.

Lea took it from me. "Daddy, you might as well fill Coley in, because if you don't, I will."

The phone was making sputtering noises as she passed it back to me. "I'm on again," I said.

And so Starbuck gave me a shorthand account of the murders and went on to briefly describe the way Clara McGuinn's accountant, her own nephew, had rigged the Santa Rosita computers to make the breakage work against the track.

"The confusing part," Starbuck growled, "is that the little bastard said the blonde told him she was working for Romeo Vetticino. But Romeo's not interested in acquiring any racetracks these days. He's been out of things for a while. A diagnosed Alzheimer case. He looks like a million bucks, but you wouldn't want him to be your partner at bridge. I doubt he can even remember his last death threat."

"Mrs. Mac's nephew got it wrong," I told him. "It's Romeo's son who's partnered with Courville."

"Son? The son's out of it. I researched the whole goddamn family. He was raised by Romeo's first wife on the East Coast. My understanding is that the kid barely knew his father."

"Maybe. But he's got his father's taste in women," I said, rubbing it in by adding, "I'm surprised you didn't know that."

"What are you talking about?"

"You told me you knew where Francie Dorn was," I said. Lea was staring at me, one brow rumpled.

"I knew where she *was*," Starbuck replied. "She was shacked up with Romeo. But she isn't there anymore. The family bounced her, probably when the old man started shorting out."

"Uh-uh," I told him. "What she did was bounce from Romeo to his son. He calls himself Mark Vetter. He's in business with Remy."

"How do you know?"

"I bumped into Francie last night at Remy's place."

Starbuck was silent, but I thought I could hear his mind whirring. Finally, he said, "So tell me about your gal Francie. How's she look these days?"

"Great," I said. "She claims Romeo's son is keeping her against her will."

"I hope you don't believe her. Not after your last go-round with her."

"My last go-round was with you," I told him. "And I'm not sure what to believe. Except that Courville and Vetter have this little concrete bunker out here that's filled with cash. And there's a file cabinet in the bunker that's most likely chock-full of in-criminating evidence. I was going to check it out tonight, except your daughter showed up and blew that plan away. If you can pull her off my back for about twenty-four hours, I just may get this job done."

"Let me talk to her."

Feeling rather smug, I handed the phone to Lea.

She listened for a few minutes. Then told her father good-bye and replaced the receiver on its cradle.

"Well?" I asked.

"Dad says that he's afraid you're falling under the Dorn woman's spell and will do something incredibly foolish and maybe even criminal. He says if I should let you out of my sight even for a minute, he will spank me until I'm blue."

"Is that all?"

"He says if your concrete bunker really exists and is not some-thing you dreamed up, we should break into the place tonight when the house is asleep."

"Break in how?" I asked.

"I'm an expert at locks," she informed me. "Picking locks is one of the things I'm really good at."

I reached past her and lifted the phone receiver.

"Who are you calling?" she asked.

"I'm canceling my other expert."

The phone rang in Jackie Parnell's room at the Alibi Motel nine times before he picked it up. "Heaven on a roll," he said.

"Jackie?"

"Hiya, podnah. Me and Mari are in bed eatin' pork chops. The thought of getting into action tonight has made me dang insatia-ble." There was a giggle in the background.

"I thought her name was Jeri," I said.

"Jeri had to go back to work," he explained.

"Well, I hate to ruin your appetites, but the job's off."

"Off? Don't gimme no bullshit, Coley."

"The situation has changed," I said. "I'm sorry I wasted your time, though it sounds like you've been keeping busy. I'll cover your expenses."

"Hell with the expenses," he said. "Damn, I was looking forward to tonight. You gonna try to bust that place yourself, aren't you?"

"No," I said, looking at Lea.

"Damn," he repeated. "And I thought we was gonna be pals on this."

"We're still pals," I said. "There'll be other locks to pick."

He hesitated, then chuckled. "You got that right. Well, you hang tough, you heah?"

I promised him I would.

42

DURING THE RAINY drive to Dogwood Plantation, I questioned Lea about her father's activities in Los Angeles. I was particularly interested in details about the murders of Irwin Matthes and Lannie Luchek. Her problem was that she did not want to be disloyal to her father, but at the same time she understood the importance of my knowing as much as possible about the situation. Both of our lives could depend on it. And though she would not have admitted it, I'd like to think that she realized that her father was an arrogant, bullheaded idiot who deserved to be disobeyed.

In any case, she spilled all she knew, which, while not every-thing, Starbuck being such a secretive son of a bitch, was considerably more than I'd known. She described the death scenes, the police reports, and Starbuck's heavy-handed investigations up to and including his pathetic tryst with Romeo Vetticino's niece.

She provided this information in a manner so competently and with such professional detachment, I began to wonder what it must have been like growing up the only child of a martinet like Starbuck. So, while she was in full-disclosure mode, we spent the last hour of the trip talking about her life with Father.

At the end of it I'd decided that Starbuck was the sort of blessed character who does everything wrong but still winds up on the plus side of life. He'd loved his wife and racing, period. Lea had, of necessity, depended upon her mother for signs of parental affection. But when her mother died, Starbuck apparently refocused his interests. Lea was his little girl, and where she was concerned, he would settle for nothing less than perfection.

She pushed herself to meet his demands. And meet them she did until, finally, she discovered that he wasn't exactly the perfect daughter's perfect father. He drank too much and his disposition was lousy and, after his wife's death, he spent too much time with women who drank too much and who had lousy dispositions.

So she moved past him to a point where she could not only tolerate him but was amused by his taunts and tantrums. And she continued to love him with a fierceness and determination that would never waver.

I told her that it was more than he deserved. She smiled and said, "He has hidden attributes."

"That's what they say about sharks and leeches and other seemingly worthless creatures," I said.

She paid me no mind. "He really loved my mother."

"It's the least he could do."

"There's only been one other woman that has had any effect on him."

"Oh?" I asked.

"Clara McGuinn."

"Too bad for him she's not available," I said.

"Too bad, indeed," Lea agreed.

Moon-faced Floyd was on the gate that night, waving us onto the plantation from the little guardhouse. I didn't blame him for not coming out into the driving rain to check the car for hostiles.

Lea was impressed by the size of the house as we drove by it. "Why would anyone need a place that big?" she asked.

"It gives you a chance to build up a good speed sliding down the banisters," I told her.

"I'll take your word for it."

I parked by Granny's cottage. Lea elected to stay in the car while I went inside and packed an overnight bag.

Granny was sitting in the small living room, watching videotapes of that day's races. He gave me a disgusted look. "You're making a king-size mistake. It don't pay to get mixed up in these people's personal lives."

"I'm trying not to. Like I told you, this is something Remy insisted on."

"I heard him talking about your woman, son. If he doesn't get her, he'll be angry. If he does, he'll treat you like dirt. Either way, your life here's gonna be miserable."

"I bet I can come up with some other alternatives," I said.

Granny shook his head. "Stick with horses, Coley. They kick you and bite you. And sometimes they even piss on you. But they never break your spirit."

"Did something happen today?" I asked.

"You left before the last race," Granny told me. "The kid, Mike, he made a bad mistake. He was on Remy's Pride, a horse that dearly loves the mud, and they were two lengths ahead of the pack. And something happened. Maybe the kid's goggles got too muddy. Whatever, he thought he'd crossed the finish line and he stood up in the irons and the horse stopped. It just stopped. The pack shot right past 'em.

"Mr. C. went nuts. He rushed down to the track and yanked the kid off the horse's back and began shaking him like a goddamned rag doll. Then he cursed him and told him how he'll never be a first-class jock. The kid was feeling bad enough, without Remy making it worse."

"Jocks make mistakes about the finish line all the time," I said.

Granny grinned at me. "Even in big races."

I nodded. The best year of my career, I was on the back of a powerful animal named Attaboy. We were closing in on the lead horse when I thought we'd crossed the finish line. There were another two lengths to go. More than enough for Attaboy to push ahead. But I was convinced it was all over. So I took hold of Attaboy. We slowed and the pack shot past me like a collective bullet. The race was the Kentucky Derby.

"It might do Mike some good if you told him about you and Attaboy," Granny said.

"First chance I get."

"Then maybe the night won't be a complete loss," Granny said.

I paused at the door to my bedroom. "You ever hear of a guy named Matthes?" I asked. "Irwin Matthes?"

Granny shook his head.

I repeated the description of Matthes that Lea had given me.

"That sounds like the fella worked at Magnolia Park for Miss Bouraine. I useta see him around. He wasn't there long. Don't know as I ever caught his name."

"Did he come out here?"

"Once, maybe. He was with her at one of the parties up at the big house. I don't suppose I said two words to the guy. Seemed a little twitchy to me. Matthes, huh? You could ask Remy. He'd know."

"That's okay, Granny. It's not important. Forget I mentioned it."

He gave me a hard look. "Come to think of it, you're looking a little twitchy yourself," he said.

43

STARBUCK WAS SITTING on the wooden plank deck behind his house, comfortable in walking shorts and a polo shirt, sipping a martini and watching the sunset, when they came for him. They moved in, two from the left, two from the right. Looking rather absurd in their Armanis on the beach. Getting sand in their four-hundred-dollar Gucci loafers.

He recognized the man in charge, Joey Lunchbox. The name had been bestowed on him in his teens when he was just starting out as a collector for Romeo Vetticino and carried the proceeds from the cribs and the betting parlors in a kids' Flintstones lunchbox. Once, on a whim, he cut off a pimp's little finger and tossed that in the lunchbox, too, getting blood all over the receipts and letting Romeo know that Joey's improvisations left something to be desired.

The hood's presence dissuaded Starbuck from any sort of defensive action. Choo-Choo was inside, working on dinner. If Starbuck were to call to him, there was no telling what Joey might do. He had his assignment, whatever it was, and he would carry it out at any cost.

Additionally, there were four of them, young and fit and with reflexes unhindered by half a pitcher of martinis. And actually, Starbuck was curious about who was pulling Joey's strings now that Romeo was at peace with the world. So he filled his glass to the rim and downed it in a gulp.

"What's up, Joey?" he asked.

"C'mon with us," Joey said.

Starbuck looked at his bare, bony knees. "Can I slip on some long pants?"

"No."

They led him around his house to the road, where a pearl-gray Lincoln Town Car with smoked windows was blocking his drive. He took the backseat, between a shiny gray Armani and a shiny tan Armani. Joey slid into the passenger seat while the midnight-blue Armani with the ponytail drove.

Their destination was the Vetticino compound in Malibu. They arrived just as the sun took a final wink and went to sleep behind the Pacific. The Lincoln eased through the open gate and parked next to a red Mercedes convertible.

They entered the house from the pool area, passing through French doors into a living room where Donna Meyhew sat perusing an issue of *Interview* magazine.

"Where's your mom?" Joey asked.

She lowered the magazine and in a bored voice replied that her mother was in the office. As they walked past, her eyes locked onto Starbuck's. She shook her head and put a red-tipped finger to her lips.

The office was at the far end of the house, past a dining room, a den, a pool room, a salon, a gym, and even a solarium. It consisted of three rooms, two of them filled to the rafters with electronic equipment—computers, printers, scanners, faxes, a bank of telephones—manned by a male worker who vaguely resembled Woody Allen and three women who might have been his sisters.

Luisa Meyhew was in the third room, seated at a large desk that was piled high with manila files. She was wearing thick cat's-eyes glasses, which she took off when Starbuck and the others entered. "Sit the son of a bitch down," she ordered Joey Lunchbox.

Joey turned to Starbuck. "You wanna sit down?"

Starbuck took a chair not far from the desk. Joey and his pals remained standing. Luisa said to Joey, "Ask the son of a bitch what he thinks he was up to?"

"Lady wants to know—"

Starbuck interrupted, by saying to Luisa, "Could you be more precise?"

"Tell the son of a bitch he is not to talk to me, for if he does, I may allow my anger to show and ask you to cut out his goddamned heart."

"Ah, Joey, could you ask the lady to explain exactly what she wants from me?"

It was, of course, his visit to St. Catherine's that prompted his appearance there. Luisa wanted to know why he (a.k.a. the son of a bitch) who had caused her brother so much grief in the past with his goddamn computer games had found it necessary to track him down at his haven of rest and torment him further.

Starbuck tried to explain, through their intermediary, that he was genuinely sorry to have disturbed Romeo's tranquillity. "Though actually, he seemed quite peaceful and healthy," he added.

Luisa Meyhew turned her head in a quick, birdlike fashion to glare at Starbuck for the first time. "What were you doing there?" she asked, her voice losing some of its stridency.

"I'd been misinformed about something," Starbuck replied.

"Tell me about it."

Starbuck thought that over and could come up with no reason not to. "A friend of mine is president of a business that is losing money when it should be operating in the black," he said. "I discovered the problem—in essence, a little faulty bookkeeping. The bookkeeper responsible told me that he'd been paid to do his number by Romeo Vetticino."

"What did you think Romeo had in mind?"

"To buy the company cheap, once it went belly-up."

She leaned back in her chair. "How long ago was Romeo supposed to have initiated this operation?"

"Well, that's the thing of it. This would have been maybe five or six months ago."

"Unlikely," she said. "Tell me the name of the company?"

Starbuck hesitated. Assuming Romeo's son was operating on his own, what would be the result of his mentioning Santa Rosita racetrack to Luisa Meyhew? Would she slap the boy's wrist?

Would she applaud his ambition and lend the family's support?
His problem was that he did not have a clear understanding of the
dynamics of the family's relationships.

Joey Lunchbox used his middle finger to tap the top of Starbuck's head to get his attention. "You was asked a question."

"The company is Southern Boy Supplies," Starbuck lied.
"Among other things, it controls a racetrack down in Louisiana."

"Never heard of it," she said.

"There's a woman named Francine Dorn—" he began, and
stopped when he saw the rage twist her face.

"What do you know about the bitch?"

"She's involved in the takeover."

"Then my poor Romeo would have nothing to do with it.
The bitch stole from him. Took advantage of his . . . condition.
So she's in Louisiana, huh?"

Starbuck didn't like the look that passed between Luisa and
Joey Lunchbox. He wasn't fond of Francie, but that didn't mean
he was pleased at having fingered her.

Joey turned on his heel and left the room. Luisa settled back
in her chair. "You know her?" she asked Starbuck.

"Not really know her. I know about her. I saw her once,
driving your brother around."

The woman leaned forward, studying him. "You're interested
in this Dorn bitch. Why?"

"She was involved in a fixed race seven years ago."

"She's a bad woman. I told Romeo to get rid of her, but he
thought it was cute to have a bimbo bodyguard."

"Bodyguard?"

"Sure. What did you think? That she was his sweetheart? Oh,
you are really something. My brother has more class than that.
Maybe he screwed her, but he sure as hell wasn't in any romance
with her."

The news puzzled Starbuck, but Luisa didn't seem to notice,
or care. "She stole from Romeo. Money and . . . some other
things. I thank you for the information on her whereabouts. If she
is in Louisiana, we'll find her. If she isn't, we may have to talk
with you again."

"There's nothing more I can tell you about her," Starbuck said.

"Joey Lunchbox can find ways to make you tell things even you don't know you know."

At that moment Joey entered the room. He looked confused. "About this Southern Boy company?"

"Yes?" Luisa asked.

"Felix, Mr. V.'s main guy in Louisiana, tells me that Marco's got a piece of it with a local named Courville and Jerry the Hat from Miami."

Luisa scowled. "Marco? That little bastard! Harvard boy, huh?" She whirled on Starbuck. "You knew this, that my nephew was involved in this company?"

"First I'm hearing of it," Starbuck lied.

"You said somebody's trying to suck the profits from the company?"

Starbuck allowed as how he'd said that.

"Who?"

"I don't know. I was told it was Romeo."

"Who's your friend in the company?"

Starbuck was getting deeper and deeper into his original lie. "Remy Courville," he improvised. "He's a horseman. I knew his father."

"Maybe it's Marco who's trying to get rid of his partners, lower the boom on the business, and buy them out."

Starbuck shrugged. "If that's true, it means he's working with Francine Dorn," he said.

Luisa leaned back in the chair and was silent for nearly a minute. "The little shit would do that. He hates Romeo. He maybe even planned it from the start, her stealing the . . ."

She censored herself and stared at Starbuck. "Your pal Courville just got lucky. Little Marco and the bitch aren't going to be around much longer to screw with the company's finances."

She turned to Joey Lunchbox. "Take the big bastard home. We know where to find him."

As soon as Starbuck and the four Armanis left the office, Joey said to ponytail, "Drive this guy back to the Marina. I got some long-distance calls to make."

As Starbuck followed ponytail through the living room young Donna jumped from the couch and stopped him.

"Was that about me?" she almost whispered.

"No, ma'am," he replied.

"You didn't say anything. . . ."

"Nary a word. I'd love to chat awhile, Donna, but this gentleman is driving me home."

"I'll drive you," she said.

"If it's all the same with you," Starbuck told her, "I always leave with the guy who brought me."

PART TWELVE

Lea and I
Settle In

44

W HEN LEA AND I stepped over the threshold to Remy's old plantation home, either the house was empty of hosts and guests or the Courvilles and the others were playing hide-and-seek in some recess I'd not been privy to. A butler with a French accent named Roger, pronounced Ro-Jay, showed us to our quarters—a high-ceilinged suite that consisted of a small sitting room with television and couch and chairs and a bedroom with splendid antiques, including a four-poster big enough for a ménage à quatre.

There were also French doors opening onto a balcony that ran across the front of the house.

Lea was impressed.

What impressed me were the contents of her canvas bag. In

addition to lace underwear and sheer nightgowns and assorted other frills, she removed a Pik-Quick set of hardened steel lock picks, a Super Slim Jim for busting into autos, a hermantle rope, a grappling hook, thick gloves, a Bali-Song knife, two Tasers, a wedge door alarm, and nunchakus, those sticks fastened by a chain that Bruce Lee used to flip so casually near his skull.

"Have you used any of this stuff before?" I asked.

"Everything but the nunchakus," she replied, which is how I discovered what they were called.

She placed each item carefully into a chest of drawers that wasn't any older than two hundred years and we were standing there wondering what to do next when there came a knock at the door.

Before we could respond with a "Come in," Remy entered with a tray containing cocktail glasses filled with a substance that looked like cold cream. "These are welcome gin fizzes to cut the chill of the wet night," he explained.

I eyed mine skeptically.

"A little gin, a little white wine, simple syrup, lemon juice, cream. When Huey Long was governor, he had a special bartender he'd take with him wherever he went so he could have his gin fizz."

"Good enough for Huey, good enough for the likes of me," I said, and took a sip. It tasted like cold cream.

"They're saying on TV that a hurricane is on the way," Remy confided, between swigs of his gin fizz. "But they always say that, the alarmist bastards." He smiled at Lea. "How's the drink?"

"Delicious," she said. Then she slowly licked her lips. Remy almost swooned.

He recovered, but continued to stare at her. "I hope the room is to your liking. According to my dad, who owned the place before me, William Faulkner once spent a week here. He was a very famous writer."

"Really? A writer. Imagine," Lea said, blinking her eyes in wonder. I thought she was overplaying her hand, but Remy didn't seem to notice.

"Anyway, I think you'll find the suite comfortable. I know the bed is. I've done some of my best work on that bed."

"We'll treat it like a shrine," I told him.

He turned to look at me as if he'd forgotten I was there. Then he frowned. "Unfortunately, we're gonna have a repeat of last night's crowd, minus the Gossoms and Delia Bouraine," he said. "Your pal Travers is down in the study now. Personally, I agree with you that he's a horse's ass, but my sister seems to go for him, and I do business with him. I'd be personally obliged if you just ignored him instead of breaking any of his bones."

"I'll try, but I'm not making any promises," I said.

"Good enough." He turned back to Lea. "Join us in the study when you can."

He let himself out the way he'd come in, without our help. Lea started to say something, but I put a finger to my lips. "Nice guy, don't you think?" I said.

"Very," she agreed. "And so intelligent," she drawled. "Knows all about writers and fancy drinks and everything."

She was pushing the act too far. I glared at her and ran a finger across my throat. She moved to the door and opened it. The hallway was empty.

She shut the door and walked to the bed. She flopped onto it. "Do you really think Faulkner slept here?" she asked.

"He had to sleep somewhere."

"Who's Travers?"

"Remy's banker. We don't get along."

"So I gathered. What's Remy need with a banker, when he keeps all his cash on the property?"

"Maybe we can find out tonight," I told her.

"Mmmm," Lea said, burrowing into the bed. "This *is* very comfortable. Think I have time for a little nap?"

"Be my guest. I'm going to check out the lay of the land."

I opened the French doors and stepped out onto the balcony. It was damp out there, if not downright wet. Our room was one of eight on that floor, four of them on this side of the house. I turned right and walked to the end of the balcony.

A light was on in the corner bedroom, making its interior entirely visible through the French doors' thin curtains. The room was empty. I tried the door and it opened.

The bedroom was much larger than ours, done up in pastels. Very feminine. On a dresser rested twin diamond earrings that I'd seen the night before attached to the lobes of our hostess, Joan Courville. The master bedroom, then.

I poked around a bit more without finding anything of interest, then started toward the balcony. I stopped when an odd flash of light swept the front of the house. I moved to a switch on the wall and darkened the bedroom.

At the French doors I tugged back the drapes. Johnson, the hairy-faced wolfman security guard, was directly beneath the balcony, his yellow slicker glistening with rainwater. He was playing the beam of his flashlight over the front of the building. He didn't seem to be concerned about the weather. Nor did he appear to have any desire to move on to another location.

I crossed the room and paused by the hall door. No sound out there. I opened the door a few inches, convinced myself that the hall was empty, and left the bedroom.

Across the way was a smaller corner suite, its door ajar. A man's clothes were tossed over the chairs and bed. Open bills rested on a chest, addressed to Remy Courville. It appeared as though he and his wife slept apart. No big surprise.

Next to Remy's quarters was a suite of similar size in which I found Mike LeBlanc's riding gear, picture books about racing, and several comics that seemed to be devoted to superheroes from outer space. And a small, framed photo of the Courvilles, smiling and hugging one another. It did not look like an old snapshot.

Judging by the clothes scattered about the room next to ours, it was being shared by the oddly engaged Mark Vetter and Francie. I was pawing through her luggage when I heard footsteps padding down the hall.

I slipped into their closet and pulled the door nearly shut just before Francie entered. I could see her through the brief opening. She was wearing a multicolored cocktail gown, very low cut, that made her look about five years younger than she had the night before.

She checked herself in the mirror, made a minor adjustment to her lipstick, then smiled in apparent appreciation of her image. She turned, dropped to her knees suddenly, and reached under the bed, withdrawing an alligator suitcase. She placed it on the bed, unsnapped it. It seemed to be filled with rolled clothes, shoes, and a bright yellow bird's nest.

Francie smiled at the assortment and brought her right hand to her breast. Then over her breast. Her fingers paused at her neckline, then darted down against her bare flesh.

When they appeared again, they held a small metal object. A key. With her free hand, she dug beneath the rolled clothes and pulled out a leather case about the size of a half shoe box. She unlocked it with her key.

From it she took two packets of money. She sat on the bed with the packets, and fanned herself with them. Then she counted each bill. There were fifty one-hundred-dollar bills in each packet.

Smiling smugly, she replaced the money in the case, locked it, and put it into the larger suitcase, which she slid under the bed. She deposited the key back into her bra and stretched the material of her gown over her breasts to make sure the outline of the key did not show. Then she waltzed from the room.

I waited until the soft pads of her footsteps faded away. Then I hopped from the closet and dragged out the suitcase. The rolled clothes were some sort of dark pant suit. The spike-heel shoes, which matched the outfit, had tramped through mud. Francie had tried to clean them, but dry dirt was still caked near the sole and heel. The bird's nest turned out to be a blond wig. Under that was a very nasty-looking pistol.

I replaced all items, closed the bag, and put it back under the bed. And returned to our suite without further incident.

45

EA WAS SPREAD out on the four-poster sound asleep and looking like Remy Courville's dream of heaven. Mine, too. A good reason to take a cold shower. Though, actually, I hate cold showers and would never think of taking one, not even in high summer.

A nice, steamy shower, then.

I'd done that, put on a white silk shirt, a silk tie with tiny white polka dots on a blue background, gray flannel trousers, and a midnight-blue blazer with crossed polo mallets on the pocket, when Lea opened her eyes and stared at the ceiling.

"Remind me not to drink any of those gin fizzes before nappy time," she said. "My mouth tastes like it's coated with mildew." She blinked and looked at my outfit, smiling at the pocket crest. "Well, gee, what's on your schedule, a game of snooker before the banquet?"

"Thought I'd see what the other half is doing in the study," I said. "Shall I wait for you?"

"Absolutely not," she said. She pushed back against the mattress, then let the springs bounce her forward. She worked up a back-and-forth bounce until she had enough momentum to leap upright on the bed. Then she hopped onto the carpet.

I applauded. "What do you do for an encore?" I asked.

"This was the encore," she said. "Wait'll you get a load of the main event."

"I hope that's an invitation," I said.

She shrugged noncommittally. "I wonder what I should wear tonight?" she asked.

"Considering the fevered state of Remy's libido, I'd dress down a little. No sense forcing the issue."

"Right, master," she said. She strutted to the bathroom, looked over her shoulder, Marilyn Monroe–like, and blew me a kiss, then slammed the door behind her. I sighed and left for the study.

On the main floor, Mike LeBlanc's girlfriend, Julie Fontenot, was on her way out, a security guard I had not met at her side. Both of them wore bright yellow ponchos. She was carrying an overnight case. "Not leaving so soon?" I asked.

She glared back in the direction of the study. Her eyes were red; she'd been crying. "Yep, I sure am."

"What's the matter?"

The security guard, a beefy type with sixties sideburns and not much sense of occasion, grumbled, "Hurricane's comin'. Ah'm taking the lady home 'fore she gets stranded here."

"It was Mark's idea," she said. "Heck, I wouldn't want to stay here, anyway. Not with him actin' so moody and all."

"He had a tough time at the track," I told her. "He'll feel better tomorrow."

"But I won't," she said. "You don't have to hit me with a horseshoe." She gave me a halfhearted good-bye wave and they were off. In the few seconds that the front door was open, the wind whipped through the room, lifting a glass globe from an end table and shattering it against the flagstone fireplace. Roger the butler seemed to materialize out of the ether. His perpetually disapproving eyes glommed onto the destroyed objet d'art.

"Looks like we're going to have to batten down the hatches tonight," I said.

He nodded solemnly and continued staring at the glittering shards as if he were afraid of them. Or the wind.

★★★

In the study, the supercharged ions were tweaking everybody's nerve ends. Remy, Mark Vetter, and Norell Travers, Jr., were in a huddle in one corner of the room, frowning, mumbling in low tones. Remy's wife, Joan, and Mike LeBlanc were in another corner near an entertainment shelf, listening with worried expressions while a mush-mouthed weatherman described the gathering fury of the storm with demonic glee.

Francie Dorn was sharing a sofa with Roberta Courville, who was bemoaning the woes of selling property in a buyer's market. Granny Hayes polished off one gin fizz as I entered and was a third of the way through another by the time I crossed the floor to stand beside him at the bar. He gestured to a row of the white drinks that Remy or someone had prepoured.

"The kid and his girl split up," Granny said. "This sure ain't his day. Where's *your* woman friend?"

"Strapping on her gun to keep Remy at bay."

"Don't jest about that, son. Stormy weather does bring out the violence in people." From the guy huddle, Travers Jr. snickered suddenly—a sound so nasty it made my skin crawl. "Brings out the meanness, too," Granny mumbled.

"Some people are as mean as ferrets, even in the sunshine," I said.

Mike joined us at the bar to fill a glass of water for Joan Courville. Granny winked at me and I asked, "Mike, you ever hear of the horse Attaboy?"

The young jockey didn't answer until he'd filled the glass from a pitcher. Then he turned to me. "I'm sorry, sir. What'd you ask?"

He was looking past me to where Joan Courville sat staring at the radio with worried brow. "It's not important," I told him. "We can talk later."

Beside me, Granny reached for another gin fizz. I asked him if he was going for a record. He shook his head. "You don't get a whole hell of a lot of hurricanes in Southern California," he said. "They're easier to take if you're pie-eyed."

Not discounting Granny's experience in such matters, I was building a scotch on the rocks when Lea made her entrance.

She'd moussed her hair and done a full makeup number on her face, shadowing her eyes with a faint blue that matched a silk dress that delicately hugged and displayed her athletic figure. She was wearing matching pearls on her earlobes and around her neck.

She smiled pleasantly at the gathering, which had dropped its disparate interests to stare at her. Remy leapt forward to welcome her and whisper something in her ear before presenting her, labeling her, for reasons known only to him, as "Coley's fiancée, Lee Ann Stanton."

Reactions were varied. Joan Courville offered a polite hello; Mike nodded shyly, avoiding eye contact; Roberta Courville was guarded; Francie gave her a tight smile, then turned her head to glare at me; Mark Vetter kissed her hand; and Travers Jr. looked from her to me and shook his head as if he'd never understand the vagaries of women.

When Remy finally deemed it necessary, he released Lea's arm and she wandered our way. I introduced her to Granny, who nodded self-consciously, picked up another gin fizz, and strolled off in the direction of the radio. "This your idea of dressing down?" I whispered.

"Would you have preferred the leather micro-mini?" she asked. She was looking over my shoulder as I fixed her a light scotch. "Uh-oh," she cooed.

When I turned, I was not surprised to see Francie bearing down on us, grinning fiercely. "So this is the beauty you mentioned last night, eh, Coley?"

I smiled weakly.

"But you didn't say anything about being engaged. Congratulations, you two. When's the big day?"

Lea draped her arm on my shoulder and began playing with the hair at the back of my neck. "Every day's a big day for us," she drawled. "And the nights——"

"I mean, when's the wedding?"

"Honey, when the engagement is this good, why spoil things?"

"Where did you ever find this lovely woman, Coley?"

"One of those Compute-a-Date services," I said.

"Oh, go on," Lea said, pushing me against the bar playfully enough to bruise a rib. "Coley and I met at the Gator Lounge in the Quarter earlier this week."

Francie gave me a raised eyebrow. "Quick engagement."

"That's just Remy being an ole smarty-pants," Lea said. "He knows we're not engaged." She ran her fingers through my hair. "Not yet, anyway."

"Roberta and I were wondering where you got that wonderful suntan, Miss Stanton."

"Make it Lee Ann, honey. And the answer is the tropics. Every chance I get, I love to jet down to the tropics. I'm tryin' to talk this galoot into springing for a little trip next weekend."

"Maybe we could all go," Francie said icily.

It continued on like that for a few more minutes, when one of the maids entered, crossed to Joan Courville, and whispered a few words. Joan stood and announced dinner.

As was the custom of the house, places at table had been assigned. I found myself between our hostess and her sister-in-law, Roberta, neither of whom seemed in a particularly talkative mood. I was not surprised that Remy and Lea were seated together at the opposite end of the table. From time to time I'd stare at them through the burning candles to find Remy gesturing wildly in the midst of some story while Lea played the intrigued listener. Considering that her other tablemate was Travers Jr., I didn't blame her for doting on Remy. Well, maybe just a little.

The hurricane had been officially christened Bruce, and there were a few comments about movie stars named Bruce and rock stars and wasn't it odd how the names we thought of as being so wimpy in our youth—Arnold, Sylvester, Bruce—had suddenly been transformed into properly macho monikers.

Joan Courville began to discuss the last full-blown hurricane, which had devastated Florida and just a tip of Louisiana. Francie and Mark, seated together, were engaged in a serious conversation that apparently had to do with Remy, since, every few seconds one or the other of them would stare in his direction. Left to my own devices, I turned to Roberta Courville and discovered a bit more than I needed to know about plantation management and the ups and downs of the sugar market.

When the after-dinner coffee was poured, I was amused to note the absence of Sweet'n Low or any of the other substitutes. I did not give in to the temptation to ask for some.

It was a little after nine when we left the dining room to the dirty-dish collectors and the sweepers. Granny slurred his adieus and staggered back to his digs to sleep away the impending storm. Mike and Joan hied to the radio to chart its progress. Roberta and the weasel challenged Remy and Mark to a rubber of bridge. "This time I'm keeping score," the weasel snapped.

"Lee Ann," Remy called to Lea, "come be my good-luck charm."

She looked at me. Since we'd decided to wait until much later, when the household was asleep, to burgle the bunker, I gave her a slight nod and she went off with the bridge players to the game room.

Francie moved beside me. "Well," she said, "that leaves us."

"I think I'll watch the bridge game, too."

"No," she whispered. "You're coming with me."

"Where?"

"To your bedroom."

"That's not a really good idea," I said.

"Don't be a fool," she replied. "This isn't about sex. It's about survival."

46

LEA HAD LEFT the room a mess. There were wet towels on the carpet. Various oils and unguents occupied every spare inch of flat surface. Clothes were draped over the bed and chairs. Francie wrinkled her nose and said, "Compulsively neat little minx, isn't she?"

"I beg your pardon?" I said, trying to look properly indignant.

"Did you really meet her in a bar in the French Quarter?"

I nodded.

"And you don't know who she is?"

"Lee Ann?" I asked.

Francie's face looked tight and hard. "Lee Ann, bullshit. She's Raymond Starbuck's daughter."

"Raymond Starbuck? The chief steward at Santa Anita?"

"Raymond Starbuck, the son of a bitch who's been persecuting me for the past seven years. How much have you told her about the Santa Rosita deal?"

"What Santa Rosita deal?" I asked.

She froze for a beat and stared at me. "Oh, my God," she exclaimed, "are you saying you're not part of the deal?"

"What are you talking about?"

"I just assumed . . ." She shook her head from side to side. "Forget what I said. But remember this. If Mark finds out who your little 'fiancée' is, he'll kill her. And you, for bringing her here. And me, because I let her follow me from L.A."

"L.A.? I thought you've been in New York."

"Oh, Coley." She looked actually pained. "You're such a mark. I think that's what I loved about you."

"What's going on, Francie?" I asked.

She put a hand to my cheek, very tenderly. "You probably were my last chance, God help us all."

"What's going on?"

"You don't want to know. What you want to do is get the hell out of here. Now. Tonight. And take the blonde with you."

"Not unless you give me a reason."

Her face hardened. "Life is preferable to death. That's your reason. Get out of here and maybe you'll keep both of us alive. But don't trust that blonde. And you sure as hell don't want to trust anybody here."

"Not even you?"

"Me? What did trusting me ever get you?" She uttered an agonized little moan and moved toward me, hugging me fiercely. "You are a sweet man. I'm so sorry." A few seconds later I was alone in the bedroom with my memories.

I wasn't particularly happy with them, so I went in search of company. First stop was the den, where the radio was issuing the good news that Hurricane Bruce seemed to be blowing out into the Gulf away from the coast.

Calmed by the report, Joan was headed up to bed and Mike was making yawning motions. I poured a finger of scotch into a tumbler and strolled to the game room, where Remy and Mark were being bad winners—ribbing Travers Jr. mercilessly as he went down three tricks, doubled.

I wasn't an expert at bridge, but I knew that one of the cardinal rules was that you never played against former college room-mates, happily married couples, or identical twins. I'm not sure if they just pick up on each other's vibes or if they work out subtle signals. In either case, the results are inevitably the same. You lose.

Travers Jr. and Roberta evidently had had this proven to them before, but there they were, challenging the odds again by play-ing college roomies.

Lea, whose chair was next to Remy's, presumably so that she

could see his cards, looked up at me. I said, "Ready for bed, dear?"

"Bed?" Remy exclaimed. "It's not even ten o'clock. Besides, Lee Ann's bringing us all kinds of good luck."

"Maybe just one more hand, honey," she said to me. "This is fun. Remy and Mark have already won nearly six hundred dollahs."

"Gee," I said. "You really are a good-luck charm. But I do think—"

"Uh, Mr. Courville, suh?" Floyd the security guard, his round baby face wet with rain and/or perspiration, hair curly and damp, stood in the doorway, dripping on the carpet.

Obviously peeved, Remy excused himself. He and Floyd took their discussion into the hall, where the deep, incomprehensible rumble of the guard's voice went on for about a minute. Then Remy, scowling, returned and said, "Coley, take my chair for a hand, huh? A little situation. I shouldn't be long."

Mark Vetter stood. "Anything I can help you with, Remy?"

"Nothing I can't handle."

"I insist," Vetter replied. Travers Jr., the weasel, hopped up, too, and joined Remy and Vetter as they followed the security guard from the room.

Lea gave me a questioning glance. I shrugged and stated the obvious. "Well, there goes the bridge game."

"Fine with me," Roberta said. "I can think of more entertaining ways to spend my money." She stood and left the table.

I looked at the suddenly empty game room. "Is it my aftershave, or what?" I asked.

Lea was frowning. "Something sure as hell shook Remy's cage hard."

"I'll go snoop," I told her. "You'd better climb up to our room and check your nunchakus."

"No need to be rude," she said.

"Francie knows who you are. She recognized you."

Lea frowned. "That's a bummer. Now what?"

"She thinks I didn't know your real identity, that I'm a doofus who let you pick me up in a bar."

"Nice opinion she has of you."

"I'm happy playing dumb, if it keeps me breathing."

"Has she told her boyfriend?"

I shook my head. "She's afraid he'll blame her for leading you here. Thinks he'll kill you first, then me, and then her. She'd like you and me to go off somewhere and never come back. Then maybe Mark won't bump her off."

"That's some relationship they have."

"Not like ours, huh?"

"Right," she said. "Anyway, she's probably right about us getting away ASAP. I vote we crack the bunker and then we're outta here."

"First," I said, "I'd better see what Curly, Moe, and Larry are up to. Pack our bags. By the way, the room looks like a bomb hit Frederick's of Hollywood."

"Are you one of those neatniks?" she asked.

I adjusted her necklace, which had slipped a bit to the right.

"You really are, aren't you? One of those compulsive a-place-for-everything *bachelors*."

I was definitely getting through to her.

47

AFTER SEVERAL FALSE turns, I finally located the Dixie version of the Pep Boys gathered in the above-the-ground basement that had once served as the plantation's stable. Remy had converted the space into a series of little business cubicles that

were used by Granny, Howard Ragusa, the horse-farm management people, and the security force.

The security area was the only active and lighted section at
ten-thirty of a stormy Friday night. I eased my way past shadowed
work pockets filled with fitness files and health records. Directly
across from all the activity was a dark cubicle where the horse
management records were kept. I slipped in and eased a chair
under me.

Through the half-open door, I could see directly into the
security offices, where Remy, Mark, and the weasel were gathered around a television monitor mounted on a wall just beneath
the ceiling. Security guards Floyd and Johnson stood with them,
looking very despondent.

It took me a minute to realize what the flickering videotaped
image on the monitor was. As my eyes adjusted to the light and
distance, Remy's stone bunker came into focus. Wind and rain
caused a tree branch to upstage the action, but you could see the
bunker clearly enough. You could also see a blurred figure in
dark pants and rain-slick black jacket standing in the rain in front
of the bunker door.

The figure bent before the door, its body hiding its hand
movements.

Then the door opened and the figure disappeared into the inky
room. Eyes glued to the screen, Vetter snarled, "Which one of
you frigging security experts was watching the monitors when
this was going on?"

Johnson coughed and said, "It was the storm cocked up the
schedule, Mr. Courville. Some of the men failed to show. And
those that did got pulled away to handle emergencies."

"Emergencies?" Vetter nearly yelled. He was not taking the
situation lightly, a spoiled rich kid who hadn't had much experience with things not going his way.

"Yessir. A section of fence got blowed away at the southeast
corner. And a couple horses kicked the hell out of their stalls and
had to be sedated. The barn was on short staff, too, so they come
to us. And Mrs. Courville needed some putty put in—"

"Dammit," Remy spit into the man's face, "you're working for me, not Ragusa or Mrs. Courville."

"Top-goddamn-drawer security, Remy," Vetter said nastily.

The other guard, Floyd, said, "I shoulda been here, Mr. Courville. It was my responsibility."

"Screw the responsibility," Vetter told him. "Just get out of here and leave us alone."

The men looked at Courville, who nodded. I didn't think I was visible, but I eased away from the door as they passed by me on their way out. When I returned to the chair, the situation on the monitor had changed slightly. A dim light appeared in the bunker. The intruder was using a flash.

"Who the hell is this guy?" Remy asked. "Where'd he come from? Who knew about the shipment, Mark? Your old man, maybe?"

"I haven't even seen him in a year. And from what I hear, he's got the IQ of a not-too-bright summer squash."

"I understand those people have moments of lucidity," Travers Jr. offered.

Mark Vetter wheeled on him. "*Those people*. He's my *father*, you fat asshole."

"All right!" Remy shouted. "Calm down. Fighting each other isn't going to get us anywhere. Norell has a point."

"Use your head, Remy. This isn't my father's style. Only one box of cash was stolen. If it'd been my father, there would have been twenty guys and we'd have been picked clean. This is somebody else's play, a small-timer. Who else knows about the cash?"

"Your guy in Miami, Jerry the Hat," Remy snapped. "But if he wanted to steal just a little of the dough, he'd have shorted us before he loaded the truck."

"What about Felicia?"

"I sure as hell didn't tell her about the cash," Mark Vetter replied. "Did you?"

Remy shook his head. "But she is damned resourceful. We know that."

"She would have broken in, herself," Vetter said. "She doesn't trust partners."

Vetter turned to Norell. "That leaves you, Junior. Who have *you* told about the money?"

"Me?" Norell squealed. "I didn't tell a soul. What about that snoop that you let Delia Bouraine bring out here, Matthes. Couldn't he have found out about . . . ?"

"Forget him, Junior," Vetter said. "He's out of the picture."

Remy groaned. "Somebody's got to recognize this geek. It's coming up now, the clearest shot we have."

On the monitor, the thief was making his getaway. He turned toward the camera and a flash of lightning illuminated his face like a strobe. He was wearing a black cap over his red hair, and his collar was turned up and the screen was blurred, but I easily recognized Jackie Parnell's round Howdy Doody face.

The others evidently didn't, but Remy said, "Dammit, there's something about him. . . ."

They rewound the tape and began watching it again. I'd seen enough to realize my time at Dogwood Plantation was growing very short.

48

LEA TOOK THE news about the preemptive break-in with typical good humor. She called me a series of names, of which "jagoff" was probably the kindest, for bringing a loose cannon like Jackie into the operation.

She ran out of steam after "butthead" and "yutz," and I told her I was going out for a drive.

"In the rain?"

"I have to warn Jackie," I said. "He has no idea of the implications of his little burgle."

"So?" she asked. "The thought of them catching up with him makes my mouth water."

"Wither he goeth, go we," I said. "And it might be good to know if he took anything else that might be of value."

My hand was on the doorknob when she called my name. "I don't really think you're a butthead," she said. "But you are a doofus."

I certainly felt like one maneuvering the rental car around washed-out roads to the nearest pay phone. It turned out to be in a leaky booth attached to the side of Alphonse's Gas & Lube, an establishment that wouldn't have been open at that time of night even in good weather. But the phone was working. The problem was, it was located directly beneath a hole in Alphonse's rain gutter.

Wondering if a man could get electrocuted by using a phone with a waterfall pouring down his neck, I deposited my wet quarter, punched in my credit-card number, and dialed the ex-senator. He picked up on the second ring.

"Hi-dee-ho," he said cheerily.

"Hi, Jackie," I said. "Having a nice night?"

"Oh, man, I just come through the door." There was a giddy note in his voice. "And I am swimmin', for sure."

"Where've you been?"

"Oh, hell, bummin' around."

"You hit the bunker tonight," I said.

I could almost hear his grin. "You was a bad boy, Coley. You just sorta forgot to tell ole Jackie that the place was floor-to-ceiling greenbacks. I've got a friggin' hunnerd grand in fifties 'n hunnerds. And there's a couple million more where that came from."

"Not for you, there isn't. There was a camera trained on the door. They've got some nice footage of you coming out. Enough for a segment on the funny videos TV show."

"Oh, shit. I found one camera and hit it with mud. I shoulda known they'd have more. Guess I'd better take a little vacation."

"A big one," I told him.

"You better take one, too. They may remember you was with me at Le Cavalier."

"That was my first thought," I told him. "I don't suppose you took anything else out of the bunker, like the goddamned files I wanted."

"I went in there with the idea of surprisin' you with 'em, Coley. You know damn well I didn't do it for the money. I never knew about the money. I thought I'd empty out Remy's desk and file cabinets and lay the stuff on you. But the sight of all that green changed my good intentions. Like Elvis says, I was a one-eyed cat peekin' in a seafood store."

"Why'd you take just the one box?"

"It was goddamn heavy, and with the storm and all I figured I'd take just the one, which they wouldn't miss. Then I'd go back tomorrow night and razoo some more."

"Not a good idea."

"I guess not. I didn't mean to blow this for you, Coley. But, my man, one hundred long is one hundred long."

"Don't spend it too fast. You may wind up with the Vetticino family after you. And/or the FBI. The money might buy you some goodwill if you haven't spent too much of it."

"Aw, goddammit. Now you're really bringing me down."

I was bringing *him* down. "Listen, you cornpone Murph the Surf," I said. "If I get clear of this with all my faculties, you're not going to have to worry about the Vetticinos or the feds. I'll kill you myself."

He was silent for a few seconds. Then: "Sorry you feel that way, podnah. Hope you mellow out when you get the time. Meanwhile, I best be moving on."

"When you get wherever you're going," I said, "do me a favor. No postcards. I won't wish that I was there."

49

STARBUCK DID NOT thank the ponytailed driver for the ride home from the Vetticino conclave in Malibu. He slammed the car door, then strode around his house and entered through the kitchen, where Choo-Choo looked up from a bowl of lentil soup.

"Don't let me interrupt your dinner, Choo," Starbuck growled sarcastically.

"I call you for food," Choo-Choo protested while moving for the oven, "but you not here anymore. I think you go for a walk by the ocean, like you do sometimes when you drink a whole pitcher of martini."

"I didn't drink a whole pitcher." He stared at the rump roast simmering in its own juice, inhaled its aroma, and said, "I'll be eating in the office."

He thundered through the house, his sandals slapping like gunshots on the hardwood floor. The phone was in his hand before his tailbone connected with the seat of his chair. That's when he received his first hint about Hurricane Bruce. A recorded voice, nasal, unemotional, hopelessly Southern, informed him that his call "could not be completed at this time due to weather conditions in the Louisiana area."

He moved a stack of magazines from in front of a seldom-used television set and pressed the number combination for the Weather Channel. By the time Choo-Choo placed a plate piled high with roast, boiled potatoes, and carrots in front of him, he'd seen footage of a darkened French Quarter, of people wandering down thoroughfares knee-high in water, of the wind uprooting an oak that was every bit as large as a California redwood. He'd heard Cajuns talking about the might of the storm and seen an assortment of diagrams with wind directions and vectors.

Before Choo-Choo could escape, Starbuck pointed his fork at the screen, where a bespectacled weather expert was explaining haltingly exactly how Hurricane Bruce was progressing. "You ever notice, Choo, how they bring out these guys when the chips are down. In normal conditions, we get hot-looking ladies with big hair and great smiles. But when the storms hit, they bring on the professors. It's their way of scarin' us."

"Yes, Mr. Starbuck," Choo-Choo said. His disinterested look indicated that whatever the boss said was fine with him.

The footage of the destructive force of the storm was impressive, and Starbuck, who had nothing but confidence in his daughter's ability to cope with any normal situation, began to worry about the suddenly abnormal situation into which he'd sent her.

He knew, because she'd told him, that we were spending the weekend at Remy's. But Lea had neglected to mention the exact location of Dogwood Plantation. Now, not only was a hurricane tearing its way through the area, Starbuck was saddled with the added guilt of having unwittingly stirred up Luisa Meyhew (née Vetticino) to the point where she was planning some sort of move against her nephew and Francie Dorn. He wanted to get that news to Lea, but he didn't know how. Not with the phone lines down.

For the next few hours he continued trying her hotel. Maybe she'd left a number for him. Or an address. Failing that, he hoped that someone at the hotel might know the location of Dogwood Plantation.

At roughly nine P.M., one of the weather scholars announced that the hurricane was shifting away from the Louisiana coast. At nine-thirty, Starbuck got through to the hotel. No, Miss Stanton left no messages, except that she would be gone for the weekend. No, he had no knowledge of any Dogwood Plantation.

Nor did directory assistance have a telephone listing for the plantation or Remy Courville. How the hell did the guy do business? Starbuck wondered. That gave him the idea of phoning Clara McGuinn.

It was nearly ten o'clock, a little late to be calling, but Clara picked up immediately. Starbuck had already formed an apology for the call in his mind, but the urgency in her "Hello," moved them past that stage.

"Hi, Clara, it's Ray."

"Oh." The disappointment was so apparent that his heart sank.

"You okay?" he managed to ask.

"Of course, Ray." Her tone was brisker now. Businesslike. "What can I do for you?"

"I need a telephone number for Remy Courville's plantation. In the morning I could get it from any number of sources. But I need it tonight. I thought you might know someone—"

"I'm sure I can get it for you."

"I'm sorry to bother you so late."

"It's no bother. I'm . . . glad to have something to do. Barry's at a taping session that should have ended hours ago, and I'm not sure if he's expecting me to wait up for him or not."

Starbuck wondered what kind of taping session it might be. Not that it mattered much, he supposed. He said, "If you get the number, call me anytime. It's important, or I wouldn't ask."

"I know that, Ray," she said, and promised to act quickly.

He replaced the phone and stared for a minute at televised pictures of the bayous of Louisiana overflowing onto farmlands and homes. That phone number wasn't going to do the trick. "Choo-Choo," he shouted. "Fix me an overnight bag."

PART THIRTEEN

In the Eye
of the Storm

50

ON THE DRIVE back to the plantation, the rain had slowed but the wind was still gusting mightily. My rental rocked, rolled, and did the 'gator, but it got me to the guarded gate and beyond.

I parked near the backdoor, raced inside the big house, and climbed the rear stairwell to the top floor.

The hall was quiet, an antique wall fixture serving as a subdued night-light. The door to our bedroom was open.

Lea had picked up her clothes and makeup, but there was a mess of a different sort. A chair had been knocked over. Bed linen trailed across the carpet. A vase on its side spilled water and magnolias over an antique tabletop.

I backed out of the room and stood in the hall, confronted by a line of closed doors. Eenie, meenie, minie . . .

A wisp of laughter floated up the front stairs, suggesting humanity below. In the den I found a contingent of hard-core wide-awake houseguests and their host helping each other make it through the night.

Francie and Vetter were side by side on the carpet, resting on sofa pillows in front of a roaring fire. Lea was sitting at attention on an overstuffed chair with Remy perched on its arm, leaning in on her. There was a bulky bandage on his left thumb.

Lea jumped to her feet and ran across the room to me. She bent to kiss me on the cheek and whispered cheerily, "Our host tried to rape me and I had to break his thumb. But it's okay."

"Well, well," Remy called out, slurring more than a little. "The wandering boy returns."

"What happened to your thumb?" I asked, and felt Lea tighten beside me.

"Oh, it was the most awful thing. . . ." she began.

"We were just playing around," Remy said, "and we had a little accident. No big woof." He wagged the splinted digit back and forth to show me. "Good excuse for a little painkiller."

"We didn't expect you back," Francie said pleasantly from the floor. "Running off in the storm like a pouty little boy."

"Hey, cut the guy some slack," Vetter told her, giving her a playful slap on the cheek.

"You men take up for each other," Francie said, pouting herself.

I looked at Lea for inspiration. "I . . . I told them about our little tiff, baby." She hugged me. "I didn't really mean all the names I called you. You didn't have to run away like that."

"I just wanted to cool off," I said, following her lead. "I'm glad you didn't mean it."

"Let's go to bed," she said.

Francie glared at us both. I could feel her mind going through a series of questions. Where had I gone? Was I working with Lea Starbuck or playing her along? What should she (Francie) do to stay clear of, or profit from, whatever was going down?

"Lee Ann, baby, you're not gonna break my thumb and run, are you?" Remy asked. "It's still early."

"Why, Remy, you know there are times when five's a crowd."

"But I count only two," he replied. "You and me."

"Well, you better just get yoahself a good accountant," she said, nearly dragging me from the room.

Outside the door we paused.

We heard Remy say, "Mark, why don't we take a drive into town?"

I looked at Lea, who was nodding her head up and down, urging them on.

"Not tonight," Vetter replied. "This is Felicia's lucky night."

"Then maybe I'll go myself," Remy said glumly.

The front door opened, letting in a sudden rush of wind. We pretended to move toward the stairs as Floyd passed us and paused at the door to the den. Remy ordered him in.

"Sir, we got two guys at the gate, want to come in," Floyd told him.

"Two *guys*?" Remy asked incredulously.

"They say they got lost in the storm and would appreciate a place to spend the night."

"I don't friggin' believe this," Remy said. "Send 'em on their way. Don't bother me with this crap. Spend the night. Unbelievable."

"Uh, they said to tell you they're friends of the Hat."

There was silence in the room. Then Vetter asked, "What do they look like?"

"Both of 'em are wearing suits and ties. One's older, got gray hair. The guy driving the Caddy is in his twenties."

"Caddy?"

"Midnight-blue Seville. Louisiana plates."

"We better see them," Vetter said.

"Escort them in," Remy said. "But check them for weapons, first."

"They're gonna get wet."

"Do it on the porch," Remy said, a bit exasperated. "Make sure there's at least two of you covering them in here."

Floyd went out without looking in our direction.

"This has got to be connected to the break-in," Vetter said.

"What break-in?" Francie asked.

"It doesn't concern you," Vetter told her. "In fact, maybe you'd better go on up to our room now."

"If that's what you want."

"No. Hang around," Remy said. "Let's keep the odds as much in our favor as we can."

"Should I get my gun?" Francie asked.

"I don't think that's necessary," Vetter replied. "What happens if they really want to stay the night, Remy?"

"I could send Coley to sleep in his own bed in the cottage and share my bunk with Blondie," Remy said, chuckling. "That'd free up a bedroom for the Hat's friends."

"Jesus, Remy, don't we have enough bullshit going on right now," Vetter complained, "without you stirring up the pot even more? If they really want to stay, set up cots in the basement. That way your crack guards can keep an eye on them."

The front door opened and the wind tore through the house again. A bored voice said, "You boys enjoy working out here in the sticks?"

Lea and I moved farther up the stairwell. The newcomers could not see us, but we couldn't see them, either. When they'd passed, we edged down the stairs again. A new security guard stood at the door to the den, facing in. A scar ran from his left temple down his cheek.

The bored voice was saying ". . . Paul Felix, and this is my associate, Richard Brody. I'm sorry but I didn't catch the lady's name."

"Felicia Deauville," Francie said flatly.

"A pleasure, Miss Deauville. We're terribly sorry to impose ourselves on you people like this. But we were headed on to Houston for a meeting with some of Jerry the Hat's friends and we sort of got stuck here, water to the back of us, water to the front of us."

"That must be an important meeting," Vetter said, "for you to try to drive through a hurricane to make it."

"Moisant Airport is shut down, and Richard, who does the driving, underestimated the ferocity of the storm. We stopped back there in a little burg. What was its name, Richard?"

"Raceland," Richard replied. His voice cracked like an adolescent's.

"Right. Raceland. No room at the inn, though. I used the car phone to get through to Jerry and he said he was sure his old friend and cohort Remy Courville would have a couple of spare beds for the night."

"I have guests for the weekend," Remy said. He didn't sound drunk at all now. "But I think we can set up some cots for you in the basement."

"That'll be excellent, won't it, Richard?"

"Excellent."

"We won't trouble you any further. We'll just go get our bags and your men can show us where to sleep. And thank you again for your hospitality."

I gestured for Lea to follow me to the room. Inside it, she said, "What in the world was *that* all about?"

I shrugged. "The important thing is that we now know what we're looking for—some physical proof that Remy and Mark are partnered with this Jerry the Hat in Southern Boy."

"Then," she said, "all we do is wait for the house to fall asleep, go out to the bunker, find the evidence, then bridge the swollen creeks and waterways and somehow carry it to civilization without being shot."

"That about covers it. I'm glad you brought your nunchakus."

"What is it about that word that amuses you so?" she asked.

"It's like Louis Armstrong said about jazz, 'If you gotta ask, you'll never know.' "

51

SINCE THERE WERE no direct flights from LAX to New Orleans scheduled for at least another two hours, Starbuck let himself get talked into one that stopped over for twenty minutes at the Dallas–Fort Worth airport. But when his plane touched down there, he discovered that twenty minutes had been a slight exaggeration.

"We've canceled all our flights into Louisiana because they have a hurricane down there," a pale, overworked blond woman in a dark blue uniform informed him.

"What about the other airlines?" he asked.

"I phoned around for some gentlemen who flew in from LAX an hour or so ago. There was nobody going in or out of New Orleans International or Baton Rouge Metropolitan. And the weather had gotten worse, not better."

"I checked my luggage through to New Orleans. Is there any way of getting it off the plane?"

"They're unloading now, at . . ." She looked over her shoulder at a TV monitor that was flickering ominously. "It looks like we're having some sort of transmission problem. But I know the luggage is being unloaded at one of the terminals."

"I'll find it," he said, and, grumbling to himself, left the ticket counter and headed in the direction of the cocktail lounge. But once he got there, he didn't go in. Another grounded passenger pushed through the door before him, allowing him to glance at a male quartet sitting solemnly at a table nursing four glasses of

Perrier. Joey Lunchbox and his Armani-clad associates. The "gentlemen" who'd come in on the L.A. flight an hour before, probably.

At least the storm was screwing up their travel plans, too. They didn't seem to mind waiting out the weather. They just had a few people to kill. They didn't have their only daughter in God knows what kind of a situation with a screw-up ex-jockey as her sole ally. Assuming he hadn't gone over to the enemy.

The big man did an about-face and headed for the bank of telephones. It took him three calls to various parts of the United States to discover the name of a pilot in the Dallas area who might be brave enough to fly him into a hurricane.

"Lambert Speed's your man," a retired air-force colonel named Mackay told him. "Tough, absolutely fearless, and one hell of a pilot before drugs rotted his brains."

"What?" Starbuck whined.

"Even with half a tank," Mackay said, "Speed can jockey a plane better than any of your goddamned commercial flyboys."

It had been years since Starbuck had spoken with Mackay. The guy sounded like he was down to half a tank, too. Maybe retirement did that to you.

"Uh, Colonel, if the guy's on drugs, maybe I'd better—"

"Hell, Ray, he got cleaned up after 'Nam. Last I'd heard, he was still off the stuff."

"When was it you heard that?"

"Eight, nine years ago. Hell, Ray. I've been looking at the goddamn hurricane on TV. If you want somebody to fly you into *that*, you damn well better hope he's on something."

Starbuck thanked the man, depressed the switch hook for a clear line, and dialed Lambert Speed's eight-year-old Dallas phone number.

It rang seven times before an ageless, accentless foghorn voice said, "Yeah?"

"Lambert Speed?"

"Is that who you want?"

The question gave Starbuck pause. "Uh, yes," he replied. "Why?"

"I need somebody to fly me to Louisiana."

"Tonight?" the voice asked.

"As soon as possible."

"How'd you get my number?"

"From Colonel Jennings Mackay," Starbuck said.

The deep voice suddenly lost its edge. "Jee-zus, how is the old guy?"

"Fine. Retired. Living in Montana."

"Retired? Man, they musta needed a crowbar to pry that son of a gun out of his uniform. What's your name, sir?"

Starbuck told him.

"Were you in 'Nam?"

"Korea was my war," Starbuck said. "Look, can you fly me tonight?"

"A friend of the colonel's? Sure."

"No problem with the weather?" Starbuck asked, wondering now if he was making a big mistake.

"The weather? Hell, I don't give a rat about the weather. I damn near had to touch down in a hurricane once."

Starbuck's heart sank. "That's what we'll be flying into," he said. "There's a hurricane in the Gulf heading for Louisiana. It's been on the news all night."

There was a momentary silence on the other end. "That's okay," Lambert Speed replied, but it sounded as if he were speaking to himself. "That's okay, I can still do that. I'm sure I can do that."

The image of Lea in jeopardy flitted through Starbuck's mind. He took a deep breath and asked Speed for directions.

Speed hesitated, then said, "I don't trust phones. Got too much to lose. Where do I find you?"

Starbuck told him and the pilot said, "Good. Pick you up at the SuperShuttle landing in about thirty minutes. What do you look like?"

"Six-three, two hundred pounds. Gray hair. Wearing a tan suit with a red tie. And I'm carrying a brown leather bag."

"Got it," Lambert Speed said. "I'll find you. Then we'll go kick that hurricane's butt."

Starbuck replaced the phone wondering if he'd made a mistake. When he turned, he knew he had.

Joey Lunchbox and his associates were standing a few feet away, staring at him. Joey said, "Hi, Starbuck. Mind if we share your plane ride?"

Starbuck knew they probably were not carrying weapons on that side of the metal detectors. The reason he'd checked his small overnight bag was because his own gun was nestled in it. Too far away to do him any good. Or harm.

But regardless of the fact that the Vetticino quartet was momentarily without arms, he was still in a difficult situation. He couldn't exactly outwalk them or outtalk them. He might appeal to the security guards, but what would he tell them? These men are forcing me to share my private plane?

He said to Joey and his men, "Let's go catch a flight. I don't know how many the plane holds, but with any luck, all of you guys can find a seat."

"Push comes to shove, Starbuck," Joey said. "I wonder which one of us stays behind?"

52

THINGS WERE NOT going well at Dogwood Plantation. Just before midnight, the storm blew out a window at the end of the upstairs hall. The crash, the tinkle of glass, and the ensuing howl of wind was followed by the sounds of hammering. Finally, someone began ringing a bell. It took Lea and me a little longer than the others to respond to it, since we had to undress and get into our nightclothes.

Roger, in full butler garb, stood in the hall with the bell and a mournful look on his face. "Mr. Courville suggests you join the others in the dining room."

They were all there in nightclothes and robes, except for Mike LeBlanc, who was wearing tennis shorts and a sweatshirt, and Mark Vetter, who'd thrown on pants and an unbuttoned dress shirt. Joan Courville's hair was in curlers. Her sister-in-law had some sort of white grease on her face and it was also on Travers Jr.'s nose and forehead.

The guests were occupying the seats at the dining-room table. The two newcomers stood wrapped in their robes by the door to the kitchen, flanked by Floyd and the scarred security guard. The older and taller man, Paul Felix, was dark-complexioned, with a rosebud mouth and understandably nervous eyes. His associate, Richard, was blond and burly, with a crew cut and the drooping jaw of a mouth breather.

A portable TV set had been placed on a sideboard and nearly everyone in the room was gawking at it as a voice-in-the-well announcer with a Dixie accent intoned, ". . . cuttin' a swath along the Gulf Coast from the Florida Keys to Mobile, Hurricane Bruce is threatening to move out to sea. If it does, New Orleans may miss this very devastating force of nature."

On the screen were scenes of collapsed homes, flood tides, sunken automobiles, and grim, tight-lipped people battling a storm and losing.

"Those bastards never get it right," Remy snapped. "I'm sorry I had to get you all up, but regardless of what they're saying on TV, the storm seems to be getting worse."

"Well, we're weathering it," Francie said archly, her hard eyes still on me and Lea. "Aren't we?"

Remy shook his head. "Honey, if the hurricane comes, and I think it will, weathering it is going to take a lot of effort. This is a solid old place that has withstood one hell of a lot of wind and rain. But it's no match for a hurricane that can do that." He pointed his broken thumb at the screen, where a giant oil rig in the Gulf had been ripped off of its moorings by the wind.

"Are you telling us we're in danger?" Vetter asked, incredulous.

"Hell, Marco," Remy replied. "I just lead a good life and let the devil take what he can."

Roger the butler cleared his throat. "Sir, the servants are a bit upset. They would like to be with their families."

"Sure," Remy told him. "Just make certain they're back here when it passes."

"If there's any here here," Roberta said.

Roger left to dismiss the servants.

Remy turned to Floyd. "What about your guys?"

"There are just four of us," Floyd said. "We'll have to make do."

"I already told Granny to dismiss as many of the barn personnel as he can," Remy said. "Those bunkhouses weren't constructed to withstand a hurricane of this force." He moved to the sideboard, found a bottle of cognac, and waved it at us. "Care for one of Remy's Rémys?"

Apparently no one did. He poured himself a healthy tot and downed it in a gulp. "When you go back to your rooms, don't sleep near a window. No sense getting cut needlessly. In fact, sleeping under the bed would be my suggestion. I've tried it before and it's a pretty kinky experience."

Wanting to get the crowd moving, I took Lea's hand and led her from the room.

"Sleep comfy," Francie called after us.

53

STANDING NEAR THE SuperShuttle bus stop at the Dal-las–Fort Worth airport, Starbuck looked at his watch for the fifth or sixth time. Lambert Speed was fifteen minutes late. Since the pilot had not sounded like a man who'd welcome four surprise customers, Starbuck had convinced Joey and company to stand a few paces away. But Joey was growing anxious.

Starbuck was concentrating so completely on the cars arriving and departing that he didn't hear the hoodlum as he approached and slapped the back of his head viciously.

Starbuck wheeled on him in fury. "What the hell . . . ?"

"Where's your friggin' pilot?"

"How should I know?" Starbuck snapped back, rubbing his head. He was wondering how much grief he'd be in for if he broke Joey's jaw. Too much.

"I don't like you, Starbuck," Joey said. "And the lady I work for don't like you. I don't know why you feel you gotta go to Louisiana, but I don't like that either. Since your pilot seems to be a no-show, maybe I dump you right here."

"Waiting for me?" a deep voice whispered from beside them. It belonged to a man of middle height who could have been in his fifties when you considered his white hair. Then you might have noticed his unlined, strangely tranquil face and said he was in his late twenties. The face of a sleeping altar boy. With granny glasses perched on his nose.

His hands were in the pockets of a weathered yellow jacket

that he wore over a faded black T-shirt. Unpressed khaki pants and Rockport running shoes completed his gear. He grinned at Joey. "Facedown on the concrete, tough guy."

Joey said, "Huh?"

Lambert Speed's eyes brightened behind his glasses. He backed away a step so that Joey and his friends could all see what he was holding in his right hand in the jacket pocket. "All you spooks," he said, smiling all the while, "down on the ground like good little gomers."

Starbuck stared at him in wonder. "How did you—" he began.

"Don't say anything," Speed cut him off. "These boys need a lesson, all the crap they been giving me lately."

Joey squinted at him. "Giving *you*? I never laid eyes on you in my life."

"Speaking of your life," Speed said, and gestured with the pocketed gun.

Reluctantly, Joey and the others got down on the ground. At some less complex period in history, passersby might have paused to observe the strange ritual, maybe even comment on it. But this was the none-of-my-business nineties, and as it was after midnight, travelers shunned them as if they were performing some distastefully lewd act.

When the four men were pressing their wide Armani lapels to the pavement, Speed told them, "Don't try standing upright like men too soon, you low-life bastards." He grabbed Starbuck's arm with his free hand and pulled him past them to an ancient black pickup at the curb in a no-parking zone.

As they drove away, Starbuck looked back at Joey getting to his feet and brushing the dirt from his clothes. "That was pretty amazing, Mr. Speed," he said. "They're tough boys."

"I wasn't sure you wasn't part of their crowd," Speed said, "until that angry little mother swatted your head. Then I knew you were on my side."

"Your side?" Starbuck asked, a bit confused.

"Boils down to this. There's only two types of folks in this world, them that are with you and them that work for the goddamn DEA, like those peckers back there."

"The DEA," Starbuck said, bemused.

"They took my house. They took my boat. They even took my goddamn wife, or I think they did. They ain't gonna get my sweet little CT6."

"What might that be?"

"My Cessna Turbo Stationair 6. That's what's gonna fly us through that hurricane like we was floating on a cloud."

Starbuck usually didn't look for answers that he didn't want to know, but he had to ask, "Why's the DEA on your back, Mr. Speed?"

"They don't need a reason. I'm on their list and they check it twice a day. They say I deal in the deadly, but I been clean since six months after the fall of Saigon City. Clean and pure and reverent. And didn't those dungbugs look fine hugging the ground back there?"

Starbuck had to agree that the dungbugs did. Nonetheless, he was convinced that Speed was flying on some very high octane. He wouldn't have minded a martini right then himself. "Ah, Mr. Speed . . . ?"

"Call me Lambert."

"Lambert, what're you gonna charge me for the flight?"

"It's not that long, and it's probably gonna be pretty damned exciting, which is to the good. And considering you're a pal of the colonel's, I'll give you my bargain rate. Twelve hundred bucks."

"Twelve hundred?" Starbuck forgot his apprehensions and fears. "Twelve hundred? You must be crazy."

"Flying a little Cessna into a Gulf hurricane," Speed replied, "I'd say we both were."

54

WITH THE WIND whipping and wailing in the eaves, Lea and I listened at the door of our bedroom as other guests shuffled past seeking their own areas of discomfort. "This is a swell night for a robbery," Lea said testily. "Not only do we fight Mother Nature, but everybody, security guards included, will be awake and on edge."

"Need I remind you that if you had not poked your very lovely nose into this weekend, Jackie Parnell and I would have done the job and I'd be on my way back to L.A. by now."

"With your picture in the mailbox of every hit man in Christendom."

I grinned. "Christendom? You really are an old-fashioned girl, aren't you?"

"Which one of us goes downstairs to see if the coast's clear?"

"Me," I told her. "No sense getting any more of Remy's bones broken. How exactly did that happen, anyway?"

"I was lying on the bed, waiting for you, and the lout tiptoed in and jumped me. I thought it was you, so naturally I opened like a petal," she said sarcastically. "Then, when I realized my mistake, I had to break his thumb."

"Just bent it back?"

"Actually, I pretended to fall off the bed and held on tight and popped that sucker. He screeched like a stuck pig. The only downside of the adventure was that his wife was one of the first to respond. I don't think she was very amused, but she took him away to apply the splint. In her position, I'd have let him writhe until it turned black and fell off."

"Hold that thought and let it warm you," I told her, heading for the door.

The dining room was empty, but the television in the den was turned on. I chanced a look inside. Remy stood before the TV set, weaving, a glass filled with sloshing cognac in one hand. On the monitor, a weary, wet newsman stood on an elevation in front of struggling men in slickers piling sandbags along the swollen shores of the Mississippi River.

The newsman was saying that Hurricane Bruce, though gathering momentum in the Gulf, seemed to be ignoring New Orleans. He warned the people of Houma, Louisiana, that it would hit them squarely. As for other towns due west, like New Iberia and Lake Charles, it now appeared that they would not get Bruce's full force.

He allowed as how Thibodaux, where the plantation was located, might get a touch of tail wind, but the big worry was over.

After two attempts, Remy punched the set's off button and grumbled, "Bullshit. It's comin' here. I can feel it."

I slipped back into the dining room while Remy staggered by. At a safe distance I followed him up the stairs. When I reached the top floor, Remy was entering his wife's bedroom. I went in to see my little lady.

She was dressed in black. Black leotard, black socks, black gym shoes, black jacket, and her hair hidden by a black cap. "Don't tell me," I said, "by day, a mild-mannered Valley girl, by night, she's the black widow."

"Are you going out in your pj's?" she asked. "Or did you bring your colors?"

I'd brought gray slacks and a black polo shirt. After donning them and covering them with my already wet dark green windbreaker, I was ready. My hand was on the knob when Lea touched my shoulder and shook her head. She pointed at the wall separating us from the hall. "Somebody," she whispered.

I turned off our light and eased open the door a few inches. Richard, the mouth-breathing newcomer, was sneaking down the hall in shirt and slacks but in his sock feet. In his right hand was a gun, complete with silencer. He paused before the door to the room Francie and Mark were cohabiting. Lea pushed past me into the hall.

She was like a panther, graceful and silent. Richard paused and started to turn just as she bounced a nunchaku off of his noggin.

Richard's mouth dropped even lower than usual. She hit him once again on his way down. Richard kissed the carpet with a thud, the loudest sound made during the complete altercation. Lea picked up his gun and hopped back to our room. She tossed the gun onto our bed.

"Who was he going for, her or him?" she asked.

"Probably her," I said.

"Why?"

"We could have asked him," I said, "if you hadn't been so fast with your nunchaku."

"He had a gun and besides . . . shhh." She went silent. All I could hear was the sound of the wind. But we were finished with conversation for a while. Instead, we waited behind the partially closed door like naughty children to see if anybody came to notice her mischief.

When nobody did, we ventured out and stood over Richard's unconscious body, trying to decide what to do with it. I suggested we turn him over to the security guards. But Lea quite correctly pointed out that we would then have to abandon our looting of the bunker, and if she'd known that to be the consequence of her actions, she would have considered letting Richard bump off Francie and/or Vetter.

So we jammed Richard into a broom closet in the kitchen and ran a mop handle through the door clasps to keep him there. Then we descended to the basement. The cots for Richard and his pal Felix had been set up in a cubicle that the vet used when he was visiting. Felix was resting on his side, the back of his head toward us, presumably snoozing. Richard's bunk seemed occupied, too, probably with pillows to satisfy any guard who might amble past.

A cot in the security guards' office was being used by a lanky gent in uniform who hissed instead of snoring. Floyd was facing a bank of monitors resting on a shelf that ran along the back wall. On the monitors were various shots of the grounds—the entrance, the four walls, the barn, the bunker. The monitor on which I'd seen Jackie make his departure was now dark and silent. Floyd's head bobbed back and forth. I thought at first he was nodding. But he was wearing tiny earphones connected to a Walkman resting on the arm of his chair. He slapped his stomach like a drum in time to music only he could hear.

As we worked our way back to the basement stairs, I studied the walls, looking for a fuse box. I found it at the top of the stairs, a long gray metal cabinet. Beneath the lid rested an assortment of breakers. I smiled at Lea and led the way to the back door. It was time to brave the elements and whatever else we came across.

The night was so dark I felt like I was stepping into the Twilight Zone. Or maybe a warm shower. The rain was strangely tepid, but thanks to the wind, it stung all the same. I led the way past trees that shook like pom-poms, past the swimming pool that was as rough as any ocean, past the barren tennis courts.

I gave both Granny's cottage and the barn a wide berth, moving near the now deserted bunkhouses.

By the time we came upon the clearing a mile and a half later, I was breathing heavily, but Lea seemed as fresh as a daisy, albeit a heavily watered one.

We were nearing the cement bunker. I heard the click of a rifle before I saw the guard. It was Johnson, his black beard soggy with rain. He'd constructed a little lean-to against a tree where he'd been sitting with a clear view of the bunker. He was moving to his feet, wet and uncomfortable, raising his rifle and pointing it at my chest.

Lea tapped him with one of her ever-popular nunchakus. He fell backward, mouth wide open. She rolled him over on his stomach, not wanting him to drown.

Recalling the angle of the video picture of the front of the bunker, I was able to spot the main camera. It was in a protective plastic ball, bolted to a pine tree about ten feet up. I pointed it out to Lea. She nodded.

I then splashed all the way back to the house, went immediately to the fuse box, and disconnected all of the breakers.

The security office seemed to be the only one experiencing the shock of sudden darkness. There were curses and grumbles and then both guards were stumbling my way.

I went back into the rain.

It took them about three minutes to locate the box and reconnect the breakers. Their office lights went back on, as did the monitors, presumably. Everything would look the same, except for the camera that had been aimed at the front door of the bunker. If Lea had been successful, and I had no doubt on that score, the camera would now be pointed a few degrees away from the bunker's door. On a night that dark and wet, it was unlikely that the switch would be noticed. Certainly not immediately.

Lea already had the bunker door open by the time I got to the clearing. She was inside, at the desk, sitting in a swivel chair with a file folder on her lap. A penlight protruded from between her teeth, illuminating the contents of the folder as she used both hands to rapidly leaf through them.

She bounced the papers into a neat pack, placed them back in the folder, and handed it to me. The label on it read SANTA ROSITA.

She winked and stood up. She was ready to go. I stopped her, gently slipped the light from between her teeth, and played it on the file cabinet. I yanked the L–Z drawer open and flipped through its collection. I came to a thick folder labeled SOUTHERN BOY SUPPLIES. I stuck it and the Santa Rosita file into my pants and covered them with the windbreaker.

As we exited the hut a particularly violent gust of air took the door from my hands and blew it inward against a row of money boxes. The boxes toppled to the floor, spilling their contents. A mini-cyclone sucked the paper money into a funnel that carried it into the wet night.

I was glued to the ground, fascinated by the sight of all that cash drifting out of the bunker. I put out my hand to grab a flock of fifty-dollar bills. But they were too fast for me.

Lea clutched my coat and pulled at me, but I really wasn't ready to go. More money fluttered through my fingers. It was like some sadistic TV game show. "Welcome to 'Catch It If You Can,' the only show that throws real money away. . . ."

She grabbed the front of my jacket and literally jerked me from the bunker. "Thanks," I told her, "I needed that."

Our plan was to head directly to her car and get the hell out of there. But we didn't quite make it. The wind literally blocked us, pushing us backward to the bunker. Another few feet and we'd be waltzing in front of the security camera.

Then the wind shifted and suddenly we were being carried in the direction of the stables. Weighing barely a hundred and twenty-five pounds, I was more than a little concerned by the way the wind was controlling me. I flew past the stables, conscious of doors slamming and lights going on inside. In front of me a huge trash can suddenly left the ground and smashed into a tree. The tree's massive branches were snapping off like twigs.

To my right, Granny was struggling to cover the distance from his cottage to the stables and making little progress. I could hear the horses now, whinnying in panic. I was whinnying in panic myself.

Then the wind subsided as swiftly as it had begun. And the rain picked up. I stood still, feeling the fat, warm drops land on my head and shoulders and liking them. My attention was drawn to Granny, who was shouting curses at the night as he neared the stable. A door opened and he went inside.

"Hold it!" It was Johnson, staggering around the far side of the stable, one hand to his head, the other holding a cellular phone. I turned and ran for the car.

Lea was already at the wheel with the engine revved. I jumped in and slammed the door. I pulled the folders from my pants while she backed up and started down the shell road to the front gate.

A Jeep was heading our way. Not a good sign. It got worse when its driver angled it across the road, blocking the entrance. Its doors opened and Floyd and two other security guards got out.

Lea threw the car into reverse, but Johnson was standing there, pointing his handgun directly at us.

"Get out of the car," he shouted over the rain.

I slipped the files under the seat and looked at Lea. She nodded and we both got out.

Johnson had every right to be out of sorts. Regardless of the way Bruce Lee could shrug off a well-delivered nunchaku, they had to hurt like hell. He was wet and his head was sore and he probably wasn't being paid enough to cover that sort of extreme discomfort. He looked as if he were going to prod Lea with his gun. I saw her tense for it, waiting.

But he opted against physical contact. "Let's go into the house," he said grimly.

I was vaguely aware of his associates coming up on the right. One of them exclaimed, "Jesus!" I knew they were pretty religious in that part of the country, but I couldn't see why . . .

And then I understood.

A tree was spinning through the rain in our direction. A huge, goddamned oak or willow, or whatever the hell it was. It seemed as big as a private jet. The wind funnel that was carrying it hit us before the tree actually arrived. It lifted me off my feet and tossed me back against the house.

Since I was being bounced like a Ping-Pong ball, I did not actually see Lea do an acrobatic somersault, using the wind to leap clear of the tree. But she was at least a hundred yards away when the tree plowed into the hapless Johnson. First it was nunchakus, then a whole bloody tree. His horoscope must have said something about staying away from wood all day.

His terrible scream was carried by the wind to the ears of the other guards, who were spooked enough by what their eyes were telling them. They turned and ran. Floyd must've felt weighed down by his gun, because he threw it away. The first two to reach the Jeep hopped in and roared off, leaving Floyd racing after them, howling in frustration.

A tree branch sailed through an upper window of the house and lights went on immediately in most of the rooms. I could hear screaming. Doors slamming. Glass breaking.

And then—sudden and complete silence and stillness. The air was oppressively warm and humid.

I ran to see if I could help Johnson, but he was past that.

Lea was watching me with some anxiety. I said, "Time to go."

"Is it over?" she asked.

"So it seems," I said. "But what do I know? I'm a tourist here myself."

"Coley," Granny called out from the barn door. "Come over here and help me get these animals secure while we can."

I took a few steps in his direction. "It's over," I called to him. "You can handle it. We've got to go."

"You ain't going nowhere, you jackass," he shouted back. "We haven't seen the half of what this thing can do. We're sittin' here right in the center of the goddamned hurricane's eye."

55

I WATCHED GRANNY run back to the barn, then turned to Lea. "You call it," I told her. "Do we stay or go?"

She frowned and looked at the lifeless Johnson. Flying trees are enough to shake anybody's self-confidence, even a woman who took obvious pride in her intelligence and physical prowess.

"I've been in earthquakes that put my heart in my mouth," she said. "But I'll take earthquakes any day over this. They don't leave you with any decision to make."

I knew what she meant. One minute everything was fine. The next, the ground shook. The walls creaked. You held your breath, or closed your eyes tight, or sat in a closet and screamed obscenities. And almost before you knew what hit you, the attack was over. You'd met the monster and vanquished it without thinking. Aftershocks were pathetic little death throes, to be tolerated rather than feared.

But a hurricane was something different. It came at you full force, then subsided, then came at you again, even stronger. Its effect was whimsical, flattening one structure, leaving its neighbor untouched. The most maddening thing about a hurricane was that it gave you some control over the situation. You could stay and take your chances, or run and take your chances.

"You're the gambler," she said. "What do you think?"

"I'm not a gambler. I prefer sure things and this isn't one of them. But I think we've got better odds here. There's some food and drinking water and a power generator and a building that's stood up to a couple dozen hurricanes. Cars get picked up and tossed around and we could wind up disappearing forever in a swamp bog, which would be okay with me, of course, because we'd be together, but—"

"All right, already. We stay."

Suddenly a family of nutria scurried past us—father, mother, and four babies. The nutria is a ratlike creature roughly the size of a cat, with yellow pointed teeth extending an inch or two over its bottom lip. Under ordinary circumstances they were pretty scary critters, but that day they were just one more life-form trying to outguess the storm. They'd chosen to run.

Lea gave me an apprehensive look. "You think they know something we don't? Like how to survive?"

"We can try a run," I said.

"No." She shook her head. "We stay."

"Then you'd better modify your Spider Woman outfit or our friend Richard might want your guts for garters."

She yanked off her watch cap and her hair flowed down over her shoulders, raindrops nestling in it like diamonds.

She gave me a quick smile that was supposed to make me think she had herself under control, then ran into the house. She told me later that the first person she bumped into was Richard, who was seated on a chair in the kitchen with a towel full of ice cubes pressed against his head. He turned at the sound of her footsteps, moaned, then closed his eyes and reapplied the ice. She could not tell if he recognized her as his assailant or not.

The last big wind had snapped both phone and power lines. But the generator was supplying enough juice to keep a few dim lights glowing inside the house and in the barn, which is where I headed.

Granny and Mike LeBlanc were trying to calm the animals while Mark Vetter nailed boards over the upper hay doors. Two of the stable hands had been severely wounded by flying glass, and Howard Ragusa had driven off with them in the direction of the nearest hospital. Most of the other ten full-time staffers had departed long ago for higher ground. Saying we were undermanned and overwhelmed didn't even begin to describe it.

Francie joined us from the house, not to help but to inform Mark that the radio had said that Lake Allemande had overflowed onto the highway. "Nearly all the roads out of this garden spot have been turned into marshlands that can't support the weight of a car. Isn't this the most goddamned fun you've ever had?"

Vetter didn't answer her. He continued hammering nails.

"Don't you think we should get out of here? Now?"

He paused and asked, "What's Remy say?"

"Haven't seen him."

"Haven't seen him? Isn't he in the goddamn house?"

"Not with us. Maybe he's already hit the road?"

Vetter scowled and hopped down to our level. He handed Granny the hammer and headed for the door. "I'll be back," he said over his shoulder. "I've gotta check something."

I thought I knew what he was going to check—if the money bunker were still intact. I doubted he'd be happy with what he found: an unlocked door, missing loot, and rifled drawers.

Francie watched him leave the barn with an amused smile on her face. "He forgot his trusty rain hat," she said.

"He better find some cover more solid than a hat when this twister starts to move," Granny grumbled.

"What are the others doing?" I asked Francie. "We could use some help."

"Joan seems to have forgotten where the storm windows are, so she and Roberta are trying to stand the pool table on end to keep the weather out. Your *fiancée* is looking for the storm windows. And I'm going back to get drunk."

"Where are the two guys who came in last night?" I wondered.

She frowned. "I think they're with sweet little Lee Ann." She gave me a salute and strode off. Granny watched her for a beat. "Damn if she hasn't changed all of a sudden," he said. "I figgered her for one of the good ones."

"I made that same mistake, once upon a time," I told him.

Mike had been trying to calm Sly Boots, but the animal was far from tranquil. He shifted suddenly and his flank bumped the boy against a wooden rail. Mike cried out in pain.

"You okay, son?" I asked.

He nodded, but he was holding his right arm away from the horse, voluntarily or involuntarily protecting it.

"What've you got?"

"Nothing."

"C'mon, let me see."

There were four serious gouges running across the back of his hand. The blood had clotted but the bump had opened the wounds. "A tree branch was coming right for my face," he said. "I'm lucky I was able to get my hand in the way. This's gonna scar up, probably."

"You better go put something on it," I said.

"Soon as we get Sly Boots comfortable."

But once that was achieved, there were nine other animals to care for.

56

STARBUCK HAD NEVER experienced anything like it. He'd been in commercial aircraft that had hit air pockets and dropped, leaving his stomach a few hundred feet overhead. He'd even been in an armed-forces transport plane that had had to plow through a snowstorm to land. But this was something else again. Fear-induced bile gathered in his throat as the little Cessna bucked and rolled and shimmied in the wind. His hands were bone white clutching his armrests.

One minute they'd be heading up at a fifteen-degree angle, driving him back against the seat. The next they were dipping and zooming down, headed directly at earth and hurling him forward with his seat belt nearly cutting him in two.

Through it all, Lambert Speed grinned and bounced in his seat like a child with his first tricycle, humming the *William Tell* overture.

Forty-five minutes earlier, driving to the hangar where Speed kept his plane, Starbuck had made up his mind to wait for a commercial jet. Lea was resourceful and proud of it; she'd probably resent his attempt to help. Speed's brain was addled, either by drugs or by nature, and it didn't matter which. And there was the ticket price—twelve hundred dollars, one goddamned way.

But the Cessna Stationair had been pretty impressive. A sleek little single-engine job complete with an assortment of state-of-the-art electronics gear. And as Speed proudly showed him all the bells and whistles, the pilot began to sound less loony and more professional. "That's a Bendix color radar," he said, pointing out a display indicator attached to the complex instrument panel in the cockpit. "And a Ryan Stormscope that tracks lightning flashes. And this King radio navigator lets you go point-to-point instead of having to stick to the regular airways routes. Hell, we can go straight to—where's that place you want to go?"

"Dogwood Plantation, sixty miles southwest of New Orleans. Nearest town is called Raceland."

Speed led him from the Cessna to an office just inside the door to the hangar, where an old geezer in a dirty gray jumpsuit sat at a desk drinking coffee.

"Ever hear of Raceland, Louisiana, Julius?" Speed asked him.

"Got a hurricane down there," the geezer said. "We'll probably catch some rain because of it."

"What about Raceland?" Speed asked again.

The geezer reached up a hand to a shelf above the desk that contained several well-worn, leather-bound books. He picked one and tossed it to the pilot.

It contained air routes throughout Louisiana. Speed flipped through the pages until he found what he wanted. He held it up and winked at Starbuck. "No problem," he said. "There's a good-size landing strip in Houma, Louisiana. Can't be too far away from your Dogwood."

"Hurricane down there, Speed," old Julius said, squinting at them both. "You flying into a hurricane?"

Speed looked at Starbuck. "Are we? It'll give me a chance to use that Ryan Stormscope."

Starbuck looked at the old man. "Would you go?" he asked.

"No. But I'd send my wife and daughter."

"Let's give it a shot," Speed said. "Half-price deal. Six bills. Barely pay for my gas."

Starbuck was not a man to turn down a bargain.

The trip started out well enough. Then Speed began to rant about the DEA and how the few trips he'd made south of the border didn't necessarily have to have been drug runs, did they?

"But try telling that to the damned DEA. Those peckerwoods just want my plane. Simple as that."

No sooner had they crossed the Texas border than they encountered their first wind and rain. The Cessna did a little sideways dance into a cloud bank, blocking them from dawn's early light. Visibility zero. Starbuck gritted his teeth and, for perhaps the first time in thirty years, thought about prayer.

Then came the buck-and-wing. The loop-de-loop. The zig-zag.

Speed seemed to dote on every lurch. From time to time he'd laugh as if he'd just heard the punch line to a very funny joke. Then he'd get back to his DEA grousing.

Finally, he said, "Hold on now."

They seemed to be heading into a dark swirling mass. The little plane shook like a buckboard then was suddenly lifted and tossed off course.

"That all you can do, you bastard?" Speed shouted, wrestling with the controls. Every light on the panel seemed to be blinking out alarms. Buzzers sounded.

"What the hell's going on?" Starbuck shouted.

"We're doing battle."

"I can see that, dammit. Are we going down?"

"Good idea," Speed said calmly, and pushed down on the yoke.

The Cessna did an abrupt nosedive. Starbuck's Ben Franklin glasses flew from his nose and he grabbed them, jamming them into his coat pocket. Then the plane leveled off and sailed into a calm gray early morning.

They were too close to the ground, Starbuck thought. Almost hugging swampland. But the wind had stopped.

In the distance lightning flashed.

The sudden calm didn't do much to relax Starbuck. He sat petrified as Speed steered them between gnarled trees that protruded from the bayous like demon fingers.

"What happened to the hurricane?" Starbuck asked.

"It's still there. And we're here."

"Could you take us up a little? Above these trees."

"Hang loose," Speed told him. "This is my kind of flying. Low to the ground."

Avoiding radar, Starbuck thought. He didn't know much about the operation of the Drug Enforcement Agency, except that they'd once confiscated the stables of a guy he knew. The stable owner had sworn that they'd planted the drugs on his property, but as Starbuck understood full well, nobody was ever guilty of anything.

"I never did a goddamned evil thing in my life," Speed was saying. "They got no cause to hound me like—"

"How much further?" Starbuck interrupted.

"Minutes. Houma is coming up on our left. I'll take it down and you'll be on your way in minutes."

But the Houma landing strip seemed to be underwater and Speed was forced to pull up to avoid two trucks that were parked on the field, trying to drain it with huge suction pumps.

The wind began to gust again. The Cessna bucked against it and continued along through the trees. Speed's eyes flicked toward his air map. "Okay, then, we'll try this other place, Thigh-bo-ducks."

At the town of Thibodaux's Happy Landing Airfield, the strip was puddled but available. The Cessna wobbled going in for a landing and Starbuck stared through the rain-blurred window in horror as the ground seemed to rise up to smite them.

Then the little plane leveled off. The nosewheel hit the tarmac with barely a bump and they touched down as lightly as if they'd landed on a pillow. Starbuck looked at Speed in wonder. "Nothing to it, when you know how," the pilot said, grinning.

The metal Quonset hut that was used for a hangar was locked up. So was the adjoining office. Starbuck circled the whole building looking for some sign of humanity, but only got wind-lashed and rained on for his trouble. He flipped up the hood of the parka Choo-Choo had thoughtfully packed in his overnight bag and trudged back to find Speed filling up the plane's tanks.

"Somebody on duty?" he shouted above the rising wind, looking around.

"Hurricane scared 'em off," Speed shouted back. "It's a self-service pump."

The lock on the pump had been sheared. Speed looked sheepish. "State of emergency. When you need gas, you need gas."

"Right now what I need is a car," Starbuck bellowed.

Speed took a long look around the premises and shook his head.

"Then I'll have to walk."

"I'd try that way," Speed said, pointing in a vaguely southeastern direction. "But we have business first."

"Bill me," Starbuck told him.

Speed grinned and replaced the pump handle. "My business is strictly cash."

"I'm not carrying six hundred."

"How much do you have?"

Starbuck put down his sopping overnight bag and got out his wallet, trying to keep its contents dry and failing. "Maybe three hundred fifty," he said.

"It's a deal," Speed told him, taking the cash. "The gas is on me."

57

GRANNY, MIKE LEBLANC, and I were still in the barn when Hurricane Bruce hit us again with everything it had.

A dormer blew off and the wind gushed in. The whole structure shook. Planks began to pop out along one wall like piano keyboards in an animated cartoon. They wiggled in a wave, then fell back into place, loose, separated, more or less useless.

The great door to the barn was thrown open and Vetter rushed in. "Is he here?"

"Who?" Granny asked.

"Remy. Is Remy here?"

"Hell no," Granny replied. "I was wrong about him, too. Son of a gun don't care enough for his animals to come out here and help us. You could give the boy a hand. . . ."

But Vetter had other things on his mind. He turned and ran out the open door, toward the house. Outside, it was as gray as dusk, with an unhealthy yellow cast to the murk. But it was light enough for us to follow Vetter's progress. Twenty feet from the barn, the wind whipped his legs out from under him and he fell heavily on his side. Leaning into the wind, he somehow got to his feet. His forehead was bleeding where it had come in contact with a rock. As if toying with him, the wind paused and he nearly fell again. His knee touched the ground and for a second he froze there in a scrimmage position. But as the wind picked up he bolted forward.

This time the wind forced him toward the house and against it with a nasty cracking sound. It pinned him to the wood, maybe a foot off the ground, within arm's reach of the back door. It paused again, and he slid to the ground. He crawled to the door, shouldered it open, and stumbled into the house. As soon as he did, the wind whooshed and slammed the door behind him, mockingly.

The clouds opened a bit and the gloom lifted slightly. "That might be the end of it," Granny said.

I looked from the rippling wall to the agitated horses and hoped he was right.

"Let's give it a few minutes more," he said. "Just to make sure it's history and not just foolin' with us."

I nodded, wondering if my voice would quake if I tried to speak.

"This your first hurricane?" Mike LeBlanc asked me.

"And, I hope, my last." It didn't quake, but I didn't exactly recognize it.

"They're part of life in Louisiana," he said, not exactly calm himself, but more relaxed than I, certainly. "I've been through four of them. Our house got blown down once. This was while my daddy and mama were still alive."

It was the most I'd ever heard him say. I supposed it was the tension we were under. "They went in a fire," he continued. "My daddy liked his pipe and his jug and he fell asleep with the pipe still going. He did it a lot, but that time it caught. I had a room to the front of the house, so I was able to get free of the flames. But the folks weren't so lucky. Or my little sister. I sure miss 'em."

"When was this?"

He frowned. "I'm not sure of the exact year. A while back."

"You must've been pretty young to be on your own."

"Oh, heck. I wasn't alone. I went to live with my uncle Boudreaux, who works at Trahan Stables in Beaumont, Texas, where they train Thoroughbreds."

"That's where I first saw the lad, Coley," Granny said. "Harrowing and watering the training track and mucking out the stalls. You were what, fifteen?"

"Fourteen," Mike answered. "I was real young then. And now, just three years later, I'm . . ." He'd started to make a gesture with his right hand. He winced in pain and lifted the ragged hand to his lips. He began to blow on the wounds.

Granny went to him, grabbed the hand roughly, and moved it to study it by the light of the open door. "That looks downright gruesome. Gotta make sure it don't get infected."

"I'll look after it. It's not so bad, but it sure as heck stings."

"You were saying something about being three years older," I prompted him.

"Yeah. Just three years and I'm an adult now, I guess," he said ingenuously. "I may even go to England to race this fall."

"Not very likely," Granny told him. "Remy's got enough work for you right here in the States."

Mike grinned. "Well, that'd be okay, too. But I sure would like to see what those British jockeys are all about."

Suddenly, a damp, warm breeze washed over our faces. Granny looked up and said, "Aw, hell. It was just playin' possum. Savin' the worst for last."

I turned to see the top lift off the barn as easily as if a giant hand were removing it.

The rafters began to vibrate. With a yell, Granny rushed down the row of stabled horses, throwing open the gates.

Above us, the loft and its load of hay began to sway.

Frantically, we tried to shoo the horses from their stalls and out of the barn.

The wind whooshed in from above, blowing out the already weakened wall. I shouted to Granny, "Get out of here. It's going."

"There's 'nother animal back there."

I grabbed his arm and yanked him toward the door. He swung on me in a fury, but the hay-heavy loft toppled over, spooking the last horse from its stall. All of us, men and horses, got the hell out of there just as the entire barn gave up with a mighty groan and surrendered to the hurricane.

Some horses raced off into the trees. Others began to circle the destroyed barn, confused and frightened. Granny and Mike stopped to stare at them. Me, I ran full out for the main house.

58

THERE DIDN'T SEEM to be anyone at home. Not in the kitchen, which had been scavenged, the dry-goods cabinet doors hanging open on naked shelves, the fridge equally empty. Not in the hall, where the generator was barely keeping a dim bulb flickering. Not in the dining room, or parlor, or the den, which appeared to have been a temporary hangout, at least until the windows shattered in, one dragging a blanket, the other tumbling a pool table to the wet, stained carpet.

Lightning flashed outside the window. The air in the den was thick and humid, but so strangely electric, the wet hairs on the back of my neck started to crawl. I backtracked to the hall and called out, "Where is everybody?"

Granny shouted back, "They're down here."

He and Mike were on the stairs that descended to the faux basement.

The others had used sheets and towels to keep the water from the center of the basement, where they sat on pillows and cushions from the upstairs rooms. Both Vetter and Richard featured bandages on their noggins. Roberta Courville's left arm was wrapped in gauze, through which a circle of blood was seeping. The weasel, in obvious pain, had removed his left shoe, exposing several toes that looked pretty well mashed. Neither Joan Courville nor the thin Paul Felix seemed to be much the worse for wear, except that their clothes were stained and torn.

Mike moved to Joan and told her how happy he was that she was unharmed.

Lea, who had gathered her hair in a ponytail, secured with a red kerchief, hopped from her cushion and greeted me with a very nice hug that I hoped was genuine and not just more of her role play. She told me of her unsuccessful attempts to find the storm windows.

Luckily, she had placed no faith in either blankets or pool table and had found a spot in the hall rather than in the game room when the storm struck the hardest. Roberta had been cut by flying glass, the weasel's foot had been in the way when the pool table tumbled.

"How do you stand with Ricardo?" I whispered.

"I haven't turned my back on him," she said, sotto voce.

"A safe rule to keep in any case," I said.

She had been the one who organized the food patrol. Gallon jugs of water had been stored in the security office, as far from the windows as possible.

"Some perishable goods, like milk and cheese and eggs, and a lovely piece of beef that we may have to figure out some way to roast are being stored in a mini-fridge I found in the horse reproduction cubicle. It was being used to store semen samples."

"I hope you didn't throw them away?"

She looked stricken. "Oh, Lord, were they important?"

"Probably," I said, smiling. "But not as important as our having food. I was just being larky."

"I'm too tired to find that obnoxious."

I spotted Vetter swigging from a Rémy Martin bottle and said, looking around the room, "That reminds me. Where's our host?"

"I haven't seen him. Wasn't he with you in the barn?"

"Un-uh," I said. I addressed the crowd. "Has anyone seen Remy?"

Vetter glared at me. The others looked at me blankly.

Vetter said, "He split. Probably in New Orleans by now."

"Not unless he walked," Travers Jr. said, wincing at his pain. "The cars are still here."

"My husband is probably inebriated and sleeping through all this like a baby," Joan Courville said, a bit shakily. "It would be just like him."

I turned and started for the stairs.

"Where are you going?" Lea asked.

"To see if I can find Remy. Maybe he's hurt."

"I'll come with you."

"So will I," Felix said. "Give me a chance to stretch my legs."

The house had not grown any cheerier. The hall light had gone out and the darkness was eerie. Then there were the creaking walls, the sudden shake every time the wind hit the building.

We went through the downstairs, looking behind sofas and under tables. We were about to climb the stairs when Paul Felix said, "Just a minute."

We looked at him. A man in his mid to late sixties. Wiry, but not exactly an imposing figure. And yet there was something about his crooning voice, the tranquil European face, and the cold blue eyes that commanded your attention. "I don't know who you two are, or why you felt it necessary to hurt Richard. He and I have a job to do, and hurricanes, floods, whatever, we'll do it. We have absolutely no business with you. Richard is upset. His head hurts. He thinks he may have a concussion, though I think not. Even so, we bear you no malice. We have no interest in any sort of payback. We are only interested in doing our job and going home to our families."

"And your job is what?" I asked.

He hesitated, then said, "That would be up to Miss Dorn and Mr. Vetter."

"Last night Richard was about to enter their room with a gun in his hand," Lea said.

He nodded. "And this is why you knocked him out."

She said it was.

"An understandable reaction, which is why we harbor no ill

feelings. We were a bit curious as to why you put him into a closet instead of turning him over to the security guards. But it was to our benefit that you did. I reiterate—we are not interested in why you are here. We just want you to let us do our job and we will of course let you do yours."

"Suppose our jobs conflict?" I asked.

"Do you think they will?"

When I didn't answer, he said, "I'm glad we had this little chat." He turned from us and walked toward the rear stairs.

"What do you think?" Lea asked.

The whole house began to shake. "I think we'll think about it later," I said. "Let's check upstairs while there still is an upstairs."

The master bedroom was in turmoil. French doors had blown in, scattering glass and broken wood all over the carpet. Past the doors I could see that the balcony was covered with broken pots and mud slush.

Bed linens trailed across the floor to the door. Pillows had been tossed. The mattress was half off of the frame, pinning down a pair of men's shoes. The black socks that had been tucked neatly into them had not been disturbed.

A dresser had tumbled, spilling several of its drawers, the contents of which were draped on overturned chairs and a dressing table with a cracked mirror. A woman's robe was caught between the dressing table and the wall.

"He's here," Lea said flatly behind me.

She was standing in Remy's room across the hall. Unlike his wife's suite, his bedroom hadn't suffered much from the hurricane. One of the windows was cracked. It looked as if it had been slammed, catching a thick-weave curtain, the tail of which fluttered in the breeze like a tattered flag.

I looked at that first, though I was conscious of the man on the floor near the bed. The bed hadn't been slept in. The upper part of Remy's body was leaning against it, hanging from one of the foot posts. His hands were pressed together under his chin, the bandaged thumb resting against the chin. His pants were around his knees.

Lea remained just inside the door. I moved closer.

He was dead, all right. His eyes were open and bulging, staring in surprise at the rattling window across the room but not really seeing it. The gold chain that held the key to his concrete bank was caught on the bed's short foot post. Part of the chain was embedded in Remy's neck, just above the crisp white collar of his shirt. Blood had flowed, but not a lot of it. It spotted the bandaged thumb and spilled down the front of his shirt, but the back of his collar was dry and pristine.

His shoeless feet were tangled in a throw rug. The dark suede loafers he'd been wearing were in the middle of the room.

Lea seemed both fascinated and repulsed by the body.

It looked as if Remy had started undressing for bed. But in his drunken stupor, he'd tripped, caught his chain on the bedpost and panicked, garroting himself.

Lea pointed to the dead man's feet. "He tried to stand, to free himself, but the pants and the rug must've kept him off balance. God, how horrible."

I reached out and patted the corpse's dry, lank hair, then touched the lifeless shoulders. "We'd better get downstairs," I told her.

She hesitated. "Isn't there something we should do?"

"Nothing that'll matter to him," I replied.

59

THOUGH THE LANDING field at Thibodaux was just thirty miles or so from Dogwood Plantation, for Starbuck they were a rough thirty miles.

Eleven of them were eaten up in a '58 Ford tow truck operated by a guy named Lew and his elder brother Charlie, two good old boys who, though operating on low candle power, were big-hearted enough to let him ride in the back, on the truck's rear guardrail, one arm wrapped around a winch boom, getting rained on from above and splashed from below. All they asked in return was twenty dollars, which he didn't have. So they settled for the leather overnight bag and some of its contents—a white pima cotton shirt, argyle socks, and a pair of Ferragamo all-weather shoes. They let him keep his Dopp kit and his one set of boxer shorts.

They deposited him on a shoulder of highway 1 and went off along a nearly washed-out macadam in search of people in distress who were carrying cash. Starbuck used his fresh boxers to mop his face. Then he unzipped his Dopp and removed his Nova 9mm pistol and his electric shaver. He tossed the kit away, slipped the razor into the left pocket of his parka and the pistol into his right. Then he started walking south on highway 1.

The wind had just picked up again when a frazzled family in a rec vehicle took pity on him and carried him another twelve miles. They were from Arkansas—a husband, wife, her teenage sister, and their two toddlers, a boy and a girl. The kids were crying, the sister was having a fit. Judging from the wife's nonstop harangue, it had been her husband's idea to visit Cajun country. She and "the kids" wanted Disney World, which had not only escaped the storm but would have been "a whole lot more fun than looking at a bunch of fat old guys sitting around a stewpot with a raccoon in it. And now, even if we escape this swampland without drowning to death or getting eaten by crocodiles or rats—" The sister let out a scream that could have been heard at Disney World.

"Calm down now, baby sis," the matriarch went on. "If Eldon's good at anything, which I doubt, it's driving this here camper. He'll get us through if the Lord wants us to get through."

Eldon, who'd no doubt been listening to his wife's incessant voice since the family left Arkadelphia, kept his mind and his eyes on the road. Suddenly, he leaned forward and wiped some moisture from the windshield. Then he slammed on the brakes.

His wife looked at him with terror in her eyes. "What is it, man?"

"Road going off to the right. Got a sign to it. Says 'Dogwood.' Isn't that the place you're heading for?" he asked Starbuck.

"I believe it is. Thanks for the lift."

Starbuck opened the rear door and started to hop out. Just then a huge nutria scurried past and the wife shouted. "Ohmygawd, you're not going out there with critters like that on the loose?" she wailed.

"Just think of it as nature's own Disney World," Starbuck told her.

60

REMY'S SISTER, ROBERTA, took the news of his death harder than anyone else in the basement. Joan Courville's head dropped and she stared at the floor, which was an appropriate gesture, if not an especially dramatic one. His business partners had other things on their minds. Travers Jr. was under a blanket, shivering and moaning, the pain from his foot evidently intensifying. Vetter, puzzled, squinted out the window at the hurricane as if by using willpower, he might quiet it.

Roberta rose, teary-eyed, from the floor and started toward the stairs, but Granny grabbed her. "You really don't want to see him," I told her.

She placed her head against Granny's chest and began to weep. Then she tore away from him and raced to the stairs. Lea and I followed.

The three of us were on the main stairwell when the roof of the house blew off. Unlike the barn, which had lifted off in almost slow-motion, this happened like a bolt.

There was a ferocious crack followed by the roar of the wind as it filled the attic. Then plaster rained down on us and a hole appeared in the ceiling. More plaster fell, and through the hole we could see the angry dark sky. I took one of Roberta's arms and Lea took the other and we more or less dragged her back to the kitchen. Plaster had fallen from that ceiling, too, making a mess of the stove and sink.

As we scurried down the stairs the others looked at us expectantly and fearfully. Even Paul Felix was showing signs of agitation. "What was that?" he asked.

"The roof heading for New Orleans," I said.

"Dammit," he snapped. "This *is* serious."

The lights went off.

"There goes the generator," Lea said.

Francie stood up, her face twisted in anger. "This shit must stop," she snarled.

Lea moved toward her. "If we can just—" she began.

But Francie wasn't in a mood to be comforted.

"You get away from me, you bitch," she yelled. She turned to Vetter. "She was sent here to kill us. You know damn well she was."

"Calm down, baby," he said.

That just made her more manic. "Her name is Starbuck and she and her old man have been trying to get me for years. Ask Coley, he knows."

Vetter stared at me. I shrugged. "I don't have any idea what she's talking about."

Francie's lower lip began to tremble. "Oh, God, he's in on it, too. I should have realized."

"Calm down now," Vetter said.

Francie tucked her chin to her chest and said, "It's gone sour. It's gone to . . ."

She paused and all color left her face. One of her hands went out to clutch the air. She was staring past us. "I knew it," she said. "I goddamned knew it."

We all turned to see what she was talking about.

Starbuck had just stepped through the back doorway.

61

"I KNOCKED AT the front but there was nobody—" he began.

"It's him," Francie screeched.

Starbuck looked at her, then took in the rest of us. He seemed to relax a bit when he saw Lea.

"Nice timing," I told him. "Just dropped in for the hurricane?"

"Who the hell are you?" Vetter asked.

"It's him," Francie yelled. "Starbuck. The bastard who's been hounding me. He spotted me last year with Romeo, Mark. Now he's working for him. He and his bitch are here because Romeo wants us both dead."

I turned to Felix, who was observing Francie with an amused smile. Richard's mouth was hanging open.

"Romeo's out of it," Vetter told Francie. "He wouldn't send anybody after us."

"Yeah, sure," she said sneeringly. "We walk away with nearly a hundred large of his mad money and he just smiles and says, 'Good work.' Does that sound like Romeo?"

"Shut your goddamn mouth," Vetter told her through clenched teeth.

"They're gonna kill us if we stay here."

Vetter slapped her hard. "Pull yourself together," he commanded.

Francie was momentarily stunned. Then she said, "If Remy's dead, they damn well killed him."

"Courville's dead?" Starbuck asked.

Vetter ignored the question. "Well?" he asked Lea.

"Nobody killed Remy," she answered. "He tripped and was strangled by his neck chain. Go upstairs and see, if you don't believe me."

The house shimmied suddenly. "Forget it," Vetter said. "I'm getting out now before this death trap caves." He asked Francie, "You coming?"

"Hell, yes," she replied.

Felix nodded to Richard, who pulled a gun from under his shirt. He aimed it in the direction of Francie and Vetter. Starbuck couldn't believe his eyes.

Felix said, "You had the right idea, Francie, but the wrong party."

"Wait a minute, now. . . ." Vetter protested. "You're not telling me my father . . ."

"It's your aunt," Felix said. "I got the impression she's not very happy with you and your girlfriend."

Vetter took a backward step. Richard swung the gun toward him.

Without a second's hesitation, Francie's arm shot out toward the person nearest her, Lea. She pushed Lea into Richard and raced for the exit.

Lea twisted, bounced Richard to the floor, and used the momentum to regain her balance. Then she turned and raced through the door after Francie.

With a snarl, Richard awkwardly got to his feet and started for the exit himself. Starbuck kicked Richard's left knee as he ran past and sent him sprawling.

Vetter seized the opportunity and beat it out of the house. Starbuck followed, tugging at the pocket of his parka. I started after them, but Richard grabbed my legs. I rolled and punched him in his bandage. He yelled. I punched him again. I knew that Felix had to be dangerously near, but I couldn't look for him just then.

A hand covered my face and eyes and I was pulled back off of Richard. Something solid connected with the back of my head.

Felix stepped around me, dropping his cognac-bottle weapon to the floor. "It's the redhead and Vetter we want," I heard him tell Richard. "Move it."

I tried to grab their feet, but my hands weren't going where I aimed them. I heard Granny call my name. I wasn't unconscious, just woozy. I pushed myself upright and tried to get my legs under me.

The wind peeked in the back door, laughed at us, then ran around the house. There was the sound of a shot. "Lea," I cried as Granny helped me up. A car door slammed. An engine kicked over.

I staggered to the steps. Dizzy, very dizzy.

More car doors slamming. Another engine starting.

I made it through the door.

The wind, though not at full force, was still strong enough to send the stinging rain into my face. The tree that had been blocking the drive was now resting against the house. The body of Johnson the security guard was gone, carried to some other part of the swamp by the wind.

My rental car was tearing away toward the highway, followed by Felix and Richard's Caddy. Starbuck was kneeling on the ground, one arm straight out in front of him, aiming a small pistol at the fleeing cars.

I blinked. Francie was in the passenger seat of the rental. Lea was driving! She hadn't been shot! But if not her or Starbuck . . . ?

A moan came from beside the house.

Vetter lay on the ground. "Help me," he cried. Blood was seeping through his jacket near his left shoulder. I gave him a quick glance and decided that Lea needed me more.

There were only three cars left. The wind had turned two on their sides. The third, a Mercedes, had had its front end smashed by a tree. Starbuck and I spotted it at the same time. I got to it first.

A key was in the ignition. As the big man leapt into the passenger seat, I twisted the key. Nothing. Not even the flutter of a battery.

Frustrated, I stared through the windshield at the now darkened road. "That's my daughter driving away with your goddamned Francie Dorn," Starbuck growled. "You really screwed this one up, Killebrew."

"Me? You're the one pushed Francie over the edge."

He glared at me and I saw a flicker of pain pass his face. Then he asked, "Will your Francie let her go?"

I didn't think so. I said, "You told me yourself that Lea was resourceful. She's bright and fast and strong. She can handle Francie."

"She better," he said. "It's a cinch she's not gonna get much help from this useless pair."

I got out of the car and went to see about Vetter. Granny and Mike LeBlanc were moving cautiously through the rain toward us.

Vetter tried to get up, but the pain was too much. I edged him into a sitting position. He was as wet as an eel. With Mike's help, I got him all the way up. Starbuck watched us silently, his hands in the pocket of his parka.

"Did Francie get away?" Vetter asked me.

"She usually does," I told him.

"You know her, huh?"

"Not as well as I thought."

"She'll kill the blonde," he said.

Starbuck stepped forward. "Maybe not," he growled. "She doesn't have a weapon, does she?"

"Who do you think shot *me*?" Vetter asked.

Before we could get back inside the house, the whole building began to shake violently. I left Vetter to lean on Granny and Starbuck and raced back into the building, Mike at my heels.

Joan Courville was helping her wounded sister-in-law to the exit. Travers, the weasel, hopped on his good foot and cried, "Help. I can't walk."

I took one arm, Mike the other and we carried him to the door.

"Outside. Must get out," Travers yelled in my ear. I wished we could have left him. He continued to shout high-pitched orders to us as we edged him up the stairs, and I to this day don't know if I banged his foot against a stair on purpose or by accident.

The others were waiting for us in the rain. Roberta seemed to be dizzy from loss of blood. Remy's widow showed no emotion at all. When another lightning bolt shot through the dark sky, she didn't even blink.

"Can you guys handle Vetter by yourself?" I asked Granny and Starbuck.

"Sure," Starbuck replied. "Nothing wrong with his legs."

"Where we headed?" the old man asked.

"Follow us," I said.

As we moved away from the main house we could see that of all the smaller cottages, only Granny's was still standing. At a distance it appeared as if it had been totally ignored by the storm. But as we neared, it simply folded over and flattened with a whoosh and a clatter. Granny shouted, "You bloody bastard," and waved a fist at the weather.

There were three or four inches of water covering the ground. And the wind splattered us with it as we trudged along. Travers Jr. was getting more annoying by the yard. "It throbs. Lift me higher," he ordered. "My feet are getting wet."

"Stop whining, buddy," Starbuck commanded. "The situation's lousy enough without having to listen to you bellyache."

"Who is this obnoxious lout?" Travers wanted to know.

Starbuck reached out an arm and plinked Travers's nose with his index finger.

Travers screamed in pain. I chuckled.

Behind us, the old house groaned.

I turned my head and saw it listing to the right. Then planking began to splinter outward, popping like an assault rifle. The spine shifted and the whole two-story structure sank downward into the basement, settling among the scattered red brick foundation. It reminded me of a movie pirate ship, sinking beneath the sea.

"The fastest demolition job I ever saw," Starbuck said.

"Dammit and what the hell, Coley," Granny spat. "Where's this place you're takin' us to?"

"Not far now," I told him, wondering if the silent Vetter had figured out our destination.

Travers the weasel was whimpering and we were all at low ebb as the bunker came into view. And then we were inside the squat edifice, unloading our human baggage. Vetter slumped in the swivel chair, his face twisted in pain. The weasel was perched on the edge of the desk. Roberta slid to the damp floor at its driest spot and leaned against a wall.

The others reacted to the small space with some curiosity. Their main concern was, quite rightly, its stability. And that seemed to be satisfactory. The only visible effect of the hurricane's might was that the place had been swept clean except for a couple of empty money boxes and a scattering of wet fifties and hundreds wedged into crevices or caught beneath the legs of the solid oak desk and the filing cabinet.

The desk had been tossed against a wall, but it was a sturdy piece of workmanship. The filing cabinet's drawers had sprung out and many of the files had blown away.

I looked at the open doorway and said to Mike, "Let's put Travers on the floor."

"The floor," Travers wailed. "It's wet and cold on the floor. My foot will get infected."

"We'll just have to risk it," I said, and we deposited him next to his girlfriend Roberta. Then we turned the desk on its side and used it to block most of the gaping door. It wasn't a perfect fit, but it would have to do.

We were a cozy crowd, sweating and breathing hard in the airless gloom. Vetter glared at the empty money boxes. Roberta cuddled the weasel and was snapped at for her efforts. Granny sat silently, lost in his thoughts. Joan Courville leaned against a wall, mumbling to herself and ignoring Mike LeBlanc, who stood beside her, not knowing quite what to do with his hands.

"Why don't you fill me in, Killebrew," Starbuck said.

"Who *are* you?" Roberta asked him.

"Killebrew's boss."

"That's not precisely correct," I said.

"Boss of what?" Roberta went on. "What are you people up to?"

I couldn't think of a simple answer that would have satisfied her. Starbuck said, "I don't know what I'm doing in this god-damned box. I didn't travel two thousand miles to sit around while my daughter . . ."

Suddenly, Joan began crying. "It's not fair. I've lost it all."

"Now, Miz Courville," Granny said, "I realize things look rough, but—"

"It's all gone, you old fool," she screamed. "Don't you realize that?"

"Aw, Miz Courville, don't upset yourself so." He thought she was talking about the house and the horses and, since Granny was a genuine romantic, maybe even her husband. But Joan Courville's next move disabused him of that idea.

She took a deep breath and pasted a smile on her face. She turned to Vetter and asked in her best gentle Southern accent, "Do you know where the money is, Mark?"

Starbuck stared at her as if she'd sprouted another head. Then he must have recalled our telephone conversation about the bunker full of cash, because he replaced his puzzled look with one of serious thought.

Vetter's reply to Joan Courville was unequivocal. "I thought it was still here. Maybe the thief who broke in the other night came back."

"Maybe," she said, and turned to me, the guy who'd led them to the bunker. "Was he someone working with you, Mr. Killebrew? Like this rude man." She indicated Starbuck.

I didn't reply.

"Maybe Remy was in on it, too. Were you and Remy planning on cheating us?"

"Remy and I weren't doing anything together," I said.

"But you know where the money is?"

"Yes," I said. That got everyone's attention, even Starbuck's.

"Will you tell me?" Joan Courville was almost batting her eyes.

"Sure."

"Well?" she asked, still smiling sweetly.

"It's *Gone With the Wind, Part Three*."

The smile disappeared. "Don't play with me."

"I'm not playing. The hurricane blew it all over the swamp."

She frowned, not quite believing me. I added, "Since you know about the money, I suppose you were part of the operation."

Joan's eyes darted to Vetter, who tried to avoid them.

"What operation?" Roberta Courville demanded from the floor.

"The money-laundering operation being run by your brother and these gents." I pointed a thumb at Vetter and Travers.

Roberta scowled. "You'd better explain that."

"Sure," I told her. "You find yourself with more money than you want the government to know about. It could come from drugs, prostitution, illegal gambling, numbers, whatever. There was once a time, in the law-enforcement Dark Ages, when you could smuggle excess loot out of the country to a bank in Switzerland or the Bahamas or the Caymans where nobody ever bothered to ask where it came from.

"But today's watchdogs know that trick. So a new plan was devised—an easier, hassle-free plan. You simply pay people—like your brother—to turn black money into ready green."

Starbuck was staring at me. Not smiling, not frowning. Maybe his mind was on Lea.

"Remy was involved in this *scheme*?" His sister couldn't believe it. "He's never had any head for money."

"Then maybe Joan was the financial expert, or his old Harvard roomie."

Neither of them seemed inclined to deny the charge or accept it.

I shrugged. "According to files I found in this very office," I said, "Remy and Vetter would take their client's ill-gotten loot and hand it over to their banker buddy, Travers Junior. He would then wire it to a bank in the Caymans, crediting it to the account of Southern Boy Supplies, a company that originally owned a few vans and a couple of uniforms and did little more than transport currency across state lines.

"Once it was safely deposited, the original owner of the money 'borrowed' it back from Southern Boy in the form of a loan. The interest on the loan was, in fact, the payment for laundering the bad cash."

"That's absurd," Norell Travers snapped back. "How long could a bank continue to wire large sums out of the country before the IRS or the FBI would come snooping around?"

"Not forever," I agreed. "So one of you got a better idea. Remy was a self-professed sportsman with a stable full of horses. What would be more natural than for him to buy a racetrack? So Southern Boy expanded its activities a little. The company purchased Magnolia Park. Racetracks run almost entirely on cash. Cash in, cash out. They're perfect clearinghouses for bad money."

"How?" Granny asked.

"Let me give you an example. A wiseguy like Jerry the Hat Hinano, a Miami pimp turned crack meister, has two million bucks he can't explain. Remy and Vetter and Junior add the money to the cash on hand at their track. They do a little midnight work on a totalizator ticket machine and provide the Hat with enough winning tickets over a period of a month for him to collect ninety percent of his original stash. Then the IRS takes its cut and the Hat winds up with somewhere near sixty cents on the dollar as legitimate income. The taxes and the Southern Boy cut are small enough prices to pay, since the Hat's rackets bring in more than any minor country can spend."

Roberta faced Joan. "You knew Remy was involved in this?"

Joan Courville didn't reply. Instead, she took a deep breath and looked imploringly at Mike LeBlanc. The boy, who had been waiting all his life for that look, rushed to her. He was rewarded by Joan's body slumping against his.

"I asked you a question," Roberta said to her.

"Leave her alone," Mike ordered. "Can't you see she's worn out?"

"Not only did she know," I told Roberta, "it's my guess she killed Remy for his share."

"Are you insane?" Joan Courville spit out. "You said yourself that Remy died by accident."

"I don't think I did," I replied. "I certainly never believed it."

Joan waved a hand in front of her face as if to dismiss the idea and me along with it. "How in the world could I have done such a thing?"

"By proxy," I explained. "You convinced young Mike that Remy really needed dying if you two were to be happy ever after. In some storybook country, perhaps, like Merry Olde England."

The boy moved closer to Joan, trying to draw courage from her.

"Excuse me for buttin' in, Coley," Granny said, "but Mike was with us in the stable."

"Think back, Granny. When was the last time you saw Remy alive, the last time any of us did? He wasn't around when the storm hit, or when we were in its eye, trying to get things secured. By then, he was already history.

"I don't know much about rigor mortis, but he was turning a little stiff when we found him. I imagine Mike strangled him late last night, or early this morning, before the storm really hit. That's why Remy's hair and clothes were dry when I found him. He hadn't been out in any weather, and he would have if he'd been breathing. His home and horses and money were being threatened."

Granny gave Mike a pained look. "What you got to say, son?"

Mike deferred to Joan Courville, who blessed him with her special smile.

I said, "There are bits of torn flesh under Remy's fingernails. When he was being strangled, he clawed at the hand of his killer. Look at the back of Mike's hand."

Mike dropped his hand from Joan's shoulder and slipped it into his pants pocket.

"He was trying to hurt her, Granny," Mike stammered. "He was attacking her—"

"Shut up," Joan shouted at him. "Don't say another word."

The rest of us stared at the boy as he took a backward step. "Then what *do* I do?" he asked Joan.

"Come on," Joan told him. "Let's take our chances outside."

"She set you up, kid," I told him. "She stayed with Remy of her own free will. She may have hated him, but she loved his money. The abuse was part of the package."

"Let's go. Now!" Joan ordered.

"She talked you into taking Remy's life," I said. "He wasn't much of a human being. It looks like he went along with some murders in Los Angeles. But that doesn't give the average citizen the right to administer the death penalty."

"You're certain he ordered the hits in L.A.?" Starbuck asked.

"And I know who did the job," I told him.

"Let's go," Joan ordered the boy. "I'll not stay with these horrible people another minute. Push the desk away from the door."

"Yes, ma'am," Mike replied obediently. He edged the heavy piece of furniture easily. As Remy had learned the hard way, jocks have a lot of strength for their size. Then Mike stepped back and allowed Joan Courville to exit before him. At the door he paused and turned to Granny. "I'm sorry if you think I'm letting you down, sir. But when you got love for someone—"

"Son," Granny got out, "please don't. . . ."

"He was a mean man, sir. He made me feel low after the race. And he made Joan feel low all the time. I'm glad he's dead. And I'm glad I did it."

"Hurry, Mike," his big romance called to him. "It's still raining, dammit."

The boy followed her out into the wind and darkness.

62

"YOU'RE JUST GONNA let 'em run?" Granny asked me indignantly.

"Who do I look like, the cop on the beat?" I asked. Starbuck snickered.

"Then I'll go," the old man said. "They'll take off and be long gone—"

"None of the cars work," I said. "If they did, I'd have gone after Lea. Joan and the kid won't get far on foot."

He gave me a disappointed look and turned to climb creakily over the desk. I waited until he stumbled into the dampness to follow him. "What's the point?" I asked, getting a face full of wet leaves. Starbuck was moving up behind me.

Granny said, "I wasn't put on this earth to sit back while a pair of killers just stroll off into the goddamn sunset."

"Sunset? Look at the sky. Does that look like sunset?"

"You know what I mean," he replied gruffly, and headed toward the road.

With a sigh, I zipped up my jacket and joined him. Starbuck, uncharacteristically silent, was at my side. The wind was somewhere between brisk and blustery. The storm seemed to be wearing itself down.

As we approached the vicinity where the house once stood, I

saw two figures disappearing into the murk. Joan and Mike were not on foot.

"That don't surprise me none," Granny said. "They both know what to do on the back of a horse."

"Where the hell did the animals come from?" Starbuck asked. I looked around. All I could see was desolation. Nothing four-footed.

"Horses know how to roll with nature's punches better'n humans," Granny told us. He paused and cocked his head, like a dog hearing his master's voice. "Listen."

I listened. What I heard was a whinny. That was followed by a horse prancing into view. It was Cajun Desire, the Thoroughbred that Remy had hoped would win the Dixie Derby. He pranced near the collapsed barn, his perfect chestnut body brightening the gloom. I don't know where he'd spent the last couple of hours, but it hadn't been dodging trees and lightning bolts.

He stood there, head held high, as if waiting for the barn to rise up from its own rubble.

"He's all yours, Coley," Granny said, grinning.

"The hell he is," Starbuck replied. "I need him to find my daughter."

He started toward the horse. I ran after him. The big man paused a few feet from Cajun Desire. "Starbuck," I said. He turned and I did something I'd been wanting to do for seven years. I hit him in the jaw with all the strength I possessed.

My hand felt like I'd broken it, but he went down hard and stayed there.

I looked at Cajun Desire. He ignored me. Keeping my eyes on him, I asked Granny, "Think you can find me a saddle in all that debris?"

"Can't you ride him bareback?"

"I don't know if I can ride him at all. I haven't been on a horse in seven years. And I never was in the goddamned circus."

I moved closer to the animal, talking to him in a calm, steady voice. "Okay, Cajun Desire, this wind's heading on and the bad stuff is over. . . . Now it's just a matter of you and me coming to an understanding."

The chestnut looked at me suspiciously. I couldn't blame him. "It's going to be fine, old boy. You're young and powerful and I'm over the hill and smart enough not to get either of us in trouble. We'll make a great team."

His whinny sounded sarcastic.

I moved closer and he didn't back away. "There's something I've got to do and I need your help." My right hand was still throbbing from its contact with Starbuck's jaw. I moved it out to the horse slowly and patted his neck. "You're a damned handsome boy," I told him, almost whispering now. "Granny has been taking good care of you. Neither of us is going to let him down, now, are we?"

A nearby tree keeled over with a crash and the horse reared up and pulled away. From the corner of my eye I could see Granny approaching with the gear.

"C'mon, old boy," I said, "You're not afraid of a dumb tree, are you?"

I reached my arm behind me and Granny passed me the bridle. My right hand was still too tender, so I took it with my left, bringing it to the animal. Slowly, confidently, I worked the bit between his teeth, looping the rein into place. Then we were both prepping him, Granny and I.

When we were finished, I stepped back and looked at him. "You gonna take a picture of him," Granny grumped, "or are you gonna ride him? Mike and Joan got a big head start."

I didn't give a damn about Mike and Joan. Starbuck and I were similarly motivated. I was going after Lea, not the lethal lovers. But let Granny think what he might.

"Well, you gonna get on him, or shall I?" he said.

"I'll ride him," I answered, annoyed. "Give me a minute."

For years, I'd mounted horses without a second's thought. It had been the most natural thing in the world. But there was nothing natural about it now. I didn't feel totally right about it and I knew that Cajun Desire would suss that out in a second. But I had to try to find Lea.

So I fell back on something I hadn't used since my novice days. I convinced myself that I was somebody else—somebody cocky and unafraid, who actually liked being thrown because it showed the other jocks that I could take it.

With a grim smile, I nodded to Granny. He bent and locked his fingers to boost me to the stirrup iron. It was a sensation both strange and familiar, being on a horse again. It brought back memories, good and bad, moments of elation, moments of defeat and pain.

Starbuck moaned from the ground.

Without thinking, I leaned forward until I was almost kissing Cajun Desire's mane. "All right, boy," I purred. "Let's see how we get along." I gave him a little jab with my heel and we were on our way.

Starbuck shouted my name and it echoed on the wind. I liked the way it sounded. He was standing back in the rain, madder than hell, and I was hanging on to a galloping animal weighing one thousand pounds, riding in darkness through a hurricane. And loving every minute of it.

The road was wet and muddy. Fallen trees and dead animals slowed our progress, but Cajun Desire was an intelligent, graceful beast. And it wasn't very long before I spotted the lights of a car in the distance.

We approached cautiously. A sedan had gone off the road into a deep ditch. I reined in the horse before the vehicle's occupants could see us.

I didn't have to get too close to know who they were. The angry voice of Richard the mouth breather carried through the dark. "Dammit! I can't *believe* we let that bitch get away from us."

"You drove us into the ditch, Richard," Felix said patiently, "not her."

"I hit their rear tire," Richard said. "They can't go much further on a flat."

"They can go miles on a flat, Richard. They're gone. The question now is—do we continue to sit here, or do we go looking for a way back to civilization."

"Holy hell!" Richard screamed. "Is that a goddamned croco-
dile?"

"This is the swamp, Richard. Perhaps we should get back into
the car and wait for rescue. Joey Lunchbox should be along any
minute to see how well we've performed our task. Maybe he'll
give us a lift home."

"Dammit!" Richard shouted again.

It was an amusing tableau, but I'd heard enough of it. I edged
Cajun Desire away from them and the other critters of the
swamp. With the assassins out of the way, all that Lea had to
worry about was Francie Dorn and a flat tire. I gave the horse a
gentle prod to move him faster.

63

WE PASSED DESTROYED mansions and flattened shacks
and overturned automobiles. Grounded dreams. A few
brave souls had left their cover to inspect the damage and they
weren't happy with what they saw. They stared at us with curiosity as we rode by, but their own problems were too oppressive
for them to give much thought to a solitary horseman who wasn't
wearing a black-hooded cape and carrying a scythe.

I stopped Cajun Desire near an ancient black man in a slicker
who was standing by the road facing skyward. His eyes had a
milky look. "Bad zen zen," he said, mainly to himself.

I asked if he'd seen any cars heading north. "While ago car
pass. Back window missin'. Tire goin' flop-flop."

"Did you see who was in it?"

"Sure. I see pretty good fo' a man wit' cat-racks. Two young wimmin. Didn't seem to know 'bout the tire. Or didn't care."

"That's the car I'm after," I told him. "Is there some way I can catch it?"

"I don't know about that, now. That tire slow 'em down, maybe even stop 'em after a while. And this road does some twistin' 'fore it hits Don'sonville. So I expect if you went straight in that direction"—his arthritic forefinger pointed to the north-west—"you might save yourself a few miles. But I dunno they be enough to catch you up with 'em."

"You okay out here?" I asked him.

"Me? I'm fine. It's the land that ain't doing so well."

I thanked him for his help, and Cajun Desire and I took off in the direction he'd indicated.

It led us through a cemetery, and the horse seemed to sense a change in the atmosphere. Probably he was just picking up on my mood.

The wind had knocked over statues and dislodged crypts. Elaborately carved wooden markers lay casually on the wet turf. Broken slabs exposed shadowy nooks that I didn't care to view. In Memory of My Loving Wife . . . Loving Mother . . . Loving Son . . . One of them read, AT FINAL REST, a claim that could now be disputed, thanks to Hurricane Bruce.

We both breathed easier once we were through that place and traveling over good, old-fashioned unconsecrated swampland. As we crossed through the middle of yet another devastated planta-tion, it suddenly occurred to me that I might be veering away from my intended destination. It was impossible to keep a sense of direction without some sort of guidepost. But I didn't know the landmarks and the sky was hidden behind layers of black clouds. And I wasn't sure that in this case, the horse would know the way.

Then I got lucky. Ahead was a huge two-story mansion that was still standing. It was one of those Greek Revival monsters, constructed of large stone slabs. Its doors and windows had given way to the force of the wind, but the place looked solid and there were people on its roof.

We circled the house, then paused in front of a stone stairwell that went up between two of the four solid columns that appeared to support the protruding triangular roof. The people on the roof were probably checking for leaks.

"Hello, up there," I shouted.

A startled white face peered down at me. "Who is it?" the man called down.

"I'm trying to find the road to Donaldsonville," I told him.

"It's out of commission. Flooded."

"I know. But I need to find some people who are trying to drive it."

"Damn fools, then."

"All the more reason for me to find them."

"Head to your left," he shouted, pointing his arm. "I can just about see the road from here. Watch out for the bogs. Where are you coming from?"

"Dogwood," I answered.

"Much damage?"

"Total."

He turned to a woman up there with him. "We were darned lucky, Louise," he said. Then he waved down at me. "Good luck finding your damn fool friends."

I maneuvered Cajun Desire slowly through the dark swampland. Bogs, the man had said. And bogs there were. As soon as I felt the animal's front legs starting to sink, I pulled him to a halt and slipped from the saddle.

I went ahead of him, testing the ground. If it was merely soft, we'd chance it; if it sucked at my shoes like a hungry monster, I did a sideways shuffle and led Cajun Desire around that area. Finally, we arrived at the paved road to Donaldsonville. I used a toppled stone wall to give me a leg up and got back into the saddle.

We'd trotted a few miles when I began to feel hopeless about catching Lea and Francie. And if I did catch them, would it be too late? Would Lea still be alive?

I should have been paying more attention to the landscape around me. I didn't hear the horse until it was right behind me. I turned in the saddle at the same time that something smashed against my shoulder and head.

Cajun Desire whinnied, reared, and carried me to the left, leaving the road. My right shoulder had taken the brunt of the impact, but I was too groggy to realize what had happened. Or what was happening.

I heard the other horse again and looked up to see Mike LeBlanc bearing down on us with a length of metal pipe in his hand. Mugger polo.

He swung the pipe at my head, but I drew away from it. And I kept going, right off the back of Cajun Desire.

The animal cantered away from me, uncertain of what I wanted from him. I felt soft earth in my fingers as I pushed myself to my feet.

"Kill him!" Joan Courville's no-longer-refined Southern voice shrieked.

I staggered backward as Mike rode his horse nearer. He hesitated before bringing down the pipe. If he hadn't, he would probably have given his lady friend everything she wanted.

I spun away and the pipe split the air in lieu of my scalp.

I ran farther into the swampland, looking for a tree to hide behind or a branch to use as a defensive weapon.

Joan and Mike moved in on me. "He'll keep after us. He'll never give up," the lady shouted. "You have to kill him. Now. Then maybe we'll have a chance."

"That's crazy," I shouted back. "I'm not after you. I'm trying to find—"

Mike didn't let me finish. He charged. I dodged again. It was obvious that he'd have me soon. My shoulder ached and I was losing strength by the second.

". . . ruined everything," Joan Courville was saying. She circled me with her animal.

I backed away. My heels stuck to the ground, made a plop as I pulled free.

Joan's horse reared up suddenly. When its front legs touched

ground again, its hooves sank beneath the soil. The horse panicked. It thrashed wildly, but it was trapped and sinking into a
swamp bog.

Within seconds, it was belly-deep.

Joan cried out. The horse was sinking fast. She tried to free her
feet from the stirrups, but the bog was already lapping at her
knees. Somehow she broke free from the frantic, whinnying
animal, but she was in the center of the bog and flailing about.

A country boy like Mike should have known better than to
ride to her rescue. But his lady was in trouble. By the time he
realized his mistake, his horse was sinking, too.

Mike leapt from its back in Joan's direction. The animal, free
from its burden, rolled over on its side and kicked its legs free.
The noise it made was terrifying, but it was a cry of triumph. Its
legs hit more solid earth and I grabbed a stirrup with my undam-
aged arm and helped it from the muck. As it ran off into the
swamp I turned to the unhappy couple.

Mike reached Joan just as she let loose a panic scream. He
didn't seem frightened at all. He put his arm around her shoulders. She tried to pull away, but she was too far gone.

She went under in midscream.

"Stop struggling," I shouted to Mark. But he didn't really hear
me. He actually pushed himself under the muck to keep his lady
company in the bottomless sump. True love.

Actually, it was the worst thing I'd ever seen, but I hope you
won't think too badly of me if I say I felt more sympathy for the
animal than the humans.

I was surprised to find that Cajun Desire hadn't run away. He
eyed me balefully as I approached him, but allowed me to take
the reins and lead him back to the paved road. He seemed as
skittish as I felt. But once we were in motion again, we slipped
into an easy, steady pace along the road.

I felt each bounce in my damaged shoulder and hand.

I hoped I had no broken bones, but I'd ridden with broken
bones before. Never on country roads, of course.

A few miles of that and a battered Buick zoomed past us, giving
Cajun Desire a bad moment. Then a truck lumbered past, its

flatbed filled with sandbags and four or five men in slickers. It looked like the road had opened, which meant I'd never catch up with Lea and Francie, even with their flop-flop tire. But there was no sense in turning back at that point.

Another mile or so and I met two young boys on bicycles, both in raincoats and hats. "Is the road open to Donaldsonville?" I asked.

"Sort of," the taller boy answered. He had a gold front tooth. "Cops letting some people through."

"How far from here?"

"Five miles maybe."

"Car tried to run the cops down," the other boy said eagerly, his freckled face breaking into a grin like it was Christmas. "Then it backed away and headed off into the swamp. Cops figured it was somebody doing something wrong. Runnin' corn. Or smokes. They say they'll go lookin' for 'em soon as things settle a bit. Car in the swamp ain't going no place, 'cept down. Specially with a flat tire."

"Any idea whether the car went to the left or the right?" I asked.

"Cops said it went over there," Gold tooth said, pointing to his left, my right.

I thanked the little lads and moved onward.

Before long I saw the lights of the police cars, then the cars themselves. The cops were in their green-and-yellow slickers trying to explain to a gathering crowd of motorists why they had to keep the road clear for emergency vehicles.

Cajun Desire seemed to want to head for the commotion, but I steered him off into the swamp in the direction the boy mentioned.

The horse and I went up a slight rise and then looked down on swamp water and land and a mixture of both. In the near distance was a dim glow.

As we approached, careful to avoid boggy patches, I saw that the glow was coming from my rental car. It was wrapped around a tree. A low flame burning under the hood.

I decided that because of the soft ground I could move faster on foot than on horseback. I ran toward the car, slipping in the mud, catching myself. My shoulder wouldn't have hurt more with a burning spear stuck in it.

Thirty or so feet from the car, I found Lea on the ground, still as death.

I no longer noticed my shoulder as I fell on my knees beside her. Her lifeless face was covered with mud and a little blood. I called her name.

She didn't move. But she was breathing. Unconscious. She seemed to have been thrown clear of the accident. Or maybe she jumped clear and knocked herself out.

"Coley!"

It came from the car.

Reluctantly, I turned from Lea.

The right side of the car had piled into a massive oak. The driver's door was open. Through it, I saw Francie in the passenger seat, staring out at me.

I went to her. The front of the car seemed to be in her lap, pinning her in. "Can't move," she said.

"I'll help. . . ."

She shook her head. "Too late. Gasoline. Fire. No time left."

She raised her arm. She had a gun in her hand. "Your blond bitch purposely tried to run us into a police car. Should have killed her then."

"She's a terrible driver," I said.

She made a noise that might have been a laugh except that it sounded too choked and grim. "She hit this tree just right. I've been waiting here for a clear shot at her. No luck there, either." She winced as pain coursed through her. "Maybe I'll just shoot you instead."

I stood still as she aimed the gun at me. Then she gave me a twisted grin. "No, baby. Don't worry. You were good to me. Should've stayed with you. I ran with some really bad people. Turned pretty bad myself. No big loss, then."

She brought the gun to her mouth.

"No," I shouted, and ran forward. The gun went off and the car exploded.

★★★

I awoke briefly. The world seemed bright. Lea was cradling my head on her lap. "You're . . . ?" I croaked.

"Fine," she finished.

"And Cajun De—"

"In better shape than either of us. We're okay. The medics are on their way. Sleep," she ordered. I slept.

64

I DREAMED OF horses and races and winning and losing. When I woke up, I was abed in a, well, highly medicated condition. Weasel words, meaning I was stoned from my toes to the crown of my skull. Lea has informed me that my exact location was a facility called l'Hôpital Evangeline in Thibodaux, Louisiana.

A doctor there decided my condition merited my being moved to New Orleans and a hospital better equipped to handle burns and concussions.

I remember nothing of the trip.

When I awoke, I was in a private room in New Orleans's All Saints Hospital, feeling wonderful. There seemed to be something stuck to my face and head. And my right arm was trapped to my side. But that was fine with me. I was floating on white feathers through a pink mist that smelled of an expensive floral spray.

Two detectives from the New Orleans Police Department

dropped by to ask me questions, but they were bright enough to realize, after only an hour or so, that I was in no condition to provide any coherent answers.

I was very near sobriety when the FBI guys showed up with *their* questions and a steno to carve my answers in electronic stone.

One of the feds asked, "Mr. Killebrew, do you think you could tell us exactly what you've been up to in Louisiana?" While I was trying to think of a properly vague reply, Lea arrived to shoo them away.

It's not easy to shoo the FBI away, and I marveled at yet another of her miraculous abilities.

With her was a man in a white smock who smelled of bay rum and who seemed to be looking at my ersatz fiancée rather lecherously. I began to think he wasn't a doctor at all, but an actor, pretending to be a doctor to get closer to Lea.

I mentioned this to him and he and Lea chuckled and I felt a flash of paranoia that sobered me completely.

I tried to pursue the topic of his lechery, but naturally he changed the subject. "You're going to be fine, Mr. Killebrew," the oily, handsome son of a bitch said. "Some fairly minor burns, a few glass cuts that we've cleaned up, and a nasty little hairline crack in your clavicle."

"Burns, cuts, and a cracked clavicle," I repeated.

The handsome face nodded. "I'll look in later," he said, and winked. He probably winked at Lea, too, when he walked from the room.

She pretended not to be mooning over the young charlatan. She sat on the edge of the bed, warming my knee. She was wearing some kind of orange outfit—an orange sailor suit, maybe. It looked terrific on her, no matter how dumb it sounds.

"You were lucky you didn't catch the full blast when the car blew up," she said. "Just enough to knock you out and burn your eyebrows a little, singe some of your pompadour."

"I don't have a lot of pompadour to lose," I told her.

"Dr. Morrison wasn't sure how you cracked your collarbone."

"That doesn't surprise me," I said. "Maybe if my collarbone

had pert breasts and beautiful long legs, he might have been more interested in it."

"My, my, but medicine does bring out your romantic side," she said.

"He winked at me. That's what I need, a doctor who winks. I'm surprised he didn't begin his pitch with, 'Hi, I'm Bob—' "

"Carl," she interrupted. "That's his name. Carl Dénéchaud Morrison."

" 'Hi, I'm *Carl*,' " I continued doggedly, " 'I'll be your doctor tonight. We have a lot of wonderful things on the menu—pills, shots, bedpans.' "

"How did you hurt your clavicle?" she asked, ignoring my feeble joke.

"Mugger polo," I told her. "We can get into it later, after you've clued me in on how I got here. We could begin with your carrying me to safety."

"I didn't," she said. "Daddy arrived on horseback. He looked quite dashing, even with the wheezes and an ugly bruise on his chin. He went for the police, who were nearby, and they brought in an emergency helicopter that carried us to a hospital in Thibodaux. A wonderful old building. L'Hôpital Evangeline. Fortunately, it was barely touched by the hurricane."

"Is your father here?"

She shook her head. "Said he'd had a long enough vacation. Went back home on the first flight he could get."

"Good," I said. "What about Cajun Desire?"

"In Granny's capable hands. He stopped by to see you while you were non compos mentis. He had to go back to Dogwood Plantation to help with the salvage. Roberta Courville's decided to rebuild the place, stable and all."

"How long have I been here?" I asked, using my free hand to touch my face. There seemed to be strips of adhesive on my forehead and chin and left ear.

"Three days. Dr. Morrison says that they want to do a little bit more on your clavicle and make sure that your respiratory tissues aren't going to swell enough to interfere with your breathing. You should be able to leave by the end of the week."

"Francie . . . ?"

"She didn't have a chance," Lea said.

"She killed herself," I said. "I saw her do it."

Lea's lips parted, but she hesitated before she spoke. "She was going to shoot me when we came to the end of our ride. She said she wasn't. But she hated Dad and killing me was going to be her payback. As soon as I figured that out, my driving grew progressively worse. I wasn't trying to kill her, but I'm not sorry she's dead."

I wanted to remind her that Francie was someone I'd once loved, but I didn't see what purpose that would serve. Maybe the drugs' aftereffects were turning me maudlin. Lea was absolutely right: Francie would have killed her without batting an eyelash.

"When we were on our ride," Lea said, "I asked her about . . . your last race. She told me something you might find interesting."

"Oh?"

"It wasn't just your hangover that caused your accident seven years ago. Francie said she slipped a double dose of Dalmane into your Ovaltine that morning."

"Dalmane?" I asked.

"A hypnotic drug. The effects of a mild overdose would be drowsiness, weakness, feeling of drunkenness, the staggers."

"Hmmm," I said. "Sounds like you've been brushing up on your medical lore with Dr. Carl."

She shook her head. "You're impossible," she said.

I smiled. "It's good news, even if it won't make any difference."

"It might, if Dad submits this new evidence to the Racing Commission."

"He won't," I said. "He won't believe Francie was telling you the truth."

She sighed. "Maybe not. But I believe her."

I told her that was good enough for me.

65

ON A CLOUDY, humid evening not long thereafter, when Dr. Carl and the FBI finally decided they were finished with me, Lea and I said farewell to All Saints Hospital and the city of New Orleans.

We spent the flight back to L.A. dining on something small and gray brown that was supposed to be a filet mignon, sipping champagne and flirting. In between we also discussed Starbuck's deposition to the FBI, which Lea had given me in the hospital and which provided me with just about all the pieces of the Santa Rosita–Southern Boy puzzle.

Starbuck had requested our immediate presence as soon as the flight touched down. As we walked into his office the big man looked up at me and said, "Your face looks like hell."

"You should talk, with your purple chin," I told him.

He glared at me. "You won't catch me by surprise again."

"I hope I won't have to," I said. "Anyway, thanks for helping to get me to the hospital."

"I had nothing to do with it. It was Lea. I'd have been happy to leave you in the mud."

"Oh, Daddy . . ." Lea said.

"Jesus, what a mess that whole thing was," he said. "Dammit, Killebrew, it would have been so simple if you'd only followed the original plan."

"The original plan didn't have a hurricane in it."

"Or Francie Dorn," Lea added.

Starbuck lowered his head and glared at me over his Ben Franklins. "Lea told me about the knockout drops your Francie supposedly fed you before that race."

"Dalmane," she corrected him.

His eyes flicked at her with impatience. "Whatever. I don't for a second place any faith in anything that Francie dame would say. But that's my own take on it. I suppose we should let the members of the Racing Commission decide for themselves. Maybe they'll be naive enough to clean your slate, Killebrew."

"Thanks," I said.

"They buy it, you could race again, if that's what you want."

"I've been out of the game quite awhile," I said. "But I'll think about it."

"Yeah," he said. "Well, to business. By the time the law is finished with Vetter and his associates, I don't think Clara will have to worry about Southern Boy Supplies' bid to take over her track." He frowned. "Maybe we should also snoop around for a legit partner for old man Bouraine's little girl."

Delia Bouraine would have loved to hear herself so described. "Maybe," I said. Then, after a pause, I asked, "Why *did* you spend so much time on Francie's case?"

"At first I just wanted to talk to her. Get her story on record. But she kept dodging me. So that made me curious and I began putting feelers out. She sent me a letter, asking me to lay off. Wrote that she was out of it. She'd made all the bets for you and put the winnings in a locker. She sent you the key. It had been your idea from the jump. All she got was five grand for her trouble."

"The letter never became part of my file," I said. "It would have really nailed me. I might have even done time."

"Yeah, well, I never put it in your file, because I didn't believe it. It was the goddamned letter that made me really go after Francie. See, I didn't figure her for the kind of dame who'd settle for just five thousand where there was so much more."

"She loved money, that's for sure," I told him. "She killed for it."

"Oh?" He seemed only half-interested.

"Lea says the police think it was a woman who killed Irwin Matthes, because of high-heel footprints in the barn area out at Santa Rosita. Both George McGuinn and the security guard, Larry Mullen, were romanced by a blonde. Francie had a pair of shoes with mud stains and bits of hay on the heels that could have come from the track. And she had a blond wig. She wasn't in Louisiana when I got there. When she did fly in, the story was that she'd been in New York. That was a lie. She later said she thought Lea had followed her to Louisiana from here.

"Remy and Vetter knew that Matthes was a snoop. They probably put her onto him while he was still down south. They paid her to seduce him and to kill him."

"Got any proof of that?" Starbuck asked.

"The shoes may be in the wreckage of the house, but I don't know if you can tell swamp mud from stable mud. Remy and Vetter paid her in cash for what they called 'doing a triple.' That would be Matthes and the security guard—"

"And Lannie Luchek," Lea added.

"Maybe Vetter will back up your theory," the big man said. "But I doubt it. He's not gonna want to add murder to his other woes."

"What're you going to do about Vetter's aunt?" I asked.

He glared at Lea. "Is there any of my business you didn't tell him?" When she rolled her eyes instead of answering, he said to me, "She's not exactly a fan of mine, but she's willing to live and let live. This was after I agreed not to spread the word about Romeo's vulnerable condition."

He pushed his glasses up on his nose and looked through them at some papers on his desk. "Anyhow, it's all history now. Francie's gone to her own reward. It's no business of mine anymore." To display his disinterest, he picked up the papers and began to leaf through them.

"You're forgetting something," I told him.

"Oh?" He was looking up at me over the glasses.

"You owe me some money."

He frowned, as if the subject of money confused him. "Oh, yeah. How much was it, again?"

"Ten thousand, plus another six thousand in expenses."

"Six thousand? For what?" he shouted.

"Planes, hotel, and hospital bills," I shouted back.

"Umm," he mumbled, calming down. "Okay. Lea, make out the check." He picked up his papers again and successfully pretended that we were no longer there.

I looked at Lea expectantly. She moved to his desk, pushed his chair with him in it aside, and opened the center drawer. She withdrew a leather-bound checkbook. She placed the checkbook on his desk, taking over his reading lamp, picked up a pen, and methodically filled out a check. Then she tore it from the book.

She reversed her actions, replacing the checkbook, closing the drawer, pushing his chair back in front of the lamp. He stared at her the whole time. Finally, he said, "Make sure you put on it, 'For payment in full.' "

She handed me the check and gave him a raspberry.

66

"IS THE OLD man always like that?" I asked Lea, slipping the check into my wallet as we marched through Choo-Choo's spotless kitchen.

"Unyielding, dogmatic, autocratic, vaguely obnoxious, and cheap? Nearly always. Are you taking me to dinner?"

"At my restaurant?" I wondered.

"I was thinking of something more intimate."

"I don't know," I said. "Intimate dinners can lead to serious romance. You may be too tall for that."

"Well, you know what they say," she told me, "the bigger they are . . ."

"Yeah. The harder *I* fall," I said, offering her my good arm.